The Dancing Mistress

Daniela Brotsack

The
Dancing Mistress

Bibliografische Information der Deutschen Nationalbibliothek
Die Deutsche Nationalbibliothek verzeichnet diese Publikation
in der Deutschen Nationalbibliografie; detaillierte bibliografische Daten sind im Internet über http://dnb.d-nb.de abrufbar.

Imprint
ISBN: 978-3-7693-0713-9
English first edition
© 2024 Daniela Brotsack, translated with help from DeepL
Proofreading: Peter Longley, Beckenham

German original title: Die Tanzmeisterin
© 2021 Daniela Brotsack, www.daniela-brotsack.com
new Edition 2024: ISBN-13: 978-3-7693-0711-5
Cover-painting (fan): © Alfred Leiblfinger
Print of fan: © Sabine Schmidt, www.westra-druck.de
Typesetting and layout: © Daniela Brotsack
Publisher:
BoD · Books on Demand GmbH, In de Tarpen 42,
22848 Norderstedt
Printed by:
Libri Plureos GmbH, Friedensallee 273,
22763 Hamburg

Life is too precious,
to waste it on trivialities!

Foreword

With this book, you are holding a very special novel in your hands. Daniela Brotsack's story takes us back to the 18th century, when Wolfgang Mozart also lived in Salzburg. This novel will whet your appetite for culture! And along the way, the reader learns many interesting facts about the history of this period.

The author Daniela Brotsack has been a member of my dance group in Salzburg for many years, where we dance contra dances from Mozart's time and English country dances. Inspired by our experiences and adventures with dance, Daniela came up with the idea for this novel and so, as today's dance master, I have the honour of writing the foreword.

We have experienced many celebrations with dance and music together and Daniela authentically describes in her novel how dancing together connects us, makes us happy and has a strengthening effect. That's exactly how we experience it again and again.

Even though the book is called "The Dancing Mistress", dance is not the main content. As I wrote in the first sentence: you are holding a special book in your hands.

Why? Because this novel can do something very special: It has the potential to spread a soothing atmosphere through reading.

It has a healing effect on the soul to experience in this novel how people in the circle around the main character and narrator treat each other with respect and dignity. How in every person, regardless of social status, it is above all being, goodwill and honesty that count. The protagonist champions these values with her own example and ingenious ideas, which she puts into practice, and takes the reader with her into her world.

Of course, it's not all sunshine and cheerfulness. The world that the author takes us into plays out all of life's pieces – from misfortune, suffering and sadness to joy, success and happiness.

The narrator Victoria and her family are characterised by how they deal with strokes of fate and events. People help each other, listen to each other, are there for each other and, strengthened in this way, get through crises together. Culture – particularly emphasised in the novel – music and dance also help. Daniela Brotsack lets her narrator listen to special gems of music or play them herself and describes them in such a way that you want to listen to every piece immediately.

And – how could it be otherwise – all these human values that make life so worth living and loving and that come to life in this novel are experienced by the author herself. Wherever possible, Daniela enriches her environment with ideas and initiatives in order to experience beautiful and thus invigorating things together.

Her two earlier novels are also characterised by these values. The first novel, "Mit dem Mut einer Löwin – der lange Weg nach Hause", is set in the Middle Ages, while the second, "Des Falken Treue" (both not yet available in English), like a sequel to the first, tells a story of our time.

I hope you enjoy reading the novel "The Dancing Mistress".

Salzburg, in March 2021

Verena Brunner
Female dance master of today

Briefly explained

Dear reader,

Sometime around 2007, I discovered my enthusiasm for medieval dances. Shortly before the 1st Paris Lodron Ball of the University of Salzburg in the rooms of the prince-archbishop's residence in 2012, I got to know and love the dances from the Mozart era and have been a member of Verena Brunner's Salzburg dance group with members from up to seven decades ever since, rehearsing historical dances with a lot of fun and joy.

In earlier centuries, everyone danced right up to the highest kings. Unfortunately, that has changed. Nowadays, dancing is often seen as unmanly. And yet many women still consider a good dancer to be particularly attractive. To counteract the widespread laziness to dance, I wanted to write about a female dancing master to inspire others to dance.

After the first forty or so pages of my manuscript, my writing flow came to a standstill. When I started working again, some of my protagonists developed a life of their own. They didn't want to accept the life I had planned for them and wouldn't leave me alone until I had rewritten everything. However, this also meant that the time frame of my story had to change.

Since a woman in the 18th century could hardly fulfil such a profession as dancing master on her own, I felt compelled to provide my protagonist with a brother who shares her enthusiasm for dancing.

Although I certainly didn't want to write a romance novel (yet again), I was confronted with the problem that a single woman at this certain time wasn't considered anything in the eyes of society, which is why my dancing master wasn't allowed to remain unmarried – and so love is involved.

I hope I have managed the balancing act between historical facts and an easy-to-read story with likeable people, so
that my readers are also fascinated by those women who
went their own way against all odds in earlier times and
were quite successful.

Despite the numerous historically documented persons
and facts, I would like to point out that my story is a novel
in which there are also many fictional dialogues and scenes.
I did not set out to reproduce every detail with historical
accuracy and took the liberty of allowing my protagonists
to act against some of the conventions of the time. After
all, who knows whether there weren't people and ideas at
the time described that were similar to the ones I had imagined?

A word about the cover: at the time described, fans were
a very common accessory. Because the ladies wore corsets
and often countless layers of fabric, a fan was at least a
small help to prevent fainting in stuffy air. I thought that a
dancing master's very personal fan could display the insi-
gnia of her art together with some drawings of dance figures. Some dance masters advertised the mastery of the following skills as a prerequisite for their profession: dancing,
riding, fencing and playing the pochette (pocket fiddle).

I gave the friends of my protagonist Victoria the names
of noble families from Bavaria who were long extinct at the
time.

As the story is set in Deutschland (Germany) and pre-
sent-day Österreich (Austria), the German names are given
in the original German spelling. The English spelling can
be found in the footnotes

I hope you enjoy the dancing mistress and her adventures!

Yours
Daniela Brotsack

"Everyone wants to have an intelligent wife, but they don't want to give them the means of understanding."

Dorothea Christiane Erxleben,
doctor and pioneer of women's studies
(1715–1762)

January 1774

It was cold and we had a respectable amount of snow. Archbishop Colloredo sent us an invitation to a sleigh ride from the Domplatz (cathedral square) to Schloss Hellbrunn, followed by a masked ball in the residence. The date was set for the next full moon on the 27th of the month, a Friday. My mamma was to entertain the prince's guests with her music at a small reception at Schloss Hellbrunn. For this reason, our family was given the special privilege of being invited to the "Schlittade"[1] itself and no one who could stand on their feet would turn down such an invitation.

Pappa broached the subject in the evening: "We have two sledges and trained horses that are suitable for a ride like this. That means there's room for all of us. Of course, I'll be driving the sleigh with your mamma myself. You will steer the second one with Victoria, Christoph."

Mamma now took the floor. "At the same time as the Monarch's invitation, we received another invitation from your Uncle Josef and Aunt Maria, offering us the opportunity to stay with them in Salzburg for the days around the Schlittade. Through the Monarch's secretary, of course, they know that we will be there. Isn't that marvellous?"

Father nodded in agreement. "Your brother Josef and his wife Maria are lovely people who I would like to see again.

I'm really looking forward to this evening. Please promise me to prepare yourselves so that nobody gets tired and inattentive. That could be dangerous with the sledges, especially in the dark. Oh yes, and to make sure my children both have fun, we'll mix up the pairs on the way into town. Christoph, you go with your mamma and I'll put myself in my daughter's capable hands and let her take the reins."

I hugged my clever father with the soft heart. He wouldn't regret his decision.

---

1   *Schlittade comes from the word Schlitten, which is a sledge.*

Christoph and I took care of the preparations in the stable and shed. First we inspected the sledges again. One looked like a wolf and the other like a feisty eagle. Both were in good condition and just needed a little cleaning. We touched up the paint here and there.

They were two really comfortable sledges that came from my father's parents. Both of them had a space under the seat where you could stow a hot brick to keep the person sitting nice and warm on their backside. And both had a screwed-on frame on the runners where the coachman stood, which was about knee-high and bent backwards at the bottom. The driver stood on it and it protected him and his legs from snow and wetness from the front, which was a great relief and not standard. In addition, both vehicles had a lantern in the centre front to illuminate the path directly in front of the horse, as well as holders for torches.

For the seats, there were beanbags sewn from bearskins, fur on the inside and leather on the outside. This protected the sitter's legs and abdomen from wind and weather.

Mamma and I had a lot of fun with the rest of the preparations. We were looking forward to this trip like children and packed clothes for two days and nights, but also thought of enough torches for the sledges.

A few days later, on the day before the spectacle, we set off on both sledges towards Salzburg under slightly overcast skies.

I was wearing winter trousers and thick boots and a simple skirt that I could button up left and right. The top layer was a long coat. When I stood behind the sledge, you couldn't see anything that might cause offence.

We gave the horses free rein on a long straight and they chased along so fast it was a joy. The little bells on the sledges and the horses' harnesses accompanied every movement and everyone in front of us heard us coming and made way for us with a hello.

When Pappa turned round to me from time to time, he looked very happy. I hadn't seen him this cheerful for a long time. I'd always had the feeling that something was bothering him recently. But he didn't talk about it.

Every now and then I would hear my mamma yowl or the loud crack of my brother's whip, which spurred his horse on even more. However, the encouragement wasn't particularly necessary, as our animals were dashing forwards out of sheer joie de vivre and none of them was better than the other.

When we arrived at Uncle Josef and Aunt Maria's house in the centre of the city, right on the banks of the Salzach, between the Mozarts' flat and the residence, the horses were reasonably dry again and we were looking forward to a warm room. My uncle's gorsoon and another servant would look after our horses and the sleighs. A stable that also rented out boxes was just round the corner and as the sleighs weren't very big, our relatives would have a suitable place to keep them.

"Welcome, my dears!" Maria embraced each of us with a warmth that was almost unbearable. Uncle Josef stood somewhat awkwardly next to her and offered his hand to everyone with a broad grin. His handshake was legendary and I wrested my right hand from him as quickly as possible so as not to get hurt. I was delighted to see them both in such good health.

"Dionys, how happy I am to see you with such a cheerful gleam in your eyes and a healthy complexion!" Josef gave his brother-in-law a well-meaning pat on the shoulder.

"I was able to enjoy the journey here to the full. I had a really cosy ride because my daughter drove me to the city limits. Thank you for the invitation." My father was in a great mood.

"Now come in at last, settle down and hurry into the warm parlour. We have a small evening party tonight with a light dinner among good friends. Oh yes, the Mozarts are coming too. So after a nice hot cup of mocha, I suggest you get some rest."

My aunt changed the subject to the latest gossip about who had got engaged and which dances they had already attended or would be attending this carnival season. Uncle Josef also knew all the latest news and rumours.

Of course, there was not only mocha, but also excellent pastries. Among other things, the cook had made a *Linzer Torte*, which my brother particularly enjoyed. I guess the cook wanted to ingratiate herself again because Christoph knows how to give nice compliments.

Although I didn't feel tired, I went to the room provided for me and lay down. After reading two pages in the book from my relatives' library, my eyes fell shut. My aunt's maid woke me up at the right time and teased me that I looked a bit sleepy. The cheeky young thing always makes me laugh.

The evening event was supposed to be completely informal. In other words, I put on an evening gown, of course, but not my best ball gown. I had Wolferl[2] Mozart as my table host. "Greetings, noble Countess von Falkenstein. You look lovely again. Before anyone else beats me to it, I'll ask for the first dance."

"Thank you for the compliment, genius Mozart. Of course I'll dance the first dance with you. It's a pleasure. Because of your travels to Italy and Wien[3] and my trip last year, we haven't seen each other for so long that I almost didn't recognise you."

Of course, this was an exaggeration. I would have recognised my old friend anytime and anywhere. But as he was also not always telling the truth, that was fine. Wolferl knew a lot to tell about his travels and, as always, he made jokes that made me laugh heartily.

"Don't tell me I'm still growing." He sat up very straight and pushed his chest forward until I laughed.

"Now that you mention it, you've grown up!" I ducked away from him and he gave me a peck on the arm and laughed out loud.

---

2   *Wolferl is a Bavarian/Austrian loving short form of the name Wolfgang.*
3   *Vienna*

People chatted between courses and a wide variety of topics came up. An elderly lady, whose name I simply can't remember, asked the group: "Which of the ladies has actually read *The History of Lady Sophia Sternheim* by that writer in Koblenz, Sophie von La Roche? It's quoted everywhere."

My aunt eagerly took the floor. "Of course I had to read that. Did you know that La Roche originally came from Kaufbeuren? She was born Gutermann zu Gutershofen, so she is a distant relative of mine."

"Oh, that's very interesting. Then somehow you have family ties with Christoph Wieland, the poet. How exciting!" came back from the lady immediately. "As far as I know, he's a cousin of La Roche."

Mrs Mozart also shared her knowledge. "They're both very talented, anyway. I've read La Roche's *Sternheim* and also a few things by Wieland. His *Lady Johanna Gray* in particular really touched my heart, even though I'm Catholic through and through." She put her hands over her breasts and looked upwards. Wolfgang started to giggle and I couldn't hold back any longer. Especially when she realised and winked at us conspiratorially while exaggerating the gesture even further.

As already announced, after the meal there was dancing in the *Tanzmeistersaal*[4], which belonged to the flat and also had a separate entrance. There were plenty of musicians in the room who were itching to dance. Among them were my mother and Wolfgang's father, who played a duet with their violins with an undetermined outcome. It was marvellous to see them both in their element. Leopold Mozart is otherwise a very rational and rather serious person. But the music makes even him shine.

"So, here comes an Anglaise[5]!" My friend Nannerl Mozart sat down at the pianoforte and tapped the keys like a der-

---

4   *Dancing master's hall, part of Mozart's apartment.*
5   *A dance in a long lane in which the first couple dances with every other couple in turn. When it reaches the bottom, it dances back to the starting point in the role of the other couple.*

vish. The rest of us danced to the cheerful and sometimes almost too fast melodies with great joy. Completely exhilarated, I briefly opened a window during a break in the dancing. Immediately there were shouts from all sides that I should close it again immediately before people died. Why is everyone always so sensitive? I must almost be dying of heat because the others start shivering at the first draught. That happened to me again and again.

I fell into bed in the early hours of the morning, dog-tired but happy. It had been an evening when I had felt completely at ease. However, it had been far too hot and I had a headache.

It wasn't until late morning that I got up again, reasonably well-rested, and got dressed. I skipped breakfast as there would be a snack at lunchtime. My first stop was at my brother's to check on our horses with him. After all, they had to look their best today and be fit for the ride. In return for a small gift of money, the stable lads at the livery stable were overflowing with kindness and wanted to take extra good care of our horses and spruce them up.

Shortly after midday, the horses were harnessed and our small group set off for the nearby cathedral square. There were already many different sledges.

"Look, Vic, there's a bear over there."

"Yes, and there's even a dragon over here. I like its green colour. It looks so poisonous."

"And there, another dark lindworm. What a difference to the radiant, shimmering gold dragon behind!"

Mamma called over and drew our attention to a sledge with a beautifully carved wolf.

We marvelled at the wide variety of sledges, some of which were real works of carving art. Other ornaments seemed to me to be rather skilfully made from papiermâché. Together with the beautifully gleaming horses and the people elegantly dressed in furs, it was a real feast for the eyes. Countless bells rang out their delicate sound, you could hear joking shouts, horses neighing and dogs barking. A joyful, excited atmosphere prevailed in the square. People came from all corners and streets to see what was going on.

And then the sleigh with the archbishop came out of the courtyard of the residence next to the cathedral.

It was adorned with a white stag with a cross between its antlers[6]. In other words, the animal from the legend of St Hubert.

His coachman, a tall man, drove to the front of the procession and off we trotted towards the town. Outside, in the open field, the pace was then briefly increased a little and I felt wonderful because I was allowed to be part of this spectacle.

The colourful procession, initially accompanied by many onlookers, made a large loop across the snow-covered fields towards Hellbrunn. Obviously the route had already been prepared in advance. Presumably to ensure safety, as you can't see holes and small ditches in the snow. I also spotted a lot of animal tracks.

The snow meant that nature had also become superficially quiet in the city, but there were still the constant sounds of craftsmen, shouts, horse-drawn carriages and much more.

All I could hear here was the gentle tinkling of bells, the snorting of horses and the cheerful laughter of people. My heart soared and I felt really happy.

When we arrived at the castle, it was still light and everything looked like something out of a fairy tale. Many servants had been specially deployed to look after the horses. The guests of the Schlittade were invited to attend a small reception in the castle's Carabinieri Hall. Champagne and snacks were served. Then our mamma played a chamber music concert with some excellent musicians for about three quarters of an hour. It was marvellous.

---

6   *Such a sledge is not documented.*

I had a seat next to a window during the performance. Everything around the castle looked spectacular as the sun slowly disappeared behind the mountains. And shortly afterwards, the sky seemed to glow. It was a marvellous sunset that I was able to watch and was incredibly impactful, especially with the beautiful music.

Back outside, the torches were lit. Of course, there were again guests who had not made any arrangements in this direction and who were dependent on the archbishop's servants to provide torches for their vehicles. Well, perhaps they had reckoned on that too and saved themselves some money. But we had made provisions for everything and so the horseboy was not forced to provide us with any further services.

I was about to snuggle into the leather sack on the eagle sledge when Pappa held my arm. "Victoria, I know that you have better eyesight at night and that you are also the better sledge driver of the two of us. So I'd be happy to put myself in your capable hands as far as the city limits and be content as a passenger."

I was surprised and delighted at the same time. So I helped my father to find a comfortable sitting position, gathered up my skirts, under which I was wearing trousers anyway in the cold, and prepared to set off. The servant who was holding our carriage looked astonished and indignant when he noticed the change. He was no doubt of the opinion that what had never been should not be. I gave him my friendliest smile and was rewarded by the fact that he no longer looked so grumpy.

Then I took off the blanket that had covered the sweating horse and stowed it on the sledge. I then took my place on the runners and looked over at my brother challengingly.

He laughed happily and my mother looked at me with a satisfied expression on her face. Just a few minutes later, the archbishop's sleigh set off back towards the town. The full moon shone on the landscape and covered everything in a silvery glow.

"You'll see that not everyone will arrive in the city in one piece. Some of the gentlemen here have looked very deeply into the champagne glass. Wait and see, we can foresee an incident." Christoph played Cassandra again. He would not be disappointed.

Not long after setting off, the first accident occurred. One of the guests didn't have his horse under control. It broke loose and ran straight to a ditch. It jumped over it and arrived safely on the other side. But the sleigh landed in the ditch along with the lady and the powerless coachman. Fortunately there was no water in the ditch, but it was boggy and the sleigh had obviously been damaged. As there were enough helping hands at work, in no time at all, we drove on and enjoyed our adventure.

"Look how beautiful the landscape is!" Mamma called out to us, pointing enthusiastically at the silhouette of the city.

From a distance, it looked as if we were gliding towards a city that was not of this world. On the Festung[7], which otherwise towers in darkness, fires could be seen blazing and fireworks were being set off on the *Gaisberg*[8]. It was like being in a pleasant dream!

"How lucky we are to be able to live such a life. Not many are granted that. May it always stay that way so that we don't have to worry too much!" Pappa looked up at me encouragingly and I picked up the pace. It was as if Christoph's and my sledge were flying over the snow. I could literally feel the horses' joy on this outing and at that moment I loved our little community even more.

The return journey didn't take that long, as there was only one big "S". When we had a closer look at the first houses, we could already see many people. My father told Christoph and me to stop and we changed positions again. Acting unconventionally is one thing, but presenting it to the public is another story.

---

7   *The achbishop's fortress obove the town, today known as Hohensalzburg*
8   *A small mountain (1287 m above sea level) next to Salzburg*

There was more light in the city and my father felt safe again as a coachman. Besides, I had had my fun and knew that I couldn't insist on my role any longer to ensure that the rest of the evening went well. We arrived back at the residence the same way we had started in the afternoon and nobody would have anything to complain about.

"Dionysius, let's go quickly to Maria and Josef. Their lads can look after the horses and we still have time to change in peace." Mamma was right, of course. Our relatives could also take us to the residence in one of the sedan chair services and the masked ball definitely required a change of clothes.

For my taste, it took far too long before we were all ready to set off again. Of course, we were still well on time, but I always get fidgety when so much time is wasted on useless activities. So I'd been sitting in the library reading for ages when the signal to leave finally came.

Like many other women, I had read the letters of Lady Mary Wortley Montagu, published in 1763, who was the wife of an ambassador in Constantinople. I had raved so much about it to Christoph that we both had father get us original Turkish clothes. Of course, we wouldn't be the first or the most original masks in Turkish style, but we would probably be among the most stylish, because they were original.

Christoph wore an undergarment with a rich floral pattern and a matching, typical şalvar, or harem trousers. Over this was a magnificent belt with semi-precious stones. The most important thing was a richly embroidered silk caftan and a matching white turban, just like the Turks themselves wear.

I also wore an underdress and a Şalvar, which was richly embroidered in the lower third. Then a gold-embroidered Turkish blouse and, on top of that, a magnificent entari with a train, as the overdress is called, which in my case was worn open from the waist down. This, I was told, was the dress of the palace ladies in Turkey.

We both wore pointed shoes made of soft leather that were specially made for dancing.

I had already had my hair braided into very thin plaits at the beginning of the day, which was not visible under my cap. I also wore a hat decorated with feathers and gemstones and an intricate veil.

I hadn't realised that father had also bought Turkish clothes for himself and mother and was surprised that they also looked like a sultan and his lady of the heart.

A short time later, we entered the residence, which was lit up with the help of probably thousands of candles. The high stucco walls – a glittering place that holds many memories for me.

Many guests had already gathered, some wearing unusual masks that showed a lot of imagination. Others, on the other hand, hadn't gone to much trouble with their costumes. They just wore a half-mask or a little hat with a veil combined with a normal evening gown.

The orchestra was already assembled and mamma was just whispering to my father which of the musicians she knew, when she stumbled and turned towards us. "Oh dear, I left my fan on Maria's chest of drawers. I won't make it through the evening without it!" Christoph made a little bow, waved his arms a little – and suddenly had mamma's fan in his hand.

"I was curious to see how long it would take for his loss to be noticed. When we left, he was lying alone on the piece of furniture and called out to me: ‚Take me with you', so I couldn't resist."

"Have I ever told you that I couldn't wish for a better son? You are a wonderfully attentive person. Thank you so much, you saved my evening." With that, she gave him an air kiss and took her fan.

It was still a pleasant temperature in the room, but with more people and the many candle flames, it would be scorching hot in a few hours.

The sound of fanfares drew the attention of all visitors of the ballroom. Of course, there were still whispers here and there. Some people just can't keep their mouths shut. But it became noticeably quieter and all attention turned to the entrance of the hall. There, the host appeared in a magnificent robe with a Venetian mask, while the orchestra played the *Entrance of the Queen of Sheba* from the oratorio *Solomon* by Georg Friedrich Händel[9]. What a performance!

Prince Archbishop Colloredo welcomed his guests and asked them to dance.

Immediately afterwards, the orchestra began to play the first dance that I had already promised my brother. It was a minuet[10].

Afterwards, I danced with my uncle Josef, who knew how to make me laugh with funny remarks or short grimaces and gestures.

It was an Anglaise in the long alley. We stood in the first third and danced down. After a good twenty minutes, we reached the bottom and danced back up again.

The dance had lasted about an hour and we had met a lot of old acquaintances. We exchanged brief pleasantries with every couple we already knew – as far as the dance gave us the opportunity. We got ourselves all heated up and went for some of the punch that was by the refreshments. It was very good, but also to be enjoyed with caution. I realised the effects of the alcohol very quickly and held back from then on.

Then, we continued with a quadrille[11]. A friend of my father's had asked me to do this dance, a good dancer and a consummate gentleman. I had adored him even as a small child. In my childish imagination, all men should be like him: Always friendly, well-mannered, nice to children and accomplished dancers. Mr Blumenau was also very

---

9   *George Frideric Handel*
10   *Courtly ballroom dance in 3/4 cadence.*
11   *Contra dance with 4 pairs*

well-read and had a refreshing wit. The dance went by far too quickly with him.

During a break from dancing, I found myself in a pleasant company where everyone had something to say. One of the gentlemen had an aunt in Berlin.

"That damn Preußenkönig Friedrich[12]! You can still remember his *Tartoffel* orders or whatever that stuff is called, can't you?"

Another gentleman spoke up: "You mean *Erdäpfel*; aren't they called *Kartoffeln* (potatoes) by the Preußen? Farmers were supposed to grow them because they were nutritious. That certainly made sense during the famine in Sachsen[13] three years ago. But by force? There were the so-called *tuber preachers* who travelled the countryside and told people everywhere that they should grow the crop."

I also knew something about the subject. "Many farmers didn't know what to do with the plant at first. They didn't realise for a long time that it was the tubers that were eatable and not the herb and flowers. This led to a number of deaths. Understandably, the farmers didn't want to know anything more about it."

One lady said: "I heard that Friedrich once even had potato fields guarded as a ruse so that the farmers would think the plants were valuable. It seems to have worked. He's a real rascal! The farmers now supposedly have to grow the plants on a tenth of their arable land. I don't like that stuff. But it still did a good job during the famine."

Finally, the first speaker continued, "It's all true. Well, as we all know, there's no accounting for taste. But now Friedrich gets down to the coffee. In Prussia, crazy Fritz imposed a luxury tax of 150 per cent on coffee! In Berlin, the beans cost many times more than from our Vic's father, from whom I always buy them – although we already pay a lot more here in the south than in Hamburg due to the many different customs duties from the north down here."

---

12 *Prussian King Frederick thee great*
13 *Saxony*

"Oh no, he's crazy! And why is that?" the lady wanted to know.

"Because he doesn't want the bourgeoisie and normal people to drink the brew. That's what my aunt told me in one of her letters. Recently, a large parcel sent to her was actually searched. As the inspectors found coffee[14] in it that wasn't labelled, I had to pay a hefty fine. What's more, the coffee was confiscated!" the first speaker replied.

"I've always been suspicious of the Prussians. I can't understand why anyone would still want to live in their territory." The lady had her own opinion.

I stood next to them and could only marvel at the ideas some rulers came up with. But not for long, because my next dancer was already standing in front of me and wanted to accompany me to the dance floor.

It was an all-round harmonious celebration. The whole day was a special experience. For me, the Schlittade was the first time I had experienced something like this, although it is organised at many courts in Germany, for example in Dresden. But I had only ever heard of such events.

For me, this day was a very special experience that I will remember for the rest of my life. The night-time drive, the people, the music, everything was just right and I felt really happy that day.

---

14 A few years later, on 21 January 1781, Frederick the Great hired out 400 veterans to act as "coffee sniffers". From then on, it was forbidden to roast coffee yourself (so that the smuggled coffee could be found).

*"We love in a young woman
quite different things from intellect.
We love in her the beautiful, the youthful,
the teasing, the confiding,
the character, her faults, her caprices,
and God knows what other unspeakable things;
but we do not love her intellect."*

Johann Wolfgang von Goethe (1824)

A look back

Childhood

I have now thrown my readers into the middle of my life and simply started to tell my story without explaining myself. I would now like to make up for this.

Let me start by saying that after some time away, I have been living again mainly with my family near Reichenhall[15] in the south of Baiern[16] since the end of 1773, where I grew up on a beautiful estate between the villages of Nonn and Karlstein.

I was baptised Victoria, but everyone just calls me Vic, because I was raised like a boy. The most important and precious person in my life is my twin brother Christoph. He is the only person who really knows me inside out – just like I know him. We know about each other's fears and dreams and understand each other without words.

Christoph and I have always been thick as thieves. We did almost everything together as children and even now we know that we can rely on each other. Together, we could and can take on any opponent – even our good-natured but very strict father.

Pappa had tried for a long time to raise us in a gender-appropriate way, the way society demands. But nothing had worked. We both stood up to him and swore that we would rather not learn anything at all if we weren't taught together.

So he had to give in and give me the same education as my brother. It didn't hurt either of us and we had fun learning together. As we got older, my father appreciated us

---

15 *The town name propably comes from reich (rich) and hall (old word for salt), which means rich of salt. Bad Reichenhall – spa since 7. June 1890 – still has a saline.*

16 *At this time the spelling was Baiern instead of Bayern for Bavaria. The y was introduced by royal decree of King Ludwig I in 1825. He loved Greece.*

both equally. Christoph says that Pappa is very proud of his educated daughter – but he never openly expresses this in public. I don't think that's fair, but he's also just a child of his time and was brought up very conservatively.

Pappa is a merchant. He has many things shipped by sea to or from Hamburg, which is why he has an office there and is usually in the Hanseatic city during the summer months.

Our mother Regina is a highly educated and very progressive woman who also campaigns for the rights of the women working here in her home. She has always been in favour of good education and congratulated us on our brilliant fraternal strategy.

Mamma is an outstanding violinist. When she plays, the audience starts dreaming. At a young age, she played in the great royal houses of Europe and she is still a sought-after soloist for concerts. However, because of father, who travels a lot himself, asking her to do so, she no longer travels so far and concentrates mainly on concerts that take place in the surrounding area. Or she plays in Hamburg when she accompanies Pappa on his business trips.

Mamma also plays the pianoforte quite well. She gave us children lessons on both instruments. She thought we both had the talent for it, but would probably never get as far as giving concerts due to a lack of hard work. I also learnt to play the flute – all my flutes were from the workshop of the family Walch in Berchtolsgaden[17] – and Christoph practised the cello. There were many beautiful pieces that we were able to play together as a family.

In our society, it was more or less forbidden for women to play wind instruments or even the violoncello. The latter mainly for the reason that a man – at least some – unfortunately also has an imagination and his thoughts might go astray if he saw a woman playing this instrument.

---

17   *Maps from the 18th century are still labelled with the name Berchtolsgaden instead of Berchtesgaden. See map at the back of the book.*

The main offence was the protruding chest and the spread legs when playing a violoncello or the inflated cheeks when using a fanfare.

The bad thing is that men generally don't learn to control themselves and their urges. Even as children, they are allowed to do anything, and at anything obnoxious everybody only smiles at instead of criticising.

Women should remain as still as possible and never be loud. Even when playing the pianoforte, we must ensure that we only play soft melodies and do not become loud and demanding. Women must always look perfect. In my opinion, some women look even more enchanting with a flute on their lips than without. Fortunately, playing the flute is tolerated to some extent. At least a woman who plays the flute is not excluded from society.

Through my brother, I learnt everything that a young man of standing should be able to do: reading and writing in German, Latin, French and English as well as arithmetic from a very modern tutor. After some initial scepticism, because he had only ever taught boys, he was delighted with the progress we both made.

But he also really knew how to package the subject matter in such an interesting way that children really wanted to grasp it. Christoph and I are still grateful to him for that today.

There were also lessons in history and philosophy. We siblings loved these lessons. Christoph and I also had fencing and riding lessons. We practised fencing from horseback and did a lot of things that were not without danger. Fortunately, no mishaps occurred during our sometimes reckless adventures.

When we didn't have to study, we went swimming in Lake Thumsee in the summer and frolicked on the ice of The unnamed lake[18] in the winter.

---

18   This small lake near Bad Reichenhall is now called Listsee.

The lesson that gave us the most pleasure was the one with our beloved Aunt Seraphia. She is our mother's youngest sister and has been a gifted ballet dancer since her youth, having danced on the most famous stages, in front of the most important monarchs in Europe and even with the Russian Tsar. Seraphia studied at the Académie Royale de Danse in Paris, which was founded by King Louis XIV in 1661.

Despite her age, she has a radiant personality and is still as pretty as a picture. Seraphia looks much younger. She is still travelling the world a lot. She sees us twins as a substitute for her own non-existent children and taught us everything she has ever learnt in between her engagements. So we had a profound education in music and dance from an early age.

When she is not travelling, Aunt Seraphia lives with us on the estate in a cosy house by the western gate with her dancing partner and a cook and maid all in one. She has been putting money aside from the start, which she could use to afford a nice retirement.

During her time here, she and her partner Heinrich give dance lessons in better homes in the region. Christoph and I have often been able to accompany them to demonstrate the steps to the students and motivate their peers.

When Christoph and I were still children, we travelled with Aunt Seraphia to München[19], Augsburg, Landshut, Regensburg and Passau for larger parties, as well as to castles in the region such as Hohensalzburg and Triebenbach, where our aunt danced at the special request of high society. We were often accompanied by Heinrich, who is an excellent violin and harpsichord player.

From an early age, Christoph and I were guests in Berchtolsgaden, at the Salzburg Residence and Triebenbach Castle, where we performed a very precisely rehearsed minuet, for example.

---

19   *Munich*

During a stay in Triebenbach in 1762, we also got to know Nannerl and Wolferl Mozart. Nannerl is the same age as us. The four of us enjoyed dancing and playing together from the very beginning. Although Wolferl is five years younger, he was involved in almost all the activities of us older ones. I help Nannerl to improve her riding skills, while she helps me to improve my dexterity on the pianoforte – to the delight of our mother.

In any case, we had a wonderful childhood in which we wanted for nothing.

Growing up

At some point, Christoph reached the age at which a young lad from better society either enters a military academy or goes to university for further education.

Now it was the same here as it had been with our entire upbringing. Christoph flatly refused to enter a university – wherever that might be – without me as a student.

In this case, we benefited from the fact that our mother had known Dorothea Erxleben and, above all, revered her art of healing. This woman had been an excellent and highly esteemed doctor. She was the first woman in the German Confederation to study medicine in Halle with the personal permission of King Frederick II and was awarded her doctorate in 1754.

The idea that women were fundamentally too stupid to study was thus rendered absurd. The director of the University of Ingolstadt, Johann Adam Freiherr von Ickstatt, therefore offered our parents a compromise in consultation with his prince: I was allowed to attend the law lectures and – to a certain extent – also take part in the students' discussions.

However, I had to sit behind the male students and would not be given the right to take an official degree. It was also made a condition that we siblings only started studying when we reached the age of 17.

In due course, Christoph and I were sent to live with my father's relatives in Ingolstadt, where we were integrated into family life. We were actually also diligent students of law.

Our temporary home was located directly on the Danube. I learnt to love the river. I could sit on its banks for hours and watch the play of light on the water or throw flat river pebbles into the water and let them bounce. Cousin Peter had shown me how to do this. He is three years older than us and had decided in favour of a military career. As a result, he was rarely to be found at home during our time in Ingolstadt.

Our cousins Luise and Kreszentia were completely different. Both are younger, Zenzi was actually still a child at the time. Both often disturbed us and stopped us from learning. But we quite like them because they are also very funny girls. They also have guts. Both Christoph and I are fond of that.

Christoph and I talked a lot about our future during this time. We agreed that we would both look for a partner that we both liked. Because our personal bond was very important to us. We couldn't imagine what it would be like to no longer have contact.

Aunt Seraphia made us very happy, because she was always in our vicinity during our student life and regularly organised get-togethers with us and our relatives in München or Ingolstadt, where we danced extensively. Some of our fellow students were also included in these dance evenings and new, sometimes intimate friendships grew, some of which would certainly last for a long time to come.

To my surprise, after completing my studies and exams, I was given an official document allowing me to practise law in public. At least in theory. Practical application is one of those things ...

It was rumoured that Director Ickstatt and Professor Johann Adam Weishaupt[20] said that they had come to appreciate me and had never taught such a sociable class of students, as everyone pulled themselves together because of me and behaved reasonably well. What's more, our grade had done everything in literally no time.

At first, they could not have imagined that a woman would be capable of such achievements. To their surprise, my contracts were watertight, and that could only be said of a few lawyers. After we graduated, my brother was allowed to spend some time learning the ropes with a lawyer in München, but as a woman I was not allowed to do that, which is why I travelled back to our parents.

During this time, I had leisure to inhale all the news I could absorb. So, I learnt that Maria Theresa's 14-year-old daughter Maria Antonia (the French call her Marie Antoinette) was married in April in the Augustinian Church in Wien *per procurationem*[21] to the French Dauphin Luis-Auguste, who was not present at his own wedding. She then travelled to Versailles, where the real wedding to the heir of the throne took place.

I could imagine that it wouldn't be easy for the young woman. Suddenly, she was more or less on her own in a foreign country, where she was also in the public eye. No matter what she did, there would always be people who would criticise her.

But I also had a lot of contact with Nannerl. Every time we visited our relatives in Salzburg, I tried to meet Nannerl. This was usually possible because the houses were only a few streets apart. Nannerl proudly told me that Wolfgang had been awarded the *Order of the Golden Spur* by Pope Clement XIV on 26 June. He can now call himself a *Cavaliere, Chevalier* or *Knight*. Of course, he is also very

20 *Johann Adam Weishaupt was the founder of the Illuminati Order in 1776.*
21 *By power of attorney – marriage ceremony by proxy.*

33

busy composing in Italy. But Nannerl has not remained idle either. She composes and plays a lot herself. She is a fantastic pianoforte player and continues to improve.

I, too, was always very interested in news from around the world. Including news of Captain James Cook, who was on an expedition to a new continent that had already been called *Terra Australis incognita*[22] since Claudius Ptolemy. Cook took possession of the eastern part of New Holland[23] for the Kingdom of Great Britain and named it New South Wales.

In July, the Russians defeated the Ottoman fleet in the three-day naval battle of Çesme[24]. Shortly afterwards, they also defeated an 80,000-strong army of their enemies. With the help of the Russians, Greece was thus rid of this foreign rule.

I'm so glad that there are no fights here at the moment.

---

22   *Southern, unknown land.*
23   *This is what Australia was called after the first discovery by the Dutch*
24   *In the Russo-Turkish War (1768–1774)*

*"To see clearly, all you need
is a change of perspective."*

Antoine de Saint-Exupéry
French novelist
(1900–1944)

1771

In 1771, we, who had a much better life than the majority of the population, also became old mother Hubbard's cupbord. The previous year's harvests had already been extremely poor due to floods and storms, and there seemed to be no end to this. Grain became immensely more expensive and also became a kind of luxury for us.

Father had the foresight to store grain in his warehouse in Hamburg and gave it out in small quantities to the needy at very humane prices. However, he had to have this store and the deliveries guarded like the apple of his eye. There were also many sacks of grain stored on our farm that only a few people knew about. In the meantime, grain prices in Bavaria had risen sevenfold.

Christoph was now back home and I helped him with the law cases he received from clients who lived in our neighbourhood. Unfortunately, all my legal training didn't help me against what befell me about a year after we graduated.

Seraphia had an invitation to a large party in Ingolstadt in September 1771, which included Christoph and me. We were all looking forward to the evening. Seraphia was hoping to make new connections that would help her career and we siblings were looking forward to seeing some of our fellow students again.

We had travelled here two weeks in advance and met up with our former fellow students and lecturers. They were fun days with lots of banter, but also exciting and serious discussions. Some had grown up compared to the first day of our studies, others had remained the same thoughtless lads.

We once attended a lecture for first-year students. It was led by Count Jacob von Falkenstein. He was a likeable and handsome man with wit and charm. Von Falkenstein included us, who were already qualified lawyers, and then seemed very surprised that some of the questions were passed on to me for answering. You could see the surprise he felt when he got exactly the right answers from me.

Von Falkenstein was a few years older than us. He supported the university as a lecturer on a monthly basis. He had come as a lecturer towards the end of our student days and we had only seen him a few times. He was likeable and good at what he did. And von Falkenstein knew how to keep students in a good mood and spur them on to work hard.

Seraphia had told us that his mother, an eccentric person, had had the ambition in her youth to become the best violinist in the German-speaking world. She was really good, but was quickly married off to the Count von Falkenstein and was thus away from the soirée stage. According to Seraphia, she never got over the fact that she could no longer play in front of larger audiences, while our mother had a career despite her marriage.

Von Falkenstein was also there for a social evening. He laughed and joked with us and I could well imagine him as a reliable friend. The two of us talked briefly about a contentious family dispute. He was quite a good lawyer and, it seemed to me, a sensitive person.

The ball and its consequences

But now to the ball that followed just two evenings later. For this very festive occasion, I wore a gold-coloured silk dress, combined with a green breast insert and green sleeves. The dress was perfectly made and relatively simply decorated.

I don't like this overloaded fashion that can still be seen at some of the big receptions and balls. It makes me feel like a cow at a cattle drive[25]. Christoph complimented me when he saw me. That's saying something. He's usually rather reserved about such things.

We arrived at a large townhouse and were introduced to our hosts. They had a wonderfully large ballroom decorated with thousands of colourful and fragrant flowers, probably from countless greenhouses.

Almost immediately, my brother spotted our university friends and we went to meet them. It was as if we hadn't seen each other for decades instead of just a few hours!

I couldn't look as quickly as the gentlemen asked me for my favour for the individual dances. I had also promised a dance to the Count von Falkenstein. Incidentally, he was the nephew of the hosts and had already asked for a dance when we were introduced to his uncle and his wife. He insisted on a minuet at a later hour.

So I danced the first minuet with Fritz, the first German dance with Konstantin, the first Anglaise with Johann and so on. Of course, I danced one minuet with my brother.

During the dance break, we stood together and drank punch. My brother gave me a poke in the ribs. "Look, something's happening over there."

I looked in the direction indicated and spotted a young lady obsessively chewing on the tips of her gloves[26], while she fixed her gaze on an older man who I had already noticed unpleasantly. "She wants to get rid of him," I said. "I understand that. I hope she succeeds!"

"He doesn't seem to understand what she's trying to tell him. Some people just don't know the secret language of ladies' gloves. Or he doesn't want to understand it." He chuckled.

It was already past one o'clock when I stepped out during another break in the orchestra to freshen up a bit and check

---

25   *In the alps, cattle are during the summer on fields high up the mountains. If the season ist successful, the lot comes down beautiful decorated in Autumn.*

26   *There was not only the fan language, but also the glove language and the language of flowers. However, I think there were often translation errors here.*

my hair in the mirror. I had the feeling that a few hairpins had come loose.

With the help of a maid, whom our hostess had assigned to deal with just such incidents, my hair was back in place in no time and I was about to head back towards the ballroom when Leonhard von Falkenstein, the younger brother of Jacob von Falkenstein, stopped me. He was accompanied by a young lady and his brother.

"Ah, there you are! Dear Demoiselle von Sommerauer, please spare us a few minutes. Rumour has it that you are good with all kinds of contracts. I would like my contract with a business partner to be untroubled. You would do me a particular favour if you would take a quick look through it with my brother. There are only two pages. So it should only be a few minutes before you can tell me whether anything needs to be changed."

Although I didn't like him, I couldn't really refuse our host's nephew. Besides, his brother and this young woman were there. So the four of us went into the library. There we sat down on two ottomans over the corner. Jacob von Falkenstein and I bent over the papers, while his brother stood up again and paced restlessly up and down.

Jacob and I were discussing the wording of a sentence when suddenly someone ripped open the library door and shouted. "Murder". At that moment, I realised that Jacob and I were alone in the room and that I wouldn't get out of this situation unscathed. Von Falkenstein looked just as shocked as I felt.

I must have sat there paralysed. Because after a few seconds, von Falkenstein put his hand on mine and whispered, "I'm so sorry. I didn't know anything about this, please believe me". Within minutes, the library was full of people.

Leonhard, the brother of twenty-eight-year-old Jacob, had obviously set out to compromise us. Now he was standing next to his companion in the crowd, looking at us in turn with a smug expression.

Jacob, on the other hand, looked like a cornered animal. He looked at me seriously for a long time, as if he was weighing things up. I sensed the moment when he steered himself, and thus our common destiny, into the path that offered me a way out of the expected ostracism of society. He went down on his knees in front of me with the words:

"Dearest Victoria von Sommerauer, may I ask you to marry me? I implore you to say that you will marry me." A little more quietly, so that only I could understand, he added: "I assure you that I will not put any obstacles in the way of you going your own way."

Applause erupted around us. There was no turning back now. With a heavy heart, I gave him my word that I would marry him. Jacob von Falkenstein was a man of honour. That much I realised at that moment.

His mother, who was also standing near us, looked petrified. It must have been terrible for her to see the daughter of her hated rival as her future daughter-in-law. Leonhard's smug expression changed to triumphant. He had driven his brother into a situation that he had not wanted.

The general commotion and the announcement, which spread like wildfire through the ballroom, caught the attention of Christoph and Aunt Seraphia. They immediately rushed to us to find out what was going on.

In the meantime, Jacob had managed to get everyone else out of the room so that we could talk in peace.

My now fiancé explained everything to my relatives and asked me to apologise again: "I should have mistrusted my brother straight away. I'm sorry that I didn't see through the whole thing. I think he wanted to present me as a cad to the company gathered here. I don't think it has anything to do with you, Victoria."

Christoph made a visible effort not to flare up. "What a terrible misfortune! Your brother is an intriguer! It was honourable of you to offer to marry Victoria. I thank you for that on behalf of our parents. My sister has given you her word that she will marry you. The reasons for this are well known.

Just believe me: as soon as I realise that you're making Vic unhappy, I'll take care of it."

I interjected here. "Christoph, that's very kind of you. But we need to get to know each other better first. I'm firmly convinced that we'll come to terms with the situation, if not more."

Jacob also had something to say. "Thank you, Victoria, I agree. I don't think it's a lack of sympathy, Mr von Sommerauer. I hold your sister in high esteem and have the greatest respect for her as a person. But it's too early to guarantee her happiness."

Seraphia looked at Jacob for a long time. "Count von Falkenstein, I know you to be a reliable and pleasant man and I think that you and my niece are a couple who are well suited to each other. It is now up to the two of you to turn your mutual sympathy into something more."

Jacob led me to the dance. He danced a minuet with me to our engagement with perfect form. He was as good a dancer as my brother. At least that was a small consolation!

After our dance, he introduced me to his best friend, Frederik von Barby. This man, a count's son, was a very handsome man, even better looking than Jacob. He looked at me with cold eyes that made me shiver. I was worried that I was going to have a problem here. I think he thought I had set things up to make a good match, because the von Falkensteins were a wealthy family.

I was grateful to Jacob von Falkenstein for this act of honour and somehow I also liked him. On the other hand, I would have liked to challenge his brother to a duel. But such a death would have been too honourable for him. Poison, perhaps? No, I was not a murderer. But I wished this man murder or even the plague on his neck with all my might.

I cried myself to sleep that night and for a few nights afterwards because – like so many women before me – I would enter into a relationship without love. I had always believed that this would never happen to me.

My parents were upset when they found out about the upcoming wedding, but they couldn't help me. However, they also promised to offer me shelter at any time if the marriage turned out to be unsustainable, even though they both largely conformed to social norms, they didn't want to see me unhappy.

I felt sorry for myself, although only a few days later I received a letter from my husband-to-be enclosing a contract that guaranteed me a life of my own. I was to manage my dowry myself and could do as I pleased as long as I didn't make my husband a laughing stock. A very generous gesture that put my fiancé in an even more favourable light.

Between the chairs

The wedding took place just three weeks later in October, on a golden autumn day. It was, without exaggeration, a glittering celebration. Jacob's mother had arranged and organised almost everything and she was unbeatable at it. Nothing was lacking, even though many people feared for their existence due to the famine.

Everyone who was anyone in the region was there. Even Elector Maximilian III attended our wedding in the Frauenkirche in München, which was celebrated by the bishop.

Although he was handsome and clever and therefore much sought-after by the ladies, I wasn't aware of any of Jacob's dalliances, as I knew them from other men. That was a relief for me. But even though I quite liked him, I wouldn't have chosen Jacob if I'd seen any other way of getting out of it without disgrace. After all, we hardly knew each other.

So the wedding with him was more of a sad occasion for me. But there was another reason, I only found out about it on the wedding night.

We were to spend our wedding night in the family's town palace in the *Burggassen*[27] and also live there in the future – at least during the cold season. With great fanfare, we were brought to the door of our wedding room by Jacob's mother – who was freezing cold towards me – and a few other relatives. There was a dressing room on either side. One led into a second bedroom, which was to be mine. My maid helped me out of my wedding dress and into a sumptuously embroidered nightgown. She undid my hair and combed it until it shone. Then I dismissed her and locked the door.

When we were finally alone, Jacob pointed to one of two chairs next to a table with a carafe of wine and glasses. "Please sit down."

He picked up the carafe and poured us both a drink. He then sat down on the second chair, toasted me, took a sip and then looked at me for a long time before he spoke.

"It's the first time you and I have been alone since the unspeakable incident at the ball. I would have liked to have spared both of us all that. I didn't know what my brother had planned. Please believe me."

He looked at me pleadingly.

"I saw your frightened face and sensed that you weren't feeling well about the whole thing. But why?"

"Oh, it's all quite complicated."

He took both my hands in his. "I knew that sooner or later I would have to marry a woman. My mother wants grandchildren at all costs. Of course, I thought that if I

---

27   *A street in Munich city*

did, my wife should at least be a good-looking and smart woman. Someone I can show off in public and with whom I can really have a conversation. You are suiting both points. So I guess I can consider myself lucky. But I didn't want to steal your life. Especially not from you, because I really appreciate you. You're worth much more than I can give you.

"I can't imagine what possessed my brother at the moment he left us alone. The only reason I can think of is that he thought I was behaving dishonourably and he could have shone as a result. He's always seen me as a disruptive competitor.

"He and my mother will make life difficult for you, I think. They both radiate such dislike towards you that it almost scares me."

"I can probably even explain to you about your mother." I told him about his mother's ambitions and her competitive thoughts towards my Mamma. "I'm sure, like Leonhard, she thought you would never marry me and is now very disappointed by your reaction."

"That probably explains it. I always knew my mother wasn't easy, but I didn't know she had this ugly streak.

"I beg you to at least give me your affection." Now he had tears in his eyes. "I like and admire you. That's why I will try to make your life as beautiful as I can, I promise you that here and now."

I must have looked as if I had seen a ghost, because he continued speaking quickly.

"I want so much for you to be a good companion and friend to me, even though I can't give you my heart. Because that already belongs to someone else."

I thought of some icy eyes that had looked at me after we had announced our engagement. Slowly, I understood what he was trying to tell me. I thanked the heavens that Seraphia had told me so much about people and that I had always listened. So I asked offhandedly, "You love a man, is that it?" and hoped it wasn't true.

Jacob looked at me, startled, like a little boy who had been caught stealing.

"Your friend Frederik? Please don't lie to me. Nobody will find out from me, I swear to you on everything I hold sacred. If you really want me to be your friend, then please be open with me now."

Again, he waited to answer and just looked at me at first. Then he gave himself a jolt. He had made up his mind.

"Yes, it's Frederik. I'm attracted to both sexes, but it's true that he's the love of my life."

My new husband knew that he was completely exposing himself and his great love to me with this confession. I could have destroyed their life – and mine – with a single word[28].

"I owe it to you to be honest. You have a great attraction for me, I can't deny that. And I also want to share a bed with you and a part of my life. I want to be a good husband to you. The nights we spend together should be just the two of us. But you should also know that I can't offer you my heart, only my affection and friendship. And you have that unconditionally because you are a wonderful person."

"Please tell me more." I wanted to know the exact circumstances that I now had to come to terms with.

"We've known each other since Frederik was at university. He's five years younger than me. After we both had some experience with the opposite sex, the two of us got to know each other a few years ago and gradually became a couple. A very happy couple.

"Even when Frederik moved to München three years ago, we continued to meet. I helped him get his first clients. He is my only close friend and the most important person in my life."

"Does your mother know about you?"

"God forbid, no! If she knew, she would have declared me mad long ago – or maybe even had me killed. But I think

28   With the help of the jurist Anselm von Feuerbach, Bavaria did not criminalise se-
      xual acts between men until 1813, long before Prussia did, following the Civil Code.

she suspects that I'm hiding something from her, because I can't think of any other reason why she hardly ever lets me out of her sight. Without Frederik, there's no doubt that I wouldn't be alive for a long time. His love alone makes me put up with my mother."

"Who knows about you?"

"Nobody. You know about it now."

Inwardly, I was deadly sad. I now had a very kind and sincere husband who would certainly treat me well, but he in turn loved a man. I was surprised that I wasn't shocked, just disappointed – and a little afraid of where this would lead.

"Thank you for your openness. I give you credit for that. Now I have to see how I can live with it. If your secret is uncovered, I'll be finished socially, too. Besides, your boyfriend worries me. You couldn't see the deadly look he gave me when you introduced us at the ball."

"He showered me with reproaches. He said I should have just dropped you. But I was able to convince him that I was also partly to blame for the situation and therefore had an obligation to you. It will be difficult to completely appease him. But at least he now believes me that you are not to blame and that my brother was the mastermind.

"Please don't worry about it tonight. It's our wedding night. I promise you that I will make it as pleasant as possible for you. I want you to be at least as comfortable with me as I am in your company."

Jacob stood up and pulled me up to him to hug me. He stroked and kissed me in silence for quite a while. I had sworn to myself that I would have a positive experience on my wedding night, so I switched off my thoughts and focussed on my feelings. Jacob made me realise that he wasn't averse to caresses either and so I carefully felt my way forward and began to stroke him. It felt right to me. We were now chained together and somehow we had to make the best of it together.

We both had another glass of wine and, after Jacob had topped up the fire again, we went to bed.

Feeling was exactly the right approach. Jacob insisted that we took off our nightgowns. He stroked me tenderly all over my body, let me explore his too and it was only after a long time of knowing every inch of each other and also telling each other our desires that our marriage was truly consummated. He actually managed to banish my fear. I didn't find the act half as bad as I had imagined from various stories behind closed doors. I am sure that I have my husband's prudence to thank for this.

When I woke up in the morning, Jacob looked at me seriously, leaning on one arm "Good morning, love," he said. "I think I have a place in my heart for you too. It feels good to have you here, Vic. I thank you for everything and will do everything in my power to make you happy."

Yes, I liked Jacob too, he was really gentle and considerate towards me. He let me sensitively discover my own desires and I am grateful to him for that. I would even go so far as to say that having sex with him was a wonderful experience and, if the stories are to be believed, such an emotional union is probably not given to many wives.

But there was still this drop of bitterness called Frederik. I kept thinking about the cold eyes that had literally impaled me. I knew I had to come up with something. I knew that Jacob would suffer sooner or later if his wife and his lover were hostile to each other. Hopefully Frederik knew that too.

Personal initiative

My mother-in-law was a terrible person. She was under pressure to control everything. Especially her older son. Leonhard usually stayed at another family home, for which I was grateful. I think she adored Jacob. But it was a jealous love, one that poisoned everything and robbed him of the air he needed to breathe.

Jacob's mother kept a close eye on him, even after our wedding. Jacob could hardly go anywhere on his own. She completely ignored me, as far as she could.

Then one night Jacob came into my bedroom. He wasn't in a good mood. It was the first time I'd seen him slightly drunk on port and his eyes were moist. "What's wrong, Jacob?" I asked him, offering him the space next to me in bed. "Please tell me. Maybe I can help you dispel the dark clouds."

He sighed and pulled me close. "I'm going mad, my dear Victoria. It's only your company that keeps me from hurting myself."

I shuddered. His condition was really bad. So I took him in my arms and stroked his back reassuringly.

"Mother has never been as bad as she has been since we got married. We've been married for a fortnight now and since then I haven't even had the chance to see Frederik. Whenever I make an attempt to get away from the house, mamma has a ridiculous task for me. I'm dying of longing for him."

"Why doesn't he come here?"

"Mother doesn't like him. She's accepted that he's a friend of mine so far, but she doesn't want him in the house. She also has a hard time with your presence. Because I can't go to you during the day either. She immediately stops me. As if she really regrets having to share me with you. It's just as well that she has no power over either of us, at least at night."

Now I realised why Jacob was never around me during the day. I always thought he wasn't interested in my company. It hurt me to hear that. So I took my time to announce the decision I had made long ago. Over the past few days, I had come to the conclusion that I wanted to help Jacob because I wanted him to be happy, even if it cost me something.

"Tomorrow we'll both go for a long ride – unaccompanied. We'll show ourselves around town first and then visit your beloved Frederik. Your mamma will make a fool of herself if she doesn't let us go out together – unaccompanied. After all, we're both adults and even married."

Jacob looked at me hopefully. Then he kissed me. "Have I already told you that I like you very much? Not like Frederik, but my feelings for you have grown in the meantime. Your strength gives me strength." He stayed with me that night. I could feel the anticipation in him every time he touched me. It made me sad and happy at the same time.

After breakfast, we saddled up our horses. "Mother, Victoria and I are going for a ride together," Jacob announced our decision.

She didn't contradict him, she just pierced me with her eyes. I didn't owe her anything. So we were able to set off undisturbed. We were already discussing a legal case on the way to the stables. The stable lads all shook their heads when they heard our heated discourse. But I'm sure they realised that we were having a great time. And that's how it should be between newlyweds.

The first thing we did was visit one of Jacob's old aunts. Aunt Cecilia was a sister of his father. Her marriage had been annulled. Jacob had told me that her brother had rescued her from the clutches of a cruel man and had demanded the town palace in *Das Thall*[29] from him as compensation for the cruelty she had suffered. This was the only way to prevent the matter from becoming public knowledge. Cilia, as she immediately let us call her, was walking on a stick, which was a result of her few weeks in a marriage.

We spent the usual time with her for a short morning visit that was only just in keeping with propriety and promised to delight the old and frail but enchanting lady with a visit more often.

---

29   *Street in Munich city*

Then we rode along winding paths to Frederik's city palace in the *Schwabinger Gassen*. We were admitted and led into the parlour where Frederik was sitting. The greeting between the two men was exuberant. I, on the other hand, was greeted a little stiffly and our hosts eyes, which had been shining with joy at first, turned cold again when they looked at me. But Frederik kept his composure. He had tea and cupcakes served and finally dismissed the staff. "Thank you, let's have a chat without further interruption, as one likes to do between friends."

When the door had closed, Jacob's first words to his friend were: "Vic knows all about us."

Frederik flinched, looked first at his friend and then at me. I could see and feel his fear.

"How could you?" he yelled at Jacob. "She'll be our downfall!"

"No, on the contrary, she's our only salvation and it's only thanks to her that we're sitting here together now."

Frederik's eyes met mine again. Less cold this time, more doubtful and searching. "It's asking a lot to entrust your life to someone you don't yet know how to judge."

"Do you have another choice? Do I have another?" I stood up and faced the two of them. "Don't think that I wouldn't have imagined a marriage differently! If I had to have a husband, I wanted one who only loved me and who I would be in love with first. You know what I got instead. I'm not happy with this situation either! And I find it hard to bear. But what else can I do but help you?

"I know that my mother-in-law will give Jacob an attendant if I don't go with him. I also know that he loves you and I can see that you love him. You wouldn't separate after all. I'd rather have the feeling that I've got things under control somehow. Even if that's perhaps just an illusion.

"I've liked Jacob since we first met. He's a good person. I want him to be happy. You will both have to live with my existence, just as I have to live with yours. However, it would be easier for all of us, and especially for Jacob, if we both at least agreed to a truce. So I offer you peace, Frederik. My life would also be destroyed if someone found out your secret, wouldn't it?"

With that, I went to a door which, as I knew from Jacob, led to the library. I felt more than saw it behind my back as Jacob jumped up and heard his "Dearest!" that carried all the longing a person can feel for another.

Then I closed the door behind me and leant back against it for a moment. Tears welled up in my eyes.

I would be lying if I said it didn't hurt. But I still couldn't complain. Jacob and I got on well. We could have intelligent conversations. Nevertheless, the whole thing with Frederik weighed on me.

I stayed in the library and immersed myself in a book until, after well over an hour, my problem stood before me. When I looked up, Frederik got down on his knees and took my hands in his. He had tears in his eyes.

"Offer accepted. I've realised that you're also just the victim of an intrigue by Jacob's brother. Jacob told me what you did for us. Thank you Vic, you make us both very happy with your support."

"That makes me happy. Then it's not for nothing." I had problems to pronounce, for my tears came back and my throat got narrow.

Frederick went on with his speach. He seems to have the same thick throat like me. "I will always be there for you from now on, should you ever need me. That's a promise. I will be a true friend to you. Just please give me a little time to get used to the new situation."

From that day onwards, Jacob and I often went for rides in the city. We also never forgot Aunt Cilia, who was getting more and more frail.

Around Christmas time, I realised that the time at Frederik's house was the only time for me outside our bedrooms when I didn't feel watched over by my mother-in-law and so I enjoyed the quiet hours in Frederik's library, which I spent studying numerous books and making plans, all the more.

"A clever woman has millions of born enemies: all stupid men."

Marie von Ebner-Eschenbach,
German writer (1830–1916)

1772

Change

My husband was under the thumb of his mother with every fibre of his being. She didn't let me breathe either. As soon as I rebelled against it, she terrorised me. She knew exactly how to impose her will on us. And she had many willing helpers.

After just a few weeks, I was cut off from the world outside of Jacob and Frederik's company and I was horrified to realise that Jacob's mother was the highest authority in the von Falkenstein household and held all the strings in her hand and played with us all like dolls. I felt like I was locked up and constantly running into walls. Somehow I no longer had any aspect of my life under control. I didn't like that at all.

I was also suspicious of Jacob's younger brother Leonhard. He was a young, arrogant dandy who didn't have much intelligence, but he had a lot of muscles that he liked to flex. He gave me a bad feeling right from the start, because as soon as he thought he was unobserved, he looked at me greedily and tried to corner me. I told Jacob and he never left me alone when Leonhard was in the house.

"When it comes to women, I don't trust my brother one bit. I've heard too many rumours for that. He also relishes every opportunity to humiliate me personally. And defiling my wife would suit him just fine. He knows that such an offence would have no consequences for him because the family would have to keep it under wraps.

"If I can't give you all my love, I at least want to protect you from him. Because you mean a lot to me. I couldn't have found a better wife than you."

I then received one of the few intimate kisses from Jacob, which showed me that he now felt more for me than just friendship.

When Leonhard also wanted to move into the palace after the Christmas holidays, I had finally had enough. I came to blows with my mother-in-law and managed to get Jacob and I to move out within a few days – to the palace of his aunt Cilia, who had died shortly before Christmas. She had bequeathed her beautiful palace with all its furnishings and servants to Jacob and me. I had already put my legal skills to good use in the quiet of Frederik's library and got Jacob to sign several deeds to prevent his horrible family from ever gaining control of this piece of our freedom.

When Jacob realised that I wasn't fundamentally fighting against his family, but for both of our freedom, he bravely stood behind me and did everything I suggested. Our last day with his family ended with a terribly ugly argument with my domineering mother-in-law, who was afraid of losing her influence over her son. We both got very loud. But I didn't give in one jot. Jacob sided with me and we won the battle and all our possessions were in our own house within days.

Just two days after our move, Jacob was looking for a ring he had received as a gift from Frederik. "I'm sure I put it on the chest of drawers in my bedroom yesterday afternoon – with some papers. The papers are still there, but the ring is gone."

I looked up from the magazine I had been reading. "I saw your ring lying there when I wanted to ask you if you could have a quick look at which dress fits better. Did you check to see if it had fallen off?"

"Of course. I crawled around the chest of drawers on all fours and was promptly caught by a parlour maid. That was a bit embarrassing." He looked at me with a grimace and we both had to laugh.

"Hm, we are intruders into the lives of the servants who have always worked here. They think they owe us nothing, but we owe them everything. Please let me do it. If he's not already miles away, you'll get your ring back."

So I sent for all of Jacob's aunt's former servants, who now worked for us in the house and in the stables.

Quite a few faces looked at us eagerly. First Jacob said a few warm words about his aunt, then he let me have the floor.

"You used to work for my husband's aunt and now we're the new bosses here. That's a change for you and us. We will have to get used to each other. I don't expect this to happen overnight without any differences.

"If you no longer wish to stay here, you are free to leave. You will receive your outstanding salary and can accept another job if one is offered to you. Of course, you will also receive a proper letter of reference from us.

"From now on, there are certain rules for each and every individual who stays here – regardless of which rules applied here before. I will now explain these rules to you. If you would prefer to leave us, please do so.

"Firstly, I can assure you that we will do everything we can to get us all through the famine. However, we also need your help to do this. In spring, we will convert ano-ther good part of the garden into a vegetable garden. From now on, we will only cook simple meals and only as much as is actually eaten. Waste is out of the question.

"I demand complete loyalty from all of you. There will be no gossiping about anything or anyone here in the house or on our land. Members of my mother-in-law's household are not welcome here and will only be granted access to the house or the stables with our express blessing.

"Remain friendly but firm towards them. You have our express authorisation to expel these people from the pro-perty. In particular, my mother-in-law and her second son Leonhard have no authority over you. I don't want them in the house without my husband or I knowing about it.

"Anyone who steals something and is caught is pub-licly reported and thrown out in a wide arc. Don't think that we don't know exactly where our possessions are or where they should be. We may well notice a missing item of clothing. The same goes for a missing piece of jewellery or other items.

"You will realise that we are also completely normal people. We are also familiar with the problems that can arise in families or among servants. So if one of you is in some kind of private difficulty, he or she can tell us about it at any time. We will then consider together how we can solve the problem. We will take you and your concerns seriously. So don't be shy.

"However, I must warn you," I said firmly "don't take advantage of our good nature. You can trust us to the extent that we can trust you. That is a promise."

My speech caused a real chatter among the servants. Everyone had something to say, but not to us. We left them to discuss in peace and retired to our rooms.

That very evening, Jacob's valet stood before me in the library. Our majordomo[30] had brought him to me at his own request. The still quite young man, who had introduced himself as Erich Hintermeier, stood before me, his head bowed and his nervous hands wringing.

"Our majordomo Heinrich said you've come with a request?" I said.

He put Jacob's ring on the small table next to me.

"Madame, I'm so ashamed. I would like to get married and got carried away without thinking. I thought I could buy a licence to marry with this ring. But it almost burnt a hole in my trousers. I realised that I couldn't build my life with the woman I loved on a lie and a theft. It would destroy everything.

"I also like you and your husband. I think you are good people. Not like the people I was with before Madame Cäcilia and not like your husband's mother, who only tells us terrible stories."

---

30 From Latin "steward of the house". He is the highest court official, comparable to the English butler.

The servant then looked me firmly in the eye. "When you spoke to us, I realised that I would have to give you the ring back. At first I just wanted to put it back in your husband's room. But then they would have suspected the chambermaids too and there would always have been tension in the house. So I had to do it personally.

"If you think it's right, then throw me out of the house today. All I ask is that you don't report me to the authorities, because otherwise I won't find a job anywhere and neither will my beloved Franzi[31] if word gets out."

I asked him to sit opposite me and let him tell me about his first job, then about his time here with Jacob's aunt and also about his lover Franzi.

According to him, his first master had been a terribly conceited man who never had a kind word for his servants. He spoke of Jacob's aunt with respect. He had taken the old lady with all her quirks to his heart and missed her.

Erich had previously held a different position and had only recently been appointed valet de chambre when Cilia felt her end approaching. She wanted all her people to remain in their positions.

The domestic servants also seemed to have a good relationship with each other. The young man spoke in the warmest terms about the efficiency of the others. At the end, when he spoke of his sweetheart, his eyes shone.

I came to a decision and looked directly at him.

"Thank you for your honesty, Erich. There will be no consequences for your actions this time. Only you and I know about the matter and that's that. You'll stay here in position and do a good job, as you probably always have. If you prove yourself, then I promise you that my husband and I will help you obtain a marriage licence – within the next two years. Is that an acceptable offer for you?"

Erich got down on his knees in front of me and kissed my hands. He had tears in his eyes when he looked at me.

---

31   *Franzi is the Bavarian short form of Franziska.*

"Thank you, Madame, you are very kind. I will do my best to do you and your husband every honour and serve you well."

From that day on, something fundamental changed in the behaviour of our entire staff, which we had taken over from Aunt Cilia and did not want to replace. Everyone became noticeably more relaxed, attentive and trusting. Jacob and I soon knew all the names of the servants, also knew a little about their backgrounds and were rewarded for our appreciation of our people with almost consistently willing staff, most of whom went about their work in a good mood.

If there were any difficulties – including family difficulties – we were consulted and always offered advice or financial support here and there.

Jacob and I had separate bedrooms, as was customary in our social class. But we also shared the same bed in our house at least twice a week.

We usually had in-depth conversations late into the night, but sometimes we also got intimate with each other.

Over time, I was able to enjoy this more and more because Jacob was a sensitive lover who kept asking me what I would like. We tried out a lot and I got to know my body in a whole new way. During our time together, he also focussed completely on me. Frederik wasn't mentioned at all.

We were both much more relaxed after being without his mother's influence. Jacob even became a really cheerful and lively person. Frederik visited us, or we visited him, almost every day. Sometimes Jacob was also alone with his other sweetheart.

I was delighted that Frederik also became a really good friend to me over time. We found things in common and met with respect for each other.

The connection with Jacob, as tricky as it was, brought me an advantage that should not be underestimated. With him, I rose into the higher aristocratic circles of München and made acquaintances there. He was successful and showed this with the woman at his side.

The fact that he was successful was also due in part to me. I worked on some of his cases in the background as a lawyer.

We worked very well together and I enjoyed having something to do. I also had a wonderful fencing and riding partner with Frederik and I really enjoyed dancing with both of them. Jacob was an enthusiastic dancer.

At home, in spring, I made sure that crops were grown in another part of the park-like garden in addition to the existing vegetable garden. I also had a greenhouse put up. I wanted at least our household to have enough to eat in the future. As it gave me pleasure, I helped with the sowing. At the end, I bought wine for all the helpers.

We all had to make do with less, but nobody had to go hungry – and our cook became very inventive. She was extremely proud every time we praised her for what she conjured up from the few supplies we had. I had instructed her to really only cook as much as we could eat and not to waste anything. The dishes were no longer as sophisticated, but still very tasty.

We shared what food we could procure from Jacob's lands and father's business connections with Frederik and the servants of both households. This gesture in turn secured the loyalty of our people once and for all. They were well fed and all of them were committed to ensuring that we all continued to have a life in which we lacked nothing important.

Hooray, a female friend

I began to build up a circle of acquaintances, visited a few ladies here and there for a chat, and even invited them myself from time to time. It was important to me to be part of this society, not least so that I could counteract rumours about "my" men straight away. Because the usual ladies' meetings consisted mainly of gossip about others. The women had nothing else to do but to think up and tell delicate stories about others. After all, in our circles they had no other role than to be decorative and bear heirs. Because so many major official events were cancelled due to the general mood caused by the famine, every bit of news was spread.

It wasn't that I didn't enjoy some of the meetings, because there was a lot of laughter and there were usually excellent drinks and sometimes exotic fruit from one or other of the orangeries. But I wouldn't describe these women as friends.

At one such meeting, which was absolutely boring for me and almost put me to sleep, two other visitors were announced. I noticed how gruffly the hostess reacted to the second name at first, before regaining control of her facial features and voice.

The two ladies entered the room. The first was probably about the same age as Seraphia, the other I guessed to be about my age. The older one was dressed in modern and elaborate clothes and her entrance caused the hostess's face to light up briefly. The younger lady, who was dressed much more simply but tastefully, made a very pleasant and dignified impression on me. I observed her and immediately sensed that she was not particularly comfortable in her own skin. Her behaviour was impeccable and she had a nice smile on her face, although it didn't reach her eyes.

I learnt that the two were Countess Aichelberg and her niece Magdalena von Sieghardinger.

That day, I had kept to the background the whole time and left it at that. So I could see that this woman, who interested me more and more, was attacked by everything she said. Not in such a way that it was immediately obvious, but in such a way that it created an unpleasant feeling.

As I wasn't paying much attention to the conversations, I was surprised when the word was suddenly addressed to me.

"What do you think, Victoria?"

I automatically reacted to my name, but didn't know what the question was about. All pairs of eyes were on me, which was embarrassing.

"Oh, sorry, I must have been dreaming. What was the question?"

"Who were you dreaming about? About your husband or your lover?"

"Neither one. I was just enjoying the little rainbows that the sunlight casts on the wall through your crystal chandelier. It's just beautiful."

The hostess replied somewhat harshly: "How can a person who normally thinks as practically as you can fall into such childish fancies. We said that we would probably have to go to the market ourselves in future because our kitchen staff were throwing money out of the window for the few things we get on the table. My cook now spends huge amounts of money on food. She probably keeps some of it herself. I can't explain it any other way."

I was indignant. At that moment, I caught the eye of the younger lady who had been introduced to us as Magdalena Sieghardinger. Suddenly she began to smile and her eyes lit up. We had understood each other.

I clearly took the position of the servants when I returned to the original topic. "You can't possibly be serious, dear Friederike. We have a famine in the country. It goes without saying that food is extremely expensive and hard to come by."

Now Magdalena also got in touch. "I went to the market last week because I wanted to see for myself. It really is devastating. There are huge crowds in the bakeries. The bread that the common people call `hunger bread´ is more than twice as expensive as normal and even smaller.

"There is hardly any product and what is available is sometimes spoilt or expensive. On the way home after shopping, you have to be careful not to get mugged and robbed.

"Our cook only goes shopping when accompanied by two strong and armed men. We are glad that she always finds ways to get hold of perfectly good food. Even if we think they are overpriced. But it will become even more difficult. The harvest is still a long way off and nobody can say today what it will look like. There are already many deaths from hunger, which of course we women are not told about because we are oh so delicate beings who cannot bear the truth. On the other hand, the men on the streets complain about their wives' ignorance of their environment. I've heard that myself."

The ladies all looked at her in dismay. Magdalena had told them a truth they didn't want to hear. She probably did this often and was therefore not particularly popular with the ladies.

She was the only one I could really call a friend after a while. She was known as a very well-read and rhetorically brilliant woman and was usually ostracised by women and avoided by men for fear of her cleverness.

I really liked her. Because I could have wonderful discussions with her and also talk about scientific or historical topics. She was always an asset to me. Above all, I could always laugh a lot with her. Magdalena is a very cheerful person who can also laugh at herself and her own shortcomings. Both, my husband and his friend, also liked this natural woman from the very beginning and regretted that she was treated so patronisingly by society.

Magdalena lives with her mother and three younger siblings. Fortunately, they own a lucrative country estate, from which they have been able to maintain a respectable, if not lavish, lifestyle. Their father was killed in a robbery of his carriage two years ago. He had also been a brilliant mind – and therefore highly respected.

Here they are again, the great differences that lie only in gender and are revealed by a single prefix. A brilliant man is held in high esteem, but a woman of the same calibre is just as deeply despised.

The art of hunting with falcons

A special feature of the Sieghardinger family, which I had only learnt through an intensive conversation with Magdalena in private, was that her father, like his ancestors, had been a master falconer at the ducal court. Until his death in 1761, he had been the chief falconer to Clemens August Ferdinand Maria Hyazinth, Duke of Baiern and Archbishop, at his court in Köln[32]. He then left the foreign country and returned to Baiern with his family.

"My father received the hunting medal *Ordre de la Clemence* for his services." Magdalena said. "He taught Friedrich and me falconry with the permission of the local prince. Our family is authorised to hunt a certain amount of game with our birds in the München area. Be it ducks, pheasants, partridges, herons, hares, foxes or deer."

"I'm beginning to realise why your brother is called Friedrich."

Magdalena beamed. "Yes, you're right, it was actually named after Friedrich II, whom my father greatly admired!"

"I would love to see a live falcon up close. They fascinate me when I see them flying above me or sitting at the top of a tree."

---

32 *Cologne*

Magdalena was pleased that I was interested. We both agreed that I should come to her in comfortable clothes. "Please wear muted colours and no glittering jewellery. Oh yes, please also refrain from wearing decorative feathers in your hair and similar things. So really very simple. Then you will be introduced to the birds. I'm looking forward to showing you my favourites."

"And how happy I am to see these magnificent birds."

Just a few days later, the time had come. I was very excited. Of course I knew Emperor Frederick II's book *De arte venandi cum avibus*[33]. Although no one in my family had ever had anything to do with falconry, we had all read it. And now I was to be given the opportunity to get very close to these marvellous birds.

I rode up to Magdalena and was warmly welcomed by her. "It's marvellous that you've come here in a man's saddle. Then we can take Friedrich and two of our birds to the *Hofmark Falkenau*[34]. There we can let the birds fly by following on and maybe we'll even have a successful hunt."

"I've heard about following on before. But I can't remember what it is." I just felt very uneducated.

"We let the birds fly free. They circle above us and stay close to us. Maybe they even feel like sitting on a tree for a while. Every now and then we lure them back onto our hand with a small treat and then they are allowed to fly on again. However, if they also chase something, we are delighted. But for now, come with us to the aviaries."

I followed Magdalena with great anticipation. There were aviaries for the birds in a separate building behind the main house.

First she showed me the different birds. "This is Sahib, a male Lanner falcon, a Lanneret. He's almost a year old."

Sahib appeared to me as a rather inconspicuous bird with predominantly brown plumage and a few lighter-colou-

---

33   *On the art of hunting with birds. This book was written between 1241 and 1248 by Emperor Frederick II = Friedrich II of Hohenstaufen.*

34   *now Au-Haidhausen, a district of Munich*

red feathers on the front neck and chest. They darkened towards the bottom. Its legs were bluish and seemed to me to be an unusual colour.

"He's beautiful. Those big eyes! He shows no fear at all."

Magdalena was already standing in front of the next bird.

"Here we have a female Lanner falcon. Thia is already five years old and our best bird."

I was amazed. "I already knew that the females of birds of prey are a lot bigger. But I didn't realise that they looked so much different."

Thia's back and wing coverts were pied grey-brown, the back of her head was reddish and her body was covered with bright, almost white feathers, interspersed only with small brown speckles. Their feet were a bright yellow colour.

Magdalena laughed. "No, it's not like that. Sahib still has his juvenile appearance. He's already fully grown, so he won't get any bigger. But only when he becomes sexually mature, an adult, will he look similar to Thia. He will change his plumage again by then and the colour of his feet will also change."

"Oh, I've never heard of young falcons having a different appearance to old ones."

"Yes, it's not common knowledge either. Many people probably still think they see different species of birds and not the same ones at different ages."

She took a few more steps to the next bird.

"And over here we have Alibaba, our hobby tiercel He is now three years old. His most striking feature is his fox-red trousers. Take a look."

I took a closer look at Alibaba. He was not dissimilar to Thia in colour. His back was brown and he was also lightly speckled with brown at the front. But he was slightly smaller than Sahib. His 'trousers' were actually a strong reddish colour. He also looked at me curiously out of his big eyes.

Magdalena went to the largest aviary.

"Here is our grand lady: Morgana is my female golden eagle. She is a very skilful hunter and also kills adult deer. She brings them down in a matter of seconds. Better than most human hunters."

"How did she come to you?"

"She was brought to us by one of the Elector's hunters. She was still very young at the time and injured on one wing. She wouldn't have survived without human help. I looked after her for months and we both formed a close bond. She is a great bird and stayed here voluntarily, even though I wanted to release her back into the wild.

"I think she enjoys always getting her food reliably and having a quiet and dry place to stay. I often let her fly when I go out riding. She has beaten game for me time and time again."

"I am completely overwhelmed by these marvellous creatures! Just the perfect plumage and the proud look. They don't seem to be afraid of me either."

"That's because both Friedrich and I and two other people in our household take it in turns to look after the animals. They're not just focussed on one person. Well, apart from Morgana, a little bit on me.

"This was always important at the royal courts. If the prince only went hunting with his falcons once in a blue moon and was otherwise unable to look after the birds – the effort involved is high and most princes don't have the time – they couldn't be focussed on a single person, otherwise the success of the hunt would have suffered."

Magdalena presented me with a richly decorated falconer's glove made of thick leather for my left hand.

"Put this on. I'll give you Alibaba on your hand. He's allowed to rest today and will now get his portion to eat."

She went into the spacious aviary and also picked up the bird with one gloved hand. She held the jesses[35] of the bird

---

between her fingers so that the falcon could not suddenly fly off.

"I don't want to put the hood on him now because we're staying here and he's welcome to see what happens."

We carefully let the falcon transfer from her hand to mine. He did this completely calmly. Magdalena showed me how to hold the bird. She gave me a piece of meat on my glove to hold and Alibaba started to eat. It was a special moment of happiness for me when the bird visibly felt comfortable sitting on my hand and trustingly ate what was offered to it. I was also surprised at how light the bird was, even though I thought it was an impressive size.

"Thank you, Magdalena. I really appreciate your trust in me." I was touched by this experience. "It means a lot to me that I can experience this."

"You are my friend. There aren't many people I would trust with one of our birds in any way – even if only for a minute. But I trust you not to do anything that would harm him or us."

The door was opened carefully and Friedrich came in.

"Oh, you're almost ready to go, are you?"

"Yes, Alibaba is just getting his food and then we can go. Are you coming with us? Then I suggest we go on a training flight with Thia and Sahib. Later, I might be able to do a following on with Morgana with Vic."

"Good idea, sister. I'll get the horses saddled and fetch our Bella. She'll love the trip."

While Alibaba was still eating[36], Magdalena filled her falconer's bag with everything she would need. Among other things, she packed a hunting knife, various spare leather leashes and some meat.

Then she checked the bells on Thia and Sahib's feet. In this case, these were two beautifully decorated small bells. The bells make it easier for the hunter to locate the fal-

---

36 *The bird eats.*

cons. They have a delicate sound and let the falconer know where his bird is and sometimes even what it is doing.

Finally, both birds were fitted with ornately decorated leather hoods so that they could no longer see anything. This kept the falcons calmer during transport.

Shortly afterwards, Friedrich came back and announced that our horses were ready to go. A long-legged and multi-coloured dog came into the room with him.

"This is Bella, our pointing dog." Magdalena said. "Our birds all know her, of course, and know exactly that she belongs to us and comes hunting with us. Oh yes, in case you're wondering, falconry dogs are always colourful. Because a brown dog could be mistaken for game by a bird and hit. Bird dogs should have a pleasant character, points game[37] but never rushes, then they are ideal."

"I realise I can still learn a lot here with you!"

Magdalena took Alibaba from my hand after his meal and put him back in his aviary.

We rode out of München to the so-called Falkenau. As the Elector had nothing to do with the falconry, it had been increasingly colonised for a few years. But there was still enough space and, above all, wide open areas next to enough trees to let the birds fly following up.

When we arrived in uninhabited terrain, Magdalena and Friedrich took the hoods off their birds and let them fly.

Friedrich mentioned something that I wouldn't have thought of. "Both are used to each other, so we can let them fly together. But that's not a given. Even in the bird kingdom there are animosities."

I hardly concentrated on my horse any more, but mostly looked up at the sky and marvelled at the flight of these noble birds. They soared into the air and swooped down again at breakneck speed as they were enticed by my companions with some feeding.

---

37 *A pointing dog indicates to the hunter that it has scented game.*

After a marvellous flight, both birds were brought back to the hand and hooded again.

Bella ran ahead of us the whole time with her muzzle close to the ground. She rummaged here, sniffed there and set the pace. Then she suddenly stopped with one front leg in the air. She had scented something.

Magdalena and Friedrich hurried to take the hoods off the birds again.

They both made sure they kept the birds at an angle to suit the wind and game. The birds looked around, roused, muted[38] and then took off. They tried to get height and in the process got ringing up[39] above us. By now Bella had followed the game on the ground and again indicated that she still had it in her nose.

When the birds were high enough for a hunting flight and in a waiting position[40], Friedrich flushed the game[41] and we saw a pheasant fly up. In excellent teamwork, the two birds pursued the pheasant and attacked it. They were above it at a speed that gave it no real chance of escape.

Thia was the one who finally hit the bird. Then she sat on her victim in the middle of the meadow and began to gorge. Magdalena ran over and gave Thia something else to eat as a replacement. Friedrich gave Sahib a piece of meat. Bella also received a treat as thanks for her good work.

"That was beautiful to watch. I could watch you and the birds all day." I said.

The pheasant was packed up and we rode back into town. The whole spectacle had taken us just over an hour.

"There's one more thing that interests me. Does every bird have its own cap?"

"Yes, the hood must fit him perfectly. It must not chafe, it has to be comfortable for the bird. If it doesn't fit, you'll have a lot of trouble because the bird won't accept it and

38 Mute is the falconry term for the droppings of the bird of prey.
39 Circling, if possible above the hunter or at least in visual contact with him.
40 The falcon waits for the game to be startled so that it can hunt it.
41 Hunting slang for flushing out game so that it comes out of cover

will always try to avoid it. As you can see, we can only cover it with one hand because the bird sits on the other. If it doesn't hold still, it doesn't work."

Magdalena looked at me questioningly. "It's not late in the day yet and if you're happy with a slightly later lunch, we can both go out again with Morgana if you want. The thermals are good today and our female eagle loves to fly on days like this."

"Of course I want to. There's no question about it!"

Friedrich promised to take care of the two birds and so Magdalena just hooded her Morgana and we were on our way again.

There was a huge difference in size and weight between Thia and Morgana.

"Morgana weighs about some times over Thia and her wingspan is twice that of our female falcon. But she's such a treasure. You'll be amazed when you see her fly." Magdalena said.

We had arrived at the open space, on one side of which there was a row of trees. Bella was with us again, but this time she hadn't been instructed to search for game. Magdalena took off the bird's hood and shortly afterwards Morgana took off on her flight. It was a feast for the eyes to watch the female eagle's flight. She soared very high. So high that we could almost no longer see her with the naked eye.

Meanwhile, we rode on a little further and talked a bit about everyday things. Then Magdalena reached into her bag and pulled out a piece of meat. She called Morgana and showed her the delicacy. The eagle came flying towards us out of nowhere with such force that my horse became a little restless. My gelding didn't know any big birds. However, he realised how calm Magdalena's horse remained and quickly calmed down again.

Magdalena threw the piece of meat upwards and Morgana elegantly grabbed it with her feet. She then sat down on a nearby tree and ate with relish.

"Of course, she can also eat during the flight, but she's a very indulgent lady." Magdalena laughed happily.

We rode on and a little later Morgana was above us again. She was circling high and looked simply majestic. A sight that makes the heart beat faster. Suddenly I saw a deer running across the plain a long way ahead of us. Morgana had also spotted it and set off in pursuit.

It happened so quickly that I can't say what happened in detail. In any case, Morgana was sitting on the head of the dead deer shortly afterwards. She had struck it in a matter of seconds and had brought it from life to death.

Once again, Magdalena removed the bird from the game and offered replacement food.

"She'll get some of her deer later. But for now, we have to make sure we get the animal home."

Magdalena had ropes with her. Together we tied the deer's legs and hung it behind my gelding's saddle. He had already had to transport game and was therefore suitable for this task.

Our journey back to the city was a little slower, but we had been successful and a piece of meat was a blessing during the ongoing famine. I got a leg of venison to take home and in the evening we had a wonderful roast.

Jacob was happy about the change in the menu and our cook was also delighted that she was finally able to prepare one of her special game dishes again. She said I could go out dressed like a poacher more often and bring fresh meat.

I persuaded Jacob and Frederik to join me at the few dance events that took place. Both were excellent dancers with whom it was a real pleasure to float across the floor. The two men saw each other and were able to chat while I had the advantage of being able to enjoy more dances than usual with really good dancers.

After one of the first events, however, I had to put my foot down when we met at home the next day.

"Are you two tired of life? Do you want to plunge us into ruin? I know what you did when you disappeared for about half an hour. And I also know where. Because I heard you moaning.

"Fortunately, I was able to save you from being discovered in time. Pray to your God that I am the only one with this knowledge! Pull yourselves together and please wait until we get home before indulging your lust. I want to be able to experience such events without fear of being discovered."

I stood in front of the two men, who were sitting next to each other on a sofa, and hissed at them. Horror was written all over both of their faces. Jacob jumped up and took me in his strong arms.

"I promise you that this was the last time. I'm sorry that we put you in danger with our recklessness. It won't happen again."

Frederik also apologised profusely to me and swore to refrain from such escapades in future.

Once we had sorted this out, the following parties were pure joy for me. I danced every dance and was in high spirits. In between, we once again had an invitation to a musical afternoon. Jacob and I accepted the invitation. Frederik was also invited. The two of them sat to my left and right during the performance.

A little later, I was standing in a corner of the parlour with some ladies when one of them approached me. "I envy you so much, my dear. You have a husband and a lover. And both are also long-time friends. It's amazing that your husband is so relaxed about it. You can really see the happiness in all three of you. I don't think it's morally right for you to show yourselves in public with both of them, but your husband doesn't seem to mind."

Another commented, "I would be happy if my husband paid any attention to me at all."

"If my husband looked at me the way your husband looks at you." One said, "I wouldn't be looking for a lover too. But they don't seem to mind ..."

I refrained from commenting on this. I had neither denied nor admitted that Frederik was my lover. I almost couldn't stop myself from laughing. But I was happy about the development, which left less room for speculation in the other direction.

When we sat together the next day, I told the two men about the conversation. And indeed, from that day onwards, Frederik often touched me or winked at me at such events, as if by chance. He made fun of fooling people.

Together we managed over time to integrate Magdalena more into society. Because she enjoyed the attention of the two gentlemen, von Falkenstein and von Barby, and they only had good things to say about her, she was finally able to enjoy the balls with numerous dancers who were suddenly vying for her favour.

In order not to buck the general trend, Magdalena was now also noticed by the ladies. And lo and behold, some of them realised that although Magdalena was smarter than them, she never offended others.

She was gradually taken to heart by some women who were obviously only afraid of being exposed by a woman who was so much smarter than them. The rest were lost anyway.

Why hadn't they excluded me? I wondered. Quite simple: hardly anyone knew that I had studied law and, besides, it was always advantageous to be on good terms with a countess – even if she is one only by marriage. After all, the ladies were not all from the high nobility themselves. They hoped to gain one advantage or another through a connection with me. For example, they were occasionally invited to a ball or to one of the house concerts that I organised at regular intervals. This brought them into conversation and made them seem more important.

Everyday life moves in

Since my first trip with my two falconer friends, I have been to Falkenau several times. Jacob and Frederik were also invited to accompany us. They were no less enthusiastic about the birds and their skills than I was. They also wanted to know everything about this type of hunting from Magdalena and Friedrich.

We learnt that the game usually has a 50:50 chance of escaping the birds. We saw many a hare making marvellous hooks to escape the bird's grasp and were able to congratulate some of them on their success. But the odd pheasant also escaped the cook's pot through daring manoeuvres.

On other days, the birds of prey had more luck and killed their prey with deadly accuracy. Some of these hunting flights were so spectacular that I couldn't think of anything better.

Jacob had lectures in Ingolstadt for a week every four weeks. We usually travelled there together and stayed overnight with one of his uncles.

The second time I was in Ingolstadt with Jacob, I came along to the lecture and sat at the back of the room. The students eyed me a little sceptically at first.

Jacob first made sure the room was quiet and then introduced me:

"Gentlemen, my wife, Victoria Countess von Falkenstein, is with us today. I ask for your attention and your best behaviour during her presence."

At first, the students congratulated him on our marriage. But then one of them complained.

"We can't have a fine lady here who doesn't understand what's being said anyway. Why do you have your wife with you? She'll only get bored. Besides, she'll throw us off course."

The student was immediately supported by several others.

Jacob smiled to the group "Perhaps I should have told you straight away that my wife has had exactly the same training as you, but unlike you, she already has her degree in her pocket. That means she could take my place here at any time and talk about our laws. Perhaps we can all discuss today's topic with her later."

They all turned to me with expressions ranging from astonishment to disbelief. I smiled at all these young lads and liked them immediately. From that day onwards, I made a habit of going to university with them at least once a week.

Jacob and I often enjoyed talking with the students there about the different types of legal cases. I loved these discussions. The students would do the work of finding a new tricky case from all over the world that we could all discuss together. I enjoyed it just as much as the young lads. To Jacob's delight, everyone learnt a lot – including us.

Was I happy? Not the way I had always wanted to be. But I wasn't unhappy either. Because I had a man with whom I had a real friendship and sincerity, even if he loved another man besides loving me – and clearly more than me. After all, I could call this man my friend and Magdalena was a real friend to me. I had also grown fond of her brother Friedrich.

A letter arrived from Nannerl in May. Among other things, she told us about the many balls and concerts they had attended, as well as a few spectacular opera performances.

"... Prince Archbishop Sigmund Christoph von Schrattenbach passed away in December. The enthronement of the new Prince

Archbishop Hieronymus Count von Colloredo was celebrated on 1st of May.

The musical work that was performed that day was Wolfgang's "Il sogno di Scipione[42]". The libretto was written by Pietro Metastasio. Wolfgang had actually written it for Schrattenbach's 50th first mass anniversary, but now it became a work for an enthronement, which is also a nice thing.

Just imagine, Colloredo has now not only confirmed my brother in his position, but has even appointed him second con-certmaster. Isn't that marvellous?

I also compose this and that, and Wolfgang has already adopted some of my ideas. But my father thinks I should leave it alone because I can't keep up with my brother's genius and you can't take women composers seriously anyway.

I am extremely sad about his statement. I know that we are not equally strong in our expression, but that doesn't mean that I couldn't do anything. What do you think? But I already know what you think. That comforts me a little ..."

Summer joy

The Falkensteins had numerous estates, some of which were widely scattered in the Inn[43] region and around Lake Chiemsee. Jacob had to visit them all at least once a year for a few weeks. Previously, he had always done this round with his mother. However, she was (luckily for us) suffering. So this year I was supposed to join him.

I think that was a good thing for everyone involved. After all, our farmers also wanted to see the new countess and we were relaxed without Jacob's mother. On the estates, we planned to organise a dance evening with all of our

---

42   *It is unclear whether the entire work or only a part of it was performed at that time.*
43   *a river which flows into the Donau (Danube)*

servants. Frederik was invited to accompany us. We sent our things, the two valets and my maid off in a carriage and rode our separate ways.

Frederik and I developed a genuine and deep affection for each other during this time. He wasn't just polite towards me, but became really attentive and affectionate. He had also made peace with the situation and learnt to accept me as a friend.

We had a relaxed and enjoyable time. Frederik and I competed in fencing skills and we all danced our feet off.

What I enjoyed most in the country was preparing the dance evenings. I always held a few practice evenings for the staff on the estates and at least one in the village inn.

At the first farm we arrived at near Aschau, everything was very stiff. All the servants were lined up outside when we arrived to welcome us.

I was introduced to everyone by name by the caretaker and quickly realised that, given the absence of the Countess Mother in our group, the general tension quickly fell away from people. I was presented with a beautiful bouquet of flowers by a kitchen maid.

Jacob addressed a few words to his subordinates:

"Thank you for your hard work throughout the year. I really appreciate the fact that you all make sure that this estate is cared for and nurtured and produces a relatively good yield of crops despite the adverse conditions. Each and every one of you is important and contributes to its success.

"As you can see, this year I am in the company of my wife Victoria and my good friend Frederik von Barby. My mamma and my brother are unable to attend and have therefore stayed in München.

"It is important to us that our visit causes only minimal disruption to the daily routine here and that the everyday tasks that need to be done are done as usual. Incidentally, we would like to be catered for here as normal and do not want a gala dinner. I will, therefore ask the people responsible here for a short chat afterwards. I will leave everything else to my wife."

I had already thought about what was important to me.

"Thank you all for this warm welcome and the colourful meadow flowers." I said "We'll be poking our noses in everywhere on the farm over the next few days. Frederik von Barby and I want to learn something and find out how the tasks are done here. Please don't let our presence disturb you.

"I also have the pleasure of announcing that there will be a dance evening before we continue our journey, to which everyone who can dance is invited – regardless of who they are. There will be a joint practice evening beforehand. We will let you know when. I look forward to seeing you there in large numbers."

There were almost always happy faces, some even cheered.

We adapted our bedtimes to the routine on the farm. This meant we went to bed relatively early and got up early. We had stews and pastries to eat. For the most part, I much preferred this to the sophisticated dishes I had often been served. It was only the pastries that made me hungry again soon afterwards. That's why I usually visited the kitchen again in between meals on these days. The first time, I had a few frightened kitchen boys in front of me. But they soon got used to my presence and were no longer bothered.

My two men and I were shown all the work processes on the farm and those that were not necessary were explained to us. We watched the fruit being harvested, stood next to the makers and much more. Here and there we had an idea for simplification and discussed whether a change would make sense.

In particular, I took a close look at the stables and the work being done there. Once, when I saw that a couple of men were trying to force a bridle on a horse that was to be driven in with the carriage and the big brown horse panicked and became dangerous as a result, I intervened.

"Gentlemen, please stop that!" I shouted. "If you carry on like that, you'll scare the horse away forever."

"This balky horse is the only horse that won't put a bridle on," remarked the stable manager.

"It seems to me that this horse just doesn't trust you. Please don't tell me now that you don't have time to spend a little of it with a difficult horse."

"No, Madame, it's not the time. But he has to learn that, too. None of the others have any problems. Only he's resisting."

"I'm sure he'll learn. What stable boy has a peaceful disposition and calm movements?"

"Our Peter here is a very peaceful soul." He pushed Peter in front of me. The boy was slightly taller than me and looked very friendly.

"I'd like to spend some time with Peter and the horse, if you don't mind. We'll try to teach the horse that a bridle isn't the devil's work."

The stable manager agreed and Peter walked with me to a small enclosure where the horse was now standing.

"Now, Peter, you go in to the horse and groom it calmly. Talk to it, touch it all over with flowing and calm movements, stroke it, give it all your attention and, if you can, your affection, too. Do not pressurise it. As soon as it shows fear, respect this and try to regain the horse's trust so that it comes to you of its own accord."

With a little guidance from me and a lot of effort on his part, the lanky Peter managed within three days to get the previously stubborn horse, who had been given the name Leo by his new friend, to lower his head voluntarily to allow the bridle to be put on. The horse had come to trust this person and would do many things for his sake.

I was sure that I had been able to watch a friendship grow that would last for many years to come. This thought filled me with joy.

The stable manager was pleased and I noticed in passing that Peter was now in a better position in the stable. He was now really needed – at least in connection with that horse Leo. The boy became much more self-confident.

Then, came the first dance practice evening. Excited chatter greeted us in front of the barn where we were to practise. We had hired two musicians from Aschau who knew all the pieces we wanted to practise. This meant I could concentrate on announcing the figures.

It was great fun! The actual dance evening was even better. Some families from the neighbourhood also came along. It was great to see that everyone was happy and that nobody had to be afraid of a tyrannical rule.

Frederik had the idea of organising a training evening like this at our next stop – which was Endorf and Hartmannsberg Castle – completely unrecognised. So the day before we left the estate, we dressed quite simply, each put on a half-mask and rode on a diversion from the other side to Endorf. We pretended to be travelling musicians passing through the country. At the village green, we announced that anyone who wanted to dance that evening should just turn up. We would show them the latest dances.

In fact, the green was so packed with people on this balmy evening that it was a joy. Other musicians had also turned up. I danced the *Tourdion*[44] with everyone, which was still quite popular with the rural population. *Branles*[45] were also dances that almost everyone enjoyed.

When everyone was all sweaty from dancing and a break was called, Frederik and I went to the centre to dance a perfect *Folia*[46] with Jacob's musical accompaniment.

Then we moved on to newer dances. From the *Indian Queen* to *Mr Beveridge's Maggot* and *Hole in the wall* to *Christchurch Bells*, we practised a few dances that everyone enjoyed. Finally, we danced *Gathering peascods* before everyone trolled off to their accommodation.

---

44   *Rural circle dance, which was quite popular.*
45   *Round dances with courtly origins.*
46   *Folia is a dancing form from Portugal, popular in baroque period.*

I announced the figures, improved them and sometimes even danced along to be able to show something better. My men and I took turns playing music and dancing with the simple people with enthusiasm. It was great fun.

Heated and happy, we later made our way to our horses, which we had stabled with a farmer a little outside the village. In the moonlit night, we trotted back to the estate where we had spent the last few days.

Jacob broke the silence between us after a while. "You know, Frederik, that was the best idea you've ever had. I've enjoyed this day like none before. Completely unrecognised, I was able to just be me today and do what is closest to my heart. Together with the two people I love above all else. Thank you both for these wonderful hours." His voice sounded full and we could hear the emotion in it.

I let my horse walk next to his. Then I kissed my fingers and placed them briefly on his lips. "I love you both for letting me spend this day with you so freely and carefree. It was simply marvellous!" I threw my arms upwards.

Frederik only let out a loud whoop, which was echoed by the nearby rocks.

The next day we arrived at the castle in public and it was announced that the Count had organised a dance evening to show his gratitude to his people in this village for their loyal service.

When this evening came a few days later and we got out of the carriage in Endorf, which was half a mile[47] from the castle, we were greeted honourably.

Jacob said a few sentences to the villagers and then asked them to dance. As I was also the one announcing the dances for the simple people that day, my voice was of course recognised quite quickly. I realised that some of them were scared stiff.

So I joined the small orchestra and spoke to the people.

---

47   Until the 19th century, the German country mile of 7,532.5 metres was in use, or
      until 1811 the Bavarian mile of 7,414.975 metres.

"Dear villagers, I beg you to dance and be merry, as if we were nothing more than a few unknown minstrels visiting you on a dance night. Behave in such a way that we all enjoy the evening. We are not here on this day as your masters, but as those who care about your well-being and want to give you a few pleasant hours."

It looked like everything was calming down again. Jacob and Frederik, like me, kept mingling with the dancers. Gradually, everyone relaxed and it became almost as much fun as the practice evening.

I saw how the women adored Jacob and Frederik and had to smile because they were constantly being looked after by countless people. But I wasn't served any less well. It was a wonderfully carefree time.

Jacob and I had become even closer since we left München and I could hardly imagine life without him. There were never any arguments between us. We did have the occasional heated discussion, but as we were both careful not to personally devalue each other, we always found common ground.

A few days later, we were riding along the Chiemsee and enjoying the wonderful landscape when Frederik teased me.

"Vic, you do realise that you've broken countless men's hearts in the last few weeks?"

I laughed. "Humbug, they're just returning the kindness they've been shown."

Jacob now made his opinion known. "No, Vic, I have to agree with Frederik. Almost all of them adore you. And not just the men. No, even the women worship the ground you walk on. You're a wonderful mistress with a heart, you're also a fantastic dance master and you manage to make everyone really enjoy dancing and actually learn it.

"Everyone is also relieved that my mamma isn't there, who no one can please, and that you are so different from her. Please stay as you are."

Frederik nodded. "Yes, stay like that, because that's how we all love you." I was touched.

Our friend travelled back to München after our stay of several weeks around Lake Chiemsee, while Jacob and I visited my parents together for a few days. It was wonderful for me to meet them and Christoph again. They all got on very well with my husband too. Unfortunately, Seraphia wasn't in the area at the time. We had rainy weather, which meant we could hardly do anything. But nature really needed the wet.

Our return to the München city palace was followed by the normal schedule of balls, other invitations and social engagements of all kinds, as well as Jacob's lectures in Ingolstadt. We also worked together on legal cases that were brought to my husband.

After the harvest that year, the granaries and fruit and other crop stores were finally well stocked again and prices fell back to normal levels. There was a great sigh of relief throughout the country.

A gift

During his visits, Frederik always brought me small and special gifts. Whether it was a small piece of jewellery from his late mother, whom he had loved very much, a precious fan, a hat in the latest fashion or fencing gloves. He knew how to make me happy.

One day I told our friend that he shouldn't feel obliged to bring me presents. What he told me in response made a plan form within me.

"You know, although I love Jacob almost idolatrously, I find women to be very aesthetic and beautiful creatures. You women have gorgeous bodies and sometimes I wish I had one too. To be honest, I like all the trinkets that are only available for you. It makes me happy to choose and buy all this stuff especially for you, even if I can't use any of it myself. And it gives me great pleasure when you wear or use the things and I realise that you really like them. Sometimes I wish I knew how a woman feels in such a beautiful dress and with all these marvellous things."

A few days later, I had Frederik's valet give me his master's measurements. Then I had an excellent tailor make a new evening gown for Frederik according to these measurements, and I also had one made for my husband, using fabrics from my father's last delivery.

I then went to my own seamstress with the same measurements and told her about a friend in Reichenhall who I wanted to make happy with a dress. She was tall and lanky and suffered from having almost no breasts but a broad back.

"To be honest, you'd think my girlfriend was a man from behind. She suffers from that. Maybe you can do something about it?"

The result was a beautiful salmon-coloured dress whose neckline was padded so that it looked as if the wearer had a firm and beautiful breast, although not a voluptuous one.

Completely satisfied, I had the parcels delivered to my home. Then I waited for a day when Jacob was travelling around the city without me and our staff had their day off.

I asked Frederik to join me, who, as so often on these days, came in the back entrance to the garden and through the patio door.

When he realised that the staff were off and Jacob wasn't there either, he looked at me questioningly. "Is Madame trying to seduce me?"

"Not quite. Just come with me and trust me."

I then pulled him into my changing room with me. There was jewellery, gloves, fans and a wig on a small table next to the full-length mirror and he looked delighted. "You have such lovely things, Vic."

"Take your clothes off, my friend, I have a surprise for you." He looked at me in horror.

"I mean it seriously. You don't have to worry that I'm going to attack you. And you don't need to be embarrassed in front of me either. I know every inch of Jacob's body and you won't look that much different, will you? I also promise not to stare at you or touch you lewdly."

Frederik hesitantly undressed. "The shirt too," I ordered him without looking.

"But, then I'm naked."

"I'm aware of that. Please trust me."

He also followed this instruction after a brief hesitation.

"Now sit on the stool here, arms up and eyes closed. And they stay closed!"

I could feel his tension. But he had to get through it. First he was given an undergarment, which made him relax a little. Then I laced him into a bodice and put a panier[48] on him. The dress itself rustled as I slipped it over his body. "Keep your eyes closed until I tell you to open them."

I then put a wig on Frederik and put a little make-up around his eyes. Finally, I put the precious necklace on him.

"Now stand up straight." I instructed.

I tied the dress, which was made in such a way that you could put it on without help, to the right fit. I could feel him trembling. He could probably already guess where this journey would end.

Finally, I helped him into his gloves and handed him the fan. With his clean-shaven chin, he really did look like a woman. A pretty woman.

"Now you can open your eyes." I ordered.

He stared into the mirror and, despite all his assumptions, couldn't believe what he saw at first. He moved a little woodenly at first. He looked at us in the mirror in disbelief. I was standing next to him and had put my hand on his arm.

"Don't forget to breathe, Frederik. You wanted to know what it feels like to be dressed like a woman. You can have that experience here and now."

---

48   *A kind of oval hoop skirt that makes the hips grow extremely wide.*

"It looks like I have breasts. It's all so unusual. The corset isn't exactly comfortable, I'd say. But I could get used to it. The dress is beautiful. I've never seen it on you before."

"You'll never see that on me either. Because this is your dress. I had it made especially for you. It would be far too big for me."

We stood next to each other for a few minutes and made eye contact via the mirror in front of us. Frederik was beaming as if I had just fulfilled his dearest wish.

"Do you want Jacob to see you like this for once? He knows absolutely nothing about any of this, by the way. So it's entirely your decision."

"Thank you from the bottom of my heart for this experience. Would you allow me a little time alone?"

"I'll be in the bedroom next door if you need me." Then I went to my room to write a letter to Seraphia.

After a long time, Frederik came and asked me back into the changing room.

He took me tightly in his arms. "Thank you, dear friend, for this wonderful experience. I've decided not to confront Jacob about it. He should only know me as a man. But maybe you'll give me the chance to repeat an afternoon like that?"

"Yes, I think that can be done." I helped him out of his clothes again, left him the undergarment and removed his make-up. Then, I left him. A short time later, the normal Frederik, with tousled hair, re-entered the salon, a happy smile on his face.

He hugged me again and gave me a kiss, from which I could read his friendly affection.

The next time Jacob and I were back from Ingolstadt, I had new coats as gifts for both men. They were amazed and delighted with these marvellous items of clothing. They put them on at the next possible event and I was proud of my two extremely smart companions.

It felt like it was getting easier for me to live with the two of them every day.

One evening, I found myself sitting between the two men in our parlour. What felt very strange to me at first, gradually turned out to be a feeling of security. In the end, my two heroes fell asleep. Jacob with his head in my lap and Frederik leaning on my shoulder. They held hands and included me in their embrace. It touched me to see how much trust they both had in me. They had both become immensely important people in my life.

Both of them were no longer afraid to touch each other tenderly in my presence. I could even see them kissing from time to time. I was also repeatedly kissed by both of them. We were now something like a family. At least that's how it gradually felt to me. Only the child was missing. But I still wasn't pregnant, which is why my mother-in-law was already teasing me.

After my initial feeling of discomfort, I realised that I personally saw it as increasingly normal for Jacob and Frederik to make love. Why shouldn't lovers kiss or caress each other? Who was allowed to presume to determine what was right or wrong? Wasn't such a loving relationship much better than one in which one partner was beaten or otherwise mistreated by the other?

So spring and summer came and went and before I knew it, autumn was shining in the most beautiful colours with colourful leaves and a still warm sun. I think I had somehow become happy after all.

Deer hunting

We received an invitation to a pack hunt from the electoral court itself. It was to take place exactly on our first wedding anniversary, in the style of the French model. Although we weren't invited as hunters, but only as hunting guests, we didn't want to miss out on this event and happily agreed to accompany it.

There was a pack of hounds with around 80 *Koppeln*[49] Bracken[50]. There were also mounted hunters equipped with trompe de chasse, a hunting horn based on the French original – and Jacob, Frederik, my brother Christoph and I were right in the middle of the colourful party that accompanied the hunters.

Yes, Christoph was just visiting München and wanted to celebrate our wedding anniversary with us.

We had already discussed beforehand that the four of us would stay together. Our horses were used to each other and had roughly the same pace. To keep the picture, I usually stayed next to Jacob.

I rushed over a hedge hand in hand with my brother, Jacob and I flew over another jump side by side and once we even managed to clear an obstacle with all four of us at the same time. Our joyful whoops could be heard far and wide.

Sometimes, you could hear the hunters' horn signals from the front, sometimes a little to the side and the whole group of riders reacted like one man and swivelled in the direction from which the sound was calling us. It was simply marvellous and a feeling of freedom and happiness spread through me.

In the end, several of the stags were caught by the dogs and literally slaughtered by the hunters. The majestic animals took their toll on me. But that's life – and death. We riders had a wonderful day, the end of which many a noble stag did not survive.

Unfortunately, Christoph left a few days later – but with the promise that he would come back for a few days before Christmas if the weather favoured him. He had a client who owned property in München and Reichenhall and

---

49   One "Koppel" is two dogs connected by a lead on their collars. A young dog is led
     from an old dog for training purposes. This teaches the young dog how to behave. In
     German pack hunts, the number of dogs is always given in "Koppel".
50   Bracen bloodhounds

who appreciated it when my brother came to München to visit him. So he could easily combine one with the other.

Dancing lesson

The winter ball season had long since begun. We were glad that the hungry season had come to an end and that opulent dance events were being held everywhere again. So the two men and I hardly turned down any invitations to the numerous ball evenings in the city.

What's more, we often held rehearsal evenings in our palace, where I taught the latest dances to interested people from our circle. Aunt Seraphia always kept me up to date. I really enjoyed teaching people to dance.

The best thing about it was that Jacob and I were able to build up a good, almost friendly relationship with most of the families through these evenings, because, here we met on a very human level.

Sometimes, there were also quite clumsy dancers, which usually led to a complete mess and lots of laughter at some point.

This is what one scene looked like. Some of the dancers were already in the wrong position at the beginning.

"Stop! The gentleman is standing to the left of the lady!" I schouted.

There was a general shuffling around in the room. I looked at everything and then stood in front of a couple and fixed my gaze on the gentleman.

"Would you be so kind as to switch to the other side of your lady?"

He looked at me, puzzled. Then, as if he was just waking up, he changed sides. I smiled at him and nodded slightly to show my agreement.

I stopped again after a couple's figure.

"No, no, not like that, please. The lady is always led around the gentleman so that she walks forwards. If in this case the gentleman has to walk backwards, then so be it! This is not about the gentleman's comfort, but about aesthetic beauty for your audience, gentlemen. You want to pay homage to beautiful women, don't you?"

I saw that in one couple the woman clearly knew what she was doing, while the man was in charge and stubbornly stuck to it.

"Gentlemen, we are not here at the negotiating table for the next battle, where you have to win at all costs. We are dancing. Dance is a togetherness – or at least it should be. Believe me, sometimes your dance partners know better where the journey is going. So don't contradict them for the sake of contradicting them. After all, you are partners for the dance in question. Sometimes – especially if you're a little unsure yourself – it's a good idea to let your partner take the lead and follow them. Even if your partner is female. Just give it a try."

Some gentlemen looked at me indignantly.

"You won't believe how many factors determine whether a gentleman is desirable to us women as a dancer. For example, I definitely prefer to dance with a gentleman who is in a good mood and a bit clumsy than one who has nice moves but makes me feel like I have to stand at attention in front of a general and will be court-martialled if I put a foot wrong."

A giggle went through the rows. One or two gentlemen seemed to at least start thinking after hearing these words. In any case, there was generally a lot of laughter during the evenings. This was partly due to the mistakes that were made, but also to comments from somewhat cheeky dancers who pointed out the peculiarities of individual participants or laughed at their own mistakes. Many a person good-naturedly tolerated a cheeky comment as long as it contributed to the general amusement and was not offensive.

Concert outing

Jacob and I had received an invitation via Magdalena from the lady with whom I had met my friend for the first time. It was Magdalena's maternal aunt and the Countess von Aichelberg who had accompanied Magdalena on our first meeting. Her husband and she have great influence in society of München and invitations to her palace were coveted like diamonds.

We were looking forward to the evening. All dressed up, we travelled to the Palais von Aichelberg together with our friend Frederik. Magdalena, her mother and Frederik were already there and greeted us right after the hostess herself.

The evening began with a concert. The *Alster Overture* by Georg Philipp Telemann was played. I liked the instrumentation very much – 4 horns, 2 oboes, 2 violins and basso continuo. I liked the music itself even more. I was completely enthralled by the work, which I had never heard before. I would tell mamma and Christoph about it.

After the concert and thunderous applause, the chairs were removed from the hall and the guests stood in groups with refreshments and chatted. The countess joined me. "I am glad that my niece has found such good friends in you, your husband and his friend. This connection is very good for her, she has blossomed and men have been queuing up to dance with her recently. I am delighted with this development. I very much hope that there will soon be a gentleman she wants to give her heart to."

"As far as I know, several gentlemen have tried to win her over." I assured her. "But I don't think her heart has been in it yet. But I'm sure the right man will be found for Magdalena too."

"I'm convinced of that. We just hope it doesn't take too much longer.

"How did you like the music? A friend advised me to hire this ensemble with this particular piece. I think he was exactly right. My guests look very happy."

"Oh yes, it was a wonderful concert. I was particularly taken with *The canonising Pallas* and *The concertante frogs and crows* of the *Alster Overture*. You can really hear the croaking of the frogs and the cawing of the crows and feel like you're close to the water. Of course, I also have to say that I particularly love the sound of the horns."

"Well, now I have to go back to looking after my other guests. Please excuse me." With that, the countess disappeared from my field of vision again.

The rest of the evening was spent dancing. It was wonderful to enjoy the music and the dancing. I had almost only good dancers this time. Friedrich also asked me to be his partner for an Anglaise.

"When are you coming to the falconry again? Bella always gets really excited when you're there. She likes you."

"I'm glad to hear that, because I really like your Bella too. She's a wonderful dog."

We were separated again and each had to do a *dos-a-dos*[51] with our partner couple.

"I also like it when you're there. You just fit in well with us and the birds are completely unperturbed by your presence."

"Friedrich, I blush when you say that."

Hand tour[52] with the opposite partner.

"You're pretty when you blush."

"Please don't embarrass me, I'm a married woman."

---

51 *The dancers facing each other circle each other without turning round. They therefore meet back-to-back at the far end*

52 *The couple take left or right hands and walk in a circle.*

"Excuse me, please. I thought I could say something like that to my sister's best friend."

A *moulinette*[53] with the partner couple disturbed our talk.

"Thank you for the compliment, Friedrich. I also value you as a friend."

"It makes me happy that you all integrate me so well, even though I'm the youngest."

Another *Dos-a-Dos* with the other partner.

"But of course. You're now part of our group and it's hard to imagine life without you."

As the conversation became increasingly difficult, also because we needed our breath to dance, as the musicians set a considerable pace during this dance, we ended our conversation. We smiled at each other every time we met, sometimes made faces and enjoyed ourselves from then on, even without witty lyrics.

Later, when I was dancing with Jacob, he made a remark that surprised me. "Friedrich is growing up. I think he's a little in love with you. You know what, I can't blame him, because you're a wonderful woman."

I thought about it. Jacob was probably right in his assessment. Friedrich had really grown up over the last year. I felt honoured that a younger man might even see me as an adorable or desirable woman.

Friedrich had been studying medicine in Ingolstadt for a few years now and I was convinced that he would make a very good doctor. He was sensitive enough to recognise mood swings in people and had a great deal of empathy.

Whenever there were a few lecture-free days, Friedrich came home to work with the birds. Alongside medicine, this was his great passion.

---

53   *Also called a mill. Both pairs take each other's left or right hands. A circle is described around the pairs of hands crossed in the centre, as with mill wings.*

The ball season

We now mostly went to the balls as a group. Usually Jacob, Frederik and I were joined by Magdalena and her mother and – if his studies allowed him time – Friedrich. The two women were so wonderfully refreshing. Magdalena's mother had a great sense of humour, thanks to which she always had willing dancers at hand.

It was simply a wonderful and carefree time. I was able to really enjoy these parties that year. Even when my mother-in-law was in the room. I ignored her for the most part. Fortunately, she only went to selected balls that were so big that we didn't necessarily have to meet.

Christoph came to visit again in the second week of December. I greeted him enthusiastically at the door.

"Christoph, what a joy! Oh, my dearest brother, it's lovely to have you here. There's a big ball tomorrow. You have to come along."

"It's not really the best weather for travelling, but I wanted to see you, dearest sister. I'm also bringing you a big parcel from our aunt."

"Don't tell me any fairy tales. You're here for your client."

"How clever you are, Vic. But I liked coming all the more because I knew that you would provide me with such wonderful accommodation and a family connection."

He whirled me round. He had already sent his luggage ahead in a carriage. His room was already prepared. Now he pressed the package he mentioned into my hand and withdrew to free himself from the travelling dust.

Seraphia had given Christoph some dance descriptions and melodies with a note.

"... these are the latest dances in Paris and London. If you want to practise these dances, you, your husband and brother will be among the first to master them in München ..."

So I invited Frederik, Magdalena, her mother and a few other friends over the very next afternoon to study the new dances. There were marvellous melodies from several operas, but also brand new dances by various composers.

Just a few days later, at another ball, we were lucky that the orchestra already knew the new melodies and we were able to show off our skills.

"What a joy. Now we can use our new skills!" Magdalena's mother cheered when the dance was announced and dragged her partner in front of the orchestra.

All our friends and their partners arrived in the alley in no time at all and could hardly wait to get started.

The hostess came over excitedly and headed towards the orchestra. "Please, you can't do this to me. Hardly anyone in the room can do this dance."

I approached her. "How about everyone learns it? It's not difficult and everyone will enjoy it."

She looked at me and the leader of the orchestra in turn. The man had a question mark on his face.

"Some of our friends have already practised this dance and the rest will certainly learn it quickly. Let's give it a try, please." I addressed her.

Looking at the hostess next to me, Jacob said, "What do you think, it's sure to be the talk of the town tomorrow that there are brand new dances from all over the world at your balls."

In the absence of a male dance master who already knew these dances, I was asked to explain and announce the figures and so the other ball visitors also learnt the dances in a short time.

The hostess later beamed at me and thanked me profusely. "Several guests have already come up to me to tell me that they are happy to be able to include this dance in their repertoire. Thank you, my dear Countess von Falkenstein. You have done me a great favour. Do you often organise practice sessions for new dances?"

I said "Yes, I do" and promised that I would invite her next time.

The pig chase

As there wasn't much snow yet, the elector invited us to a *Sauhatz*[54] at short notice. I had never been to a hunt like this before, which is why I watched everything closely and had this or that explained to me.

The finders were at work first. These were agile dogs with a fine nose. They tracked down the wild boar and barked at them. Then the larger boarhounds were deployed. They chased the game out of cover. Hunters and other hunting guests followed every movement of the dogs and game. The so-called packers – English mastiffs in this hunt – would finish off the wild boar until the hunters shot the sows and boars with a short spear. It was all very exciting and sometimes not without danger. The boars in particular were formidable opponents in the fight for survival.

The hunting guests were all waiting on their horses at some distance from the action, so that everyone could see what was happening, including us.

Suddenly, two pigs broke through the circle of dogs and hunters and ran straight towards us at an incredible speed. I gave my horse a heel and whip so that it jumped to the side in fright and got out of the way.

But Jacob's gelding did not manage to flee from the attacking boar's path in time because he initially resisted the action of his rider, who had perceived the danger first. As a result, the boar headed straight for the gelding. The latter lost his balance shortly before the impending collision because, to make matters worse, he had stepped into a hole.

---

54   *boar hunt*

He toppled over and Jacob fell to the ground right in front of the boar. The animal rammed its tusks into his chest. My heart stopped. I heard Jacob's agonised scream. In a matter of seconds, the boar made another violent thrust and fled shortly afterwards.

This probably only lasted a few seconds. I was shocked out of my wits. Jacob!

My husband was lying motionless on his side on the field. Frederik and I were with him at the same time, followed a second later by Christoph. We gently turned Jacob onto his back together.

The injuries to his chest were huge and were bleeding profusely. But my husband was still alive. I pushed aside the thought of the terrible thing that had happened in front of my eyes and just functioned as I sat on my knees at Jacob's side, trying to stop the bleeding with my jacket and scarf.

Frederik bent down to his lover and laid his head infinitely gently on his own hunting coat, which he had taken off and rolled up. Then he took Jacob's hand.

I looked imploringly at Frederik and grabbed his arm when I saw the tears and fear in his eyes. "Don't do anything rash now," I sobbed, "please!" At that moment, I was also overcome with fear. For Jacob and his life, but also for Frederik and me, for our life together, which I had thought would go on for years.

Hot tears ran down both our cheeks.

Jacob opened his eyes. He saw our faces above his and with his last breath and a wry smile on his face, he spoke with obvious effort: "I love you both from the bottom of my heart and thank you for the great happiness I was able to experience with you." Then he took another rattling breath before a twitch ran through his body and it went limp. I think I let out a scream.

I took Jacob's head between my hands and kissed my husband one last time. Then I looked for Frederik's gaze. He understood my intention. I hadn't kissed Jacob as Victoria alone, but also on his behalf.

As hunting helpers took Jacob away on a stretcher, I hugged Frederik. "We'll get through this. Please be strong for both of us and keep up appearances."

Christoph also hugged me and expressed his condolences. He was friendlier towards Frederik than he had ever been towards him. He had probably realised that a very special friendship had come to a cruel end.

Later, when we were alone for a moment, my brother spoke to me about it. "I could hear his last words." He said. "Is that what I think it was?"

I couldn't control my voice and my answer was laced with sobs. "His great love was Frederik, yes. Nevertheless, we both learnt to appreciate and love each other. I don't know how everything will be without him. Frederik and I are also very close. But on a different level."

My brother hugged me and gave me comfort.

He and Frederik stayed in our house at my request after the accident. Christoph because I didn't want to do without his support and Frederik because I didn't want him to be alone. I wasn't sure whether he wouldn't hurt himself if he was alone with his grief.

The three of us sat together in the salon that evening like lost heaps of misery. Frederik started to say something several times. But again he pulled himself together and kept quiet.

"Frederik, say what you have to say. I vouch for my brother. Nothing that is said between us will reach other people's ears."

Christoph gave Frederik a serious but friendly nod and stood up. "I think I'd better withdraw and let you two grieve together. You can trust me, Frederik. Because I would never do anything to harm my sister or her friends." He put his hand on Frederik's shoulder, gave me a quick hug and then left the room.

I sat down next to Frederik and took him in my arms. "Come on, let's cry for Jacob." We both cried for our friend and lover.

The next day, I was sitting in my changing room in the morning. When I heard noises in the next room, my heart was pounding and I expected to see Jacob enter at any moment. Then I remembered what had happened and I started to cry.

When we were both out of tears, Frederik and I shared our memories a few days later.

"Do you know how much it hurt me when I found out that Jacob was getting married? And when I consciously saw you for the first time at the announcement of the engagement, I felt a real hatred inside me. I thought you were going to ruin everything. I thought you had seduced him and he had fallen for your beauty, although I already knew at the time that he valued you for completely different qualities. He had raved about your legal expertise.

"Jacob implored me to be kind to you, because it was all his fault with his thoughtless behaviour. He said he wouldn't be able to cope if we were enemies. That made sense to me. Then I watched you. I wavered in my decision to hate you. Because you were so friendly and lovable.

"I danced with you at your wedding and realised that I couldn't hate you, but it wasn't until your first visit to me that I really understood Jacob's decision to marry you after his brother's betrayal.

"I have known all these years how much Jacob had suffered under his mother. She is a thoroughly malicious person who likes to harm others. After only a short time, you managed to do what he would never have managed without your help: to separate from this all-consensual person. It was only after you moved into your new palace that Jacob learnt to really enjoy life. He blossomed and since then has been a happier person than I had ever seen him before. I love you, Victoria, for this great deed and your understanding of our connection as well as your constant support. Please continue to be the friend I so desperately need right now."

"Frederik, I've grown very fond of you over the past year. I don't want to lose you as a friend either. When Jacob spoke of his love for you on our wedding night, it shattered my dream of a happy marriage. But I liked you from the start, even though you seemed to want to kill me with your eyes the first time we met. Over time, I came to understand Jacob's feelings for you better and better. You are a wonderful person and the most important person in my life after my family."

"Jacob had a big heart and deserved a better and, above all, longer life." Frederik sniffled. "I miss him so much."

"Jacob wasn't the love of my life I had always imagined, but over the months he had won a firm place in my heart. I also miss him dearly. How he was able to remain such a generous person in such a selfish and hard-hearted family as his is nothing short of a miracle."

"How am I supposed to get over my loss? I can't live without Jacob!"

"Frederik, Jacob would want you to find happiness without him. I beg you to be strong for me now, too. Because losing you, too, would be unbearable for me. You are so important to me as a friend whom I love dearly.

"You have to be especially careful now with everything you do and say. You can just be yourself towards me and Christoph and also show weakness. Apart from that, we benefit from the fact that everyone thinks you are my lover anyway. Nevertheless, you can't afford to make a mistake with anyone else.

"One thing is certain: you can always count on my friendship in the future. No matter what this future brings us."

Farewell

My husband was to be buried in the family crypt in the country, but his mother let me know in no uncertain terms that I was not wanted at the funeral. However, as I also wanted to say goodbye to my husband and Jacob had been very well known and popular, I had a mass said for him in München beforehand.

At this very well-attended funeral service just a few days after the terrible hunting accident, I stood on the side of the women between Magdalena and her mother in the front row of the church. The two of them comforted me and kept other people at a distance. Of course, my mother-in-law was also there. She was sitting in the same row right at the centre aisle.

The tough woman didn't pay any attention to me and afterwards she scolded everyone who would listen that her daughter-in-law and her lover had driven her son to his death. The way she behaved was unworthy.

I invited the mourners to a drink and canapés at our house. A lot of people came. Of course, the Sieghardinger family was also there. Magdalena and Friedrich took great care to make me feel a little better again.

Nobody had known that Jacob had made a will, but on the same day an executor turned up at the door and demanded to be let in. Jacob's mother wanted to throw him out, but I silenced her. "You may be my mother-in-law and Jacob was your son. But I am the mistress of this house. The man is welcome to stay."

I offered the gentleman a seat and some refreshments.

"Your husband has left a last will and testament with me. If you like, I can read it out here today. But we can also arrange another date."

"As I don't get on well with my mother-in-law, I think today is exactly the right time. Everyone who is concerned is probably here and we are on my territory."

While I was still chatting with my guests, Friedrich took care of the notary at my request. I wanted him to feel welcome in Jacob's house. My young friend fulfilled this task very well. I saw the two men having a lively conversation.

When most of the guests had said their goodbyes, Jacob's last will and testament was read out to a small circle.

"I, Jacob, Count von Falkenstein, in full possession of my mental powers, decree the following in the event of my death:

My wife, Victoria Countess von Falkenstein, born von Sommerauer in the municipality of Reichenhall, is to own our town house with all its contents. For the first time in my life, I am experiencing a truly happy time in this house and with her. Furthermore, Victoria is to receive an annual allowance[55] of 1,000 guilders until the end of her hopefully long and happy life.

Our marriage was forced by a compromising situation that had been brought about by my brother without our knowledge or consent. I have forgiven Leonhard. Because I have learnt to love you, Victoria, my darling. You always help me to have incredibly happy moments in life, dearest Vic. I am very grateful to you for that.

To my long-time and dear friend Frederik von Barby, I leave my hunting horses, my two dogs, which he has always envied me for, and all personal belongings to which Victoria has no claim.

I trust that you two will come to an agreement, because you are the two people who mean the most to me. Your love and friendship has enriched my life.

I have nothing to leave to my mother, whom I have loved all my life, but feared even more. Because I know that she will be well looked after. Mother, I only ask one thing of you: let Leonhard live! No matter what he does, you must not interfere.

My brother Leonhard, who, should I leave no descendants, will succeed me as Count after my death, is well provided for with the inalienable property of the family. All I ask of him is to manage with foresight and hold back on gambling.

---

55   *Allowance is a compensation customary in aristocratic circles for persons who have no claim to the inheritance but should be able to live in keeping with their status.*

In the event that Victoria and I have sons, Leonhard is to receive our property near Endorf am Chiemsee. So that he can live his life independently.

We were never close, but there are sides to you, my brother, that I honestly like. Swim free of mother's influence while you can, otherwise you will become a lonely and unhappy man like I was for a long time. She will want to control you now, as she has done with me all my life.

Find a woman you can love and respect. Then you won't need a mistress and will have a happy home and be able to weather all storms.

I bequeath my valet Erich Hintermeier a sum of 250 guilders for a wedding plus 50 guilders for the initial period. I hope you will be happy with your sweetheart, Erich.

Our majordomo should not have to get used to a new master again. Heinrich Summerer is therefore to receive 1,500 guilders to sweeten his retirement as soon as it gets too much for him with us. Thank you Heinrich for your many years of loyal service to my esteemed aunt and to us.

I wish you all a happy life.

Signed on 31 January 1772, Jacob Count von Falkenstein"

The latter two men sobbed when they heard that their master had been so generous to them.

Frederik was sitting next to me with wet eyes. I squeezed his hand, tears welling up in my eyes myself.

So, I became a wealthy count's widow at the age of just 22. However, this fact did not make me happy. Because I had lost a good friend and companion who had shared my passion for dance and much more.

"When a Woman says ‚Everybody',
she means: every body.
When a man says ‚Everybody',
he means: every man."

Marie von Ebner-Eschenbach,
Author (1830–1916)

1773

Life goes on

Christmas was a sad holiday for me. I had Christoph and Frederik around me, but the grief was still too fresh. So it was a very quiet time in our townhouse. Magdalena and Friedrich visited us and brought a little Christmas cheer into the house. They invited us to a courtship hunt to take our minds off things. This strategy was very good because I didn't have to think about Jacob all the time that day and was even able to laugh in between.

It's strange, because this year I was really grateful that Christmas is such a quiet time in our region and that there are no dance events until Epiphany.

I've always thought it was a shame that we don't follow the tradition of the British Isles, where dancing, singing and laughter are in high season between St Stephen's and Epiphany. This year, however, I was thankful that I didn't miss out on anything, as we didn't have any balls during this period.

It helped me in my grief that all the servants expressed their condolences and almost everyone told me some nice anecdote about Jacob. My maid Katharina also told me that she had admired my husband because he was always kind to everyone and so elegant.

"Only once did he come back from a trip and he was filthy from top to bottom. You had gone out then, Madame. When he saw me staring at him with my mouth open, he said, yes, that's what you look like when you lose a discussion with a high-energy horse. He laughed at that and warned me never to argue with horses.

When I told him that I would still rather do that than never sit on a horse, you know what he organised."

"Oh, that was the reason for teaching you and his valet how to ride?"

"Yes, I had probably looked at him with such longing that he decided to put me on a horse and give me lessons."

"We've seen that you have a talent, Katharina. Jacob really enjoyed instructing you. I can promise you that you will ride again and again in the future."

At the turn of the year, Christoph set off home again. Equipped with letters from me to our parents and aunt, he set off. I hoped he would arrive safely, as there was now more snow – especially further south. But it would be months before all the roads were clear of snow again.

I stayed in München. Frederik grieved more than he let anyone see. But I knew that it was very difficult for him to find his way back to everyday life. For me, it would have been a betrayal of Jacob to leave his lover completely alone during this difficult time. By the time Christoph left, Frederik had returned to his own household, but we met up almost every day for a ride or an exercise session together.

The news spread that Frederick the Great was now calling himself King of Prussia. The topic distracted Frederik a little. He was annoyed and grumbled to himself. "He simply created the province of West Prussia by decree and he's already the king of all Prussia. If only life were that easy for all of us!" he said, knowing some of the background and cultivating a few connections to high-ranking diplomats.

I had a few new dresses made that were appropriate for my widowhood. I didn't feel really comfortable in them because they were so sombre. I also dreaded not being allowed to go dancing in public for a year.

I complained to Frederik. "I don't think I can keep it up without dancing for a year. It's my favourite pastime. Normally, I can forget all my suffering when I'm dancing. And that's exactly what I can't do now. It's just awful!"

"I understand what you're saying. But there are several ways out of your dilemma. For one thing, we can dance the minuet together. And then let a little time pass and we can invite a few friends round to my house. We'll dance there. As long as it's in a private setting, nobody will be able to say anything. As much as I like dancing, I really don't feel like a party at the moment."

Frederik was right. I wasn't even interested in celebrating, but only in the comforting movement of dance itself.

On my own, I practised all the dance steps I knew over and over again. I was also able to accompany myself with the pochette[56]. At no time did I have the feeling that I was dishonouring Jacob's memory. I often fenced with Frederik. The concentration during the fencing lessons helped us both to keep our minds off things.

I made good use of my time in München and looked through Jacob's possessions. I sent papers relating to the count's properties to the family's town house. Frederik picked out the personal items he wanted. He asked me with each item whether I still needed or wanted it.

"I just want to keep his secretary and the large portrait from the parlour. You shall have the marvellous miniature with his likeness as a memento, Frederik. Jacob would have loved it. Whatever else you want, take it with you. Clothes and jewellery too, as long as something suits you and you like it. I can't use any of it." He beamed and took home numerous mementos of the love of his life.

On closer inspection, I had found letters in the secretary's secret compartment that Frederik had written to Jacob. Despite my curiosity, I hadn't read them. I had recognised the handwriting immediately and didn't want to interfere in things that didn't concern me.

I placed these letters in a beautifully decorated wooden box and handed it to my husband's lover. "I don't know the contents, although I have a hunch," I explained.

He opened the box. When he realised what it contained, he put the box aside, walked towards me and took me in

---

56   Pochette (from the French for little bag) is a mini-gig that a dance master usually
     used. He could show the dance steps during the game. The pochette could easily be
     hidden in the pockets of the men's overskirts.

his arms. "I understand that you want to travel back to your family first. Can I visit you when you're back home, dear friend?"

"Of course, I'd be sorry if you didn't visit me."

"I am so glad that with your help Jacob and I had almost a whole wonderful year in which we were able to live our love.

"At first, I was unspeakably jealous of you because you were able to spend more time with him and officially belonged to him. But then I realised that we both shared a similar fate and that it was pointless to envy you. Because you had just as much reason to envy me. Maybe even more, because Jacob kept assuring us both that I was the love of his life.

"Basically, with your sheer presence, you gave us the security from discovery that we never had before. If I'm honest, I also liked myself in the presumed role of your lover."

Frederik grinned.

"With you by his side, Jacob became happier than I have ever seen him before. He felt liberated from his mother and was able to enjoy life."

Frederik was able to laugh again. That gave me hope.

Another ray of hope for me was a letter from Nannerl Mozart. She wrote to tell me that Wolfgang's opera *Lucio Silla* had premiered in Milan on 16 December. She also told me about some of the balls she had already attended that season, who had been where and which girls from well-known families had been newly introduced to society.

"... Wolferl will probably arrive back in Salzburg in the next few days. On 17 January, his motet "Exsultate, jubilate" was performed in the Theatine Church in Milan, but the permanent position he wanted there cannot be realised. He is quite depressed because he had pinned his hopes on Milan. But he was told he was too young.

The next time you come to visit us, you have to come to Hannibalplatz[57]. We're moving to the Tanzmeisterhaus there

---

57 *Hannibalplatz has since been renamed Makartplatz. This is where the Mozart family moved from Getreidegasse (the Salzburg shopping mile) in 1773.*

soon. I'm already looking forward to it. There's a proper dance hall there. Finally enough space when we meet up to dance. It's going to be fun ..."

I was pleased to have received a mostly cheerful letter from my friend and soon wrote an answer. That was the best distraction for me.

There was still a lot to do. The university, which I had of course informed immediately that my husband had passed away, asked if I would be gracious enough to take over the teaching on an interim basis. They were currently looking for a suitable successor. I wrote to them saying that I would be happy to do this and that perhaps even Jacob's best friend could take on this task. After all, he was also an excellent lawyer who had worked on many a case with my husband.

So just one week later, I travelled with Frederik in tow to Ingolstadt to visit Jacob's uncle and give a talk to Jacob's students. The week went well. The students mourned the loss of a teacher whom they had liked very much and who had been incredibly good at communicating very dry topics in an amusing way so that they had understood everything well.

Frederik had a long conversation with Baron von Ickstatt and was given the professorship in the end. I introduced him to the students and he gave the last lecture of the week.

"Frederik, that worked out wonderfully." I told him. "They like you. You got a lot of advance trust from the boys because you were Jacob's best friend. If you treat them the way you treat me, you'll have their loyalty for all time. I'm sure Jacob would be proud of you!"

"Thank you, dear friend. You have given me a job for which I will always be grateful. It's wonderful to teach the students something!"

"Fortunately, Jacob's uncle likes you and will also provide you with a room in the future."

"I feel comfortable with this man, as if he were my own uncle. I find it pleasant to have a kind of family connection here."

One week passed into the next. It slowly became a little easier for me to get some structure back into my daily life. Even the loss of Jacob gradually became a little easier.

I started to occupy myself with other things again. For example, I read the magazines that had been delivered in the last few months. In the *Frankfurter gelehrte Anzeigen* I found a rather interesting overview of reviews of the Turkish Bible, which had been translated from Arabic by David Friedrich Megerlin.

This Megerlin must have been a very narrow-minded person. For he left nothing good about this scripture, which the Orientals call the Koran, and labelled its prophets as antichrists.

How did it actually come about that everyone thought they had the right and only blissful faith and that everyone else was an unbeliever? Why can't we all just be human and treat each other with respect? Isn't it actually the same God to whom all religions turn? Faith is just packaged differently in all of them. There are various commandments and prohibitions – the sense and nonsense of which can be argued about. I think our Catholic faith has also done a lot of damage over the course of time. All the crusades – in the name of faith! Then the woman who is supposed to be subservient to the man. What's the point of all this? Shouldn't the person who is blessed with greater wisdom be in charge, regardless of gender? Is God really a man or rather a divine energy that has no gender? But I will certainly not solve the problem of faith.

The entire servants knew that I would be leaving at the end of April to go back to my family. They had all been honest and loyal to Jacob and me. I had sought and found good positions for all of them and written the best references for them. The majordomo wanted to stay in the house with two helpers and take care of it. Only Katharina would accompany me. I had grown fond of them all and I could already feel that it would be hard to let go.

Memorial dance

On Holy Saturday I had Jacob's portrait hung in our dance hall from the parlour and fresh flowers brought in from the greenhouse.

On Easter Sunday, Magdalena and Frederik were invited to my house for Easter dinner. Jacob's place was decorated in his memory.

That day, I asked Magdalena to play a few minuets on my pianoforte in the ballroom and Frederik to dance with me in memory of Jacob. We danced as if Jacob's image were a monarch on his throne, to whom we paid homage. All three of us were completely lost in music and movement. As a result, we only realised late on how all the servants gradually gathered at the back of the hall and watched with open mouths.

When the dance was over and my people realised that they had been discovered, Heinrich Summerer, our major-domo, stepped forward.

"Excuse us, Madame, it was beautiful! We don't usually get to see such an elegant dance as the minuet for a lifetime and I think I speak for everyone when I say that we were all enchanted by your dance. It is touching that you honour the memory of our late master in such a beautiful way and that is why we wanted to join you. We all know how much our master loved to dance. All the servants honoured him very much, Madame.

"Just like you, he addressed us by name without exception. We all know that it is not common in aristocratic circles to know your servants by name and even their life stories. That is why some of us will leave this house with sadness in our hearts." Everyone nodded vigorously in acknowledgement. "I ask that you forgive us for our uninvited intrusion."

I approached the majordomo. "Thank you, Heinrich. My husband would have loved you all watching. He was truly a passionate and marvellous dancer!

"I know that my Jacob wouldn't have wanted us to go a whole year without dancing. But other people don't think like we do. That's why you have to keep it quiet from people who don't belong to our household."

My maid curtseyed to me: "Madame, would you perhaps do your servants the honour of introducing a few common dances before you leave for your parents?"

I hadn't expected that at all. But the proposal made me happy. "Yes, that would really make me happy, Katharina." I turned to Magdalena and Frederik. "Would you support me?" They both looked at me in surprise. But then they nodded with smiles.

Turning to the servants, I asked: "Do any of you play an instrument?" One of the stable boys, Felix Hartinger, stepped forward. "Yes, Madame. I play the fiddle."

"You'll report to me the day after tomorrow right after breakfast with your fiddle." He bowed briefly and then left the room with the others.

"That will be marvellous! Should we just teach them the dances that are common among the servants, or one of the brand new dances of the upper class, what do you think?"

We discussed which dances would be appropriate and agreed on a few dances with beautiful melodies, although some of them were a little challenging to perform.

Barn dance

So just two days later, I gave Felix a lesson in which he learnt to play the new melodies on his fiddle. He hadn't known that I played the pochette and violin and was therefore very enthusiastic about our playing together.

The whole thing ended with us going to the stable and neighbouring barn together and spontaneously playing a dance for the servants. In the course of this, I introduced a new dance, which was received with enthusiasm.

It wasn't long before Magdalena and Frederik appeared with their horses in hand and demanded a place for their animals in the stables and for themselves in the ranks of the dancers. There were calls for more and more new dances. This was granted.

We had such a good time! In between, I asked for a break. "I really need something to drink. Don't you?" I pleaded.

The kitchen staff were reluctant to bring drinks for everyone. There was only fruit juice mixed with spring water. Magdalena was delighted. "Oh, how refreshing and good it is! We only ever have tea, chocolate, water or alcoholic drinks. I think I'll have to have a word with our staff."

At first I noticed that the girls and women adored Frederik and hardly dared to look at him, let alone take his offered hand during the dance.

The men and boys felt the same way about Magdalena. But without exception, they became bolder and bolder. The women first observed Magdalena's movements very closely and then tried to make her posture their own. As time went on, they danced more and more gracefully and it looked beautiful.

The men also followed Frederik's example. After a while, some of them had flowing movements that made their dance look very classy. There were some real talents among them.

Right from the start, Felix and I took it in turns to throw ourselves into the dancing fray while the other continued to play.

"Bravo, bravo!" I shouted. "You are marvellous! If your next dance with other servants looks this graceful, I can be really proud of my people!"

Everyone gathered around Magdalena, Frederik and me. They thanked us profusely and curtseyed or bowed in farewell. We promised to organise another evening like this before I left, to which staff from other houses would also be admitted. My friends immediately agreed to give their staff the evening off and I also wanted to lobby other houses to allow at least a few people to come. I also came up with a plan that I had to implement as quickly as possible.

First I wrote a few urgent letters to the south, then I sent for a shoemaker who employed several journeymen. I ordered good shoes for my staff in a fortnight's time that would be suitable for a ballroom and would allow everyone to be seen on the street. Whether the shoemaker wanted to do everything himself or call in other shoemakers was up to him. I would pay and negotiated a fair price straight away. A deposit for the material made the deal perfect.

Just a few days later, an internal dance evening took place exclusively among friends at Frederik's Palais in Ludwigstraße. I was blessed to be able to experience an evening of my favourite dances with our closest circle of friends. We also took turns playing that evening. But most of the time, one of our friends, who had difficulty dancing due to a war injury to his leg, sat at the pianoforte..

During a break from the dancing, I told our friends that I was organising a dance and music evening for the servants as my farewell present. If they wanted, our friends could have their staff come too – and come themselves if they weren't too shy to dance with the servants.

Some looked at me piqued. Then one of the gentlemen dropped the crucial question. "What, you want me to dance with my wife's maid?"

"As if that would be worse than dancing with your mother-in-law!" came the prompt reply from his friend, followed by general laughter.

"Oh, you know, they're only human. And as long as you behave decently, your reputation won't suffer, provided you're in good standing with them at all."

I asked that rather plain clothing be worn on such an evening, as this would be appropriate and would not emphasise the difference between master and servant so much.

A few more days passed, during which I packed up what I thought I absolutely needed for my first time at home.

Then I had a few guest rooms prepared. I didn't know exactly how many would accept my invitation, but I knew that I would have visitors.

A divine finalisation

And then, they were all at the door in the last week of April, mamma and Christoph, Seraphia with Heinrich, as well as Nannerl and Wolferl. How happy I was! I immediately invited them into the parlour.

"Child, I'm glad that you seem to be doing well despite your grief." With these words, mamma hugged me.

"You have a wonderful palace here. I didn't realise you had such a grand residence. If only I had found the time to visit last year!" Seraphia was still sorry that she had only seen my husband at the ball and wedding and then never again.

"Settle in first. My staff will show you to your rooms. We have already prepared everything."

That evening, Frederik was present for dinner. As the two of them had only met at the wedding, I introduced him to mamma again.

"Mamma, do you remember Frederik von Barby? He was Jacob's best friend and has also become a very loyal companion to me, whom I wouldn't want to miss."

Frederik bowed. "Mrs von Sommerauer. I owe a great deal to your daughter and see in her the lovable sister that my own unfortunately never was."

When everyone had renewed their acquaintance, we sat down at the table. My cook had outdone herself, the food was so delicious.

"I almost think she's hoping I'll take her with me," I remarked.

Frederik winked at me. "No, dear friend, she wants to ingratiate herself with me because she's moving from here to me."

I laughed. "That could be the case, of course. I think she wants to make us all happy. And she's managed to do that."

After the meal, I sent for the cook and praised her in front of my guests. She was beaming all over her face as everyone applauded her artistry.

"Madame, I could never have done this without my hardworking kitchen helpers. They are all wonderful."

So these were also fetched and praised, which coloured some cheeks red. It was already late and my guests were understandably tired from the journey. So we went to bed early.

The next day we went for a ride. Frederik had provided us with two horses because there weren't that many riding horses left in my stable. He, Magdalena and her brother Friedrich accompanied us on their own horses. All three of them would also spend most of the next few days at my house.

After a quick midday snack, everyone retired to practise their respective instruments. Music could be heard from almost every room in the house, or so it seemed to me.

We came together again for dinner. It was a welcome break. After a delicious meal, I had drinks brought to us and then dismissed the servants. "I'm sure you'll want to prepare a few things for the dance and music evening the day after tomorrow. And we would also like to carry out our preparations undisturbed.

"I'm asking all the servants to gather here in the hall tomorrow at 11.00 a.m. as I have to make an announcement. It won't take long. Please tell everyone. For now, I wish you all a pleasant evening."

Once we were among ourselves, all the instruments were unpacked. Wolfgang had a new *pianoforte concerto in D*

major in his luggage. We had a lot of fun rehearsing the whole evening. It wasn't quite perfect yet, but with another evening of rehearsals the following day, we would be able to get it ready for performance. Especially as Nannerl played the keys of the pianoforte brilliantly. At some point, we decided to leave this piece for a few more hours, as everything was new for us string players.

Nannerl clapped her hands and asked for something else that we had already mastered. "Seraphia and Vic, I would like the *Brandenburg Concerto No. 4* by Johann Sebastian Bach. I know you know how to play it beautifully. Everyone can play it, can't you?" She switched from the pianoforte to the harpsichord, which was also in our ballroom.

Mother took on the solo violin, Wolfgang, Heinrich, Magdalena, Friedrich and Christoph the other parts, Frederik played his bass viol.

Seraphia and I tuned our flutes and then we played. I felt like I was in heaven. I hadn't felt this wonderful for months.

Out of sheer desire and whim, I also asked that we play *Aria Sopra La Bergamasca* in D major by Marco Uccellini. Magdalena and Friedrich had to pass because they didn't know it. In this piece too, Seraphia and I played the two main parts with the flutes instead of violins.

Magdalena jumped up enthusiastically when the last note had faded away. "Oh, this piece is simply enchanting! It sparkles with joie de vivre when you play it. You really must perform it the day after tomorrow. I think our guests will fall at your feet! It's simply going to be a marvellous party!"

We went to bed relatively early that evening too. As a result, we all had breakfast quite early again. This was followed by a walk into town to do a few errands.

Shortly after we got back, the cobbler and four helpers and, almost simultaneously, my employees came into the entrance hall.

I had the shoes distributed. We heard one cry of delight after another. Obviously, almost all the shoes fitted beautifully.

However, our running boy was sent to the well first by the cobbler. With a thunderous voice, he announced. "If you want your shoes to be nice shoes for more than a few minutes, then only put them on with washed feet. I don't want to see such dirty feet in my new shoes. It hurts my soul!"

When silence had returned, I asked for attention. "You know that tomorrow is our big day with your dance party. I expect you to have refreshments ready for our guests and all of us in the evening and to wear your best clothes – as well as your dancing shoes, of course.

My family, friends and I have prepared a surprise for you. We really hope we can make you happy with it. We've already had a lot of fun with it ourselves."

We also practised that evening and in the end we could be proud of our hard work.

The following day was all about the servants' ball. I had ordered a simple breakfast and we were invited to Frederik's house for lunch. This gave my servants enough time to concentrate on the preparations for the evening.

I had agreed with my people that there would always be someone at the front door to welcome or saying farewell to guests. They were to take turns doing this. I left everything else to the staff themselves.

The first guests arrived at seven o'clock in the evening. They were Magdalena, Friedrich, their mother and Frederik. They had a large basket with them containing countless simple but beautiful fans. The sticks were made of wood and the fabric was plain red, blue or green.

"The girls and women should all receive a fan from us as a gift so that they will remember this evening for a long time to come." Magdalena said. It had been Frederik's idea. Magdalena had found the manufactory that had made the fans in such a short time. They were very simple, but really pretty.

The first invited servants arrived and a little later some of our friends. All the ladies received their fans as they entered the house. And regardless of their status, all the women were delighted with this little gift.

None of the invited guests had cancelled after word got around about who my guests from Salzburg were. Anyone who hadn't seen and heard the Mozart family in their prodigy days was naturally hoping for a feast for the ears today. Anyone who had experienced them back then wanted to hear more of them.

After only a short time, our ballroom was full and all the invited guests were here without exception. I asked for silence and stood under Jacob's picture to greet the guests.

"Dear guests, I would like to welcome you to the palace of the late Count Jacob von Falkenstein. My husband was an enthusiastic dancer and someone who did not see the differences between people primarily in their public position, so today I have invited you to a servants' dance in his memory. With this evening, I would like to personally thank all our servants for their loyalty and marvellous service. I would also like to thank our friends, with whom we were able to spend wonderful times during our marriage. In the next few days, I will be leaving München for the time being and returning to my parental home.

"For your pleasure and mine, I have invited other guests. First and foremost my beloved mother, the famous violinist Regina von Sommerauer, then my friends Anna Maria and Wolfgang Mozart, whose fame as child prodigies is still on everyone's lips, my dear aunt and famous dancer Seraphia von Neubauer and her companion Heinrich Winkelmayr, my dear friends Magdalena von Sieghardinger and Frederik von Barby, Magdalena's brother Friedrich with their mother and my absolutely indispensable twin brother Christoph von Sommerauer.

"I don't want to waste too many more words. Just this much: before the first dance, we will perform a new concerto for pianoforte and orchestra by Wolfgang Mozart. Then we will alternate between playing and dancing and in between we will play two more pieces of music that we ourselves love very much.

"Please drink alcohol in moderation and men: keep your hands to yourself. Because anyone who misbehaves will be immediately and irrevocably removed from the house. Regardless of the social class to which they belong.

"Don't worry, none of the servants have to go to work early tomorrow morning. It has been agreed with your employers that you won't have to start work until midday tomorrow. Now I wish us all a wonderful evening!"

Applause broke out and the curiosity was palpable. Everyone wondered what was in store for them.

For many of our guests, it was the first time they had heard a concert. Everyone listened with bated breath from the very first note. It was as quiet as a mouse in the hall while we played. I saw a lot of watery eyes at the end. There was almost no end to the bravos.

It gave me immense pleasure to see this childlike enthusiasm in the faces, which otherwise too often had a haggard expression. Yes, this evening was something very special for everyone present. Our friends also confirmed this.

One of them complimented the festival: "I would regret it forever if I couldn't experience this evening. It's just wonderful what's happening here, Vic. At first I thought there couldn't be anything more mundane than a servants' ball. But you and your family and friends have made a jewel out of it. I've never been to a ballroom where there was such an exuberant atmosphere and so many happy faces. So far, I haven't seen a single bored expression. Everything seems to be pure joy."

After some searching, I discovered our stable boy Felix and made my way to him. "Where's your fiddle, Felix?"

"But, Madame, I can't compete with you and your friends."

"Nonsense. We don't have a competition here. You're a marvellous musician, you've proven that. Get your fiddle and we'll both play your favourite Anglaise. That's an order." He winced briefly, but then went to fetch his fiddle.

With his head down, the boy followed me to the pianoforte. I announced the next dance and we played, accompanied by Nannerl's marvellous playing. Wolferl and mamma also joined in. It was a wonderful recital.

My shy groom was beaming all over his face as all our servants applauded him. They were proud that one of their own was on stage. Wolfgang patted Felix on the shoulder. "You can now justifiably claim to have played with famous musicians as a fiddler. You can be very proud of that. And I'm sure your grandchildren will still be telling their own grandchildren about it."

Magdalena asked Felix to accompany her to another dance. He did so, beaming with joy. Later, he danced again himself. He was literally besieged by the chambermaids and scullery maids who wanted a piece of his new fame.

The two flute pieces with orchestral accompaniment during the dance breaks completely delighted our guests. Even many of our friends had never heard the Uccellini before and later told us how beautiful they found this melody.

Seraphia and I did dance steps to our play, as we had often done at home. This went down incredibly well with everyone. We did it more for our own enjoyment, but the joy was infectious, it seemed. By the end of the play, the whole hall was heaving with joyful people.

The evening was a complete success across the board for everyone who was able to experience it. Everything went like clockwork. Everyone behaved impeccably and it was a pure joy to see the happiness written on so many faces.

It would soon be dawn when I finally fell into bed. I was still in silent dialogue with Jacob. I was sure he would have enjoyed the evening.

By midday, the servants' dance with the famous musicians in the late count's palace was the talk of the town in

München. It, therefore came as no surprise that Frederik's palace was completely overrun two days later.

"Imagine, even high-ranking personalities have asked whether there is still a possibility that they could get an invitation. Something like this has never happened to me before." Frederik was completely overwhelmed.

We then received an invitation from the Elector asking us to organise a private concert at his house the following day. We were happy to do so, as we hoped that it would be useful to Wolfgang sooner or later.

The evening at the Elector's also lived up to its promise. We played with great enthusiasm and received unique feedback from our audience. Even though Wolfgang was not commissioned for the moment, our host was impressed and had nothing but praise and appreciation for the composer in our midst. It was clear that he had enjoyed the concert very much.

The next day, I said goodbye to every single member of my household who could not remain in my service. Each person received an additional gift of money from me. Some of them threw their arms around my neck and gave me a big hug. Everyone thanked me for their favourite experience and wished me good luck. Yes, I also wished good luck to everyone who would now be taking up a new position.

I had already given my staff more freedom last week. They should all be able to enjoy at least a few extra hours or even a whole day off before I left them.

Then, my family, the Mozarts and I travelled back to Reichenhall and Salzburg together. Seraphia and Heinrich had another engagement in Neuburg an der Donau, where Seraphia was supposed to dance.

Saying goodbye to Frederik was much harder than I had expected. Damn, he had been my husband's lover – and yet I was still attached to him. It's strange how life works sometimes.

It had rained a little, but carriages were still able to drive and we made good progress. We spent the night on the route and arrived home safe and sound.

The first time at home

As my grief was still with me, it took two weeks for me to settle in again. I now had my lovely family around me again, but I missed Frederik, Magdalena and Friedrich very much.

I really enjoyed the courtships, our fencing training and the good conversations.

I thought about Jacob throughout the service on Ascension Day. It had been almost exactly six months since I had lost my husband, lover and friend. He had been a wonderful person who deserved more happiness than he was given.

It made me happy that I had at least been able to help him find a little peace and joy. I thought of the many wonderful hours we had spent together. If I was honest with myself, I missed his tenderness, his big heart and his cheerful laugh.

And yet I hadn't known so much about him. He had truly been a remarkable and admirable person, so multi-faceted.

Two weeks after his death, I had only learnt through another appointment with Jacob's notary that Jacob offered his support to young women who had become pregnant unmarried and, therefore lost their jobs and homes. He had a small network of people who thought like him and with whom such women found a new home and work.

To this end, Jacob and a few rich widows had set up a foundation to help these women financially during a difficult time. As Jacob's heir, I was now also his successor in this matter.

After this enlightening information, Frederik and I got in touch with the other helping people – most of whom were women – ourselves. We wanted to continue Jacob's work in his spirit. Magdalena and my mother also got involved. Within a short space of time, we took in a young woman in need as one of my parents' servants and placed two others from here at Lake Chiemsee.

At Whitsun we went to mass in Salzburg, where a beautiful cantata was sung by a choir. *Also hat Gott die Welt geliebt* by Johann Sebastian Bach. Mamma explained to me that the text of this song was written by Christiana Mariana von Ziegler[58]. There are nine verses that spread very comforting words about a loving God like a protective cloak around the listener.

Shortly after Whitsun, Seraphia came home for a short time, where I visited her. She probably realised that I wanted to tell her something and asked Heinrich and Apollonia to leave us alone.

"I'm here for you, Vic, if you need a confidante. I'm sure the grief will stay with you for a while."

"Thank you for your words. Do you know how happy I am that I have learnt so much about the world from you? Your stories about the many people you've met have helped me a lot over the last year and a half. You always approach people with an open mind. I don't know how I would have fared if I hadn't had you as a role model."

"You're talking in riddles, Vic."

"Jacob's greatest love wasn't me, Seraphia. It was Frederik."

She gasped, then took my hands in hers. "I would never have guessed that. I'm so sorry for you."

"Jacob made it easy for me to come to terms with the situation. He was a generous and wonderful person and in the end I loved him. You know, he was a very tender and sensitive lover. That's why I did everything I could to see him

---

58 BWV 68. *She founded one of the first literary-musical salons in Germany. J. S. Bach set nine of Ziegler's texts to music for church cantatas.*

happy. At some point, he confessed his love to me – even if I was only in second place.

"His last words were for Frederik and me. He told us that he loved us both from the bottom of his heart and thanked us for the wonderful time we had together."

"Frederik is a very good-looking and likeable man. I like him very much." Seraphia said.

"Yes, that's him. There was tension between us at first, but gradually we became really good friends. I would never have believed that he would grow so fond of me."

"Did he desire you too?"

"No, I don't think so. But he enjoyed making the people around us believe that he was my lover when the rumour started. And I'm a close friend to him, who also let's me in on his sectrets."

Seraphia laughed softly. "I think that was a clever move with the rumour against the background you gave me."

"Seraphia, apart from us, only Christoph knows about this. He was there when Jacob died. Let's keep it that way."

"Of course, we'll keep it between us! I feel sorry for Frederik. He's a fine man and doesn't seem to have a family, does he?"

"Sure he has. His old father and older brother, with whom he doesn't have much contact. Frederik lives off an annual allowance from the family estate and his income as a lawyer. Then there's a married sister, her husband and their two children. But they are pretty snooty and would despise him if they knew about his lifestyle."

"I hope you invited him to visit us here?"

"Yes, of course, as soon as he has no commitments, he'll come. We write to each other often. He's become an important person in my life. And I think I'm just as important to him. Because apart from him, I'm the only one who knew his great love as he remembers it.

What I never asked you ... and please don't be angry with me ... it's none of my business, but ... is Heinrich your lover?"

Seraphia smiled. "Yes, that's him. He's been by my side faithfully for 15 years now and has never complained. I love him very much. But you know that a dancer isn't worth much once she's married. Heinrich knows that my great love is dancing. But he can live with this competition."

"I hope I find a man I can live with like you do with Heinrich. Because I don't want to get married a second time. I never want to give up my freedom again."

"I can understand that. Vic, I wish that for you with all my heart. For now, all I can say is that I'll stand by you whenever you need help."

And now what?

In my life so far, I have often had to learn that very few people – unfortunately including women – trust a woman to be able to think or act independently. For example, I've never had a client here in the area because, despite my title Assessor iuris, I'm denied the ability to work as a lawyer.

This fact tugged at my nerves. I knew that I was better than many a man, but nobody cared. And for one reason only: because I was a woman. I couldn't score points with my practical experience, because in the eyes of society that would have tarnished the memory of my deceased husband or, alternatively, that of my beloved brother.

So I can only practise in silence, working with my brother without the knowledge of some clients. He is brilliant in his own right, but together we are unbeatable when the law is on our side. Now I help my mother around the house and organise our servants.

I loved doing all this, but it wasn't my calling. All my life, all I wanted to do was dance and share the joy of it with other people. But my father wouldn't hear of it.

His daughter, a widowed countess, as a dance mistress, unheard of.

"It's enough that your aunt does crazy things like staying unmarried and travelling the world with her lover to dance. You're not going to do that!" He shouted. "What do you want people to think of you? Or of me, if I let you get away with it? Marry again, like any other sensible woman! You're still young and not every man has such a horrible mother as your late husband."

"So you're mainly worried about what other people might think of us? How pathetic! They think what they want anyway. If they want to think well of us, it makes no difference and if they want to think badly of us, they'll always find something to take offence at, Father!

"If a man has lovers, he is admired for it, if a woman has a lover, she is stigmatised for it. It's all so hypocritical."

"As far as I know, your husband never had a lover. That speaks in your favour, my child."

"Leave that alone. I'm not a child and what do you know about my husband and me! Maybe he was just a big secret-keeper? Not every man brags about his mistresses, and I also think that any widow with a bit of sense should refrain from marrying a second time if she can afford it. Because only as a widow can she take her life into her own hands. As such, she is not accountable to her father or anyone else."

"As long as you live in my house, you are very much accountable to me."

"Then I'll just change that again and go back to München immediately to live my own life there!"

"You're not!"

"Oh yes I am! And you're not going to stop me!"

My father's breath caught in his throat. He knew that I could and would do it. He changed the subject.

"Is it true that this Frederik von Barby is your lover?"

"No, that's not true. Anyway, it's none of your business. It's my life." I shouted back before I got silent.

"Pah, after my experience with a terrible mother-in-law and brother-in-law and a husband whose lover was a man – even if I really loved him with all my heart – I would certainly not marry again.

"In my experience, most men are also like roosters. As soon as they see a female, they puff themselves up, tell us again and again in the most boring way how great they are and allow themselves to be admired. However, they don't let us get a word in edgewise. Especially when they know that we are clever. Or they don't listen to us because they don't think it's worth listening to our opinion. They only accept the word of a woman if they are of the same opinion or if it serves their own praise and otherwise we should keep our mouths shut if possible.

"In the event of marriage, they have all rights over us women and can keep us like dogs without anyone being able to take action against them. Not even legally!"

If I ever fell in love, I would take a lover like Seraphia, but I would never marry again.

Fortunately, Christoph supported me in my position. My brother didn't let me completely lose hope that there would be men who would grant their inherent rights to self-determination to all other people.

Mamma always said that she didn't know how the situation could change because almost all men were brought up so terribly. They were constantly told by their nurses, teachers, fathers and mothers that they were the biggest and best and that women were of no importance.

"And if you listen to some of these birth machines, they're just pretty-looking dolls who have never learnt to use their brains to think, which again seems to confirm the prevailing opinion." That's what mamma originally said.

I threw some of this at our father and he actually listened to me. I realised that he was starting to think for himself, so I tried something else.

"Father, you once told me that your father was strictly against it when you announced that you were setting up your business. For similar reasons, too. After all, as a nobleman, you shouldn't work as a merchant and so on. It was your dream and you've been living it ever since. Nobody could stop you. Why do you think my dream is worth less than yours?"

At that moment, mamma called out that she needed my help. So I left my father. I had a very small hope that his opinion would change.

A visit to Salzburg

To take my mind off things and to simply spend time together again, Nannerl had sent me a message with an invitation. She wanted me to spend a few days visiting her family.

Full of anticipation, I travelled to Salzburg with a couple of friends from Nonn. After I had settled into the Mozart's guest room, Nannerl and I played the harpsichord four-handed. We sang along with some of the pieces and had a lot of fun. It felt so good to do something with a friend for once!

Later, we took a short walk through the town towards the River Salzach. We passed the brewery "bey der Stiegen"[59], which seemed to be a lively place. Travellers passing through liked to stay here, some townspeople went there in the evening for a pint of beer – or even several – and others had their own pint filled so that they could empty it at home in comfort. My hosts all liked the palatable dark brew.

Nannerl and me stood together by the river near the state bridge and looked out over the water.

---

59   *The brewery on the Gstätten was founded in 1492 and was originally located where the Haus der Natur now stands. The Stiegl Keller can still be found in the Festungsgasse. The "Stiegl Brauwelt" is located at Bräuhausstraße 9.*

"Isn't our homeland beautiful?" Nannerl wanted to know. I wholeheartedly agreed with her. "Yes, the river, the mountains, the countryside surrounding the city – it's simply marvellous here."

The next day was the weekly market[60] and we two friends browsed early through the numerous stalls selling a wide variety of goods. We were particularly fond of the wreath market at the end of Siegmund-Haffner-Gasse, where ornamental flowers and wreaths are on sale alongside birds. Once again, we marvelled at the beautiful flowers and exotic songbirds. How I would love to have a bird like that at home. On the other hand, I wouldn't want to lock such a marvellous creature in a cage.

Beneath the sound of birds we were also accompanied on our way by the sounds of the Glockenspiel[61] and the Salzburger Stier[62]. Nannerl had to pick up something her father had ordered from the Hofapotheke[63] while I indulged my passion outside the pharmacy: People-watching. I love thinking about how people live, what they do, who they might be travelling with and so on.

When we had done all the important shopping that Mrs Mozart and my Mamma had told us to do, we took our baskets home and went into town again. First I wanted to go to the bridge on the quay. There was the Mayer's shop[64], where our family loved to buy buttons, trimmings and lots of other things. There is a marvellous selection of buttons there. It's always nice to browse there and choose buttons and trims to match new and old clothes. I needed some hooks and some lace for a new dance dress. As always, I found exactly what I was looking for.

---

60 Today, the popular Schrannenmarkt is held every Thursday on the square in front of St Andräkirche.
61 The carillon sounded for the first time in 1703 in the tower of the new residence.
62 Salzburg Bull: the world's oldest horn mechanism still in operation.
63 In Mozart's time in house no. 7 on the Alter Markt, since around 1910 in house no. 6
64 The "Knopferlmayer" on the bridge has existed since 1758. 1804 the shop moved to the old town hall on the Kranzlmarkt and is still a sensation.

We took a detour to stroll through the whole of Getreidegasse from the west. I was supposed to get a few dozen horseshoe nails for Seraphia from the blacksmith[65]. She always had some with her when travelling in case a horseshoe came loose and there was no blacksmith nearby.

After our shopping, we sat down in the "Staigersche Caféhaus"[66] for a cup of chocolate and a piece of cake. I love this café, which I believe is the oldest of its kind in Austria. It has such an international flair. The people who frequent it make anything but an everyday impression on me. That's why I really enjoy watching the people inside and outside. Nannerl also made a few comments that made me laugh.

"Look, Vic, a lady is walking past outside the window and her servant is carrying a dog that looks like the spitting image of her." I almost choked with laughter because it really was like that. I wonder if anyone had ever noticed that before?

In the evening, when Nannerl's father came home from his work as bandmaster to Archbishop Hieronymus Count Colloredo, he talked about his time at university and his temporary accommodation in the "Löchlbogen"[67] before his marriage. He had some amusing stories to tell about his bachelor days. I wouldn't have believed him to have a good sense of humour after all. How deceptive you can be if you only know people superficially.

---

65 A smithy has been housed at Getreidegasse 28 since the 15th century. The Wieber family has been running the locksmith's workshop since 1976.

66 Founded by Johann Fontaine, who was granted a licence to sell chocolate, tea and coffee in Goldgasse on 31 March 1700. In 1764, today's Tomaselli moved to Alter Markt 9 and 10, where it still is today. It is the oldest surviving café house in Salzburg, the oldest within the borders of Austria and possibly the oldest continuously operating café house in Central Europe.

67 Today the inn "Zum Eulenspiegel", which is advertised as the most original restaurant in Austria in a house that is almost 700 years old.

I really enjoyed my time with the Mozart family and especially with my friend Nannerl. It was good to be distracted from my brooding for a few days.

Travelling

Seraphia realised that I wasn't happy in the situation I was in.

"Vic, I think you need to get out of here. Would you like to accompany Heinrich and me on our performance tours this year?"

I would never have dared to hope that Seraphia would make me such an offer. I told her the same thing.

"Well, now that you're a respected countess dowager and not an unmarried young lady who needs a chaperone at every step, nobody can take offence at such a journey, can they? I also have a few ideas for new choreographies[68]. I need to try them out with someone. And who better than my niece, who did exactly what I had just thought of as a child.

"Perhaps we can make a difference with Bach and Uccellini in our luggage? What do you think? Besides, Apollonia has asked me, if she could visit her family. She's usually there as my maid."

My response was to throw my arms around Seraphia's neck.

We set off just a few days later: Seraphia, Heinrich and I with my maid Katharina, who I had brought with me from München and who would also be at my aunt's service during the journey.

We had a closed two-horse carriage and two riding horses with us. We women wore practical clothing, i.e. light

---

68   *Written dance: Greek choreos = dance and graphein = to write*

riding breeches with equally light skirts over them. When we rode, it was only in the more comfortable men's seat. I would never want to ride such routes in a side saddle[69]. After all, this wasn't just a short ride in the park, but a strenuous journey where we were travelling many miles.

Our first stop was my München townhouse, where we only wanted to spend two days. Seraphia had an engagement for one evening at a party in the Residenz. I wanted to talk to Frederik about a few things. So it all fell into place.

I had, of course, written to my majordomo and informed him of our arrival. He and the few servants who had stayed to look after the house wouldn't have too much trouble.

Frederik had quite naturally invited us to his place for dinner on the evening of our arrival. 'You don't have a cook any more and I'll tell your old and my new kitchen pearl who she can entertain,' he had written to me.

When we arrived at my palace, Frederik and Magdalena were already waiting there and greeted us warmly. We hadn't seen each other for a few weeks and had a lot to talk about again.

Katharina was welcomed like a long-lost family member. When she wasn't helping us, she was putting her heads together with her former mates and her special friend, the cook.

The evening in Frederik's Palais was marvellous. We laughed a lot and at the end we all played music together. Such a single evening with good friends, tasty food and music made up for many weeks in which life seemed rather tedious.

The next day, I ran some errands that mamma had asked me to do. She had asked me to have the things sent to her directly by post. I organised everything.

In the afternoon, Seraphia was at the residence with Heinrich and Katharina for the engagement. So I visited

---

69   It was not until around 1170 that the first saddles with a saddle horn appeared, which made the side seat somewhat more secure. The side saddle as we know it today has only been around since the 19th century.

Magdalena first to have a chat with her and her mother. There was even time for a short trip with the birds to the Falkenau. How I had missed those rides! As usual, I was riding in a man's saddle and only had a simple skirt over my breeches.

This time, however, I was probably very inattentive. Magdalena let Morgana fly. I watched the majestic bird and was fascinated as always. Especially when it came swooping back to us. My horse, on the other hand – a different one to my previous hunting trips – was anything but enthusiastic, it was frightened, bolted and wanted to flee.

I suddenly found myself hanging inelegantly from his side along with the saddle. I had no way of pulling myself up again. So I ended up letting myself fall while somehow managing to keep hold of the reins, which stopped the animal from escaping. I landed somewhat roughly on the meadow.

"Damn!" I groaned.

Then Magdalena's voice came through to me. "Vic, oh dear! Has something happened to you? Can you get up?"

I took stock of the situation. "No, I'm not injured and I can get up. I'm just afraid I'm going to have a backside that shimmers in all colours for the next few days."

I could laugh again. "It's my own fault. Firstly, I didn't realise that this horse didn't know Morgana, and secondly, I knew that the boy would puff up when saddling up, but that he could hold out for so long … After all, I tightened the girth twice."

"Well, if the whole saddle slips, then of course there's no stopping it – and the horse gets even more scared because the situation is so unfamiliar."

In the evening, I was back at Frederik's door. He had invited me to dine with him again and had also asked me to discuss a few legal issues with him. It wasn't socially acceptable for the two of us to be alone in the same room, but who was going to find out? Besides, Frederik had been my lover for a long time, as society thought it knew.

I immediately told him about my mishap and he laughed about it. "That gives me hope that you'll get through the journey without an accident. I think every rider lands roughly on the ground from time to time. You were lucky that it was meadow and not the hard ground in the city and that you didn't have any unwanted witnesses."

During the meal, I realised that my dear friend had coped much worse with our loss than I had. We mainly dealt with legal issues and were also able to clarify the questions that had been bothering him for some time to his satisfaction.

Later, we sat on a bench in the back garden and talked about Jacob. Frederik wanted to talk about him.

"I can't express how much I miss Jacob in everything." He told me. "I could always discuss my cases with him. But sometimes we just sat and talked about life, our friends, the latest gossip. I miss his closeness, his touch so much."

"I realise that no one can replace Jacob. Not even in my life. But you don't have to do without everything. You have friends you can talk to about anything. You have friends who are happy to discuss legal issues with you or give you a hug."

I then embraced my dear friend. We both really needed this kind of closeness. It was a long time before we separated again.

"Frederik, I just can't see you suffering like this. You know I'm your friend and I want you to be happy again. I think you should get away from München for a while." I suggested. "Would you like to accompany us to Bayreuth and Erlangen?"

He hugged me again and leant his head against my neck and shoulder, as he had often done in the past. We sat there for a long time and said nothing.

Without speaking another word, I left my best friend after this heartfelt embrace and went to my own house.

The next morning, I only went for a leisurely ride with Frederik to nurse my backside. Afterwards, we fenced with each other for two hours until we both ran out of energy. Frederik then stood in my way when I wanted to leave.

"I will accompany you to Bayreuth. From there, I will then travel on to my family's estates. I think it's time to have a talk with my father and my brother. Who knows how much longer my father will live. I want to put an end to the discord between us."

I hugged him and kissed him on the cheek. "That makes me happy! Oh, it's going to be a wonderful journey!"

Bayreuth

We set off the next day. Katharina and Seraphia with our luggage in the carriage in front and Heinrich, Frederik and I on our horses behind. As we were well armed and within sight of a stagecoach, we had no further concerns. We took it in turns to drive the coach. Only Katharina couldn't steer the carriage, but she knew how to ride.

On the third day of our journey, we arrived safely in Bayreuth. There, Seraphia was to dance before Elector Christian Friedrich Carl Alexander of Brandenburg-Ansbach and Brandenburg-Bayreuth. He usually stayed at his hunting and country estate in Triesdorf and only paid a compulsory visit to the town for which he was responsible.

After the death of the margrave couple Frederick of Brandenburg-Bayreuth and his wife Friederike Sophie Wilhelmine von Preußen, the current one became the new Elector in the absence of a male descendant as the nephew of the Margrave couple. His wife, Friederike Caroline von Sachsen-Coburg-Saalfeld, lived separately from her husband at Schwaningen Castle.

Alexander of Brandenburg-Ansbach's cousin, Elisabeth Friederike Sophie of Brandenburg-Bayreuth, was still married to Duke Carl Eugen of Württemberg, but had been living in Bayreuth again since the death of her mother, as her marriage was in tatters and she wanted to return to the place of her childhood.

Her cousin's rare visit was the reason for the celebration and brought all the splendour to life once again. The city is without doubt magnificent. Elisabeth's mother, Wilhelmine Margravine of Brandenburg-Bayreuth[70], had been the favourite sister of the Preußenkönig Friedrich II. During her reign, she had turned a sleepy provincial town into one of the most attractive places in Deutschland.

I was lucky enough to meet an elderly lady on my walk through Bayreuth who approached me as I was admiring the statues on the roof of the opera house.

Suddenly she stood next to me and smiled at me. "Beautiful, isn't it? Still, it's hard to imagine the splendour that lies behind this façade"

I smiled back and showed her my approval.

"You know, I was in the service of Margravine Wilhelmine for many years – God rest her soul. She created such wonderful buildings!"

"She?" I asked back.

"Yes, you see, the Margravine drew some of the designs herself and above all had the ideas. I'll tell you what she alone made of the Hermitage, a real gem. And Sanspareil, a marvellous world that presents itself to the viewer."

"Sanspareil? What is that? And above all, where is it?"

"Zwernitz Castle lies between Bayreuth and Bamberg. Wilhelmine laid out a wonder garden there with a belvedere castle[71], a theatre ruin and numerous other beautiful things. Whimsical little houses were built on the rocks to serve as retreats. I no longer know which lady-in-waiting

---

70   Frederick II's eldest sister, she was admitted to the Accademia dell'Arcadia in Rome in 1751. She was a composer, musician (harpsichord, violin, lute), singer, director of the court theatre, actress, librettist, dramaturge, painter and designer of interiors and gardens. Her memoirs are particularly interesting to read.
71   In this case a small castle with a beautiful view = italian: Belvedere.

it was in 1746 who exclaimed ‚*Ah, c'est sans pareil*[72]`, at the sight of the rock garden. In the same year, Margrave Friedrich had the village of Zwernitz renamed Sanspareil."

"Oh, what a lovely story. Thank you for sharing your knowledge with me."

"Oh, you know, there aren't as many interesting people here as there were when our Margravine Wilhelmine was alive. You looked so likeable to me and I thought I would like to get to know you. I haven't socialised much since my husband, Baron Karl von Murach, died five years ago."

I really liked this pleasant lady and she seemed to know a lot.

"I'm sorry to hear that. My name is Victoria Countess Dowager von Falkenstein. My brother-in-law is now the new count and I have withdrawn from my husband's family. During my year of mourning, nothing keeps me in places where I was with my late husband and everything reminds me of him. So I'm travelling with my aunt and her dance partner. My husband's best friend has accompanied us this far. He wants to visit his family in Thüringen[73]."

Sibylla von Murach invited me and my travelling companions to a small party three days later.

It was a successful evening for Seraphia and Frederik. My aunt got two more engagements through guests she was introduced to by our new acquaintance. And Frederik met up with an old friend who now ran a county in his father's neighbourhood.

I kept a low profile that evening, but learnt a lot more about the history of Bayreuth on a few walks with Sibylla von Murach.

As always, Seraphia knew how to inspire with her art. In our accommodation, we practised dancing and making music for many hours.

I was so happy that Frederik seemed to be doing much better thanks to our presence. He became happier again

---

72   *That is unrivalled*
73   *Thuringia*

and drew new strength from all our endeavours. We both practised fencing again, and were also particuarly enthusiastic about dancing the minuet.

By invitation, we all attended a concert together with Sibylla, at which a march for some regiment by Princess Anna Amalia of Prussia[74] and pieces by her sister Wilhelmine von Brandenburg-Bayreuth and her brother Frederick II, as well as the flute sonata by Anna Bon di Venezia[75] and a symphony for two oboes, two flutes, two violins and basso continuo by Anna Amalia von Brunswick-Wolfenbüttel[76] were performed. This concert and other events were held in honour of the high visit of the Margrave and his relatives.

Thanks to Sibylla's intervention, we were given box seats. In order to accommodate as many people as possible, the auditorium downstairs was not equipped with chairs. I wouldn't have missed this evening for the world.

The Margravial Opera House shone in the light of countless candles. The stage seemed endless and its construction was elaborate and sophisticated. The entire structure with its three tiers of boxes was made of wood. The exquisite carvings, the abundance of gold and the magnificent paintings ... An angel here, a deity there, everything looked so noble.

Frederik and I rode one day to the *Eremitage,* a park half a mile or so outside Bayreuth. This park next to the old castle is beautifully laid out and of a considerable size. It contains a relatively small new castle with a mosaic façade and a beautiful fountain with various fantasy animals and gods, a theatre ruin and much more. I was particularly impressed by the Chinese pavilion, which stands on the 'snail mountain'. A magical vantage point. Frederik favoured the lower grotto with the water features which

---

74 Youngest sister of Frederick the Great and abbess of Quedlinburg Abbey,
75 A female musician from Bologna who dedicated her Flute Sonata I to Margrave Friedrich von Brandenburg-Culmbach-Bayreuth in 1756.
76 Anna Amalia was Duchess of Saxe-Weimar and Eisenach. She was a regent, patron and composer

reminded me of the grotto in the park of castle Hellbrunn in Salzburg.

My personal highlight during these days, however, was another evening at the Margravial Opera House, where a travelling stage was performing the tragedy *Romeo and Juliet*[77] by William Shakespeare. I went with Frederik. Luckily for us, he had managed to get a box seat. So at least not everyone could see that we were both in tears as the play drew to a close. I couldn't contain myself for a long time afterwards. The play had moved me like no other in a long time. We stayed in our box for a long time and talked about the play and the author, about love and life.

The opera house in Bayreuth is the most magnificent opera house I have ever seen. The paintings are marvellous, as are the carvings around the royal box. When the candles are lit everywhere, it's a dream.

The rich bourgeoisie had also been invited to a ball in the Redoutenhaus right next door. Unfortunately, I couldn't dance because of the mourning period. But I went anyway and kept discreetly in the background. I had some interesting people to talk to. Frederik gave up a few dances for my sake and accompanied me on my way through the hall.

All too soon it was time to say goodbye again. This time from Bayreuth and Frederik. We wished our friend all the best and that he would have a better relationship with his father and older brother in the future.

Erlangen

We were on the road again. During the journey, the horses suffered from the many insects that would not leave

---

77   *The Bayreuth Opera House was actually home to a travelling theatre at the time, which performed Romeo and Juliet in German, among other plays.*

them alone on hot and humid days. The horseflies in particular were very annoying, which is why we attached leather straps to the head pieces so that the horses could fend off the flood of flying pests.

Once we were really lucky. Seraphia was driving when one of the carriage horses was hit by several horseflies. The horse became hysterical and was close to bolting. Fortunately, Heinrich was able to ride alongside and scare the horseflies away, which calmed the horse down again.

Our next stop was Erlangen. Seraphia was invited to dance in several performances at the Hochfürstliches Komödienhaus. And I was supposed to support her in some of these performances. As we were unknown here and would also be dancing with masks, I didn't want to miss this opportunity to dance.

This theatre was opened back in 1719. So it has seen a lot. I like the decor almost as much as the theatre in Bayreuth. Someone told me that up to 6,000 candles are burnt in the theatre in one evening.

The theatre, the Redoutensaal and the Marstall are located in a building complex near the palace gardens. There is an orchestra pit for 40 musicians. The opera and comedy theatre was built by Margrave Georg Wilhelm von Brandenburg-Bayreuth.

We were invited by friends of Seraphia to stay with them while we were in Erlangen. In the bedroom assigned to me hung a hunting painting[78] that I really liked. At supper, I asked the lady of the house, Philomena, who had painted the picture.

"Oh, this is from one of my friends from Bamberg, Anna Maria Treu. The whole Treu family are artists, you must know. Her sisters Rosalie and Catharina[79] also paint very harmonious pictures, but each of them specialises in a different area. Catharina paints particularly beautiful ceremo-

---

78 *In painting, a hunting scene or a still life with game, weapons, etc.*
79 *Catharina Treu becomes the first woman to be appointed titular professor at the Academy of Art in Düsseldorf in 1776*

nial still lifes and Rosalie is praised for a few paintings of high lords."

"How wonderful to have a friend who knows how to paint so beautifully!"

"Have you ever heard of the Royal Academy of Arts in London?"

"I seem to remember reading a note about it in the magazine. But that was probably a few years ago. Do you know more about it?"

"Anna told me that thirty-four important artists and architects were present at the foundation in 1768 by George III. Among them were the marvellous painter Joshua Reynolds and the painters Angelika Kauffmann and Mary Moser. My friend Anna knows Angelika Kauffmann, who is of Swiss-Austrian origin. I don't understand why Anna wants to stay in Bamberg, even though there are so many opportunities in the world for people as talented as her."

Seraphia intervened in our conversation.

"You know that there is also the Académie des Arts in Stuttgart? In 1762, Anna Dorothea Therbusch from Berlin, at that time court painter to Duke Carl Eugen, was appointed an honorary member. She now lives in Paris, where I once met her at a reception. By chance, I recently read *Mystification ou histoire des portraits* by Denis Diderot. Imagine, Therbusch even plays a role in this work, as it is based on true events."

I was very interested in the story. "You mean the philosopher Diderot, who, initially together with Jean Baptiste le Rond d'Alembert, and later with Louis de Jaucourt and with the help of a network of scribes, published this all-encompassing encyclopaedia of the sciences, arts and crafts? My husband owned all 28 volumes that were published up to last year."

"Yes, that's the one I mean. As far as I know, Diderot has a close confidante, Sophie Volland, if I remember correctly. They seem to have a close friendship, like you and

Frederik. At least that's what I've been told. I wouldn't be surprised if she had also contributed to this encyclopaedia."

It's always exciting to see who knows who and what people know. I was so happy to have come on this trip. Of course, I wrote to my mother and Christoph every few days and told them in my letters what new things I had learnt and whom I had met. And I continued to write letters to Nannerl and Magdalena and to Frederik every week, all of which were answered very eagerly. In his first letter, Frederik told me that he had made peace with his father and that he would now be spending a lot of time with his brother. He would be back in München in August.

'... I'm glad I don't have to be the future count. My brother does all the work and takes care of everything, but the old man has sole power. If he likes it, my brother ends up with nothing. They rub each other up the wrong way because they have completely different opinions on a lot of things.

On the other hand, they are so similar again, but they don't see that.

I don't understand why Pappa hasn't just handed everything over a long time ago and enjoyed his retirement. He says he's tired of it, but can't let go.

So I try to mediate between them as best I can. It's difficult. Especially from my position as the younger one who has long been ignored. But I still feel it's my duty to improve the situation for the good of all. Because the servants are also suffering ...'

His last letter so far gave me hope.

' ... in very small steps, something actually seems to be changing. I think Pappa is slowly realising how his behaviour is hurting everyone and has now agreed to make a few admissions. He realises how happy this makes my brother and how it takes a burden off him. I certainly hope that he will leave more decisions to his son and heir in future ...'

I wrote to my friend to wish him continued success with his mediation and hoped that his brother appreciated his commitment.

Seraphia and I rehearsed and rehearsed. It was a minuet in which we both danced with violins[80] and played the leading melody in two voices. As far as I know, there has never been a minuet danced and played by two women like this before. At least we haven't heard of it. We had the last two rehearsals together with the orchestra in the theatre. Heinrich, our toughest critic, was thrilled. In addition, Seraphia wanted to dance *Passacaglia* by George Frideric Handel, a solemn and noble dance, and we both wanted to dance *La Folia* by Arcangelo Corelli together.

"You look so graceful and elegant. Two women fiddling and dancing, moving like queens. It's beautiful. I think the audience will love you." Heinrich said.

He was right. The audience were absolutely thrilled. They clapped and cheered for a long time and wanted to see us on stage again and again. Nobody knew who was hiding behind our elaborate half-masks and particularly sophisticated wigs, which was a special attraction and also helped me to maintain my mourning widow position.

On our penultimate evening, we were invited to a performance of Antonio Salieri's opera *Armida*, which had premiered in Wien the year of my wedding. I have to admit that although I like operas, they often have the same effect on me as sleeping pills. They just make me sit still for too long and I find that very difficult. Especially when not much is happening. When the music gets really slow and quiet, I'm tempted to fall asleep. I managed to stay awake that evening, but only with difficulty.

After the performance, I asked Seraphia to help me with my Italian. Because there were definitely passages where I didn't understand everything. I practised diligently over the following days.

---

80   *A pochette is too small for a large concert hall due to its lower sound volume.*

Furthermore on the road

We sent Katharina home with one of the horses and some of the luggage in the wake of a stagecoach. We were travelling from Erlangen to Paris and we had to pay customs duties everywhere for people, horses and luggage. We didn't want to overstretch our travelling budget. Because Seraphia and I can be each other's maids. And we'll find a solution for big occasions.

The journey took almost three weeks and we weren't always lucky enough to find comfortable accommodation. I spent one night sitting entirely on an armchair because the bed was so obviously crawling with bedbugs and other creatures that I couldn't bring myself to lie down on it.

But as Seraphia remarked so beautifully: "At your age, you can still cope quite well with an uncomfortable night like that. Later on, it becomes increasingly difficult."

She had the better bed and in return gave me her place in the carriage for the following day and sat on my horse instead of me. So I was able to rest for a while next to the coachman, Heinrich.

We had a bit of rain on a few days, but as I have a coat that can withstand a bit of water thanks to its waxed surface, I also survived this trip well. I did have a little cold halfway through, but otherwise I was in good spirits.

When we stayed overnight at a large monastery, we were invited to attend a performance of Claudio Monteverdi's *Vespro della beata vergine*[81]. This is a vocal work that made me dream. The church we were sitting in was only sparsely lit with individual candles, so nothing could distract me from the music.

In terms of atmosphere, it was a bit like the Angel Office or the so-called "golden mass" on the Saturday after St Lucia at home. In some places they are also called Rorate mass. A solemn breeze wafted through the room and I

---

81   *Known as the Marian Vespers.*

completely surrendered to the marvellous sound of the many voices.

As a journey like this is boring without any entertainment, we talked a lot. We were accompanied for part of the journey by a pleasant gentleman who joined us for his own safety. He came from Hanover and wanted to visit a distant aunt. He told us about his good friend Friedrich Wilhelm Herschel[82] and his sister Caroline[83].

"Caroline has travelled to Bath after Friedrich, where he works as a composer and musician. She is a little sparrow, but a very talented singer who performs at his concerts. I very much regret that she followed her brother to England, because we often played together as children and always got on well afterwards. She went to the garrison school for a few hours every day and that's where we got to know each other. She wrote to me from Bath. I think she's in her element there."

"Oh, Caroline was allowed to go to school? Her parents were very progressive!"

"Well, more the father. After school, she had to help with the housework at home. Her mother insisted on it."

"And now he's a musician and she's a singer? That's wonderful. Could it be that they both come from a musical household?"

He laughed. "Yes, that's right, with a father who is a military musician, nothing else could really come of it, could it? I didn't have much to do with the other three brothers when we were children and I'm not in contact with them now either. But I still keep in touch with Caroline by post. I always let her know all the news from Hanover and she lets me know everything that's happening in London and Bath.

---

82   *Herschel discovers the planet Uranus, among other things, with reflecting telescopes he has built himself.*

83   *Caroline decided against a career as a singer and became an important astronomer who was appreciated by many scholars and crowned heads.*

"The two siblings don't just work together musically. Fritz is a man who is very interested in astronomy and he shares this passion with his sister. She grinds and polishes the mirrors of telescopes that they both make. Fritz says that this task requires absolute precision. Caroline is extremely skilful at it."

I enjoyed these hours with our travelling companion, who only had a packhorse with him and liked to hear himself talk. He was never boring, always knew lots of stories and also told me some regional legends.

One evening at a post station where we had also found accommodation, Heinrich discovered a harpsichord in the dining room. As we and the stagecoach passengers still had to wait for dinner, we decided to make some music. So Seraphia and I unpacked our violins. This lifted the mood, which had been depressed by the fog, and we even got talking.

Among others, there was a merchant from Lübeck and a noble lady from Mannheim with her companion. There were also two young men who were on the Grand Tour[84].

After the meal, there was even dancing by popular demand and it was a very pleasant and enjoyable evening for everyone. We also introduced a few new tunes and dances to the travellers, which everyone clearly enjoyed. Seraphia left it to me to announce the figures and dance steps. I always had to make sure that I announced the next figure to be danced in good time so that everyone could react and actually dance it. Fortunately, I'd had some practice with this by now. With most pieces, you can easily hear from the music when there is a change of figure.

The next morning, the landlord met us with a smile before we travelled on. "My wife and I really enjoyed last night." he said. "It was peaceful and all ate and drank a lot. We enjoyed the music and dancing so much that we decided to charge you not for everything. We've also prepared some travelling provisions for you because we enjoyed

---

84 *Educational journey of young noble men, common since the Renaissance.*

it so much. It would be nice to host guests like you more often. Thank you for the wonderful change."

He pressed a large cloth full of delicacies into my hand. Our spontaneous idea had brought joy to many people – and in the end to ourselves as well. Our travel fund was well filled, but we were still delighted with the landlord's gesture.

Paris in August

We finally arrived in Paris safe and sound. Once again, Seraphia's contacts helped us with our accommodation. We were invited by a patron to stay at the Hotel d'Angevillers like Madeleine-Sophie Arnould[85]. When I saw Seraphia's friend for the first time, I was thrilled. She is a beautiful woman with a fine face. I liked her character straight away. She is friendly but has a biting wit when it counts. She likes to question things and loves to surround herself with clever people.

On the second day of our stay, Madeleine invited us to watch a performance with her at the Paris Opera.

During the intermission, I had a lively conversation with a lady sitting in the box next to ours. I liked her thoughts on operas and theatre performances in general. She introduced herself to me as the Marquise de Montesson[86]. A fascinating personality and also quite good-looking.

"You know, my husband and I actually live at Le Raincy Castle. But I really wanted to buy a few things personally in Paris. There are some things you just don't want to leave to the servants, no matter how honest they are. I also wan-

85 Madeleine-Sophie Arnould was a French opera singer and salonnière of the Enlightenment
86 Charlotte-Jeanne Béraud de la Haye de Riou, Marquise de Montesson

ted to visit a friend who is very dear to me. So my husband did me the favour of letting me come here for a few weeks.

"I try my hand at writing theatre plays in quiet hours. It's so nice to bring them to the stage – even if it's only our own for now!"

My conversation partner was bubbling over with joy. She has wit and I can imagine her performing self-written pieces with great vigour. We chatted for quite a while and laughed together at a few bon mots[87] that she dropped

Afterwards, Heinrich, who once again seemed to have his informants everywhere, explained to me in a whisper that my interlocutor had been the maîtresse en titre[88] of Louis Philippe I de Bourbon, duc d'Orléans, to whom she had been married in a morganatic marriage[89] in April of that year.

"Just imagine, she received Sainte Assise Castle in Seine-Port as a wedding present. I'd like to have a gift like that," Heinrich explained.

"Then you'll just have to marry a rich duke." Seraphia's whispered voice came from the background, from where she was trying to spy more with a theatre glass. I laughed and almost choked.

"Heinrich, you probably don't know this yet: this Philippe d'Orléans was a patron of the Mozarts when they travelled to Paris as infant prodigies. Nannerl once told me that when we were talking about that wonderful time."

"Really? No, I wasn't actually aware of that. I'm glad we have you with us, Vic. You always enrich my life with unexpected information." He bowed to me with a mischievous smile.

Seraphia reminded us to pay attention to the performance. "Let's get on with it, you two chatterboxes."

---

87   Humorous, witty remark
88   Official mistress
89   A marriage in aristocratic circles that was officially concluded, but usually excluded the wife (often of lower rank) and her children from a previous marriage from the (title) inheritance.

I was overwhelmed by Madeleine's pure soprano voice. No wonder she was the audience's favourite. She played enchantingly and sang very expressively. The admirers piled up in front of her dressing room after the performance.

Back at our accommodation, I thanked Madeleine for the invitation and showed her my enthusiasm in the form of a warm hug: "You were simply marvellous on stage. You should be very proud of yourself, Madeleine!"

"I hope I can call you a friend. Thank you, Vic. Such praise makes me especially happy when it comes from people I really appreciate myself – and when I realise that it's meant seriously."

La Reine de la danse

In addition to our rehearsals and Madeleine and Seraphia's performances, we organised as many joint activities as possible. We went to the theatre, went out, were invited to soirées and literary salons.

A few days later, we happened to meet Seraphia's friend Anna Heinel[90] in the park. She had a pretty face and was very pleasant to be with. Seraphia introduced us.

"How lucky you are to be here this year. This time last year I was in London and would have missed you. First things first. Just think, Seraphia, I've finally made up with Gaetano[91]."

"That's marvellous that you've finally buried your quarrel. You look so happy, Anna. I almost think you're in love. Is it Gaetano?"

---

90 *Anna Friederike Heinel, born in Bayreuth, was a famous dancer. She was celebrated as the "Queen of Dance" at the Paris Opera.*

91 *Gaetano Apolline Baldassarre Vestris, Italian dancer and choreographer, dance master to King Louis XVI and member of the Opéra National de Paris. He and Heinel married in 1792.*

Anna shook her head cheerfully. "Perhaps. In any case, I'm glad we're getting on after he used to see me as a rival. That really put a strain on me. I just can't stand it when people I admire see me as an enemy. I would be so happy if you could come to the performance in the next few days. Please say you'll be there!"

We could only nod as Anna continued to gush.

"Seraphia, you've always told me that Vic is such a good dancer and that your Heinrich also dances excellently. I have an idea." She clapped her hands at her enthusiasm. "Please come and see me tomorrow evening." She pressed a card into Seraphia's hand and with a wave she was gone.

"Is your friend Anna always such a whirlwind?" I asked.

Seraphia was still staring at the card in her hand, taken by surprise. "I think so. Her ideas are usually really good. And they almost always involve a lot of work."

The next day we drove out of Paris. On the way, we came across an open carriage in which Madeleine recognised Madame Jeanne Du Barry. A beautiful woman who, according to our information, also had a pleasant personality.

"She was a courtesan before she was married to Count du Barry. He and his brother managed to make her palatable to the king. This naturally gave both men more influence at court," said Madeleine.

"She looks very good and doesn't seem to be ten years older than me. For heaven's sake, how many years older is the king than her? 30 or more?" I shuddered at the idea of having an old man in my bed.

"Over 30 years older. Yes, if you want to achieve something at court as a woman, you can't be squeamish." Madeleine's comment sounded very dry. "In any case, she can draw from the full."

"Thanks, that wouldn't be for me. I'd rather stick to men who are about my age."

"Which in turn usually favour young geese for their bed as they get older." Seraphia was so right.

"Yes, that's true. But there are quite a few women – especially in aristocratic circles – who also have quite young lovers," Madeleine reported.

We spent the evening with Anna. She received us in a parlour where several guests were already staying. There was no performance at the opera that evening. A few more people arrived after us.

"Oh, how nice that you're here!" Anna said. "Now we're finally complete and I can present you with my plan."

She introduced all those present who did not yet know each other. The director of the opera, Monsieur Vestris, and other dancers were there, as well as some musicians and singers, including Madeleine.

"Here's what I have in mind: We invite the king and the high nobility to a very special performance. It should be an evening of music, singing and dancing. No opera, no theatre, no ballet. Just catchy melodies by great composers from all over Europe, combined with the angelic singing of our favourite singer Madeleine and her colleagues, the dancing of the best dancers at the Paris Opera, and the particularly impressive dancing of my esteemed friend Seraphia von Neubauer and her niece Victoria von Falkenstein along with their dance partner Heinrich Winkelmayr.

"As I know that the latter three are also excellent musicians who have a great command of a few special pieces, I would also ask for their performance. I imagine a show in which one highlight follows another, one that enchants all those present and after which everyone, without exception, is happy to have been there. A unique performance that will not be repeated.

"Of course, I would like to see this performance at the Opéra National de Paris, Salle du Palais-Royal in Rue Saint-Honoré. What do you think?"

The following hour was full of suggestions. Everyone present agreed that a special evening as suggested by Anna would be an excellent idea and that this and that could also be realised. Faces glowed, eyes shone ...

It was decided to organise this evening within three weeks. Admission would cost many times more than for a normal performance. Half of this money was to be donated to charity. Each performer would receive a portion of the proceeds as a fee. This meant that we could expect a lot of work, but also a fair wage and, if successful, almost certainly fame and further engagements.

After we had finished the evening, we found it hard to part. Someone always had an idea. But Anna decided that it had to end now and kicked us all out to go to sleep. After all, she had another performance the next day.

That very night there was a great disaster in the city. I was woken up by a tremor in the earth. It didn't last long, it was short and intense. Then I felt nothing more. But shortly afterwards I heard screams outside. The others also woke up and we were told by someone on the road that a street with all houses near our accommodation had collapsed.

The next day we saw the collapsed houses. It was terrible. Like after a war in which everything was destroyed. The ground had given way and the houses had collapsed like houses of cards, killing many people. A lot of people were trapped and people from the neighbourhood helped the survivors.

I enquired in more detail how this could have happened and learnt that there was a large network of medieval quarries under the outer regions of Paris where limestone had been and still is quarried for buildings such as Notre-Dame de Paris.

Since the expansion of Paris, it has happened now and again over the last few centuries that the ground has given way and one or more houses collapsed with it.

I was really glad that we had found accommodation in a house in the medieval town centre. At least there were no underground quarries here. I felt sorry for all the people who no longer had a roof over their heads.

That's why I spent the whole day helping to rescue some of the buried victims. It was hard work, and a lot of rubble had to be removed. But in the end, we helpers were happy to have rescued at least a few people. I fell into bed like a stone because I wasn't used to this kind of work.

A few days later, we attended a ballet in which Anna was the prima ballerina. She is a divine dancer and even Seraphia is completely enchanted by Anna's special elegance and graceful movements. Her famous *pirouette à la seconde*[92] was particularly impressive to watch.

Social gossip

Our stay in Paris consisted largely of rehearsals and Seraphia's performances here and there, but we also had the opportunity to meet some very interesting people at a few of Madeleine's parties.

These included Denis Diderot's confidante Sophie Volland and Jean-Jacques Rousseau. Unfortunately, Diderot himself had left for a trip to Russia in June.

"Tsarina Catherine II, who is a patron of Denis, invited him over ten years ago. Now he has set off to publish his encyclopaedia in Russia," she explained.

Volland told us that Diderot would probably be travelling for at least a year.

"I'm curious to see what he'll tell us about the monarch afterwards. It's rumoured that she has numerous love

---

92   *A turn in which the free leg is held horizontally to the side.*

affairs. She supposedly has a private room with furniture decorated with genitals. Can you believe that?"

I commented: "Well, she can certainly afford to have changing lovers. She has the power. Male monarchs are no different. But it's normal there and hardly anyone talks about it. We probably won't find out whether the gossip about the furniture is true. But the idea is a bit disturbing."

One of the authors of Diderot's encyclopaedia had another piece of news to report from Russia.

"Did you know that in June of this year, the Tsarina promised to tolerate all religious denominations? I think that's marvellous. After all, I have extensively studied all faiths. I find all of them perfectly acceptable in moderation. It's the extremes and the urge for one religious community – always the right one – to have sole power over all people that makes it bad."

Another agreed with him. "Yes, I've heard that. But also that Jews are excluded. So it's not as tolerant as you might think at first glance."

On another evening, Rousseau was not there, but Friedrich Melchior Baron von Grimm[93] was. I got talking to him.

"Baron von Grimm, the Mozarts would like me to send you their warmest regards. They speak very highly of you and are grateful to you for supporting Nannerl and Wolfgang during their stay in Paris."

"How are the Mozart family? Are they well? The two children impressed me deeply with their playing. When was it? I think it was in 1763, which is another ten years! In any case, please give me a warm greeting back to Salzburg."

"Yes, they are doing well. Wolfgang has already had some successes. He composes wonderfully. Nannerl still plays the pianoforte like an angel. However, my dear friend is

---

93 German writer and diplomat in Paris. He published the history of French literature from 1753 to 1790 as Correspondance littéraire, philosophique et critique and was involved in the Encyclopaedia. He was probably in Berlin in July 1773.

no longer allowed to perform in public. Her father doesn't allow it and wants her to get married."

He looked at me in amazement. "That's giving away her talent! She was a marvellous musician, the likes of which I have only seen a few. But the young woman will probably have to follow her father's wishes."

Now I was getting annoyed. "Yes, like so many other women who have great talent! It's a shame that women aren't allowed to live their lives like men. I also had to get married and become a wealthy widow to finally be free of these constraints."

"I'm sorry for you, my dear. Men are smarter than women. But let's go to the others now. They seem to have quite interesting topics."

This statement made me furious. "My arse! It has nothing to do with intelligence, but with a lust for power. You men are masters at that. If men gave women the same opportunities, they'd be amazed at how clever most women are."

I was boiling inside and left him standing there. Men always think they know the truth that applies to everyone. For them, it's important to have power over everything. They don't care who or what suffers as a result. Even if it affects their own wife or the children they claim to love. Well, they see them more as mindless property to be moulded according to their own will than as independent beings with intelligence. I thought of Christoph, Jacob and Frederik. They were different. I could only hope that more of their kind would grow up. I went out onto the terrace briefly to calm down again before joining the others.

It was in this circle that we learnt that Benjamin Franklin[94], who was in London, had caused a scandal that did him no good at all. It was he who had sent the so-called Hutchinson letters to Boston, which had recently been printed and made public.

---

94   *Boston printer, publisher, writer, scientist, statesman and inventor.*

There was a lot of talk about the Bostonian because he made all sorts of interesting inventions and seemed to be quite an impressive person in other respects.

He wanted to dissuade people from their superstition that lightning was a punishment from God. So he tried to prove that lightning is nothing more than electricity made visible.

In an attempt during a thunderstorm on 15 June 1752, he and his son flew a kite with metal attached to the tip. A string hung from this metal, to the end of which he had attached a key. His experiment (*which is not to be imitated!*) was a success.

The kite drew powerful energy and sparks leapt out of the key at the end of the rain-soaked string. Franklin had thus proven that electricity had been channelled from the tip of the kite directly to the key. This gave rise to the idea of a lightning conductor, which is now used on numerous buildings.

I listened with interest to the stories of the clever people around me. Benjamin Franklin is a very impressive man and I regretted that he wasn't here himself.

In my opinion, his most exciting invention three years ago was a pair of glasses with two different lenses mounted in a frame in such a way that you can see everything clearly both close up and in the distance.

Everyone except us seemed to know the gentleman personally. He had probably been a guest at Madeleine's meetings several times before.

I had a good time after all. At last I was able to talk to people other than Seraphia and Heinrich about all sorts of interesting topics. And I kept finding out things that I hadn't even realised before.

As I had actually read all the entries in the encyclopaedia and also looked at the illustrations, I made comments here and there when asked by the authors present at the evenings about details that I had missed in one topic, that I thought were a little too complicated in another topic and so on. Of course, I also praised a lot. Because I am still enthusiastic about the work as a whole.

One of the gentlemen came to talk about anatomical wax models. He was obviously completely fascinated by the subject.

"It is a great pity that the Académie des sciences does not support women. Marie Marguerite Bihéron in particular is such an accomplished woman who creates incredibly faithful wax models. A few years ago, she exhibited a very detailed and lifelike model of a pregnant woman with a foetus at the Académie. The model even had removable parts."

"That was certainly an excellent model. But wax melts in the heat," objected another.

"That's true, but Bihéron is said to have developed a process that guarantees the strength of the wax even at higher temperatures. She now lives and teaches mainly in England because she can make a better living from her work there."

"As far as I know, Bihéron is in constant contact with Franklin, who was mentioned earlier today."

"Bihéron is not the only woman who is an outstanding wax sculptor." the man said. "I met Anna Morandi Manzolini during my trip to Italy as part of my Grand Tour. She is known for her extremely precise anatomical wax sculptures. Especially of human organs and body parts. Oh yes, and she even teaches anatomy as an honorary professor at the University of Bologna. I imagine it was not least because of her that Pope Benedict overruled the papal bull of 1299, which stated that the dissection of human corpses for scientific purposes was desecration of corpses."

"I wonder if the two women know each other?" My question disturbed the men a little because they didn't know the answer.

"Oh, I'm afraid I don't know that. But I assume they at least know about each other."

"Now that you've been in Paris for a few weeks: Do you already know Madeleine Angélique Neufville de Villeroy[95]?"

"No, I've heard her name before, but I don't know anything about her."

"She is already an elderly lady and a well-known salonnière[96]. Her second marriage was to Marshal Charles François II de Montmorency-Luxembourg. Her salons are very popular. However, I've heard that she often doesn't want women at her events because she doesn't think they're very entertaining."

"If that's the case, I have no great desire to get to know her. Then let her be happy with the gentlemen."

One of the men laughed. "Well, she has quite a spiteful tongue sometimes. But she's beautiful and has a sharp mind and I've also heard that she's quite natural and honest, too."

We didn't meet De Villeroy, but we did get an invitation to Fanny de Beauharnais'[97] salon. She had already dedicated herself to poetry in her youth. Her work "Lettres de Stéphanie" had just been published. Of course, there were immediate enviers who did not believe she was capable of this and therefore attributed it to the male guests in her salon, as if a woman could not write a correct sentence. She is also an admirable woman. She knows how to assert herself and has many followers.

Once, at another invitation, I got talking to a writer who tirelessly stands up for us women. Her name is Madeleine d'Arsant de Puisieux.

"I know the book *Le Triomphe des dames*. I'm sure it was written by you and not, as everyone thinks, by your husband," I said after we had been introduced.

She smiled at me. "My husband is also a writer, but he has so much to do as a lawyer and ambassador in Switzerland that he doesn't get much time to write."

---

95 *In 1775, her salon was one of the 10 busiest in Europe.*
96 *Hostess e.g. of a literary salon: social gathering in private rooms.*
97 *Born Marie-Anne-Françoise Mouchard.*

Seraphia joined us. "I heard that Denis Diderot wrote about you. How exciting!"

Madame de Puisieux was in a good mood. "Yes, he did. We once had a close friendship. But we haven't seen each other for a long time."

"He's currently staying with the Tsarina in Russia, as we've been informed," I said.

"That's good to know. Then I don't have to worry that he might not be able to see me dressed up enough anywhere." She giggled.

"Speaking of the Tsarina ... Have you ever seen the marvellous busts by Marie-Anne Collot? Unfortunately, our artist travelled to St. Petersburg with her master years ago and hasn't been seen here in Paris since. What a pity about this talent!"

Seraphia was interested. "Who is that? Unfortunately, I've never heard of her. But I'll try to see something of her before we leave again."

"I actually know very little about her. She was a student of the sculptor Étienne-Maurice Falconet about ten years ago. She has already created some remarkable busts in his studio. They must have been in St Petersburg for over six years now because of a commission from Tsarina Catherine II. It's supposed to be a larger-than-life statue of Peter the Great," Puisieux knew.

My head was starting to buzz from the many new impressions and the numerous names that I carefully wrote down in my travel diary every day. Otherwise I would have forgotten them long ago.

I thought it was a great pity that Émilie du Châtelet had died before I was born, because I would have loved to have got to know her. She was still spoken of with the greatest respect. She must have been a very interesting lady.

Émilie was a philosopher, physicist, mathematician and translator and translated Newton's Philosophiae *Naturalis Principia Mathematica*. She went to the Café Gradot, the meeting place for scientists, in men's clothing and had several prominent lovers, including Voltaire. Voltaire said of her: *"I have not only lost my mistress, I have lost half of myself. She was a great man whose only fault was being a woman ..."*

For me, the most significant sentence from her says: *"If I were king, I would abolish an abuse that sets half of humanity back. I would let women share in all human rights, especially spiritual ones."*

Every single evening with all these highly interesting people was exciting. Another time we talked about fencing techniques. Heinrich was asked a question on the subject. But he referred it to me, as it wasn't exactly his favourite pastime.

"No, gentlemen, I can't tell you anything about that. In the art of fencing, I am completely overshadowed by our Victoria. She is by far the better of us." He smiled at me.

Everyone looked at me as if I had come from the moon or some other distant star. "I'm not the first woman to be able to hold a sword. Think of Philippe de la Tour du Pin de La Charce[98] alias Philis de La Charce, the heroine of the Dauphiné! Or perhaps Émilie du Châtelet, who, under the current king, challenged the commander of the Royal Guard, Colonel LeBrun, to a fencing contest.

So, which of you gentlemen would like to cross swords with me tomorrow? I would be very pleased to be able to train again."

After a brief consultation, a gentleman was found and we arranged a time and place for the following day. It was the younger son of a baron called Jaques. A pleasant man about my age.

At the agreed time in the garden of our accommodation, almost everyone who had been with the company the previous evening turned up. I was wearing trousers, of course. Jaques had organised blunt weapons.

"It might not be for the thrill-seekers, but I'm keen that we can both really give all without hurting each other too

---

98   French war heroine. She received the favour of Louis XIV and a lifelong honorary salary of 2000 livres.

much. I prefer to keep my skin intact and hope you feel the same."

"Thank you for your foresight. After all, I only want one training session. After all, we're not enemies and we both just want to have fun. Besides, an injury now would be fatal before the big performance with Anna Heinel."

We started off rather calmly and each of us measured our opponent's skills. At some point we both realised that we were about equally skilled and stepped up our attacks. Jaque's eyes flashed with pleasure and I also enjoyed the exercise immensely.

Two groups of spectators formed to cheer us on. I was delighted to see that Jaques was just as skilful as Frederik and sometimes even tried the same tricks, all of which I already knew.

Our companions were so loud that at one point the owner of our accommodation and a uniformed gendarme[99] from the Maréchausée[100] came running up. They were afraid it was a real fight and wanted to intervene. But Heinrich stopped them.

"Stop. Please leave them alone. They are just blunt weapons and they have no intention of hurting each other. Watch and enjoy the showdown. It's a feast for the eyes."

Neither of us managed to clearly defeat the other. So shortly after this incident, Jaques and I left it at a draw and shook hands, laughing.

"You're good, Madame!"

"Thank you, I was just about to pay you the same compliment, sir."

"Madame?" Our landlord looked at me in alarm. Only then did he recognise me. "Is that you? Mon Dieu! I've never seen a woman fight before. That was very impressive. It looked very elegant. Almost as elegant as your aunt's dance."

The man in uniform must have been equally impressed. Because he bowed to us and thanked us profusely for an exceptionally beautiful fencing style.

Jaques and I bowed to our wonderful audience and the whole group received a free drink from our landlord.

Every now and then I would go for a stroll on my own. On these occasions, I almost always met someone. Some are not worth mentioning here. But one encounter in particular has stuck in my memory. In a park where I was sitting on a bench, a woman came up to me. I invited her to sit with me. That's how we got talking.

"I've just stolen an hour. I like to come here on occasions like this. You know, I've been in Paris for about five years. Before that, I ran a pub with my husband – God rest his soul. But that's just not my vocation. I think a lot about morality and the power of men."

"In that case, we have a common theme. I also think a lot about it," I encouraged her.

"I like to observe the people around me and learn."

She looked at me a little more intensely. "Do you live in Paris?"

"No, I live in the south of Baiern, just on the border with the archdiocese of Salzburg. That's quite far from here. I'm travelling with my aunt, Seraphia von Neubauer. And I myself am still in the year of mourning for my husband."

"Ah, I've already seen your aunt dance. She has a fascinating charisma. I found it a special experience to see her." We introduced ourselves. Her name was Marie Gouze and to my surprise she asked me how I liked the name Olympe de Gouges[101].

---

101 Among other things, she wrote the Declaration of the Rights of Women and Citizens in 1791 and was executed in 1793 – partly because of this and her personal enmity with Robespierre.

"I don't want to use my real name for the writings I'm currently working on. So I need a nice-sounding pseudonym." She looked at me confidentially.

"You must know that my biological father was a marquis. But he didn't want to pay for his bastard's expenses or for my mother. That's a blatant injustice, don't you think?"

"That's probably true. I hope we'll be hearing and reading a lot more from you. In any case, I will read your publications as soon as they appear. I won't miss out on that."

We chatted for a while about trivialities. Madame Gouze told me that she would take every opportunity to improve her French as she had grown up speaking Occitan[102]. I had already wondered about her accent, from which I couldn't make out where she came from.

I said goodbye and later regretted not having spoken to her longer. I'm sure the world will be hearing from her more in future.

On stage

Anna's evening was getting closer and closer and now it was finally going to happen. I was very excited. Even in the morning, I was already completely excited. Even the king had announced his attendance, accompanied by his mistress, Madame du Barry, and all the ecclesiastical and secular dignitaries had immediately followed his example. Nobody wanted to be inferior to the king. This meant that a few days beforehand, all the seats were completely sold out.

Seraphia gave me a friendly hug. "Please go for a ride or a walk. If you don't work off some of your energy, you'll collapse on me by the evening, Vic."

---

102 *Romansh language in the south of France*

"I'm excited too, but that's part of it. Please don't drive yourself crazy. You can do everything perfectly and you know it."

She knew what she was talking about. So I followed her advice and actually went for a ride. It did me good and I was soon much calmer.

During my tour, I met my conversation partner from my first concert visit, the Marquise de Montesson. She was accompanied by a gentleman and was obviously pleased to see me again. She approached me straight away.

"So you're still in Paris. How nice! Are you also going to this special concert tonight, which even the king wants to attend? My husband and I have come back to Paris especially for this evening."

At the words "my husband", she looked up at the gentleman at her side. So this had to be the Duc d'Orléans. An imposing man. She introduced us to each other.

"My friends Nannerl and Wolfgang Mozart have already told me about you, monsieur. They are still talking about how you generously supported the family when they were on a concert tour," I said to the duke.

Turning to his wife, I said: "Of course I'll be there tonight. My travelling companions and I will even be part of the performance."

She clapped her hands. "Oh, I'll be so pleased to see you on stage! Look, my dear, now we know another lady who is taking part. I can't wait to see what's in store for us. As I was already fidgety with excitement, my husband suggested we go outside for a bit. How glad I am that we have met you. I wish you all every success with the performance."

We parted again and I headed back to our accommodation. When evening came and we were getting ready for our performances in the dressing rooms, I could only marvel at Seraphia. She seemed to be such a calm person.

"You're so calm, as if nothing could touch you, Aunt Seraphia."

"Oh, if you only knew. I have the worst excitement you can imagine. Most artists have jitters beforehand. As soon as they're on stage, their stage fright is gone. It's the other way round for me. I'm calm beforehand, but as soon as I step onto the stage with one foot, I'm shaking like a leaf. Believe me, it's not funny. But as I'm an artist, I guess I have to live with it. As soon as I get off to a good start, it goes away quite quickly. Fortunately, I usually have a good start."

After this explanation, I was glad that I was only suffering from the general jitters before the performance.

Everything went well and it was a truly wonderful evening with incredibly beautiful music, soulful singing that brought tears to the eyes of all of us backstage and uplifting dancing whose beauty almost made us float – as far as we had the opportunity to watch.

No matter what was performed, the music filled the room and our hearts almost to bursting point. Whether solemn or cheerful, the sounds touched our innermost being and transported us into dream worlds from which we no longer wanted to emerge at the end.

For me, it felt as if we were all one. One with humanity, with nature, the divine, the universe.

I see us as blessed because we were able to experience something like this once. It was as if that everything went by itself. All the participants said afterwards that they had felt no effort at all and that everything felt like it just was floating. I also had that feeling very strongly.

My favourite of the evening was the lament *Lascia ch'io pianga* from the opera *Rinaldo* by George Frideric Handel. Madeleine sang it like an angel. Anna and Gaetano danced a perfect *Sarabande à deux* to it.

After the last piece, the auditorium was silent. The curtain fell and there was still silence. At that moment, I realised that it had been as quiet as a mouse in the opera house since the first few performances.

Only after what felt like two minutes did applause begin in the royal box. Others joined in. Cautiously at first, then more. The applause continued to grow and would not stop. The curtain was raised again and we all bowed to the king.

When we stood up again, we saw that everyone was standing. Even the king was standing and clapping as if possessed. The bravos got louder and louder and I felt completely happy.

That night, all the artists stayed at the opera. First there was a reception in honour of the king, where all the performers were introduced to the supreme regent at his request. Anna was beaming because her idea had been such a resounding success. Vestris looked at her in love and we were sure that these two would one day be a married couple.

Long after daybreak, when we finally got to our accommodation, I wrote a letter to Christoph and told him in detail what had happened. I also wrote to Frederik and Magdalena and conveyed my enthusiasm for our stay in Paris, which was now coming to an end.

On our last Sunday, we learnt about a special performance in a lesser-known church in Paris that we attended. It was the motet *Spem in alium*[103] by the Englishman Thomas Tallis from the last century. It is written for eight choirs of five voices and is a very special treat to listen to. My mind floated in other spheres while listening to the singing. The acoustics of the church interior helped the sound to come into its own.

I can't describe what was going on inside me. In any case, I felt grateful for all the wonderful things I had already experienced. I felt blessed that I have such a privileged life and hardly know any insurmountable problems. Even the grief for Jacob became much easier to bear with the music.

---

103 *Hope for another. For all those interested, here is a tip on Alessandro Striggio: Missa sopra Ecco sì beato giorno.*

Go on, go on ...

Now we travelled on to Wien. Our route took us via Stuttgart and München – with a short stop at my palace, which we used to wash ourselves and our clothes. We travelled for a month to cover this long distance.

This time, once again, not everything went smoothly. At one point we were stuck for two days because a carriage wheel broke.

On another day, we arrived at our accommodation covered in mud from top to bottom. One of the horses lost a shoe and had to have a new one forged. Then a lead riped on the carriage, which had to be replaced as quickly as possible. Heinrich fell off his horse and sprained an ankle. Incidentally, after a few days his back turned all sorts of colours.

It wasn't funny and I admired Seraphia more and more because she had to travel a lot year in, year out for her engagements. I also began to understand my mother, who was now quite happy about her arrangement with my father and no longer has to travel so much.

Of course, we also attended mass every now and then on our trip. I don't think I'm sinning if I don't attend mass every now and then, but I love church buildings. For me, they are places of silence, contemplation and somehow also of togetherness.

In folk singing, everyone present has the same right. And neither money nor influence can buy a beautiful voice.

It was a Sunday in September and apparently a pilgrimage was being held at the place where we were resting. The final mass was accompanied by an Italian ensemble and I was completely enchanted by this impressive music. Seraphia and Heinrich were also in raptures.

The music brought tears to our eyes. The singer was an alto with a powerful voice and the musicians obviously had an unerring feeling for the music and the acoustics of the building.

Fortunately, we had the opportunity to talk to the musicians after the mass in the nearby pub, who were happy to give us information.

"Today you have heard *Nisi Dominus* by Antonio Vivaldi[104]. Vivaldi was a great composer in our home country of Italy before he was increasingly forgotten about 30 years ago. His music no longer corresponds to current tastes, but we find some of his pieces absolutely worth listening to. Like this mass."

Yes, I had already heard of Vivaldi. Mamma liked to play one of his pieces often.

"It was heart-wrenching how your singer interpreted the music. The accompaniment had just the right intensity. Thank you for this marvellous hour!" I was still hovering a little above the ground.

We had the time and opportunity to copy the sheet music. Heinrich always had prepared music paper with him, as there were many pieces of music that were either not available in printed form or not easy to obtain. So we joined forces and were delighted to have another treasure in our luggage.

Autumn in Wien

We also arrived safely in Wien, where Seraphia had further engagements. A sister of Heinrich's lived there, who was well married and offered us accommodation with a family connection for a moderate fee. By now it was already mid-October. However, the weather was in our

---

104 Vivaldi's music was increasingly forgotten during his lifetime. It only became popular again in the 20th century.

favour. It was still warm in early autumn and the forests were a riot of colour.

Seraphia and I also had a few gigs together in this city, where we danced and played the violin or the pochette at the same time. It went down well with the audience and we were able to further improve our funds. Seraphia also had several engagements in the theatre and at several royal houses, for which she was richly remunerated.

Heinrich's sister and her circle of friends booked several dance lessons with us to practise the very latest dances that we had brought back from our trip.

We also received a few invitations. Among other things, we were invited by Marianna von Martines[105] to a musical soirée, where we were also asked to contribute something. Nannette, as she was called, had only been accepted into the *Accademia Filarmonica di Bologna* this year, which is a very high honour for composers.

She played the harpsichord like a goddess and also had a marvellous singing voice. I really wanted to know who her harpsichord teacher was and asked her about it.

"Joseph Haydn lived in our house and gave me lessons from an early age. I learnt a lot from him. He was a very pleasant person. He is currently working as a bandmaster for the Counts of Esterházy. We only see each other rarely, although he is sometimes in Wien. He is a very good composer and musician."

"Yes, I've already heard a few pieces by him. Really an outstanding composer. But you obviously are, too, dear Nannette. Otherwise you certainly wouldn't have been accepted into the academy."

She blushed slightly. "Oh, there are so many really good musicians and composers. Soon every small town will have one. I don't think I've done anything that others couldn't do."

---

105 *Her piano sonatas in E major and A major were published in 1760 in an anthology by the music publisher Johann Ulrich Hafner (1711-1767).*

"That's what we women do wrong." I said to her. "We always think others are just as good as we are. Men, on the other hand, think they are the centre of the world and that each of them is a genius. Men always advertise their art – no matter how meaningless or even disappointing it is." It always outrages me how small we women make ourselves.

"There's some truth in that," said Nannette.

"We also always see composers and musicians as male. Although there are at least as many good female composers and musicians. Even though the number of those who get the chance to learn is still very small and even smaller for those who actually become known."

"Yes, I agree with you there, too."

"Well, I could certainly devise a dance choreography to your compositions and play along with my pochette, but I've never tried composing. I don't think I need to either."

We both laughed.

"You're also acquainted with the Mozarts, aren't you? I got to know the family and I have to say I like playing four-handed with Wolfgang. He's a great musician and has so much imagination."

"Yes, he really is a treasure. But his sister Nannerl is in no way inferior to him on the pianoforte. In my opinion, they have a similar wit – only Nannerl's is a little more refined."

Nannette was called to a small group of guests and I strolled through the lavishly decorated room on my own. The walls were hung with very lifelike landscape paintings.

There was a young girl there that evening who fascinated me. Maria Theresia von Paradis[106] was blind, but played the pianoforte excellently. If she kept practising like that, I thought, she would soon be a famous pianist. It was simply marvellous how she played the keys so confidently without sight.

---

106 Paradis was very popular as a pianist in Vienna from 1775 and gave numerous concerts.

Of course, there were also men on site who showed what they could do. But that was a matter of course for all of us. I suddenly felt small and insignificant amongst so many wonderful artists. And then I was caught again in the trap of women that I had mentioned earlier. I'm not world-famous and maybe I never will be. But I'm good at what I do and don't need to hide behind others. Nevertheless, I always hide my own light under a bushel, even when no one else is doing it for me – which is unfortunately now and then the case.

At some point, Seraphia asked the group who could accompany one of our flute showpieces. Several people actually volunteered to play the Bach. So we had a small but fine orchestra to accompany us to the *Brandenburg Concerto*. Seraphia and I played our flutes with enthusiasm and got the audience involved.

Our hostess came up to me afterwards. "You may not be composers, but you are both very good and sensitive musicians. Your interplay is so captivating that I felt as if I had been transported to another realm. Your dance steps here and there – simply enchanting! I've never seen a performance like this before."

Shortly afterwards, the Duke of Innpruck approached Seraphia. "Dearest Madame von Neubauer, if I had known that you could also play the flute so wonderfully, I would have booked you in this discipline for the performance on Friday evening right from the start! May I ask you both to play this piece on this special day, which is dedicated to my wife's birthday, in return for another generous payment?"

We both bowed to the Duke, who openly showed us his enthusiasm. Seraphia said there was another piece we wanted to play especially for the Duchess. "... Mr Winkelmayr will accompany us on the harpsichord. It's quite a short piece, but it's bursting with joie de vivre and is sure to please the ladies and gentlemen."

"Anything you want. Decide for yourself what you want to contribute to my wife's day of honour. I will reward you handsomely in any case. Oh, it will be a marvellous celebration."

The duke clapped his hands enthusiastically and walked away again with a self-satisfied expression, leaving us both with renewed energy.

So it was agreed that we would also play the Uccellini and dance our parade minuet. That meant practising again. But I was really looking forward to it. And it also meant that our travelling budget was still in good shape.

On this trip, I had traded my skills for a good wage for the first time in my life and I was extremely pleased with myself. I had my own money! That felt so special. Now I could finally understand how Christoph must have felt when he was paid for the first case he had taken on.

In fact, I now knew how satisfying it could be to be well paid for a service. No wonder so many men are bursting with self-satisfaction.

We had already practised another piece in Paris, which was now ready for performance. With Heinrich on the harpsichord, me on the violin and Seraphia with her transverse flute. It was the first movement *Allegro assai* from the *flute concerto in D major* by Frederick the Great.

The next day, we were invited to a countess's house in the afternoon. She was an extremely arrogant woman whose name I couldn't remember. But what she had to say was very interesting, even if she was just trying to make herself important.

"You know, my husband and I were among the first to see the elephant when it was brought to the menagerie[107] at Schönbrunn Palace[108] in 1770."

Seraphia has always been very interested in animals. She wanted to know whether it was an Indian or an African

---

107 *Today's Schönbrunn Zoo is the oldest continuously operating zoo in the world. It was reserved for the imperial family and their visitors until 1778, when it was opened to the public, at least on Sundays.*

108 *Schönbrunn Palace and its park were remodelled and extended in their present form from 1743. The park has been open to the public since 1779.*

elephant. "We've already heard about this elephant. But no one has been able to tell me which country it comes from."

"As far as I know, it was accompanied by at least one Indian man. It is an impressively large creature with incredibly thick legs and a trunk with which it can carry things and which it uses to bring food to its large mouth.

The animal is about the size of two riding ponies on top of each other, I would say. But it weighs at least eight times as much. I wouldn't dare get too close for fear of being trampled. Cumbersome is the word that comes to mind. Simply cumbersome. I always thought an elephant had bigger ears. But these don't look anything like the pictures I've seen before."

"Maybe the pictures were of an elephant from Africa. They have very large ears, as a gentleman who was on an African expedition explained to me. Asian elephants, on the other hand, have smaller ears. They both look huge to us."

"Be that as it may. It was certainly an impressive experience to see this huge animal. In comparison, all the exotic birds, monkeys and other animals in the menagerie are just tiny."

Otherwise, the countess had little to say that was worth remembering. I would have liked to have seen the elephant, though. But there was no more time. I had to be content with knowing that it was an Indian elephant.

The birthday of the Duchess of Innpruck was celebrated with a lavish party in the Upper Belvedere Palace[109] and in the garden with the beautiful fountains facing the Lower Belvedere. I think she was 40 years old.

Fortunately, the weather was still reasonably warm. In the evening, it was getting quite chilly, but it could still be seen as the last gasp of late summer. Numerous high-ranking ladies and gentlemen from the nobility were present.

---

109 From 1754, Belvedere belonged to the court archives (tangible and intangible assets of a state), but the Habsburgs continued to decide on its use.

There were also many dignitaries from the church and the military.

In the afternoon, when the weather was still sunny and warm, the guests strolled around the garden and admired the flowers that were still blooming profusely and the trees and shrubs that were already colourful.

Some also enjoyed the view over Wien from the side facing the city. St Stephen's Cathedral could be seen in the centre. St Charles' Church and the Salesian Church were also prominent in the picture to the left and right.

Many musical performances then took place during the banquet. We were not the only ones to shine, but also other world-class musicians and dancers that the Duke had brought together for the celebrations.

The day was a great success for Seraphia and also for our small group. It was overwhelming how enthusiastically the audience received everything that was presented to them. Contrary to the widespread bad habit of audiences chatting and laughing during a performance – even in the theatre – at the Duchess's birthday, out of respect for the art-loving hostess, everyone actually listened to all the musicians. I found this very appreciative and pleasant.

It was already dark outside when all the guests, musicians and dancers were asked to come outside. Everyone, including the servants, was to witness what was going on there. There was to be a performance on the area under a kind of terrace in front of and between the gardens with the fountain.

A whole orchestra formed behind us on the balcony. Seraphia suddenly beamed. "When I look at the cast, I can just imagine what's coming. Imagine, that I can still experience this!" She beamed as if her heart's desire had been fulfilled.

It was indeed a very unusual orchestration that built up before our eyes: over twenty oboes, nine horns, nine trumpets, thirteen bassoons, kettledrums and strings.

I couldn't do anything with it. "So, what's next? Because I don't know."

Seraphia smiled cheerfully at me. "If I'm not mistaken, we're going to hear the *Firework music* by George Frideric Handel."

A short time later, the trumpets and timpani began, accompanied by the strings. But it wasn't just the music that started. While Seraphia was still standing enthusiastically facing the musicians, I plucked her by the sleeve. "Look!" I shouted enthusiastically.

The first rocket had risen into the sky. It was followed by numerous others in the most beautiful colours. For the next few minutes, the sky was lit up by fireworks that were almost perfectly composed to the music. The usual exclamations of "Ah" and "Oh" came from the audience, who cheered extensively. At the end of the *Overture*, there was a brilliant finale to the fireworks. But that was not the end of the show.

Where the most important guests were gathered, the area around the fountains was lit up with torches and lanterns. Two riders suddenly appeared between the fountains on their gleaming white Lipizzaner stallions[110]. They performed a dance on horseback to the music. It looked incredibly elegant. They rode a *Pas de deux* par excellance[111] until the musical parts *Bourrée* and *La paix* were over.

La Réjouissance was joined by another six riders, who were spread out between the planted garden areas. From them we saw exercises from the high school of equestrianism. They showed *levades, piaffes, pesades* and *capers* and everything that the war horse of a warring ruler had to be able to do, or at least had to be able to do in the past, in order to guarantee the ruler the longest possible survival.

I was completely overwhelmed by this performance and was very happy that I was able to witness it. Seraphia and

---

110 *The Vienna Riding School has existed since the 16th century. The Lipizzaners were added later*

111 *Pas de deux comes from ballet and is a duet. In equestrian sport, a pas de deux is ridden as a mirror image. This one is performed to perfection.*

I held hands and were just so happy to be in this place right now. It was a real pleasure to see and hear all of this.

As the Duchess was an enthusiastic horsewoman and had mastered the high art of riding, her riding master and his friends from the imperial and royal riding school had joined forces in her honour to give her a treat. Yes, it was a pleasure – not only for the jubilarian, who burst into storms of enthusiasm.

We returned to our accommodation exhilarated and satisfied with ourselves and the world.

Before we left Wien again, we went to the theatre – the theatre next to the castle[112] on Michaelerplatz. Wolfgang's *Ascanio in Alba* was performed there. He had composed it as a commission for the wedding of Archduke Ferdinand of Austria to Princess Maria Beatrice of Este – based on a libretto by Abbate Guiseppe Parini.

I was very impressed how our friend Wolfgang, who was only 15 at the time, had created this two-and-a-half-hour work in just a few weeks.

So we had a pleasant end to our stay in Wien that couldn't have been better.

Back home again

We were lucky that we started our return journey in mid-November. At first, the weather was still really autumnal. But from Linz onwards, we could already feel an unpleasant snow wind blowing over us. The snow finally reached us when we were just outside Salzburg and forced us to spend another night with our relatives before we travelled the last three miles home in the driving snow.

---

112 *Today's Burgtheater has only existed on Vienna's Ringstrasse since 1888.*

There was a big hello when we returned home. We were first given time to unpack our belongings and sort out our souvenirs, as we had staff to take care of the rest. We also had a hot bath, which I really enjoyed.

In the evening, we all sat round a table for dinner. Seraphia, Heinrich and I were asked to recount everything that had happened. We reviewed our entire trip and were delighted with the eager listeners who hung on our every word.

After that evening, I went to bed with a feeling of satisfaction and gratitude. I had had a wonderful and exciting time and was now safely back home. What more could I wish for?

During the quiet time that followed, father told me a few things that had happened during the last year that had passed me by. For example, that the rock called Nocken in the Salzach near Laufen had been blown up.

"For the life of me, I can't remember exactly when that happened. But definitely this year."

"Yes, that's a very good thing. Skippers have died often enough due to a collision with the Nocken north of the headland in the Salzach loop. But how do they do it now with the water level measurements? Didn't they also have something to do with the Nocken?"

"That's right, the Nocken was actually the most important measuring point for the water level. But I'm sure an adequate solution was found. By blowing up the obstacle, which was a danger to all salt ships at both high and low tide, the skippers have been greatly helped.

Did you know that the name of the town of Laufen comes from the Old High German word loufa, meaning cataract? A clever man told me that on my last visit to the town."

We were briefly interrupted because our maid, Nina, brought us a carafe of wine.

"Oh, something else very important has happened. Firstly, Pope Clement XIV has banned the Jesuit order. The order's money was used for the reforms of our elector and the school system, as one hears. Then the public holidays in Baiern were also reduced. And they were reduced to twenty-two."

"But public holidays were already cut last year. Before, there were 124 days. The feasts of the Apostles were abolished and a few more. After that, there were still around 100 days. And now there are only 22? That's a very big cut in all our lives!"

"Well, who knows how well or poorly compliance will be monitored. We'll see."

Father and I always had interesting conversations. But of course he also had to work a lot. He had a lot of correspondence to do. Sometimes I helped him with his letters to various dealers around the world.

I also read the three volumes of Gottfried Taubert's[113] *Rechtschaffener Tantzmeister, oder, gründliche Erklärung der frantzösischen Tantz-Kunst,* published in Leipzig in 1717.

This reading is only possible bit by bit. It's always said that men don't say much. But I think they mainly spread this rumour themselves. Lordy, this dancing master might have a lot to say. I think he likes to express his opinion in a lot of well-chosen words. But it's also amusing – perhaps also because he digresses so much.

In his foreword, Taubert rails against so-called "dance cobbler" and "bunglers", which is in itself a pleasurable reason to read the work.

My father couldn't understand why I was reading the book. His mantra on the subject was: "As a member of the better society, you won't be a dancing master. Especially not as a woman. As your father, I could never give in to such a request. So why do you read books like this?"

"Father, my life is dance! I have already earned money with it on our journey. I have both taught and danced on stage. I love having my own money. It gives me so much joy. And I have no plans to get married again. But I don't want to be on anyone's pocket either."

---

113 *The first volume can be found in Google Book.*

"You receive an annual allowance from your late husband's family. You have a townhouse in München. You don't have to work like someone of lower class."

"I would also like to work as a lawyer. But people don't trust me to do that because I'm a woman. Besides, I enjoy dancing even more. There are so many ossified and old-fashioned dance masters. Why shouldn't I, as a woman, pursue this honourable profession? I wouldn't be the first or the only one in this profession."

"No, no and no again. My daughter doesn't work for money."

"Well, if you don't give me your blessing, then I'll go back to München next spring and try it there. Because Father, with all due respect, I am no longer a young and unmarried girl. I am a widow and as such I have the right to make my own decisions about my life. If that is not possible here in the bosom of my family, then I will withdraw from the family and live my own life in München."

"We haven't had the last word on that, Vic!" Father left the room, snorting with rage.

As if I wanted to be a blacksmith. What is contemptible about dancing? It is a respectable occupation that is also practised and honoured by the very highest people in our society. What's more, I've already heard of a few female dance masters abroad. That certainly gives me courage. I thought.

When I got to Taubert's third book, I found the following lines, which were described by some dance masters as prerequisites for being a dance master. Taubert, on the other hand, holds[114]:

'There are some masters who, ex Luciano, insist with all their might that a true master of dance must necessarily have studied, and especially in history, geography, mathematics, anatomy, poetry, and logic, even in the art of painting and the French language, as well as in riding and fencing; because these disciplines are all essential to the subtlety of the delicate art of dancing. For

---

114 *Text from a 1976 reprint by Heimeran Verlag München (translated)*

it would be far from enough for a master, by virtue of his good nature and industrious elaboration, to dance in a manner and with a noble air; but he would also have to be a good philosopher in particular, and of a clever mind, so that he could not only be a good logician and historian in the composition and composition of many an artistic ballet, so that he could take everything from a high level of invention, so that he could make a correct copy and outline of the whole work as a skilful painter, as a well-practised mathematician would accurately measure and form all his steps and figures according to the mathematical principles in their proportional lines, triangles, squares, whole and half circles, as a well-read historian would know how to dress every dancing nation according to its customs and habits; but he would also, as a well-read anatomist, have to understand exactly how these or those limbs have their articulation and joints in each main move-ment, and what muscles are actually flexing in them, as bent steps, when the legs, knees and feet are flexed, extended, adduc-ted and abducted, as well as when the arm splints and elbows are moved and guided upwards, forwards and backwards in the Porte les Bras. [...]

Alone! It seems to me that this has gone a little too far out of the right way, and is called a mistake. For although I do not deny that these things all have their use in dancing, I must also say that they are by no means requisite essentials, but only adjuncts, ornaments and accessories of the existing dancing profession. They are not mainly required for this, but most of them are only trifles, by which a master can qualify himself before others who, apart from this profession, have hardly learnt to read and write, and can more consistently insinuate himself among the intelli-gentsia than perfect his dancing art.'

When I thought about it, Christoph and I were able to live well despite these requirements. I wasn't very good at drawing, but I could still put dance steps on paper. I had at least some idea of the other requirements mentioned.

By the time we looked around a bit, it was actually December again. My year of mourning was now over and I was officially allowed to dance again without being ostracised from society. However, we first had to get the dance-less Christmas period behind us.

When it was around the anniversary of the accident, I naturally thought a lot about Jacob. I wrote a long letter to Frederik and invited him to spend Christmas with us. But then the snow became more and more. At some point, a letter came back from him saying that, in view of the weather, he would be celebrating the holidays with Magdalena and her family.

We decorated the house with lots of greenery for Christmas. Branches of fir, holly and mistletoe hung everywhere in the house. One of our serving girls had a knack for these evergreen arrangements and loved doing them. She was released from her usual duties for a few days to take care of the decorations. She was allowed to make decorations for her family and friends or for sale from the leftover material in the time she was given. She thanked us for this permission with some truly marvellous works.

To celebrate the Christmas mass, we went to the Pankraz church, which is enthroned high on the Pankraz rock near Karlstein and can be seen from afar. It was a challenge to climb to the top, although many hard-working hands had already cleared the path. At times like this, I wish I was a man. They don't have so much fabric around their legs to hinder them and can stride out bravely. I was only wearing a simple, warm dress under my coat, like the peasant women wear, but it's still a hindrance when you have to walk up a snowy mountain.

This was not the only reason why I was very grateful that men from our servants carried our instruments up the mountain. I arrived a little more relaxed because I didn't have to carry anything except my own weight. Nevertheless, I worked up a sweat. It was pretty chilly in the church. But I was prepared for it and had an extra scarf with me.

The local farmers and cottagers all gathered in front of the little church shortly before midnight and the atmosphere was wonderfully festive and full of expectation.

Mamma, Christoph and I accompanied the organist with our violins. Christmas was always something magical for me. And I was as happy as a little child every time I was able to contribute to this feeling for others. We immersed ourselves in our music and the worshippers with us.

The priest gave a really good sermon that went straight to the heart and the candles gave the church a warm glow. After the mass, I only saw beaming faces around me.

Afterwards, we all stood outside in the snow and looked up at the night sky. In a few days the moon would be full and even now it was already quite bright. It seemed like nobody wanted to go home. The mood of those present was simply dreamlike – as if everyone had taken a little look at the sky and wanted to capture this image.

"The law of women
is mostly retained bad in the hands of men."

Anita Augspurg,
female lawyer (1857–1943)

1774

The turn of the year was quite quiet in our family. We attended mass in the church in Nonn because it had snowed heavily again and the walk to St Pankraz seemed too strenuous.

I read a lot and wrote letters. I also went for a few leisurely rides in the neighbourhood with Christoph. As much as I could with all the snow. But after all, the horses needed to be trained.

Just a few days after the Schlittade in Salzburg, I received a letter from Frederik.

Dearest friend Vic,

I hope this letter will find its way to you quickly. Everything is still covered in deep snow here. The world looks simply marvellous with this white covering. The city is much quieter and everything that was ugly before shines in pure white! Well, at least, where there are no large chimneys spreading soot. After a while, their surroundings look rather bleak.

Although I love spring more than anything, I can also recognise the beauty of winter. I even enjoy riding out in warm woollen clothing. The horses enjoy the snow and are lively and sprightly.

I miss you, Vic. I don't have a fencing partner who is my equal at the moment and I'm eagerly awaiting our next meeting. Not just because of the fencing. The intellectual exchange with you is also always a special pleasure for me. Letters can't make up for personal conversations.

You have taught me to appreciate our German literature. There are remarkable minds among our poets and thinkers. For example, have you read the poem "Der Bauer an seinen durchlauchtigen Tyrannen" by Gottfried August Bürger, which was published last year? I enclose it.

Of course, I had to think of Jacob and the fact that there are very different people among the nobility: the kind and compassionate, righteous ones who think about and weigh up the consequences of their actions and those who exploit others without consideration for their own personal gain. Jacob belonged to the first category, his brother Leonhard is of the second.

I feel sorry for the people who live and work on his country estates. Leonhard is a nasty slave driver and his mother is no better. Why did Jacob have to die so young? I would have wished his people many more years of peace and prosperity.

But now to other, more refreshing things. Just imagine, by chance I came into possession of two volumes of sheet music with trio sonatas by a certain Mrs Philarmonica[115], which I like very much. I will copy them and send them to you soon. I'm sure your family will like them. A client of mine could not raise the whole sum for his lawsuit, but he offered me these notes from his father, who had been violinist to the Elector, for the balance. As I value this client for his integrity, he is completely unmusical and the sheet music actually has value to me, I agreed to this kind of payment.

I've been to various dance events with Magdalena and her family. She's been one of my favourite dancers since you left. She has such an ease and it's a joy to dance with her because she hardly puts a foot wrong. She's also an intelligent woman with her own opinion, which – as you know – I really appreciate.

The next time you are in München to visit us, I would like to organise another dance for my servants. I think they deserve to have a ball like this for themselves at least once a year. Will you be there again? I need you above all for the preparation, the dance lessons, so that everyone can enjoy taking part. You are such a wonderful teacher. Even proven clumsy people learn to dance with you.

Now I have to finish my letter because I have to get dressed for another ball.

I wish you and your family a wonderful time!
In deep solidarity,
Your friend Frederik

---

115 Until today unknown composer of the late baroque.

I was happy about the lively exchange with my friend. He seemed to be doing well. After visiting his family last summer, I have the feeling that he is much more relaxed. His father and he are talking to each other again and he has also gained a good relationship with his brother. His brother has now also called in Frederik as legal adviser for his concerns.

Frederik spent Christmas with Magdalena's family. My two dear friends sent me a joint letter after the holidays. That made me very happy. Especially because Magdalena obviously had an admirer. A Franz von Cottenau. I'm curious to see whether Magdalena will marry him.

Whenever possible, our family got together with our friends to dance. We rehearsed in small companies and often went to local balls together. As there were only experienced dancers in our family, we were often invited. However, it could sometimes be a burden to be one of the sought-after dancers. Especially if the partners still wanted or needed to learn a lot.

The Mozarts also organised another small and exquisite masked ball in the Tanzmeistersaal at their home, which provided us with a wonderful and funny evening.

Development in America

The day at the beginning of February started slowly and sluggishly in my opinion. The light was already past 9 a.m. and I had been awake for some time, but I couldn't bring myself to get up because my room wasn't heated. The sun slowly tickled my nose through my bedroom window and I stretched out comfortably in my cosy, warm duvet. I thought about what I was going to do that day.

Christoph had travelled to a friend in Laufen for a few days. The two of them wanted to go to an evening party, which I didn't fancy. So I was going to be on my own today. But first I wanted to have breakfast.

Then I gave myself a jolt and got up. I quickly toddled into the dressing room, which was reasonably heated by the tiled stove on the ground floor, and got ready. The first thing I did afterwards was to go to the breakfast room. The tiled stove there had already spread a cosy warmth and I found my father sitting at the table reading his correspondence. Contrary to his usual behaviour, he didn't look up when I entered the room.

"Good morning father."

No reaction from his side. I approached him. "What's got you so captivated?"

Pappa startled briefly and looked at me as if he had just emerged from another world.

"I'm startled now! Good morning, Vic. I've received mail from Mr Krümmelbein. He has news from the New World. We've often heard that the colonies there are opposing England as the mother country and insisting on independence. And now, apparently, some people have openly rebelled.

On 16 December last year, several men dressed like Indians stormed three ships in Boston Harbour and threw the cargo overboard. They were East India Company ships carrying tea, they didn't even belong to the crown itself. Three ships – imagine the amount of tea ... and the value of the goods! Almost a quarter of it is said to have been green tea."

Of course, father saw the economic catastrophe first and foremost as the businessman that he was.

"The English and Americans always with their masquerades. For what purpose did the men do that? If it was all private property, they could hardly have hit the crown, could they?"

"Hm, I think that has more to do with the fact that the East India Company was given a monopoly on tea imports to the colonies last year. But also because the taxes are supposed to go to England."

This was, of course, important information. "I can imagine that the colonies' desire to gain their independence will be taken seriously by King George III and Parliament after such an action." I said. "It often takes a blatant approach to be taken seriously."

"Yes, that's probably true." Pappa agreed. "But simply destroying so much good Chinese tea! I think, we will certainly find out what consequences the British draw from this."

I put my arms on his shoulders from behind. "As long as your goods aren't affected, the Americans are welcome to rebel against their mother country."

He shook his head and put his hands on my arms.

"Our ships are travelling on other routes. But it's always a nail-biter until everyone is back in the harbour and the cargo is unloaded."

Yes, I understood that. I gave him another hug and then sat down to eat my breakfast and drink some tea. I especially love green tea! I also read a book from 1752 that I always had lying around to fill in the gaps: *Das neue gelehrte Europa*. The weekly journal, from which I usually read every word, was still on my father's desk. I didn't want to snatch it from him, even though he was still busy with the correspondence.

Tea dansant

During the winter, Aunt Seraphia usually spent her time in her little house on our estate or with friends in the neighbourhood. This meant we could often meet up to dance. Not only at the balls in Salzburg and Reichenhall, but also in her parlour or in our dance hall to learn new and old dances or think up new choreographies.

Before such an informal afternoon of dancing at Seraphia's, she read to Christoph and me a letter that she had received just a few hours earlier:

Dearest friend Seraphia,
Ah, I think so often and fondly of your visit last year. Our evening together at the opera is still a topic at all kinds of events. We made a statement and enchanted people.

The news, which is actually no longer news, is that Gaetano and I are a couple. We have found love in each other and are happy. Whether we will ever get married is written in the stars. But at the moment, all that matters is that we are together.

In my last letter to you I mentioned that I would be travelling to London for a short time to perform at a private party for Queen Charlotte.

It was a real adventure. Imagine, instead of staying in one of the usual simple hostels or guesthouses, I was put up in a newly opened "Grand Hotel"[116] in Covent Garden. I am more than delighted with this accommodation.

It is a stately home and I felt like I was staying with aristocratic friends. Each guest has a suite and everything is well heated. The luxury is remarkable. The beds have down duvets and the furniture is like that of any aristocratic friends.

On the ground floor there are the usual rooms for the general public, but much more elegant than I have ever experienced in any other holiday accommodation. Everything is cosy and luxuriously furnished. The only thing missing was the family atmosphere, although this was compensated for by the fact that all the guests were in a particularly good mood and dined together.

The staff are trained and very discreet. They literally read every wish from the guests' eyes. I hope this Grand Hotel idea catches on and there will soon be hotels like this in all major cities.

---

116 *The first grand hotel in the world was probably the Grand Hotel in Covent Garden, which was opened on 25 January 1774 by David Low, a barber. Hôtel was the French word for the townhouses of the aristocracy, or hostel in old French for a place of accommodation.*

The festival itself was opulent in terms of the decor. There were numerous great artists on site who gave excellent performances. It was a good opportunity for me to observe and learn.

I wish you could have been there to experience this.

A special piece from Paris was dedicated to Mademoiselle Françoise Prévost[117], who, as you know, was the prima ballerina of the Paris Opera for around 30 years and whose fame still outshines many today. Naturally, this dance piece was danced with the shoes that were customary in her day. This was very strenuous, as we are no longer used to it.

You have no idea how grateful I am to the late Marie de Camargo[118] that she introduced the heelless dance shoe and that we ballet dancers no longer have to struggle with the usual heels.

Now I'm on my way back – don't ask about the state of the roads, it's terrible! – to Paris, where my presence is contractually requested again from March.

I expect to be in Bayreuth next spring to visit my family. Where are your future engagements? It would be nice if fate would lead us to the same place again to make a meeting possible.

I admire your art and would love to learn more from you. I am so glad that you encouraged me in my decision to become a dancer. Because my profession makes me truly happy.

Please give my warmest regards to Victoria and Heinrich.

Your very dear friend

Anna Friederike Heinel

Christoph jumped up. "A letter from *La Reine de la danse*? Oh, how exquisite!" Then he looked at me with shining eyes.

"Do you know that she's two years younger than us? Born in Bayreuth and now the *queen of dance* in Paris." He did a rather unsuccessful pirouette.

---

117 Françoise Prévost (ca. 1680–1741), French prima ballerina at the Paris Opera and teacher at the Académie royale de danse.

118 Marie Anne Cupis de Camargo, known as Marie Camargo (1710-1770). Among other things, the French dancer introduced the heelless dance shoe and the technique of the entrechat quatre (leap) to ballet.

"Of course I know that. I've already danced with her. And I've told you that she's a beautiful woman and a real dancing angel."

Then my brother looked at Seraphia again. "She should dance the *pirouette à la seconde* perfectly. Have you seen it, too?"

Our aunt smiled at her nephew. "I've never seen you gush like that before. Yes, of course we saw her last year when we were in Paris – with her pirouette too. She's a fantastic dancer and doesn't have this title of honour for nothing."

In the meantime, I was amused because Christoph was so enthusiastic about a woman he had never met before. I'd never seen anything like it in him. But then I became impatient.

"And she is happy with her Gaetano, who is twice her age."

"Do you always have to bring me back to reality so hard, sister?"

I gave my brother a quick hug and placed a peck on his cheek.

"Come on, let's dance. Old Playford[119] is waiting for us. It doesn't matter how old he is. The dances are still unique – where is Heinrich?"

At that moment, the door opened and Heinrich entered as if on cue. Behind him followed Appolonia, our major-domo Johannes and the siblings Susanne Schiffelholz and Severin Schadwell, our neighbours. The widowed Severin had taken in his sister and her husband a few months ago, as the house was far too big for one person and Susanne's husband, a senior civil servant, had been transferred here. Her husband wasn't much of a dancer and was happy for his brother-in-law to stand in for him whenever his wife asked to dance.

---

119 *John Playford (1623-1686), English music publisher, published numerous collections of dance descriptions and the accompanying melodies from 1651 onwards.*

Now our troupe was complete and we could dance. We wanted to take turns with the accompanying music. Because playing and dancing at the same time is quite exhausting with experienced couples. Besides, the pochette is far from being a concert instrument. What fun it was for all of us! There's nothing better than dancing with people who have roughly the same level of skill. There's not much pushing, pulling and improving to be done.

We were just taking our first break when there was a stormy knock at the front door. Heinrich looked at Seraphia, who just raised an eyebrow and then shrugged her shoulders. So she knew nothing about another visit.

Heinrich must have just opened the door when a powerful male voice began to sing a song from an opera. So the Mozarts had arrived. How nice!

Wolfgang stormed into the parlour and immediately chose a dance partner, singing happily, while Nannerl pushed me off the piano stool and enthusiastically hit the keys without further hesitation. Wolfgang handed out dubious compliments to everyone present like an overzealous flower girl.

When the door knocker was pressed again just a few minutes later, our parents were at the door. They were both also keen dancers and they were the ones who had invited the Mozart siblings for a few days.

We danced for quite a while until there was another knock. This time, half of our staff stood outside, laden with baskets heaped with food and wine. They were greeted with a hello. Mamma had had a few things prepared. We hungry dancers pounced on it immediately and emptied the plates and bowls in the hour that followed.

Then we continued dancing, a little more moderately after the filling meal. Seraphia and I took it in turns to announce the dance steps of the lesser-known pieces until everyone was familiar with them. Every now and again, someone didn't pay attention and there was a tangle of dancers who no longer knew where to go, which led to a burst of laughter.

We had so much fun that at one point my stomach even hurt from laughing.

We would only be able to attend three more balls before Ash Wednesday on 16 February and the start of Lent, when such great pleasures were no longer allowed.

Tea Party again

One morning in early March, it was already quite spring-like outside, Pappa and I met up again for breakfast while mamma and Christoph were still asleep. He waved a letter at me after wishing me a good morning.

"Another letter from my dear friend and partner Krümmelbein. He has received news that there has also been an incident in Philadelphia involving a tea delivery[120]. Just nine days after the masquerade in Boston.

It was another East India Company ship and it was probably the largest cargo of tea ever shipped by the company."

"Was the whole load destroyed here, too?"

"No. They were more merciful there. The captain was threatened with being tarred and feathered if he didn't leave for England immediately with the damn weed. He must have taken the warning seriously and sailed back to England the next day without unloading the cargo. I'm very curious to see how things will develop there and whether it will actually lead to independence."

"That's a really exciting thing. When will you actually be heading back to your office in Hamburg? I hear the roads are all snow-free by now and the weather should hold out

---

120 *Over the course of 1774, there were 10 "Tea Parties" in America.*

for a while. I can see that you're already restless and want to get going."

"Oh, you already know the signs? That's what I wanted to tell you anyway. I'll have my luggage strapped onto the stagecoach the day after tomorrow morning, but I'll ride alongside myself. The weather looks stable and I think it will be more comfortable for me to ride the route than in these often inadequately sprung vehicles, in which you often share the already cramped space with unwashed people – or those who reek of smoke.

"Your mother will also come to Hamburg after Whitsun and then stay with me until the winter. Everything has already been discussed with your mamma. By the way, she is due to play a concert in Salzburg on Easter Monday. I'm sure you'll be spending the Easter holidays with her brother and his family. Around Whitsun she has a big gig in München and then a series of concerts in Rosenheim. From there, she will probably be travelling further north."

The door opened and Nina came in with a cup of hot chocolate, which she served. I drank the morning treat, which I usually had once or twice a week instead of tea for breakfast, in small sips and daydreamed a little.

During the time that Pappa was in Hamburg, mamma would certainly have more engagements in the area again. Christoph and I often accompanied her. If it was only in Reichenhall, we could ride or drive home the same evening. Easter would be at the beginning of April, and then a rather boring time would begin. Seraphia had already left three days ago and Pappa wouldn't be here for a while either.

So Christoph and I would take more care of training our horses again. We were happy to do this ourselves because we love working with these marvellous creatures.

This year, we would finally be able to go dancing again without restraint. I was planning to go back to München at the end of May and establish myself as a dance master there – whether Father liked it or not.

Anton Adner

Shortly afterwards, Johann came in and reported an early visitor.

"Mr Adner[121] is asking whether you would like to take delivery of wooden toys again, Mr von Sommerauer."

"Oh yes, the old man is just in time. Bring him to us. Tell him to have breakfast with us."

Pappa grinned. "The rogue always knows when I'm leaving for Hamburg. He's never been late."

Adner entered the room with a loud and cheerful "Good morning, everyone. Thank you very much for the invitation, which I am always happy to accept."

He put his box full of wooden goods next to my father's seat, then sat down opposite him and rubbed his hands in anticipation, as he always did. I had known Anton Adner since I was a child and liked the somewhat cranky old man. He always had a lot of anecdotes to tell.

I had already got up when he was announced and had put together a plate with all the goodies for him. I now placed it in front of him. As children, Christoph and I had actually called our guest Uncle Anton on his six-monthly visits. Since we returned from our law studies, he has simply been Anton.

"Thank you very much, girl. Have you settled back in here? It's just the nicest place at home, isn't it?"

---

121 *Anton Adner (allegedly 1705–1822) was the oldest inhabitant of the Berchtesgaden valley basin. The peddler travelled far and wide with his Kraxe (wooden frame to carry goods, like a backpack) to sell mainly local wooden goods.*

"Yes, that's true, although I also like the rural areas along the Inn. The Isar is also a beautiful river. It's just that life in the city doesn't have the same appeal for me in the long term. But that could also be because my mother-in-law in München is too close."

"You're a country person, just like me. Even if you're a rich country person and I'm a poor one, right Vic?"

"That's probably the case. Where are you off to this spring, Anton?"

"It depends on your father now. If he buys the whole stock from me, then I have to walk again to Berchtolsgaden and get new ones. My woodcarvers will be delighted. If not, then I'll go to Reichenhall first to see if I can find any customers. But after that I want to walk to Laufen. There's a widow just behind the Nocken who always buys a lot from me at this time of year. She sells all the stuff to the skippers who come by."

I let him eat first and Pappa looked at the goods. Johann came back with another large mug of chocolate for Anton. Christoph swam in in the shadow of his keel. A big hello followed between him and our visitor.

"What do you want for everything?" This simple sentence from Pappa after a while kicked off a haggle between the two men that was a joy to listen to.

Basically, it always went the same way, but they both had a lot of fun with the process. First Adner quotes a horrendously high sum. Pappa then says that it's not silver-plated, it's just wood and makes a very low offer. Then Adner praises the individual pieces and the quality of the respective carver, whereupon my father raises the price a little.

This goes back and forth for at least half an hour, during which the faces of the two merchants glow with amusement and in the end, Father pays a very fair price, which Adner says he does not usually receive in the region. But in the north there are some merchants in the trading towns who actually pay even more for the goods from

Berchtolsgaden. Ultimately, both men are extremely happy with the business.

Christoph and I sat next to the scene and were just as amused as the two gentlemen. We laughed at Adner's Bavarian swear words, which we had learnt in similar conversations over the last few years and, as always, made a point of remembering a new one. By the time mamma entered the room, the exciting scene was already over. Anton stood up and bowed respectfully to her.

"Good morning, Madame. You look like the sunshine himself today. I'm delighted to see you in good health."

Mamma grinned. "You old sweet talker. It's nice to see you healthy again. You're lucky again to find my husband still here. Have you come to an agreement yet?"

"Yes, my darling, I bought everything from him and he will have to make his way back to Berchtolsgaden today to get new goods."

Mamma raised an eyebrow and looked sharply at Pappa. "I'm sure you'll find something he can take with him so he doesn't have to hike with an empty satchel?"

"Yes, Mr Adner, I actually have a small delivery for your provost that arrived here yesterday from my business partner. It's some spices that were ordered from us. I'll give you a letter and you'll be paid for the delivery there."

It was done as discussed. The wooden goods were well packed by a servant for transport on the stagecoach and, after a very sumptuous breakfast, the pedlar was equipped with the spices and the letter for the *Probstei* and travelled back to Berchtolsgaden.

Father left the day after next. The farm became quiet again and everything slowed down a little.

Once again, a letter arrived from Frederik. He told us about all the events he had attended and much more. However, there was also a very interesting section in it.

... By the way, a friend of mine, who you don't know yet, spent a few years in Italy. He has just returned home and told me that the volcano Vesuvius erupted again on 12 January. He happened

to be nearby on a relative's estate when the volcano started spewing fire. I am quoting his description here:

'The animals had been behaving strangely the whole day before. The birds weren't singing and seemed to be fleeing from something. Many flew past our farm to the east. Our sheep were also behaving unusually. They were restless and obviously uncomfortable. On the large pasture, the sheep were all at the end furthest away from Vesuvius. It was the same with the horses.

At some point, the earth began to shake. This tremor became more and more threatening. There was a roar and it became dark. The mountain spewed glowing red lava over its crater rim and a dark cloud of ash hung over the whole region. Fortunately, my uncle's farm is to the east of Vesuvius and on a not insignificant hill, so we didn't have to be too alarmed when we saw the extent of the eruption. Nevertheless, we were all relieved when the mountain calmed down again. The ash settled on everything in the following days and turned the area grey and black. It was not a pretty sight.[122]'

Easter time

Good Friday morning. I was sitting at the breakfast table with our relatives in Salzburg. Christoph came rushing in with an indistinct "Good morning" on his lips. He sat down and immediately began to eat as if he hadn't had anything for several days.

"What are you reading that's so interesting, sister?"

"The archbishop has announced that everyone who comes to mass in the cathedral on Sunday will receive a lard biscuit on the way home."

"Now that's a word! I think it's very generous."

---

122 *Jakob Philipp Hackert painted the eruption of Mount Vesuvius in 1774, but the devastation was obviously limited.*

"But that also means that you have to be very quick after the mass to get hold of one of these noodles. That means you have to sit strategically in one of the last benches on the very inside of the aisle."

At that moment, Uncle Josef came into the room. He looked round, saw us and wished us a good morning.

Christoph spooned up his soft egg on the side. "Uncle, Colloredo has lard biscuits distributed to everyone after mass on Sundays. Isn't that a nice gesture?" He said.

"Oh, that's good news. I like it that way." Uncle replied.

Aunt Maria entered the breakfast room and the news was repeated by the men. I couldn't help but smile in my journal and she must have seen it. Because she laughed quietly.

"Oh, darlings, I know when it comes to food, you like to believe in the generosity of an archbishop. But since there's a special date on the calendar today, I think Vic just sent you to April Fool's Day."

She winked at me and sat down to pour herself a cup of coffee.

"What, that's not true about the lard biscuits? You'll get a terrible revenge, sis." Christoph's anger was feigned because he laughed. I could see that he was annoyed that he hadn't been the one to think of something like that.

On Sunday, we were all at the cathedral early because mamma was due to play Johann Sebastian Bach's *Easter Oratorio* with the archbishop's orchestra. Mamma loves this composer's music as well as that of George Frideric Handel.

The performance was marvellous to listen to and moved me to tears. Mother was only one musician in an orchestra, but it was the playing of each individual that mattered.

After the solemn mass, our aunt invited us for hot chocolate and small cakes. We stayed the night with our relatives and had uplifting conversations about God and the world.

After mass on Easter Monday, we made our way home. Nature was already beginning to green and blossom and new flowers were appearing every day. It was simply beautiful to see.

I also collected a lot of wild garlic along the river Saalach on the way home. Our cook was delighted with the unexpected "delivery" and immediately prepared us a dinner flavoured with wild garlic.

A busy few weeks followed. Mamma was often out and about. Sometimes we accompanied her, sometimes we stayed at home. We trained our horses in all disciplines, went to dance and music events and had lots of other things to do.

Christoph had a new case that he didn't need my help with and I read the travelogues of Charles Burney. This English composer and organist travelled to France and Italy, among other places, and wrote down his experiences on the subject of music.

He reported that in Venice, for example, there is a music school of the Mendicanti where all the instruments are played by women. He does not use any of the common attributes for these female musicians that are generally used for male musicians, such as precise, impressive, ingenious, brilliant or others. No, he speaks more of cute. This shows me that he doesn't want to show most women who have learnt an art the same appreciation as men, who are certainly no more talented.

His reaction to Marianne Martines is completely different. He writes that she is the most perfect singer he has ever heard. She sings really beautifully and I am also convinced that he knows something about music.

I spoke to Christoph about this and asked him where such an attitude on the part of the men could come from. He asked me to give him time to think about it. It took several days before I got an answer. I don't like it at all, but it sounds plausible.

Christoph had spoken to several friends because he wanted to find out for himself. He came to the conclusion that all men at all times regard men as the norm. Man equals man. Women are the deviation from the norm and therefore, they are not trusted with anything, they are not given any rights and they have to submit to men.

"Vic, I don't see this as a good starting point for a marriage either. But that's probably mainly because I was brought up differently by my mamma than other men. Our mamma has always been my role model in some areas and I couldn't imagine her as our father's subordinate. Because she never was. She always contributed to the family fortune with her performances."

"And yet father doesn't want to see me as a dancing master." I reasoned.

Christoph gave me a warm hug. "I spoke to him again before he left. I think I gave him something to think about, dear sister."

Literary Salon

Christoph and I were invited to a literary salon in a community centre in Reichenhall.

One of the gentlemen there with an incredibly pleasant voice read from the epistolary novel *"The Sorrows of Young Werther"* by Johann Wolfgang von Goethe. I could have listened to him for hours – even if it had been a text that I wouldn't have liked nearly as much.

I like Goethe's novel and I'm going to get it myself. He really uses his head to think and not just to parrot the words of others. And he expresses his opinion in his texts. For example in his speech about bad humour:

'... *Is it not enough that we cannot make each other happy, must we also rob each other of the pleasure that every heart can still sometimes grant itself? And name me the person who is in a bad mood and is so good as to hide it, to bear it alone without destroying the joy around him! Or is it not rather an inner displeasure at our own unworthiness, a displeasure with ourselves that is always linked to an envy fuelled by foolish vanity? We see happy people whom we do not make happy. And that is unbearable ...*'[123]

I would like to get to know this poet.

Naturally, the young poet was discussed after the lecture. "My aunt's cousin lives in Koblenz and knows the La Roche family. She firmly claims that the young Goethe modelled Lotte in *Werther* on Maximiliane La Roche. The two are friends. But she married a merchant more than twice her age in January. I think his name is Brentano or something like that."

The narrator was a delightful old lady. Without being a real gossip, she was happy to pass on interesting information. She was particularly happy when she could announce positive news. She generally kept things that could harm other people to herself. That made her extremely likeable. She was small and dainty, always elegantly dressed and had eyes sparkling with joie de vivre, although her snow-white hair and the deep laugh lines on her face showed that she must be quite old.

Goethe's *"Götz von Berlichingen"* was recently premiered in Berlin. Of course, people talked about it, too. I couldn't contribute anything, but I listened with keen ears.

In addition, a continuation of Hofrath Christoph Martin Wieland's satirical novel *"Die Abderiten – eine sehr wahrscheinliche Geschichte"* (The Abderites – a very likely story) was read from the journal *"Der Teutsche Merkur"*, which

---

123 *From: "The Sorrows of Young Werther" by J. W. Goethe.*

was published for the first time last year. Wieland writes in a style that I liked. His texts are witty and humorous. I will definitely be following this novel.

As there has also been a literary magazine aimed specifically at us women since this year, we naturally also read from *"Iris. Vierteljahresschrift für Frauenzimmer"*[124]. Although I think it's good that there's finally a magazine for women, it's noticeable that almost all the texts in it are written by men. I hope this will change in the near future.[125]

The ladies and gentlemen present then spent some time discussing the texts. In between, a lady sat down at the piano and appetisers were served. These were new impressions in relaxed company.

A heavy blow

It was the middle of May – just before Whitsun – and we were out riding. In a few days' time, we wanted to set off for München because mamma was due to play in front of the Elector there and then at a few concert evenings in Rosenheim. I was already looking forward to seeing my friend Frederik again. I also wanted to stay there at least until August and try my luck. Even if it meant I wouldn't be able to attend the Leonhardiritt[126] in Holzhausen, which I had always wanted to experience.

"Vic, I thought you were coming. So where are you?"

Typical of my brother. Nothing can go fast enough for him. He had probably already forgotten that I was riding with a complete beginner.

---

124 Iris. A quaterly magazine for women
125 From the 2nd issue onwards, there were texts by Sophie von La Roche and other women. La Roche was the first female editor of a magazine in 1783/1784 with "Pomona für Teutschlands Töchter".
126 A ride in favour of Saint Leonhard with a clerical blessing for all riders and horses.

"I know that a lot of things are new to you and you have to look at everything first. But please don't forget to put one foot in front of the other. Look, unlike me, you have four of them – and a very long one at that. You can do it a bit faster! Come on, little one." I gave the gelding a good talking to and pushed him into the flanks, so we took the bend behind which Christoph was waiting.

He snorted at my last words. "Little one is good."

My young mount was by far the biggest and heaviest horse in the stable. I normally have a preference for more graceful and manoeuvrable horses, but I took this large and lovable youngster to my heart the moment he entered the yard. The gelding was so curious and had his 'beak' in or on everything. You couldn't stand next to him without him nibbling at your hair or clothes. You really had to save everything from him. Especially leather things. That's why I wanted to take over part of his training myself.

"Here we are already! The little one had to familiarise himself with a nasty puddle first. It was definitely going to jump on him."

Christoph laughed at me. "Well, it's his first trip into the countryside. So far, he's only known the area behind the stable under saddle. But he's pretty relaxed anyway, as far as I can see." Christoph smiled first at the horse and then at me.

"I feel the same way. He's a lovely guy who wants to do everything right. The boy has a wonderful character. And he's incredibly playful and cuddly."

"You both look quite happy, if I'm interpreting his expression correctly."

Now it was my turn to snort. I just imagined a stupid grin on my horse's face.

After a relaxed gallop across the meadow, we arrived back at the house, heated and satisfied. A travelling carriage was parked there and some of the servants were running around as if scared up.

Suddenly the majordomo stepped out of the house and saw us. He waved two lads over and then ran towards us. He looked a little shaken. "Please, let them look after your horses and come with me. Something bad has happened."

Fear immediately rose up in me. I still had no concrete clue, but it must be really frightening. Because I had never seen our Johannes so distraught. I only knew him as a man with nerves of steel who couldn't be rattled by anything.

"Please go into the salon," he called after us.

I saw that Christoph's hands were also shaking as we both hurried towards the door of the salon. I briefly took his hand and squeezed it. He looked at me, nodded and then opened the door. When we entered, the first thing I saw was Mr Krümmelbein, our father's esteemed assistant, standing at the window, white as lime. The first moment he turned towards us, he had a blank look on his face that made me shudder.

"Good that you're both here. I've just brought your father. He's in a very bad condition and has been taken to his bed. Your mother is with him now. She asks you to speak to me in her place. The doctor has been sent for. "

I approached the man and asked him to sit down. "You, too, Christoph."

Nina came in with a tray of hot tea. I poured a cup. Mr Krümmelbein gratefully took a smoking cup and his features smoothed out a little. He took a sip and then put the cup down again.

"Well, your father suffered a collapse and has been very restricted in his movements ever since. The doctors are sure he will recover, but it will take time. I was in a quandary and at first I couldn't decide whether to send an urgent message to your mother or set off on the journey with your father. Then I decided in favour of the trip. After all, a few days wouldn't change his situation and I wanted your father to come home. Because he has better care here. I also need instructions from your mother because your father can't give them himself at the moment. He has problems with speaking and also with writing."

I imagined the worst and Christoph was probably feeling the same. He squirmed back and forth on the armchair as if he wanted to conquer the fabric.

"Mr Krümmelbein, can you tell us how this happened?" asked Christoph.

"It's a tragedy. I hope for all our sakes that we can come up with a plan to save your father's business. I've been racking my brains, but without your active help there would be no point."

Christoph stopped Mr Krümmelbein. "Please tell me from the beginning. What happened?"

The man wrung his hands. "Yes, well, your esteemed father had already had a partner for two years, Mr Wappler[127]."

"We are aware of that. But father doesn't seem to have fully integrated him into all business matters."

"That's right, he was only entrusted with certain business."

He was interrupted. Johannes arrived with the carafe of cognac and glasses, followed by a footman with a huge portion of sandwiches and plates and Nina with another pot of tea.

Now Christoph got active. He poured us all a drink and encouraged Krümmelbein to eat some of the bread.

I also realised how hungry I was and took a bite. After a while, Krümmelbein continued.

"As I said, Wappler, he seemed quite competent at first, but we've all been taken in by a foaming-at-the-mouth and a good-for-nothing, as we now know. He was also taken in

---

127 *Colloquial Austrian insult for an incompetent person who pretends to be competent. Here is a name that says it all.*

by a swindler himself, whom her father had already rejected.

"Wappler did business with him anyway, was dazzled by the good conditions and now a complete shipload of spices and cloth disappeared never to be seen again and with it a large part of the business's capital and also money from our customers, who had been persuaded to invest by Wappler.

"When the matter came to light, Wappler disappeared overnight, presumably out of fear of the consequences of his actions, and now your father has to answer for everything. The news has knocked him down. Fortunately, I was able to speak to most of the customers. They want to give us time because your father was always honest with them and they see him as an honourable business partner who is not to blame. But the delay is not unlimited, of course. That's why I need signatures, authorisations and other help from you.

"We need to come up with a battle plan for the next steps. There's a lot of money at stake. Fortunately, the shares in the deliveries from Baiern to Hamburg are not affected because Wappler had no access to them. I see a small chance for the future because a ship with yarn and fabrics arrived before I left.

However, a large proportion of the new goods still have to be sold at good profit. I have samples of everything with me."

Mr Krümmelbein looked tired. I communicated with my brother by looking at him.

"Dear Mr Krümmelbein. I would like to thank you – also on behalf of the whole family and our servants – for bringing our father home. You are exhausted from your journey and have earned some rest. A hot bath should be ready for you now and a room has also been prepared for you. Let's talk more about everything tomorrow. Because it was a shock for us too and we have to digest it first. I wish you a good night's sleep."

I felt his relief as he made a swift bow. "I'm so glad they both took everything so calmly. I had the worst fears ..." Krümmelbein looked crestfallen.

Christoph, who is sometimes so wonderfully emotional, spontaneously hugged our father's assistant. At first, Krümmelbein was stiff as a board, but then he returned the hug. It seemed to do him good. The otherwise stiff gentleman seemed to need the hug. His eyes became moist with emotion. I turned away and poured myself another cup of tea.

When the door closed behind Krümmelbein, Christoph hugged me too. We just stood there and drew strength from not being alone. Just like we had been used to since we were children.

Mamma entered the room. Without saying a word, we waved her over and took her into our embrace. She cried and was really shaken by sobs. Only slowly did the sobs subside and she looked at us with teary eyes.

Then, she freed herself and sat down. She reached for a loaf of bread. We didn't bother her. It was important that she ate. Because our mamma would need all her strength.

After a few minutes, she began to speak. "Your father is resting now. Please let him sleep and don't see him until tomorrow. The doctor says your father will recover, but it will be a long time before he can take over his business again. What is our economic situation? Is there any hope?"

Christoph explained. "According to Mr Krümmelbein, there is still a glimmer of hope. But for that we need customers who will pay a good price for goods that arrived before he left. He has samples with him. The customers who have invested money in the lost company will grant a deferral of payment, as they assured him."

I thought about it and then gave myself a jolt. "I have my townhouse in München. I'll try to rent it out at a good price. I'll write to my notary there and Frederik first thing in the morning. The two of them should take care of it.

I also have my husband's allowance. I'll ask for it to be paid into my father's business account."

"In that case, we have a more than good chance if I add my savings from my clients' legal disputes. I hadn't even thought about your money, Vic." Christoph looked much more hopeful. But then, he changed his mind. "And your plans?"

"The family is more important now. Once Pappa has found his way back to his old form, there will still be enough time to realise it."

Christoph gave me another hug. "You're the best daughter a father could have. I'll tell him that, too."

Mamma nodded, lost in thought. Then she straightened up and lifted her head.

"Christoph, please arrange for all the servants to gather here shortly. I don't want rumours to spread and everyone is affected and should therefore know what has happened. And before they sleep badly because they know nothing and make up horror stories.

"Victoria, I would ask you to send messages to our relatives as soon as we know more tomorrow. I want them to know how things stand with us before the gossip. If Mr Krümmelbein, whom I've come to know as very reliable, says we have a chance, then we'll make the best possible use of it. We'll have to cut back in the near future and part with one or two valuables, horses and perhaps even servants. I'm not willing to give up!"

"Just two days ago, an acquaintance showed interest in our young gelding." Christoph suggested. "However, he can't train him himself and doesn't have a stable manager who is good enough for this quality of horse. I'll find out what he wants to pay – for the horse and training." Christoph drummed his fingers on his thighs.

At my hissed "Please!" he stopped knocking and looked at me sheepishly. He knew I couldn't stand it. It was due to his nervousness and I couldn't be angry with him. He got up and complied with our mamma's request.

Within a very short time, all the servants were gathered in the parlour with mostly anxious faces. They must have been hoping to find out more.

Mamma took the floor when everyone was quiet and looking at her expectantly.

"I'm sure word has already got around that my husband has been brought home from Hamburg seriously ill. The trigger for this was a fake business deal that his partner got involved in. It involved a lot of money, which has now been lost."

A murmur of dismay went through the servants.

"We have no reason to give up yet. My husband will gradually recover and everything is not lost. The most important thing now is that we fight for my husband's business to survive – and all of us with him! We need your help to do this.

"Save, where you can and where it makes sense. Let us know if you learn that someone wants something from our property and is willing to pay a good price. Only buy the essentials – including food. I would like my husband to have beef and chicken broth. But the rest of us won't be eating meat for the time being and will do without things that are luxuries.

"There won't be any major invitations in the near future and we can do without elaborate pastries and chocolates – unless there are people willing to pay for them.

"Only if we all help together and are prudent can we avert even greater misfortune. If one of you receives a good job offer, he or she is free to leave on the same day. As soon as we are well again – I very much hope for the future – everyone can come back. Everyone will be paid as soon as we can. I just can't promise when that will be yet. Work orders that are not absolutely necessary must be stopped and contractors may have to be asked to defer work that has already been completed."

After Mother's announcement, a murmur and discussion began among the servants.

The stable manager stepped forward. "Madame, if I may say so, we have a mare in the stables who is extremely fast. We think she could win prizes. One of the gentlemen in town is always taking part in races like this. And I hear he has a lot of money."

"Good idea. Give me the gentleman's name and I'll get in touch with him." Christoph was visibly pleased with the suggestion. I knew that he didn't care much about the animal anyway because the mare had a difficult character.

Then, one of the house servants suggested: "Can we take care of the hole in the roof above the kitchen from last week's storm ourselves? The master's valet is very skilful at such things and I could help him. I've done work like that at home too."

Mother beamed. "Thank you for your suggestions. Yes, please, do everything yourself that is possible and that you feel you can do. I'm sure nobody will be reprimanded for working just because it's not their actual job. But please be careful on the roof. Thank heavens we have such wonderful staff. Thank you to each and every one of you. We will get through this crisis together, I'm sure of it."

I realised we were really lucky to have such people in our service. Without exception, they were loyal and willing to work.

Nevertheless, I slept badly that night. I had wild dreams of pirates and other crooks taking other people's things and of ships sinking. The sea was covered with the most beautiful and precious cloth and the fish were sewing these huge lengths of fabric with our threads. From above, it looked as if a new continent was being created.

Before going to bed, I had written two urgent letters that had to be sent to München as quickly as possible.

The next day, we all had a late breakfast by our standards and then sat down with Mr Krümmelbein.

He looked a little more rested than yesterday and I realised for the first time that he was a good-looking man of my late husband's age. Only the beard he wore just didn't suit him. It made him look too old. But it wasn't my place to point this out to him.

Businesses in women's hands

Father had always discussed his business with Mother when he was at home. So she had enough of an idea of who the usual customers were, what brought how much money and who was happy to buy which fabrics at good prices.

Thanks to her contacts with the tailors and seamstresses of Salzburg and Reichenhall and her visits to the houses of the nobility as a musician, no trend remained hidden from her.

Our Aunt Seraphia always played her part in my father's business by reporting on her visits to London, Paris, Mannheim, Bamberg, Bayreuth, Wien, Moscow and Prague and which fashions were currently enjoying great popularity there. My stay in München had helped me to make and deepen acquaintances and I would make use of this.

Mr Krümmelbein, who showed the patterns, was particularly reliant on our mother's continued cooperation. They were extraordinary fabrics in bright colours and the finest yarns for various purposes. We looked at everything together and discussed the goods for a while before mother turned back to Mr Krümmelbein.

"Best quality. I already know who will wear a dress with this fabric and who will buy these yarns from me with a kiss. Yes, Mr Krümmelbein, we can actually think of someone for almost every pattern who is just made for it."

Mamma's joy was infectious. "Christoph, please send someone with these patterns to the tailor in Reichenhall. He has the right customers for them. He knows the procedure. I need another courier to the best tailors and seamstresses in Salzburg. I'll prepare cover letters for all the addressees immediately. Vic, what's the situation with the aristocracy in München?"

I answered her. "I'll get back to my desk immediately." I turned to my brother. "The letters to the notary and Frederik are ready in the foyer, Christoph. Johannes will take care of it. I know a few people who are sure to be interested in our goods."

Mamma beamed at Mr Krümmelbein. "We're going to make a good profit and have already cleared the first hurdle. Please tell us what activities were planned and what next steps you advise us to take, Mr Krümmelbein."

Obviously surprised by mother's energy, the man told us what purchases and sales were already planned and what he had in mind for the near future. The good man now looked a little more hopeful than the day before.

Mamma and he had a few more legal questions for Christoph and me, which we took care of immediately while they discussed other points.

I wrote several letters to various acquaintances who could either help us with information or by purchasing goods. Of course, I had to put everything into words that didn't suggest we were in trouble. I advertised the goods as exactly fitting and that only they would look good in them or something like that.

I had only been honest with Frederik. In my letter to him, I had described how things stood with us. I also asked him to take care of Krümmelbein and to support him in his business in München if possible.

I also wrote to Magdalena with honest words and asked for her active support. She was always a little ahead of her time when it came to fashion and was therefore a role model.

My letters were immediately taken to the post office, as the stagecoach was due to leave just a few hours later.

The following day, numerous other papers were signed and witnessed.

We received orders from Salzburg and Reichenhall within three days. In München, Krümmelbein would be expecting more in the post at my townhouse, where he was to spend the night.

With all this, further recommendations, plenty of provisions and many good wishes, the faithful Mr Krümmelbein was seen off again just a few days after his arrival on his long and arduous journey to the river Elbe with a stopover in München.

At first, mother wanted to stay with our ailing father and cancel her gigs in München and Rosenheim. But then we persuaded her to do it after all.

"Mamma, you'll be paid very well for these gigs. We need the money now and can't afford to do without it. So do it. Shall one of us accompany you? Christoph or I will be happy to stay here and look after father. We've already talked about it. We want you to play. And don't argue, mamma. Father will be fine."

So mamma got into the stagecoach with Mr Krümmelbein and Christoph accompanied them on horseback. I was sad not to be able to see Frederik, but I gave them a heartfelt letter for him. I was curious to hear what they would say. Especially about Rosenheim.

Since the early years of this century, there has been a bathhouse in Rosenheim near the Loreto Chapel with alleged healing properties. A Mr Wolfgang Jakob Ruedorffer had it built and ran it for a long time. After him, his son Johann Jakob ran it. He sold the baths to his son-in-law, the wine merchant Franz Carl Gaigl, in 1770.

The afore mentioned Gaigl has now helped to organise a concert week for special guests after Whitsun this year. Well-known musicians from Baiern were to come and show off their skills.

So while my mother and Christoph were away, I had my hands full at home organising the servants and looking after my father. He slept a lot. When he was awake, I often read to him. Father found it very difficult to speak.

He often took a very long time to say a sentence. But I tried not to let my impatience show. I realised that his thoughts were often with our mother. But, like us, he had also insisted that she could not turn down the invitation to play for the Elector.

When the weather was good, I had Pappa carried out into the garden. There, in a sunny corner, sheltered from the wind, was an armchair in which we put him cosily so that he could get some fresh air. I entertained him there until he got tired again and wanted to sleep.

Then I discussed all the day-to-day tasks and plans with our cook Johanna and Majordomus Johannes and listened to other members of our household about their ideas and problems. I'm still glad that everything was easily solved.

Happy turnaround

The two weeks or so passed surprisingly quickly for all of us. Mother had received a considerable amount of money for her solo performances and for her participation in Rosenheim and I had entertained Pappa well in the meantime.

Of course, my brother informed me of the news from München as soon as he got home.

"Your friend Frederik has actually already found a baroness for your townhouse who wants to move in in the autumn and will pay from June. She will also take over all the servants who are still there."

"That's very good news! How does Frederik look? How is he?"

"He's doing very well and looks great. mamma and I were only there for three days. But Frederik and I found time for a longer chat. He always speaks very highly of you and I really like him now. I think he loves you in a special way. We fenced together once and also went for a ride along the river Isar.

"He also seems to get on quite well with Krümmelbein. Both are always ready to help us. What a fortunate family we are. There are so many people who are well-disposed towards us!" Christoph gave me a big hug and whirled me round the room.

"What was Rosenheim like?" I asked. I didn't know this town well and I knew very little about the spa.

"Rather quiet, but the concerts were really good. And also well attended. Given that you can't compare Rosenheim with München, I have to say that I was very surprised by the high quality that was on offer there.

I met our fellow student Wendelin there. I spent most of the time with him when my mother didn't need me or wanted her peace and quiet. The surroundings are quite beautiful. We had a snack with us and rode to the Simssee. It's only about a mile away."

Friends like gold

I woke up just as dawn was breaking. A single blackbird was chirping outside my window. It seemed to me that it was giving a concert in which each of these little bird throats was on top form. Shortly afterwards, the singing and chirping outside was a real joy.

In the midst of the bird concert, I fell asleep again for about an hour. Later, I got ready to go out, rode a solitary round to the unnamed lake and then went for breakfast. There was a letter from Frederik at my place, which had probably been delivered that morning. I broke the seal and read the lines addressed to me.

Dearest friend Vic,

I give you a big hug, because this is the second time you've been the architect of my happiness. Yes, you read correctly and I love you for it.

But first things first. I've found a tenant for your townhouse. But you already know that from Christoph.

The lady is a widowed baroness with two children and only wants to use the house in winter, but wants to pay for it all year round. She agrees to your price. Isn't that a small miracle?

In accordance with your request, I will soon pack up your and Jacob's remaining personal belongings and have them brought to my house so that the Baroness will find a tidy house when she arrives.

Before your Mr Krümmelbein arrived, I had a few hours alone there. Don't be angry with me for looking at all your remaining clothes again. Many memories of our wonderful dance evenings came back to me. It was such a happy time with you and Jacob.

I also found the garment you had tailored for me back then. The memories have overwhelmed me. I miss you so much, even though we are in constant correspondence with each other.

Andreas Krümmelbein was therefore welcomed by me. In order to fulfil his mission in the best possible way, I offered him my support. So far, he has been more successful than he could have dreamed of. The whole world wants your fabrics! I also bought something from him. You will be amazed!

As we were invited to an elegant party and he didn't have the right wardrobe, I took the liberty of giving him some of Jacob's

clothes. The two of them have exactly the same stature. You know I don't do this sort of thing lightly. Anyway, I'll keep him company until I know he's safely back in a carriage to Hamburg in a few days' time. We've became good friends.

You'd be amazed if you saw him now. I've prescribed him a visit to the barber[128], which has turned him into a new man. Now I must surely fear his competition with the ladies. Only joking of course.

As soon as I have taken care of everything important here, I will also leave and visit you to finally honour your repeated invitation. Don't tell anyone about my arrival. I don't want you to prepare anything especially for me.

Oh yes, to come back to luck ... At the same time, a payment of a tidy sum of 950 guilders, which I won last Saturday playing Pharo[129], will be received via your notary. I hope it will help to alleviate your financial hardship.

I'll see you soon. I look forward to being able to embrace you again, my dearest friend.

In heartfelt solidarity
Your friend Frederik

I read the letter twice and smiled to myself. I was so happy about the good news that I called Christoph and strutted off with him to my father's bedroom.

A maid came out just then. "Your father is awake."

I stuck my head through the door and saw Father sitting upright. Mamma spoke to him. Then he saw me and pointed to the door with a pleased expression. Mamma turned round. Christoph and I entered the room.

I waved the letter in my hand. "There's good news. Frederik has written. He's transferring his Pharaoh winnings of 950 guilders to us. What do you say now?"

---

128 *Barber: He was responsible for personal hygiene and was also usually a surgeon or doctor for the little people.*

129 *Pharo or Faro is a card game with 2 decks of 52 French cards each, which was played a lot at the time and often for high stakes. There were usually also gambling rooms at ball events.*

"Your friend Frederik is a kind-hearted person. Heaven bless him." Mamma clapped her hands and looked far more relaxed than she had a few minutes ago. Father's lips softened too. "Thank him," he said with difficulty. He's still struggling to speak, but we can understand him much better and it's going a bit faster.

We left our parents again so as not to tire father out.

A letter arrived from Seraphia in Paris. As soon as Johannes handed it to me, I went into my room and read it over a cup of hot chocolate.

Dearest Vic,

Thank you for informing me immediately about your father's illness and the work you all have to do. Of course, I will try to win customers for your goods here at court. That will be my most important concern alongside my dance appointments. I already have my first customers in mind.

Incidentally, I was invited to the opera here in Paris on 19 April by one of my admirers here. Heinrich was a little jealous. But I was able to appease him again with particularly intense affection. 'Iphigénie en Aulide' by Christoph Willibald Gluck was premiered under the direction of the composer. It was rumoured beforehand that Gluck criticised the artists very harshly until everything was to his liking. This attacked them in their vanity, as the French are generally very confident in their abilities. But it was worth it. The performance was exquisite.

Marie Antoinette is also said to have been very fond of it. She is Gluck's patron, as far as I know.

It occurs to me that an opera by Gluck was also performed at the wedding of Maria Antonia Walpurgis Symphorosa of Baiern and Friedrich Christian of Sachsen in 1747. Incidentally, this princess was a patron of the arts.

She is a successful composer, soprano opera singer, painter and poet and is an excellent harpsichordist. She was also accepted into the Accademia dell'Arcadia in Rome, an internationally active literary academy, in the year of her wedding. A very interesting woman, who I had the honour of seeing perform one of her own operas in Dresden a few years ago.

Have you also heard that Wilhelmsburg burnt down in Weimar on 6 May? It must have been a huge fire that broke out in a kitchen chimney due to a lightning strike. Only the tower and gatehouse remain. A tragic thing and a loss for the town. I wonder whether the young Duke Carl August will have the castle rebuilt.

As a young woman I once danced at a party there in front of Duke Ernst August II, Constantine of Saxe-Weimar and Eisenach and his wife Anna Amalia. The palace – and especially the grounds around it – were very impressive.

Imagine, there was even an 'Aufritt'[130] up to the second floor in the Wilhelmsburg. On one side, you entered the Himmelsburg (the church) and on the other, the forty-metre-long oval-shaped ceremonial and guard hall. A magnificent room with slender marble columns and a surrounding gallery.

The invited guests crowded the banqueting hall. A large table had been set up there. The musicians stood on the floor above around the oval opening in the ceiling, which was fitted with a balustrade. The acoustics were really excellent.

However, what caused the most sensation was the unusual lantern that illuminated the table from above. Unfortunately, I can no longer describe it. I only remember that the overall impression was really impressive.

There was also a Knights' Hall in the Wilhelmsburg. Ernst August founded the House Order of the White Falcon in 1732 and had the portraits of the founding members hung there. I think it was their meeting place. I don't know what these Knights of the White Falcon were dedicated to. I have not looked into it. ...

---

130 *You could actually ride on horseback up the stairs to the second floor.*

She also wrote about a few rumours and other news, but they weren't that important. The greetings from Anna, Madeleine and all the other friends made me particularly happy.

Solstice dance

Mamma decided at short notice to organise our annual dance evening with friends on Solstice Day. We wanted to show normality, which would be important for the business.

What was needed beforehand was a practice evening for everyone to rehearse the latest dances.

We didn't have a ballroom, but it was warm and it wasn't the first time we had our servants lay a dance floor in the garden. The wood was all stored in the coach house and our people were already used to preparing everything perfectly. Torches were made, storm lanterns were put up and coloured lanterns were hung.

The musicians stayed in the house, with the doors open to the garden, which could be accessed from two rooms. Both rooms were lit up so that the light could also illuminate our dance outside.

Among friends, it was customary for each household to contribute something to make the event a success. Either of a musical or culinary nature. As a result, quite a sizeable orchestra came together that evening and the buffet became increasingly sumptuous.

Almost all our friends from and around Reichenhall and even from Salzburg had come. We were most pleased by the presence of the Mozarts. Wolfgang flirted with all the ladies present. He ploughed through the ranks at the dance like a whirlwind, always with a snappy phrase on his lips.

We danced until the early hours of the morning and greeted the rising sun with a cheerful dance.

The next day, a new letter arrived from Krümmelbein to my father.

... There is still no trace of Wappler and the missing money. But our creditors are appeased after the large payment and remain loyal to our business. They trust the old von Sommerauer and will continue to buy from him in future.

You can be grateful for such a wonderful family and loyal friends who are so committed to your business. I was afraid I would have to look for a new position. But this thought was unfounded, as it now turns out. I am proud to work with your family. They are all capable and understanding people.

I find working with your wife a pure pleasure. You should involve her more in the business even after your full recovery. Madame has very good ideas and also a flair for the cloth trade. That's what some of our competitors lack: a woman's business sense.

A closure of Boston Harbour came into force on 1 June. The "Intolerable Acts" are the British reaction to the Boston Tea Party last year. It's just as well that this doesn't affect us directly.

The new delivery of cloth from the Orient arrived yesterday. I am pleased to inform you that I already have binding contracts for half of them and we just have to wait for the money and the collection of the goods. Some of the München customers recommended by your daughter are also worth their weight in gold. Three of them have already placed follow-up orders for certain fabrics and the matching yarns in considerable quantities. ...

Dancing Playford

Seraphia was home for a few days on her way from Paris to Prague. She had asked me to join her alone. "Oh Vic, I'm heartbroken about the circumstances that have put you in trouble.

You are as dear to me as a daughter and I know that you will support your family to the best of your ability until your father is out of the greatest financial difficulties again. So I have an offer for you. I have a great treasure that hardly anyone knows about because it is very valuable to me. I would like to keep it that way."

I stared at my aunt and nodded very seriously.

"Therefore, I will grant you, and only you, access to my treasure. You will acquire the essence of it and, together with your brother, pass this knowledge on to your customers."

Completely confused, I was still staring. What was she trying to tell me? Which customers did she mean?

Seraphia wanted to say something, but then looked at me invitingly and said: "Just come with me!"

I climbed with her to the upper floor and entered her private bedroom for the first time. Then she picked a key out of the folds of her dress and unlocked the large chest that dominated a wall between two windows.

With a gesture towards the contents, she then said: "This is my great treasure, which has already opened many doors for me and will also help you and Christoph."

I looked at the old books, which must have been around for several decades and were all showing signs of wear. Then I recognised a name and knew at that moment what it was. All my aunt's dance books were well stored here. The title *"The Dancing Master"* by John Playford caught my eye. The last expanded edition had been published in 1728[131] and the existing copies were not easy to find these days and were also exorbitantly expensive. I only owned one volume myself and had always wanted access to the others. I got down on my knees in front of the chest.

---

131 *All editions taken together, the Dancing Master describes 1,053 dances including melody, 186 melodies without dance and 3 songs.*

"These are the complete dances collected by Playford in the original edition from 1651 to the last edition of 1728, all about 900 dances. I have a few customers who would also like to be taught these dances. Due to your current situation, Christoph and you will take over."

"Oh, you're just the best auntie anyone could have!" I hugged Seraphia and then sat down.

"That suits me very well, as I have many other engagements this year and am therefore, mostly travelling. These gigs are much better paid than the dance lessons here. So it's a financial advantage for me that you do the dance lessons instead of me. If you take over the clients, at least they won't go to another maître de dance[132] and if one day you don't want to continue, I can do it again.

"It has already been discussed with your father. Despite the preparatory work you both did, it wasn't easy to convince him. But in the end, he's in favour of anything that helps to save the family and the business. But only if you work together with Christoph for the time being, Vic."

"The main thing is that I can teach!"

"Of course you only go to the best families. I have already negotiated the prices – the usual ones – for you with your first customers. You are both capable of doing this and will start on Monday. I am convinced of your success. In addition to your great dancing skills, you are also exactly the right people for such a task. And your age will also help you. Because many of the students are children or young adults. You will both get on particularly well with them."

I was overwhelmed and had to close my mouth, which was still open.

"Dearest Aunt Seraphia, do you know that you have just fulfilled one of my greatest wishes? I've always imagined how wonderful it would be to have access to all of Playford's volumes. And I've always wanted to teach other people to dance like you."

I got to my feet, hugged her tightly and gave her a kiss. "You are our guardian angel. Thank you for your trust. We won't let you down."

She solemnly handed me the second key to the chest.

"I'll guard it like the apple of my eye, Seraphia! Thank you so much!"

We immediately discussed which of the generally popular dances we should rehearse with our customers as soon as possible. Seraphia then showed me a few dances with very catchy melodies that I was not yet familiar with.

"Have you danced them all at some point?"

"You'll laugh, during our training, our ballet troupe set their minds on dancing through them all once. I think we actually pretty much managed it. We were helped by two musician friends who could sight-read everything and also knew a lot of the unnotated dances from other sources." She bent down again and reached into another part of the chest.

"Here, take these with you and learn the dances. These are the latest contra dances[133] that are currently popular in the country. You have to know them, of course."

It was a pack of handwritten and printed notes or booklets, some with drawings of the dance figures and precise descriptions. It also said which piece of music the dance had been choreographed to.

In recent decades, more and more well-known melodies from popular operas had found their way into the dance halls of Europe. All self-respecting composers composed dances to increase their own popularity and not limit their work to the opera house or concert hall.

---

133 *Translated "dance against each other". Two couples face each other and dance figures together – in periods of 8 bars.*

Dancing mistress

Our parents still needed the support of Christoph and me. We wrote letters, made connections, drafted or checked contracts and also made sure that everything around our home ran as usual. Mamma was usually with Pappa.

Nevertheless, the very next week we had our first dance lesson in a house of a Reichenhall's citizen. There were seven children there who were to be introduced to dance. We started the first session with the basic steps. It went remarkably quickly because our students all wanted to learn. I suspected that at the beginning they wanted to get rid of us quickly. They all had a remarkably good sense of rhythm.

This meant we could quickly try out a few simple circle dances with our basic steps. I realised that the girls and boys were enjoying it more and more. As there were four girls and three boys, I usually played my pochette and Christoph danced along so that there were enough of us. From time to time, I also sat down at the pianoforte in the practice room. When we performed something, Christoph and I did it as a couple.

The following week we tried out the first Anglaise[134] with our students.

"No, no, the lady is opposite." I instructed. "There is a ladies' row and a men's row. These two rows are opposite each other."

It took a while for everyone to understand.

"Yes, just like that. I am the orchestra. Top of the line is here with me. Now the first four form a circle. The pair closest to me is pair one. All the others join in one by one as pair two. Who is pair one? Hands up."

Surprisingly, the right couple came forward.

---

134 *Anglaise, which is danced in a long double row. The men stand opposite the women. There are always 4 or 6 people in a set. With each round or verse, the couples move forward one place, so that new dance couples meet again and again.*

"Exactly. You dance downwards. The others are the pairs number two. They dance upwards. The pair number two that has reached the top pauses once and then dances back down as pair one. The same applies to the pair of one that has reached the bottom. After a pause, it dances back up as pair two. As soon as the first pair number one has reached the top again as the second pair, the dance is over."

Seven pairs of expectant eyes were fixed on me.

"That's why everyone will not only remember what they have to do, but also what the other couple is doing in the meantime."

The eyes of many a pupil widened.

"It's not that bad, we're taking it slowly now. Step by step. First, we'll do everything in the current set-up. Then we'll change positions and practise again."

Christoph and I showed steps and figures.

"What, I'm supposed to dance this *hand tour* with a gentleman?" grumbled one of the lads.

"If you never want to shake hands with another gentleman or dance a *dos-a-dos* with him, then you should give up dancing right now and perhaps specialise in hunting or astronomy. The fact is that we act with both sexes. Fencing is also similar to dancing with an opponent. You wouldn't chicken out there either, would you?

As long as we dance with dignity, this will not jeopardise our position in society or any existing respect for us. Louis XIV was a passionate dancer and a great ruler."

The boy was somewhat mollified and stayed in his seat. The dancing continued.

After a while, I interrupted. "Please, gentlemen, more poise with the reference. You look like wet sacks that someone has hung over the wall to dry." A giggle shook the youngsters. "You bend your upper bodies forwards without making a hump. And the ladies may bend their knees, but not like a servant. Keep your back straight! Otherwise a lady might be mistaken for her chambermaid. You must look dignified."

Our pupils also learnt the Anglaise quite quickly. So quickly, in fact, that they were keen to show their parents the progress they had already made. So a request was made via the majordomo to see if they were willing to attend a short performance. They came and watched their children's progress with an increasingly proud expression.

"Oh, how well our children can dance already! It looks very sublime, I think." The lady of the house clapped after the performance and beamed.

"These two young people managed to turn our wild bunch into well-mannered dancers surprisingly quickly. I would never have thought that."

Turning to us, the gentleman added: "You have pleasantly surprised me. We will continue to use your services and recommend you to others." He then addressed Christoph: "How is your father doing?"

Christoph spoke to him while I had a brief chat with the lady of the house. We had done a good job.

My brother and I walked home in high spirits. We were on foot as it wasn't very far.

"Sister, your playing on the pianoforte is getting better and better!"

"And your reference would be worthy of an emperor. You look very good when you dance. If you weren't my brother, I might even fall in love with you."

He grinned.

"We got a letter of recommendation from the landlord. Isn't that marvellous? I'm very happy about this."

We presented this letter of recommendation to Father just one week later. Apparently, the voices of our young pupils had been included. Because it was truly a document that reflected the joy of participating in our lessons. I had the impression that father was proud, although he didn't say anything about it.

Ancient philosophers

Father had always had new publications from some philosophers sent to him.

A parcel arrived with a book by Johann Gottfried Herder entitled *Auch eine Philosophie der Geschichte zur Bildung der Menschheit*[135]. I immediately pounced on it and read it to my father in the evening.

At the same time, I had my thoughts on the scholarly texts. I had to agree with Mr Herder's statement about Egypt:

"... Now an industry arose such as the blessed, idle hut dweller, the pilgrim and stranger on earth, had not known: arts invented that he neither needed nor felt the desire to use. ..."

During my time in München, I had seen how the shops were piled high with things that made no sense to me and which, in my opinion, our world simply didn't need.

"... The world became wider: the human race more united and closer. With trade, a lot of arts developed, a whole new artistic instinct in particular, for advantage, comfort, opulence and splendour! ..."

For some paragraphs, I wondered how they would be read in a hundred years' time, for example. Would we still be able to agree with Herder's text or would everything be completely different by that time?

As I realised that Pappa was getting rather tired of the text, I picked up a work by Christoph Martin Wieland that we both already knew and enjoyed again: *Musarion oder Die Philosophie dr Grazien*[136]. It also featured a few philosophers who acted in a surprisingly human way.

Father and I enjoyed these hours. And it was a relief for mamma to know that she had undisturbed time for business work or for her violin.

---

135 *A Philosophy of History for the Education of Mankind*
136 *Musarion or The Philosophy of the Graces*

In those days, I came across an article in an old magazine that amused my father greatly. It told of a Frenchman who had lived about two hundred years ago and was the personal physician of a cardinal. He travelled with this cardinal to Holland and Italy and was thus on several seashores, where he loved to observe sea creatures. Among other things, Guillaume Rondelet told of a shark in whose stomach a complete suit of armour was found.

"What do you think, Father: was the knight himself there when the armour found its way into the shark's mouth? And did Rondelet also find the knight's bones?"

Father chuckled to himself.

I laughed. "But unfortunately the text doesn't reveal that. Perhaps the owner of the armour was already digested." I laughed.

We speculated for hours about which century and which country the armour could have been from and how old and tall the knight it belonged to must have been. Which helmet might it have been wearing? What did the gloves look like? Did the kneepads have spikes or not?

We also speculated about the type and size of the shark. We only knew that there were different species from quite handy to very large, but neither of us had ever seen a shark before. We had a lot of fun.

Father solemnly presented me with a contract stating that he would gradually pay me back the money from my allowance and the rental of my palace. Of course, I don't have to have it all back, but I think it's very decent of him to have done this. After all, it would give me a lot of peace of mind if I had some money at my disposal again.

A visitor

Then Frederik arrived with us. I gave him a big hug as he was led into the parlour.

"Vic! I'm so glad to see you!" Frederik hugged me tightly. He placed a kiss on my cheek.

Mamma looked a little piqued at first.

"Victoria, did you know about this visit?"

"Yes, mamma. Everything is ready. Frederik doesn't want to experience any culinary marvels here, he wants to visit me. He's aware of the somewhat tense situation. I told you about his letter."

"I've asked Vic not to say anything to anyone so there's no fuss about me." Frederik said.

Mamma stood up and offered him her hands. "You are very welcome, Mr von Barby. And thank you again for the money you gave us from your winnings. It helps us immensely."

"Thank you for your kind welcome, Madame von Sommerauer."

"Mother, please forgive me for taking Frederik away from you again. Come on, I'll show you my mare that I've always raved about. And you absolutely must see the little one. He's been sold, but we still have him here in training. The gelding is such a wonderful horse. He's brought us a lot of money. You'll love him, the rascal."

Mamma looked at me reprovingly. "But Vic, why don't you give your visitor a rest first?"

"Thank you, Mrs von Sommerauer. But, that's all right. I'm so happy to see Vic again that I don't even want to rest now." Frederik bowed respectfully to my mamma.

I pulled Frederik behind me and he was amused by this attempt.

I stopped between the house and the stable. "I'm sorry I'm not even letting you catch your breath. But I'm bursting with curiosity. You and Krümmelbein?"

"Yes, me and Andreas. I've freed him from that unspeakable sailor's undergrowth that some people call a beard. He looks stunning. I wanted to keep him company because he was alone in a strange city. The first thing I did was drag him to the barber. We had a long and intense chat. Within the first few days, I was pleased to realise that I had found a new friend. I then fitted him with Jacob's clothes. He looks classy in them. Almost as stunning as Jacob himself.

"I helped him negotiate with a few people you had already written to and introduced him to new customers. That helped a lot to establish a basis of trust that he would never have gained on his own.

"At some point in the second week, I noticed how he kept looking at me. I asked him why he was doing that and he replied that he always liked looking at beautiful people. And suddenly we were lying in each other's arms and kissing.

"Later, I told him about Jacob. He said that he had always admired you, but now, with his new knowledge of you, he almost worshipped you. He agreed that I could tell you – and only you – about us. At first he didn't want to, but I convinced him that I could never keep such a development a secret from my best friend. I am happy. Even if we won't see each other for a while."

"I'm so happy for you, dear Frederik." With that, I joined him and we walked the rest of the way to the stables. He was delighted with our horses and asked to ride the little one, which I of course allowed him to do.

Frederik and I had a little race in the meadows of the river Saalach and he was entranced by our young horse.

"I was almost tempted to buy him. I hope he ends up in good hands. A horse like that is like a life insurance policy. The boy wants to please at all costs and reacts very sensitively."

A few days later, I rode into town with Christoph and Frederik. There met up with numerous acquaintances. Some of them, who weren't part of our close circle of friends, hadn't seen me since before my wedding to Jacob and brought me up to date with their lives. However, the most interesting news we heard was not from the city, but that the French King Louis XV had died on 10 May.

"And on the very same day, his grandson Louis XVI was proclaimed king. He was married to this Austrian woman, a daughter of Maria Theresa. I can't think of her name right now." Frederik said.

I laughed. "You can't remember anything, can't you? That's Maria Antonia or Marie Antoinette, as she calls herself now."

"Yes, that's right, that's her name, the emperor's daughter, who will now probably become queen of France."

We gossiped and laughed a lot and in the evening we attended a small, private ball together.

It was a wonderful time with Frederik. His new love gave him renewed vigour and he radiated a joy that I had last seen in him the morning before Jacob's death. I was also happy for our Mr Krümmelbein. He had always had a somewhat sad expression in his eyes, which I had noticed. I was sure that this had also changed with the new situation.

Although Christoph and I had a few dance lessons to give, we still had enough time for fun with Frederik and other friends.

We held a dance afternoon with friends, customers and neighbours, which was also attended by the Mozart siblings.

Wolfgang stormed in some time before the start. "I've composed a marvellous dance. Vic and Christoph, I need suitable figures for it. Not too easy, please!"

We immediately set about creating a choreography, which we enjoyed.

We practised a few lesser-known dances in addition to Wolfgang's piece. The hours passed far too quickly. Frederik's stay was also coming to an end.

Hellbrunn Stone Theatre

After two weeks of his visit, Frederik invited Christoph and me on a special excursion. There was a public opera evening in the Stone Theatre at Schloss Hellbrunn. The opera *L'infedeltà delusa* by Joseph Haydn was to be performed.

We had ridden to Salzburg the day before to visit our relatives and continued on to Schloss Hellbrunn in the morning. Frederik had a good friend from his student days among the court party. This man had originally invited him and at Frederik's request he was allowed to bring us along.

The Archbishop himself was not expected there until a few days later, as he still had business in the city. So it was an informal crowd that was hanging around when we arrived at Hellbrunn.

Frederik's friend, Willibald von Dachsbeck, welcomed us in front of the castle at lunchtime. Our horses were handed over to the stable lads and Frederik introduced us to his friend.

"Willi, here are my good friends Victoria, Countess Dowager von Falkenstein, and her brother Christoph von Sommerauer."

"Welcome to Schloss Hellbrunn! I've been hoping to welcome you here for a long time, Frederik. We haven't seen each other for years."

"I'm visiting the von Sommerauers and thought I'd take advantage of the opportunity. Since you raved so much about the Stone Theatre and my friends also love new experiences, I'm all the more pleased that we can all be here together."

After a small snack, we walked through the area of the trick fountains, which were created around 150 years ago by Archbishop Markus Sittikus. We were joined by a few of Willi's friends. It was quite a fun group.

Our new acquaintance had a lot to say about the marvels that a long-dead genius had devised here.

I quote the next lines from my letter to Aunt Seraphia.

First of all, Willi led us from the palace park to an extraordinary mechanical theatre, which was commissioned by Archbishop Andreas Jakob Graf Dietrichstein and built between 1748 and 1752. We stood in front of it and marvelled for a long time at the many details of this marvel of craftsmanship.

Various craftsmen were shown at work. They sawed, hammered, slaughtered and much more. We also saw soldiers and people from different classes, from farmers to nobles. There was always something new to discover in this amazingly large theatre, where so much is going on.

"There are 141 movable and 52 immovable figures. So you don't need to count. I had a long chat with the man who maintains the mechanics. It's like clockwork, with lots of cogwheels, wires and water wheels. He showed me the back of it. Simply fascinating," explained Willi.

To drown out the noise of the drive waterworks, the theatre also plays an organ. You can choose from three pieces by the court music director Johann Ernst Eberlin. Truly a masterpiece of mechanics. I couldn't get enough of this sight. We really did stand there like little children, wide-eyed in front of a stall selling the most beautiful toys.

But now onwards ... the rest of the area with the water features is also extremely interesting. There are five smaller grottoes with water machines with the themes of crafts and mythology.

Then, there are a few larger grottos. In my opinion, the Vogelsanggrotte[137] is quite magical. Three different bird calls can be heard there in a deceptively realistic way. They are created by water and dry whistles. But the Neptune Grotto with the grimace rolling its eyes and a long tongue sticking out towards its nose is also marvellous. And I love the Midas Grotto, where a jet of water lifts a golden crown and holds it aloft.

---

137 *bird singing grotto*

Willi is now very familiar with the mechanics there and here and there we were surprised by sudden fountains that he set in motion. Water even sprayed towards us from the tips of the antlers of the deer heads that adorn the entrances. But as it was a very warm day, it was all joy and laughter.

Now that I thought I knew Willi's sense of humour and that of the builder, I was careful not to sit down at the princely table. I avoided the onset of sunstroke and headed for the shade. As it happened, I was the only one of our illustrious group who didn't have a wet backside when we left the area. ...

Towards evening, we walked to the Stone Theatre with a few servants carrying baskets of food and drinks to watch the opera performance. As the plot is set in Tuscany, the location of the performance was just perfect. I also found it refreshing to see an opera that didn't feature any gods. It was a treat for the eyes and ears.

Meanwhile, we spectators enjoyed a cosy meal and the warm summer evening. Only the little midges became a real nuisance at the end, as we made our way back to the castle in the slowly fading light along torch-lit paths between the meadows. Some of us loked like they were participating in a grotesque dance as they tried to swat at the insects. It amused me so much that I almost didn't pay attention to how many bloodsuckers were attacking me. In the end, it wasn't as bad as I thought it would be.

The last of the twilight brought the three men and me past the archbishop's wildlife garden to the episcopal summer residence in Anif[138]. Willi was a guest there and had arranged for us to spend the night. It is a rather simple building. I wouldn't have called it a castle.

We were met by a handsome gentleman our age. "Welcome to Schloss Anif. Willi, I'm delighted that you've found your way here after all – and that you're bringing such nice guests with you!"

---

138 Today, Anif moated castle looks more like a dream made of icing. Unfortunately, it
is privately owned and not open for public.

The two hugged each other warmly and patted each other on the back, as men like to do.

"Good evening, dear Konrad. Yes, I'm glad to finally see you again, old friend. I've brought my dear friend Frederik from Barby with me. I think you still remember him? Victoria, Countess Dowager of Falkenstein, was the wife of his best friend Jacob. And here we have Christoph von Sommerauer, Vic's twin brother.

Friends, this is Konrad von Ehrenfels, who keeps things running here. We know each other from university in Ingolstadt. However, he studied medicine and I studied philosophy. We used to go for a drink together now and again. It was always a lot of fun with him!"

"Don't believe everything he says! Willi likes to tell stories. And not just philosophical ones."

"Yes, yes, but what you have to believe is the fact that you're facing three excellent lawyers right now. So pay attention, my dear. Vic is the woman who also studied in Ingolstadt at the time and who we regretfully never got to meet because we missed that damn ball ... remember, because of that foaling mare I was supposed to help you with. I think you were already more focussed on animals back then."

Konrad laughed. "Maybe, my friend, but the evening was very nice with all the stable lads and you had a fling with that chambermaid afterwards." Willi rolled his eyes and I had to control myself not to laugh.

Konrad now looked at the three of us curiously. His first surprised, then admiring gaze lingered on me for a long time.

"I've heard the wildest stories about you. People around Lake Chiemsee say that the Count and Countess of Falkenstein appeared unrecognised as street musicians in Endorf and encouraged everyone to dance. Is that true?"

I laughed. "Yes, that's true. It wasn't my idea, though. But, it was a marvellous evening!"

Konrad invited us inside the castle.

"Have you already eaten or would you like another snack?"

Willi answered for all of us. "I think we'll all be able to fit something in, despite the food in the theatre."

We were served a simple and wonderful evening meal of freshly baked bread with tender beef and various cheeses, accompanied by strawberries and an excellent Burgundy.

The room in which we were served looked cosy with the dark red wallpaper, and the table was just the right size for our company. The chairs were upholstered and very comfortable.

"Konrad, what is a doctor doing at the bishops' summer residence when the bishop isn't even here?" Frederik wondered.

"Oh, that's quite simple. I'm not only a doctor for people, but also for animals. After my studies in Ingolstadt, I did another one at the 'Lehrschule zur Heilung der Viehkrankheiten'[139] in Wien. The bishop has a personal physician who always has to be around him. I, on the other hand, am partly responsible for the people in the bishop's service and partly for his particularly valuable animals.

As we have both a sick steward and an injured hound here at the moment, I'm in Anif without my employer Ferdinand Christoph von Waldburg-Zeil until both have recovered. Until then, the whole court will probably be here. That's why it's good that you've come to visit at this time. I would hardly have been able to accommodate you here later and I wouldn't have had the time."

"I think it would be very interesting if you could treat people and animals in the same way and help them to feel better again. That must be a very satisfying thing, surely?" I was interested in Konrad's profession.

"Oh yes, it's very nice to see how things pick up again after an injury or illness. But unfortunately there are also

---

139 *School for healing of animal sicknes*

downsides. Like probably everyone, I don't like to see a creature die, but that comes with my job, to experience that.

I also have to save some animals from pain and decay myself. The worst experience for me so far was when I had to shoot my beloved hunting dog Brutus after he had been seriously injured by a wild boar."

I thought about Jacob and suddenly felt sad. Konrad immediately realised that my mood had changed.

"What's wrong with you, Vic? Did I say something wrong? I'm sorry if I hurt your delicate feelings with my description." Konrad looked at me, startled.

"It's not you and it's not the descriptions themselves. You couldn't have known that my husband was so badly injured by a wild boar attack that he died just minutes later. The memory still pains me. It was a terrible moment when we had to witness his death."

Konrad also turned pale. "If I had only suspected that ... I'm terribly sorry that I dragged this memory back into the light of day with my thoughtless remark. Please forgive me for making this faux pas."

Frederik, who was sitting to my left, took my hand on his side and gave it a friendly squeeze, then also spoke to Konrad. "Yes, it was a dark day for all of us. Jacob was my best friend since my student days. But how could you have known?"

I now had to occupy myself. As I had already seen a harpsichord standing in a corner, I pointed to it. "May I?"

"But of course, dear Vic. Especially if it helps you take your mind off things."

I sat down at the instrument and played a funny tune that I had learnt from Nannerl. Then I tuned into another student song and sang along with the words. For the next half hour, the men stood around me and we sang some of the old songs together, which reminded us of our student days in Ingolstadt.

It turned out to be a very nice evening and Konrad told us about some funny adventures with animals.

"So I'm sitting on the bench in the sun after the strenuous treatment of a labourer who has half severed his hand with a saw, when suddenly a large dog darts round the corner. Before I can even react, it sits on my lap and licks my face. So I'm sitting there in shock with a dog weighing about 130 pounds[140] on my lap. I try to fend him off somehow as a boy runs in my direction and keeps shouting "Kuno, Kuno!".

As he stands in front of me, he pulls the dog off me. ‚I'm sorry, sir. Kuno can smell blood from at least twenty *Klafter*[141] away.‘ He looks at me and grins. ‚At least your face is completely clean now. Even if your clothes aren't.‘ He walks away again, scolding the bloodhound."

We laughed as we visualised the situation.

Christoph and I talked about our study experiences and Frederik about his last encounter with his brother. Willi had a few amusing stories from the Salzburg court to contribute.

We all went to bed late, full and satisfied.

As the gentlemen were not yet up when I reached the ground floor in the morning, I took a short walk around the garden and was completely enchanted by my surroundings. Konrad soon joined me. I felt very comfortable in his presence.

He showed me a few beautiful corners with a pavilion, a small pond, a hidden bench here, a tree with a swing there.

"Vic, I don't want to seem intrusive, but I'd love to know if I could come and visit you sometime. I'm glad to have met you all. It's so wonderful to have people around who you can talk to about anything and who have a similar sense of humour to you."

I nodded. "We would be delighted to welcome you as our guest."

Just then we heard Willi's call. He came towards us. "We don't want to have breakfast without you, but we don't

---

140 One pound was about 360 grams back then
141 A bavarian Klafter or 6 feet was 1.751155 metres.

want the eggs to get cold either. Come on, you two. The garden won't run away within the next hour."

Just when things were getting interesting, he had to interrupt us. Always the same! After a hearty breakfast, we rode back home. Willi and Konrad accompanied us as far as Berchtolsgaden. So we still had some time to chat. But Konrad and I didn't manage to continue our conversation. I did, however, tell him our address and how he could find us.

Dining alfresco

Just a few days later, we went on a trip. Willi and Konrad were also invited. Frederik was driven by me in the chaise[142], Christoph rode alongside with Willi and Konrad. In beautiful summer weather, we travelled in this formation to Reichenhall.

As both Christoph and I are fascinated by the two graduation houses on the Traunfeld, which are connected by a footbridge, we naturally showed them to our visitors. They were also absolutely entranced by the sixty-five-foot-high[143] structure, which is about fifty *Ruten*[144] long. I found the air there very pleasant, especially in summer. In my opinion, it was a bit like the air in Hamburg harbour. A little humid and aromatic-salty.

The graduation houses here were built to save energy. The salt content of the brine was increased by the water trickling down the blackthorn branches, saving the boiling process, which required a lot of wood.

---

142 *Lightweight, two-seater carriage with movable half canopy.*
143 *1 Bavarian foot = 0.2918592 metre*
144 *1 Ruthe = 10 feet = 2.918592 metres*

Our friends Katharina and Michael Tonhauser also joined us in a chaise in the direct neighbourhood of the graduation works, at the former Achselmanstein Castle, which had housed a cotton embroidery for a few years. Michael was a lieutenant colonel with his own battalion and was on home leave.

Together we drove and rode on to Marzoll, where the Lasser zu Lasseregg family had invited us to dine *alfresco*[145].

But first, our hosts and a couple from the Gmoa[146] wanted to join us on a short ride to the outskirts of Salzburg. Everything was green and colourful. The most beautiful flowers were blooming everywhere in the meadows. It was a simply marvellous summer. At Marzoll, instead of the intense smell of wild garlic in spring, we could smell the freshly cut grass wafting from the meadows.

On our return, we were welcomed in the courtyard of Marzoll Castle[147]. A few servants took care of our horses and we were led into the castle garden, where a marvellous array of food was waiting for us on a meadow between the fruit trees. There were various types of meat, roasted vegetables, bread, cheese, small cakes and fruit. We settled down and each received a glass of champagne from a liveried servant. It all looked so stylish.

We feasted and laughed. At some point, I jumped up and took my pochette out of the chaise. As I re-entered the orchard, I played a dance. Everyone jumped up and the Lassers clapped their hands enthusiastically.

"What a wonderful idea! That's exactly what we needed. Let's dance!"

We danced anglaises and quadrilles, but also dances for six people, such as *Upon a summers day*, which we all loved dancing.

---

145 *Outdoor dining. The term picnic was only coined later.*
146 *Today, the Gmoa is divided into two parts: the Austrian village Großgmain and the Bavarian Bayerisch Gmain.*
147 *The castle is private property now and not open for the public.*

It was a wonderful afternoon. Such days with friends are truly a gift. We danced long-known dances and practised new dances with great pleasure.

After almost three weeks, our friend Frederik travelled back to München and invited Christoph and me to visit and stay with him.

"Now that you've rented out your townhouse, you'll need company for a visit. I hope that doesn't put you off, Vic. I've really enjoyed my time here with you, my friends. Thank you for your hospitality."

"Hospitality is good. You got the simplest food and gave us money, too. Thank you my friend. You are deeply rooted in my heart." I hugged Frederik and laid my head on his chest.

Our mamma also said a very fond farewell to Frederik. He had been so attentive and had also helped her with Dad's business. She and father had also taken my polite and lovable friend to their hearts.

I was sitting comfortably in the garden under the shade of an oak tree, reading. After a while, father came to me. He had been using a stick to walk more safely since his illness, but at least he was able to move around independently again.

He sat down next to me. "You want to read, don't you?" It sounded a bit like an apology because he was disturbing me in my solitude.

"No, Father, the book won't run away from me. If you have something interesting to tell me, I'll gladly put it down and listen to you."

"Hm, I'll have to think about that first." Pappa was silent for a few minutes while I waited.

"I don't think I ever told you that I once met a real Moor."

I put the book on my lap. "Really? No, you haven't told me that yet. When and where was that?"

"It was on a trip to Halle around 1745. I was still a young lad and had been taken along by my uncle. When he had an important meeting with a general there, he told me to wait in the park. I met the man there. He had dark brown skin from top to bottom and black curly hair. He sat down next to me on the bench and introduced himself to me when I apologised for staring at him so cheekily.

"The man's name was Anton Wilhelm Amo and he was a very learned man. He came from Ghana in Africa and could speak at least five foreign languages. Amo studied philosophy and liberal arts and even gained a doctorate. A very pleasant person. Unfortunately, he had an appointment of his own and left me very soon."

"That fits in perfectly with what Seraphia told me. She learnt from a friend in London that last year she attended a literary meeting at a high house in London where an African woman who writes poetry was a guest. Phillis Wheatley[148] enjoyed a very good education in Boston in America and now wants to publish more of her poetry, she was told."

"Which in turn shows us that, contrary to popular belief, black people and women are also intelligent and, with the right education, very educated people."

We sat in pleasant silence under the oak tree for a while and waited to be called to dinner.

The letter

Almost two weeks after our last trip with Frederik and our friends, a letter arrived. It was addressed to Christoph.

148 *The first African-American woman poet to have her work published.*

When he opened it – still at the breakfast table – a second letter fell out. That wasn't unusual, because every now and then each of us received letters containing a second one for another family member.

Only the sender was remarkable in this case. It was Konrad von Ehrenfels. He thanked Christoph again for the invitation to the trip and said that he had really enjoyed the excursion with our friends. He had felt very much at home in the group.

The letter to me amazed me.

Dearest Victoria,

I was very impressed by you the first time we met in Anif. But now, after our second meeting with your friends, I can't stop thinking about you. In my eyes, you are a beautiful woman and a simply wonderful person. The fact that you don't conform to the image of women who are treated as role models by society is very refreshing and I think it's one of the most important reasons why I feel attracted to you.

I know you have made it clear to me that you are not interested in a steady relationship with a man – at least for the time being. I accept that and, therefore, humbly ask if there is room for another good friend at your side? I would be honoured to call myself your and Christoph's friend.

Please allow me to invite you and your brother to a ball at his summer residence in Anif, which the bishop is organising in September. It is a masked ball to the theatre play "A Midsummer Night's Dream" by the Englishman William Shakespeare. Do you know it?

I would be very happy if you would come. In any case, I'll be there dressed as Puck with a magical flower.

I have reserved two rooms for you in the inn near the castle. So please let me know as soon as possible if you are coming.

In deep reverence
Konrad von Ehrenfels

I told Christoph that Konrad had invited us to the ball. He was immediately hooked. Above all, he liked the theme of the ball.

"It's one of my favourite plays. Even if I've only read it so far. You like it too, don't you, sister? Besides, if you like Konrad even a little, you can't disappoint this lovesick man. He's adored you since we first met."

Christoph clearly knew more than I did. As quickly as I realise when someone I know is in love, I'm pretty insensitive when it comes to myself.

Yes, I liked Konrad. He was an interesting person. He had a sense of humour and also liked to dance. He was also an excellent fencer. I could still learn a lot from him. And I definitely wanted to.

"Yes, I'd like to go. Will you text him that we're coming?"

"Of course, sister. I wouldn't want you to be the talk of the town."

Almer pilgrimage

On 24 August[149] – day of St. Bartholomäus[150] – the annual Alm pilgrimage took place on the Hirschau peninsula in Königssee. There was a big mass for all pilgrims, at which we were asked to play music. Important dignitaries from Baiern and Salzburg were invited by the prince provost[151] Franz Anton Josef von Hausen-Gleichenstorff and they had of course been guests at the hunting lodge next to church of Sankt Bartholomäus for a few days.

So we arrived in Schönau am Königssee on Tuesday and spent the night in a guest house assigned to us by our cli-

---

149 *The pilgrimage is – at least for now – always on the Saturday after 24 August.*
150 *St Bartholomew's Day*
151 *Berchtesgaden was a princely provostry. The sovereign united spiritual and secular power.*

ent. In the evening, we took a walk along the shore of Lake Königssee and looked for the spots with the best views of the lake. The atmosphere was wonderful and the evening was balmy.

On Wednesday morning, a bright summer's day, we went to the landing stage with our instruments.

A boat was already waiting for us there to take us across. The whole mountain massif that surrounds the Königssee is highly impressive. On one side is the mountain Jenner, on the other, behind Bartholomäus, our destination, towers the east face of the mountain Watzmann[152] and at its foot the Eiskapelle[153].

As a human being, I felt extremely small and vulnerable on this large and deep lake in the middle of these mighty mountains. I wonder what the lake looks like from up there? You certainly have a magnificent view of the sunrise and sunset over the Alps from the peak of the Watzmann[154].

Mamma and Christoph also sat in the boat, which was rowed by two Schönau fishermen, in amazement.

Although I had already seen the lake, I had never been on it before and when the pilgrimage chapel of St Bartholomew came into view, I was enchanted.

"Look, Christoph, isn't the church impressive against this mountain backdrop?"

"Yes, marvellous! Look at the ensemble. The building has two different onion domes! I like that."

I turned to our rowers.

"Do you know more about the pilgrimage taking place today?"

One of them nodded and gave us some information.

"This pilgrimage has been around since 1635, my grandmother said. It was founded by citizens of Salzburg as thanks for surviving the plague. The pilgrims come from

---

152 *The middle Watzmann peak (2713 m above sea level) is the highest point in the German part of the Berchtesgaden Alps.*

153 *Ice Chapel – it's a permanent ice field. It is getting smaller over the last years.*

154 *The first ascent of the Watzmann was in August 1800.*

Maria Alm in Pinzgau over the Funtensee and through the Steinerne Meer. The route is very strenuous. I think they are travelling for around ten hours.

Grandmamma also knew that in the early days of the pilgrimage, pilgrims crossed the lake and then walked on to the church in Dürrnberg. But on 23 August 1688, over 70 pilgrims drowned while crossing the Königssee. That is why the final destination of the pilgrimage has been St Bartholomäus ever since."

Mamma felt sorry for the drowned people. "Oh dear, so many people!"

"It was certainly very tragic, but it was a long time ago," our skipper reassured us.

"If you have the time, you should go to the forest chapel of St John and Paul. It's also very beautiful – and only a quarter of an hour's walk from Bartholomew in the direction of the ice chapel."

This time Christoph was curious. "Thank you very much for this information. But what is the ice chapel again?"

"The ice chapel is the name given to a large field of snow that does not melt even in summer. There is always a large cavity in it, which is why it is called a chapel. But please be careful, because it is not without danger. It's better to look at it from a healthy distance."

Mamma turned to us. "Children, we're very early and if the Prince Provost doesn't have another task for us, we can go to this chapel of St John and St Paul first. What do you think?"

Christoph and I are always up for a detour of some kind.

The two skippers were also fishermen. They wanted to pick us up again later in the day. We said goodbye to them and first went to the church of St Bartholomäus.

The large meadow in front was already teeming with people. And you could see that more were still arriving. So these were the pilgrims from Maria Alm. A little further back, we saw a lot of different vendors selling their wares. Mainly fish and bread from the people from Schönau, but also beer and other drinks, small relics, rosaries and crosses. I also thought I spotted a shoemaker who must have had a lot of work to do with the walkers' shoes.

We were greeted at the church by a servant of the Prince Provost, who immediately approached Mother.

"I hope you rested well and had a quiet crossing, Madame. I'll show you round."

The man showed us the gallery where we were to play and had also prepared a jug of water and cups for us.

"You still have more than enough time before the mass. Do you need anything else?"

We were shown the premises where we could relieve ourselves and told him about our plan to visit the small chapel briefly. So the man sent for a boy called Sepperl to accompany us.

"Sepperl, these are our musicians. Please take them to St John and Paul. They want to see the chapel. And no big detours, do you hear? The ladies and the gentleman mustn't be late for mass, otherwise it could be bad for you."

The bright boy skipped happily along the path in front of us. It was a beautiful path through a forest. After only a short distance, we reached our destination. The chapel is quite beautiful, but also small.

Very close to the chapel, Sepperl showed us four springs. "We call them fever springs. The old people say that their water has healing powers. I can't say whether that's true. I've never experienced a miracle. Haven't been ill either. But the water tastes good."

Even without a miracle, we savoured the fresh spring water. It did what Sepperl had promised. After a short prayer in the chapel, we went back to fulfil our mission at mass.

Before we were sailed back across the Königssee by the same fishermen, we were treated to a delicious meal in an adjoining room of the hunting lodge.

We spent another night in Schönau and saddled the horses for the ride home the next day.

At the Chiemsee

Most families were at their summer residences or visiting relatives during the summer. So, we hardly had any clients for dance lessons. Christoph had a client in München that he was supposed to see. So, we both decided to travel to München for a few days. This way I could visit Frederik again.

We sent our suitcases by post and rode behind with a little luggage ourselves. I rode in a gentleman's saddle with a very wide skirt. Because if I have to sit in a side saddle for long distances, I get back pain.

What is demanded of us women just for the sake of propriety is, in my opinion, outrageous. At Lake Chiemsee, we stopped in the village of Prien, which was founded by my late husband's ancestors.

My brother rented two rooms in the inn there for an overnight stay. That evening, Christoph and I were sitting in the parlour when a young girl brought the food. She looked at me, curtseyed deeply and stammered "Madame, it's good to see you well. We miss you and our master, your late husband, very much. His brother is very different from him. He was only here once, very briefly. We are afraid of him."

Fortunately, I remembered her face. She had also served in the large manor house when I had visited it with Jacob and Frederik.

"Thank you. Oh dear, I'm afraid I can't remember your name. Yes, I miss my husband a lot, too."

"Of course you don't remember my name. You only saw me briefly back then. My name is Kathi."

I pointed to Christoph. "My brother, Christoph von Sommerauer, is accompanying me to München, where I hope to meet up with a few friends from my time as a married woman."

Kathi curtseyed to Christoph, who smiled at her. "You gave a doll to my little sister Liesl when you visited with your husband and his nice friend because she cried so much when our mamma died. Liesl still has the doll with her all the time and loves her dearly. Thank you very much again, Madame."

"Yes, now I remember: the little sister Liesl, a very pretty and lovely child. If you get another visit from Leopold, the new count, please remember that he pursues all girls and women who are pretty. He probably promises a lot, but it is unlikely that he keep any of it. And I am very sure that he will take whatever he wants without consent. I recommend avoiding being alone in a room with him.

"If a girl becomes pregnant – no matter from which man, who does not want to or cannot marry her and she loses the position, then I can probably help her with a new position somewhere else. But also, if any of you have a legal problem, just get in touch with us. I can normally be found in Reichenhall with the von Sommerauer family." I gave her my card.

"Thank you, Madame. I'll remember it and tell everyone else too." She curtseyed again and slipped the card into her pocket.

At that moment, the landlady called gruffly for Kathi. She was already tapping one foot impatiently. Kathi ran past her and whispered something to her.

I waved to the landlady. "I'm sorry for keeping Kathi from her work," I called out. She then bowed briefly and withdrew.

Coffee house

We arrived in München the next evening, where we were warmly welcomed by Frederik. It was a pleasure to see him again.

After a pleasant night's sleep, our host was full of energy.

"Come along, dear friends, we'll first show ourselves around the city together and then we'll go for a cup of cocoa in the courtyard garden under the arcades! A Venetian has recently been granted a licence to sell coffee, chocolates, lemonades and other wonderful 'refraichissements'. You'll see that there are some marvellous things there[155]."

We did the round on foot, as he suggested. All three of us really enjoyed walking. I personally thought it was an imposition on the horses if you only rode a few houses further and then stopped again. And we had to stop often enough on foot because we kept bumping into people that one of us knew and with whom we could at least exchange a few polite words.

We met a slim man with fluid movements, who was probably about Frederik's age and I liked him straight away.

Frederik was delighted to see him and introduced him to us.

"This is Andreas Dominikus Zaupser. He has just been appointed Expeditor[156] and Court Councillor[157]. I have already told you about his book *Bedenken über einige Punkte des Criminalrechts*[158], which he published last year. Very informative. You really must read it. By the way, my friend Andreas is also working on an *Idioticon*[159] *des Bairischen in*

---

155 *The founder of the current "Tambosi" on Odeonsplatz was the electoral lottery collector Giovanni Pietro Sarti from Venice, known as Pantalon*

156 *An employee in the office of a public authority who was responsible for recording and registering correspondence and much more.*

157 *Associate judge of a court*

158 *Concerns about some points of the criminal law*

159 *Former term for dictionary – description of an idiom, in this case for 3 administrative regions of Bavaria with different dialects.*

Ober- und Niederbaiern sowie der Oberpfalz. I'm really looking forward to that!"

Andreas looked at Christoph. "I suppose you're a lawyer, too, Mr von Sommerauer?"

Frederik beamed at us all. "We are all lawyers. Victoria also graduated in Ingolstadt. She puts many of our colleagues in the shade when it comes to logic and accuracy."

Astonishment and definitely doubt were on Zaupser's face. "In that case, I would like to have a word with you, Madame."

"Only in that case? To test me? To see if my poor female spirit is really emulating the divine male one? You're too kind, Mr Zaupser." I couldn't help but react snappishly.

He actually took a step back at my attack. "Madame seems very belligerent to me ..."

Frederik interrupted him. "With good reason. Vic is understandably tired of being constantly belittled as a woman, as if she wasn't an independent thinker like us men. She doesn't need to be scrutinised. She's brilliant. You can take my word for it. After all, I've known Vic for a few years."

Zaupser was a man of intelligence. But, it took him a few seconds to compose himself. "Please forgive me, Madame. It was not my intention to question you or your mental abilities, or even to put you on a lower level."

"I know you men are so used to never being confronted with female intelligence and only see women as a piece of jewellery or an annoyance at best, that you don't even think about the fact that it could be different from what you've always been told."

Things were obviously getting too hot for Frederik's acquaintance. He brought forward an important appointment, said goodbye and quickly left.

When we had separated again, Christoph put his hand on my arm. "He'd like to tear you apart, I could really see that in his eyes. I understand your resentment. But, we're not going to change that any time soon."

"You mean this boundless astonishment and the great doubt of all men who learn that Victoria has studied? To be honest, it's starting to annoy me too. After all, we know that women can be just as brilliant as men – if we give them the opportunity." Frederik was completely on my side.

I beamed at the two men. "Thank you for understanding me. That's worth a lot to me." I hooked up with both of them and we continued the round.

The bar in the courtyard garden delivered what Frederik had promised. I opted for a lemonade and was delighted with the fine, fruity flavour.

The next day, a visit from Frederik's friend Willi was announced. There was a big "Hello" when he appeared.

He had an invitation to a special soirée for us all. The overture to Georg Philipp Telemann's *Hamburg Admiralty Music* and a selection of Jean-Baptiste Lully's works were played there. I particularly enjoyed the *Marche Royal*. This piece is truly royal and I really love the horns and timpani.

Willi also had some news in his luggage. "Vic, as I've heard repeatedly, you've made a great impression on my friend Konrad. I think he'll do everything he can to see you again."

"Oh, really true?" Christoph acted bored. "He invited us to the Bishop of Chiemsee's ball at his estate in Anif."

After these wonderful days in München, we travelled back home and continued to give dance lessons in the region.

The bishop's ball

Christoph and I set off for Anif via Berchtolsgaden. It was still quite warm and the ride through the woods and past the fiefdoms in Bischofswiesen and Berchtolsgaden was beautiful. I am always amazed by the sleeping witch, which looks relatively the same from both sides of the mountain massif, and the completely different views of the Watzmann, which present themselves differently to the traveller from different angles. But the Untersberg, which we partly circumnavigated, also impresses me anew every time. Some of the trees already had autumn-coloured leaves.

"Oh, what a marvellous place we live in!"

"Yes, that's probably true. It's a privilege to be able to live in the middle of these mountains, lakes and rivers. When I think of Hamburg ... also beautiful, but all flat and lots of heathland. Well, our forests were certainly more beautiful when there wasn't so much deforestation. But the wood is urgently needed for salt boiling."

We saw a majestic stag strutting along a little away in front of us. Here and there, our horses flushed out a bird. Mostly quails or pheasants.

"Magdalena would like it here, I think. I should invite her. What do you think?"

"Please do that, Vic. She's a very pleasant person to talk to, at least. Not some no-good city trine. I'd like to know more about falconry. The last time I spoke to her, she told me more about it. You probably know all about it already. I actually envy you a little in that respect. You've been hunting with her and seen her falcons and the female eagle take game. I envy you that privilege." Christoph sounded almost envious.

Do I hear more than just a little interest in falconry? I decided to send Magdalena a specific invitation with my next letter.

We passed the rest of the journey by chatting and playing word games, as we always liked to do. We arrived in Anif in the afternoon and moved into our rooms.

After a good plate of stew, we lay down and rested for a few more hours.

Konrad had organised a local maid for me at my request. She helped me get dressed and did my hair perfectly. She was a real treasure. I would never have thought that this peasant maid had such a flair for everything and, above all, such expertise.

My costume for the ball on the theme of *A Midsummer Night's Dream* consisted of an older dress from my München days that Katharina had remodelled. The fabric was green, very light and I had delicate wings made from a wire frame covered with pale yellow fabric at the back and golden silk flowers in my hair. I also wore a delicate lace mask that only left my eyes and mouth exposed. So, I was the servant of the fairy queen.

Christoph went as an enchanted bottom with a papier-mâché donkey's head. He looked adorable – the donkey's head. Clearly not the most intelligent of grey animals. That was exactly my brother's idea of humour.

We entered the ballroom when it was about half full. An illustrious crowd had already gathered in the rather plain room with its ornately painted walls. We were immediately caught up in the cheerful atmosphere. Christoph had entered the room a few minutes before me and I was with a small group of ladies. That way we couldn't get mixed up. We would be dancing the third dance together anyway and until then we would look around and stroll a little.

I soon spotted Konrad near our host, the bishop. He was wearing an adventurous costume made of various fabrics with Renaissance-style powdered sleeves and matching, tight, two-coloured leggings. His mask showed a laughing elf and he held a large silk flower with different coloured petals in his hand and pretended to enchant a guest every now and then. That had to be him.

I noticed how his eyes kept wandering over the crowd. Maybe he was looking for us? I had written to him that I definitely wanted to keep the second and last dance on the programme free for him. So for the moment, I was still enjoying the fact that Konrad hadn't recognised either Christoph or me.

For the first dance, I was asked to dance by a somewhat chubby but cheerful Oberon. He was a surprisingly agile and good dancer with fluid movements. He wanted to find out who I was, but I just laughed and told him that he could see that I was a fairy. He had to be satisfied with that.

After the dance, he thanked me politely and asked for a later *Deutscher*, which I promised him.

Konrad was still standing there searching. I walked a small loop and approached him from the side.

"Master Puck, you promised me this dance, I believe."

Konrad turned towards me. Although I couldn't see much of his face, I noticed the joy he was radiating. "Yes, indeed, it is my pleasure. I am very pleased to see you, dear fairy." He offered me his hand and we joined the line of dancers.

There weren't many opportunities to talk at this dance, but Konrad sent me glances that told me a lot about his admiration, but also his desires. His touch completed the picture and I knew that I wanted to get to know this man better. Whether despite or because of his attraction to me, I couldn't say. I liked him, but I didn't really know how I felt about a closer relationship with him.

Although the dance lasted a really long time, it was over far too quickly for my liking. We arranged to meet for the next break in the punch corner.

Afterwards, I had a dance with Christoph, who, while we were waiting for the music to start, brought up Magdalena again. "Fortunately, I know that I can enjoy the dance because my partner is such a good dancer. My first dance was torture. The lady was so reserved that she didn't dare speak to me or really dance forwards. That's a pain in the arse. The second one was a bit too chatty for my taste. But it's all good now. It's a shame Magdalena isn't here. She would have loved it, too!"

"Oh, my dear Bottom, I'm really sorry about that. I had two good dancers and a lot of fun with them. And now I can completely relax again. I really enjoy it that way. You're right. Magdalena would certainly enjoy this ball. I hope she visits us soon."

"Are you going to invite her, sister?"

"She knows she's always welcome here, but I'll issue another specific invitation if that makes you feel better."

"Yes, please do that. She's the kind of woman I like because she's my equal. And I know you like her a lot, too." He leant towards my ear, which wasn't so easy with his mask. "I'd like Konrad too, by the way, sister."

We danced on, exhilarated.

Konrad was later my partner in a minuet. I enjoyed his closeness and the fact that he is such a good dancer.

The night was over far too quickly and when it was almost dawn, a carriage took us back to our accommodation, where we both fell contentedly into our beds.

Konrad had asked me to stop off briefly at the summer residence on our way home. He wanted to accompany us part of the way. We made him happy, which was also our pleasure. So we had pleasant conversations with a new and still very interesting friend until beyond Bischofswiesen.

##

Pappa was reading the latest monthly magazine and called me over. "Look!" And indeed, he had found a piece of news that had not yet reached us. Pope Clement XIV had died on 22 September. He had been ill since March.

"Who will follow now?" That was the biggest question in this case.

"One thing was good about Pope Clement." I suggested. "He also had women sing soprano parts in the churches and not just castrati[160], as many did before him. Women

---

160 *During his curatorship, around 4,000 boys were still castrated every year.*

were also allowed to perform on the Vatican stage again. I give him credit for that. So he wasn't the worst pope we've had so far, I think."

"You're certainly right, Vic. I think it was Pope Innocent XI who banned women from church music in the last century. Give me that book over there."

I handed him the book. He leafed through it intently.

"Ah, there it is! This is what he said on 4 May 1686: ‚*Music is highly detrimental to the modesty of the female sex, because it distracts them from their real business and occupations'*."

Then I followed to turn the next page. "Well, what the music critic and composer Johann Mattheson had to say about it: ‚*... that we trample the gift of God underfoot if we do not allow women to perform church music under important hypocritical pretexts ...'* That's completely in my favour. Clever man, this Mattheson."

"We'll see who becomes the next pope, but that will take a while yet," Father concluded.

I was pleased that it was possible to have a proper conversation with my father again. He still spoke slowly and deliberately, but it was getting better and better. He, who used to be one of the absolute fast talkers because he wanted to express as many thoughts as possible at once, had been forced to slow down.

I didn't really care who would become pope. It was much more important to me that Father was doing really well again. I think he understands me better now.

Magdalena

Then, Magdalena came to visit at my invitation. I was very happy to be able to embrace my best friend again.

"My mamma sends her love and Friedrich is very sad that he couldn't come with us because of his studies. My brother always talks about you, Vic. He says that, in his eyes, we are the only two women other than our mother that he can imagine as real friends."

Christoph spent the first few days with a friend at a hunt organised by Johann Josef Joachim Ferdinand von Schidenhofen in Triebenbach. I had known Joachim for a long time, but he was never a person with whom I had a particularly close friendship. So I didn't regret that Magdalena and I spent our time differently.

We rode to Salzburg and were guests of the Mozarts. Nannerl and I played the pianoforte four-handed, while Magdalena sang along with her pleasant alto voice. We took turns and had a lot of laughs until Frau Mozart served us cocoa and cake.

The whole family joined us. Wolferl told us that he had a lot to do. "I've already composed masses this year, a concerto for bassoon and much more. I've also thought of a few themes for serenades that I still have to write down. Now I also have a commission from Elector Maximilian, who wants a new comic opera for the carnival inn München. Father and I will be travelling to München in December for the premiere[161]. So our stay in München has borne fruit after all. I have you to thank for that, Vic. I have fond memories of our visit there. It gave me a lot of pleasure."

"Yes, it really was a great thing to have you as support for the servants' ball. The whole town has been talking about nothing else for days." I also had news to tell. "Christoph and I have taken over Seraphia's dance clientele and added

---

161 *This was moved several times and took place on 13 January 1775 in the Redoutenhaus on Prannergasse.*

a few new students. We really enjoy teaching these mostly young people. They learn so quickly and with such enthusiasm."

"I can well imagine. Your students will probably have a lot more fun with you than with some of the ossified dance masters I've met. I'm not saying anything against their skills. They are often far too stiff and you both radiate such joy. Your own enthusiasm is very infectious. I've experienced that myself!"

I was very happy about this assessment and gave Wolfie a hug and a peck on the cheek.

We went for walks together and I gave Nannerl some more advice on how she would get on better with a horse. We went on a trip to Hellbrunn and I noticed the insecurity of both horse and rider. At one point, Nannerl's horse even bolted.

"Ride a big circle and get smaller until he stops, Nannerl!" I called after her. My friend managed to stay on top and eventually her horse stood still.

"This horse has no respect for you." I explained. "You have to show him that you are the leader, Nannerl. Your mount will try to see how far it can go with you every time. Only if you show him that you set the pace here and no one else will it be a fear-free outing for you, because the animal can also accept you as the leader.

"You have to give him clear commands. If you don't know what you want to do, the horse will feel insecure and want to lead itself because it feels more secure in this role.

"You are simply too good for this world, dear friend. Only if you give clear instructions and your horse listens to you can you praise it and cuddle it if you want to. If it does what it wants, you will do nothing of the sort! This is a serious instruction, my dear!"

We visited the archbishop's game preserve right next to the castle park. There were chamois, pheasants, ibex hybrids and lots of fallow deer. There were even white stags to spot. Everything was beautifully laid out.

Magdalena longed for her female eagle. "Oh, if only Morgana were here with me now. I'm sure she would love this area."

"Yes, especially the choice of game would be right for her. But I think you'd both have a problem with the archbishop." I said. We laughed at the idea of Morgana killing one of the archbishop's bucks. Preferably also in the menagerie[162] at Hellbrunn

Nannerl wanted to know everything about Magdalena's birds that I hadn't told her yet. So Magdalena talked and her cheeks turned red. She was in her element.

By the end of our outing, Nannerl was already sitting much more confidently in the saddle and the horse was behaving quite well. The two of them had decided to try again with the original division of roles.

We said goodbye to the Mozarts again and rode home. Christoph had already arrived there.

He greeted Magdalena with an exuberance that I have rarely seen in my brother. He fussed over my friend all evening and the following day and she seemed to enjoy it. He asked her about falcons and hunting, was interested in her talent for drawing and constantly complimented her.

Magdalena had the room next to mine during her stay and she used a dressing room with me. It was relatively warm there thanks to the tiled stove, so we sat on a spacious stool and chatted before going to bed.

"Your brother is a very charming man, Vic. I like him very much."

"I have a strong feeling that the feeling is mutual, dear Magdalena. I think he wants to court you and offer you marriage – if that's what you want. But tell me, what about this Franz von Cottenau that Frederik wrote about?"

"I also like him a lot. He has wit and is just as charming. But he's not at all enthusiastic about our birds. And if I'm

---

162 *The menagerie became today's Hellbrunn Zoo*

honest, I couldn't commit to a man who rejects falconry and dismisses it as a sentimental folly.

He has already let it be known that he would not allow such barbecues, as he calls them, at his wife's house. In his opinion, it takes up too much time. He wants a woman with fine talents. He really likes my painting here. He doesn't really care that I'd rather sew a lure[163] than embroider a tablecloth."

"Do I understand correctly that this Franz only accepts a woman who does what he imagines?"

"Yes, I think so. On the one hand, it looks like he somehow admires me too, but he would like to mould me to his will. No, that's not a man for me."

"I understand you only too well, Magdalena. After my acquaintance with my family by marriage, I already take a very close look at my friends. You'd better let this Franz go. No matter how much influence and money he has. That can never make up for the freedom he robs you of. I also can't imagine that you would submit without resistance. That can only end in conflict.

"I can assure you of one thing: I would be delighted to have you as my sister-in-law. And I would give my brother hell if he treated you disrespectfully. You can believe that."

Magdalena hugged me warmly. Then she looked at me mischievously again. "What's going on with Konrad?"

I played with a silk ribbon that I had taken from my dressing table. "Oh yes, Konrad. He's a darling and I really like him. But I'm not quite sure whether I should enter into a relationship with him. I didn't want to get married again and my mind is still made up. I've already made that clear to him. I think we both need some time to realise what we really want. Even if we decide to enter into a relationship without a marriage licence – where should we meet?"

"That is indeed a problem. He has no property of his own and it wouldn't work in your father's house either."

---

163 *A dummy prey attached to a long leather strap for training a bird of prey. It consists of a leather body with the wings of the game bird to be hunted attached to both sides.*

"In any case, I wish you with all my heart that you will have a loving and attentive husband, just as I had one. One who will take you with him and give you delights that you can't imagine until you've really experienced them. I can imagine that Christoph could be that man.

I've spoken to him openly about the subject of love and I think he's very close to Jacob in the way he deals with it. Which is not to say, of course, that he will tell me what happens in his own bed."

I thought about it for a moment before I continued.

"Even if you marry Christoph, who really is an honest man and wouldn't cheat a woman, I recommend that you only take this step with a contract that leaves your property in your personal care. I would advise every woman to do this. I'm happy to help you with that."

"Thank you for this good advice. I value you not only as a warm friend, but also as an excellent lawyer, Vic." My friend was very serious.

Magdalena chewed on her lower lip.

"Out with it. What do you want to know?"

"Please tell me what you like about physical love. What does the woman do and what exactly does the man do? I don't know much about it yet, like probably most unmarried women."

"And many of the married women don't know much more either, believe me. They only know the mechanical act, but the fewest know about the pleasure you can feel from it." I told her what it had been like with Jacob. What we had done when we were intimate. I described my sensations to her and the pleasure that came from a sensitive man who wanted the woman to get her money's worth.

I also told her that I knew that my brother had a lover during our time in Ingolstadt who had taught him a lot. "I even met her once. She wasn't of high standing, but she was a very smart and likeable person who you just had to like. She got married a short time later and since then I've never known of any particular woman in Christoph's life."

It was nice to have a confidante to whom I could tell such intimate things. Magdalena had become a very dear friend to me and I really hoped that she and Christoph would become a couple.

As far as possible, I left the two lovebirds alone from then on. I wanted them to get to know each other properly. I knew that my brother wouldn't take advantage of the situation to Magdalena's disadvantage and so I was only prepared if the two of them wanted to do something in public.

Mamma was in the picture with Magdalena and also had a serious conversation with Christoph. But then she also left the two of them alone. We didn't have to be afraid that my brother would be abusive. He was a well-mannered man who wouldn't deliberately compromise a woman in public and wouldn't get too close to her unless she explicitly wanted him to.

When Magdalena left us again, she and Christoph were a couple. However, they had agreed that they would wait until our father's business was stable again before getting officially engaged. We believed that it would only be another six months or so before then.

In remembrance of a witch

One October day, I found mamma sitting in the drawing room, lost in thought.

"Is father getting worse again?"

Of course, I first thought of my father, who had made such a good impression over the last few days.

"No, Vic, he's fine. I just always think about a very sad day in my life at this time of year."

"What happened that day?"

"24 years ago, a 16-year-old maid was executed as a witch at the Schranne[164] in Salzburg. She was first killed by the sword and then burned at the stake."

I'm always appalled by what people do to each other. Sometimes simply out of malice or envy. How can people who believe in a just God be so unjustly themselves at the same time! "And you saw that?"

"At the time, I was visiting my brother Josef in Salzburg." I explained. "I wasn't at the execution. But I passed the pyre a day later and the smell that emanated from it made me sick. Poor thing!"

"I don't know the case. Please tell me more about it," I asked my mother.

"Maria Pauer was a maid of the hell smith Jakob Altinger in the Katharinenvorstadt in Mühldorf am Inn[165]. She was accused of being in league with the devil. She allegedly let tools fly around and the shutters slammed open and closed by themselves. She was imprisoned for over nine months. First in Mühldorf and then in Salzburg. I can't imagine what the young girl had to endure until she was released by the executioner. How cruel people are!"

I hugged my mother. "I understand that this experience bothers you, even after so many years. And I love you for it, mamma!"

Of course, we had also heard about witch trials during our studies. I now remembered a few dates.

"1756 was the last witch trial on the soil of Baiern to date. The 15-year-old Veronica Zerritsch was executed in Landshut. As an orphan who had been rejected by her mother's second husband, she did not have a good life and had to beg for money. As a child maid, she was seized at the cradle with a knife and later confessed to having made a pact with the devil. I don't want to know what they did to her for her to make such a desperate admission."

Mother was really shaking it now.

---

164 *Today the weekly market on the Mirabellplatz*
165 *Mühldorf is a town on the river Inn and 75 km away from Salzburg*

"Did you know that even in 1769, just five years ago, an *amtliche Instruktion zum Malefiz-Inquisitions-Prozess*[166] was introduced at the Electorate of Baierns district courts?"

Mother was horrified. "Seriously?"

"Yes, mamma." I explained. "People aren't getting smarter. If they are, they're getting crueler. There are the most accurate teachings on everything that concerns sorcery, witchcraft or black arts."

"And I always thought that in this day and age, people had already achieved a certain degree of enlightenment. But, apparently that's not the case. If something doesn't go as expected, it must always be someone else's fault. That's an antediluvian way of thinking."

"Of course it is. During my time in München, I found old issues of the *Churbaierisches Intelligenzblatt*[167] from Aunt Cilia. They contained very interesting adverts dealing with the witchcraft issue. Aunt Cilia had bought and kept all the numerous writings on the subject. Very interesting. It almost seems like a war[168] is raging on this issue.

"A little later, at an official reception organised by the Elector, I met a theatine priest who was also a diligent author on the subject. His name was Ferdinand Sterzinger and he was trying to stamp out foolish superstition. I think he's in a difficult position.

"We talked a little about the law and he said that it was very difficult to push through any changes, especially in Baiern, which you could see from the fact that the reform of the law by the *Codex Iuris Bavarici Criminalis* 1751, the *Codex Iuris Bavarici Iudiciarii* 1753 and the *Codex Maximilianeus Bavaricus Civilis* 1756 did not change much.

"But let's move on to more pleasant topics," I suggested, "so that you can get out of your depressed mood."

---

166 *official instruction on the Maleficent Inquisition trial*
167 *Monthly newspaper published since 1765 with trade news, official announcements and scholarly treatises etc.*
168 *In fact, a few years later there is talk of the Bavarian Witch War.*

This conversation with my mother circled intensely through my thoughts for a few days. I wanted to find out how people can be so cruel, but I couldn't come up with anything. Some things simply remain incomprehensible to me.

Visit to München

A few days later, I said goodbye to my family and with my maid Katharina visited München. Frederik wanted to organise another servants' ball and had asked me to help him with the rest of the organisation and running. I also had personal reasons. Firstly, I wanted to meet my dear friends again. And I wanted to pay a courtesy visit to the baroness in my palace.

I also wanted to visit a few high-ranking personalities and show them my father's goods. Krümmelbein had already sent samples again. I took Katharina with me because she could be helpful in part and also wanted to visit her best friend, who was now working as Frederik's cook.

I was invited to stay with Magdalena's family while I was in town. So her house was my second destination. First, I dropped Katharina off at Frederik's. She was happy that I gave her the time to renew her friendship with the cook.

As the landlord was not at home, I rode on to Magdalena. I received a warm welcome. I was also welcomed by Magdalena's younger siblings, Angelika and Josef. Angelika had been married for a few months and was visiting her family, while her husband was spending time with his friends.

"Our Friedrich is still in Ingolstadt, but he'll be home for a short time in a few days. He wouldn't miss Frederik's ball for the world." The lady of the house hugged me in greeting.

"By the way, I've invited your friend from Barby to dinner tonight." She continued. "He often spends time here and has almost become like another son to me. He is a very pleasant young man and a true friend of my two eldest. We like to take him to balls. He's an excellent dancer and not at all pushy."

"I can hardly wait to hold Frederik in my arms." I said. "I'm really happy to have such wonderful friends like you all."

I just had time to freshen up and change before we all gathered in the dining room.

We had a lot of fun over dinner. Each of us had something to tell. I brought greetings for everyone from my family and to Magdalena and Frederik from other mutual friends from Reichenhall.

We talked about the preparations for the ball. What had already happened? What was still missing? Had anything been forgotten? Who should do what from the remaining points?

The Redoutensaal in Prannerstraße was booked, drinks and food had also been ordered, as well as candles and floral decorations. Mother and Christoph definitely wanted to come. We made a few more plans and were already excited in advance.

After the meal, Magdalena's mother shooed us both and Frederik into a small and cosy parlour. "We'll leave you alone for a while. I'm sure you have a lot to talk about among friends."

As soon as we were alone, I pulled a letter out of the folds of my dress. "I don't want to let you stew any longer, Magdalena." I handed her the letter from my brother.

"From Christoph? Oh, how I've been eagerly waiting for this." She sat down in a corner and began to read after breaking the seal.

"Frederik, will you come with me to my tenant tomorrow? I'd like to pay her a quick visit and see if she's happy with everything."

"Of course, I'd love to come with you." Frederik replied. "Do you think we could do some fencing practice in my house afterwards?"

"Not tomorrow, my friend. I want to make a few visits as quickly as possible for my father's business. But the day after that, I'm looking forward to a practice session with you in the late afternoon."

Meanwhile, my dear friend sat there with a transfigured face and pressed the letter to her heart.

"Christoph writes that he loves you and wants nothing more than to finally be reunited with you," was my prediction.

"How can you even consider anything else?" Magdalena said with an enraptured look on her face.

We talked for a while, then Frederik left us and we went to bed.

The next day, my friend picked me up in a chaise to take me to my palace. I had sent my tenant a little note saying that I wanted to pay her a short visit and she had agreed.

The baroness was an impressive personality. She greeted us cheerfully and invited us to join her for a bite to eat. "You know, I usually spend a lot of time on my own." She said. "So I enjoy any kind of visitor who can give me new insights into life."

She told me that she had accepted an invitation to Scotland next summer and that she would therefore not extend the lease on my house for the rest of the year.

"However, I feel very comfortable in this palace and you can tell that it was inhabited by good people. I feel a lot of joy, but also sadness within these walls. Do you want to tell me what happened? I've only heard rumours and I don't know what's true."

I was surprised that this woman turned out to be so sensitive. "My husband's aunt lived in this house for a long time. She was a very friendly woman who enjoyed life. She died at the age of seventy-four. My husband and I lived in the palace after her. During that time, it experienced much happiness and joy. Until Jacob lost his life in a hunting accident less than a year later. I stayed here for a few more months. Jacob's death was almost two years ago."

"Then it's true. I'm sorry for your loss. I wish you much happiness and love in this life, my dear. Although I don't really know you, I'm convinced that you deserve it."

We left the baroness on good terms. As Frederik had kept the day free for me, he accompanied me to other members of high society, to whom I brought the latest fabric and yarn samples because they had expressed an interest in father's goods.

This allowed my friend to get to know a few more people a little better. I praised Frederik's skills as a lawyer everywhere. I did this with a clear conscience, because he was really good. He had in-depth knowledge and a very sharp mind. He knew how to take opponents apart.

We also made a few visits the next day. Afterwards, we fenced in his house. I had men's clothes with me especially for this. Even though I had already practised in a dress, I much preferred uncomplicated trousers.

A few days later, Magdalena's brother Friedrich returned home. He gave all the family members a big hug, as was his way. He also hugged me as if I was one of them. Something seemed to have changed in his demeanour. I just couldn't work out what.

Over dinner, I noticed that Friedrich had become a lot more masculine in recent months. A year ago, he was still trying very hard to appear suave – which he didn't always manage to do with his very youthful appearance. Now he had such a charisma without any further effort. He now looked completely like the man he was now by the number of years he had lived. I was delighted by his clever comments on various topics. He had become a man to be taken seriously, and not just in appearance. Friedrich was now about to complete his medical degree.

Frederik's ball

Mamma, Christoph and Nannerl arrived in München the day before the ball.

Frederik and I had once again come up with something special for the ball. All the servant guests who didn't already have some because of their position received simple, white cloth gloves from us.

We also had a few fans left over from last year for a few new arrivals.

In the ballroom, the podium with the musicians was initially hidden behind a large sheet of fabric.

Unlike at the formal balls of the nobility, the guests here were quite punctual. Everyone wanted to experience this evening from the very beginning. That made us very happy.

Frederik greeted the guests from the stairs in a firm voice.

"Welcome to this year's servants' ball. As many of you know, last year the Countess Dowager of my best friend Jacob von Falkenstein held a ball for our servants in his honour, which was an incredible success. This year I have invited you to such a ball and I am delighted that so many of you came.

The evening begins with two compositions played for you by an orchestra behind this fabric. Afterwards, you will of course also be able to take a look at the orchestra as it plays for us to dance to.

Now, I wish you all a wonderful evening at the ball. Enjoy the music and games."

The music started and the ball visitors listened to one of the violin concertos by Maddalena Sirmen and the overture to *Sofonisba* by Maria Teresa Agnesi Pinottini.

Applause broke out after both pieces. While the bravos were still being shouted, the cloth fell in front of the orchestra. I heard many surprised exclamations. Because there wasn't a single man in the orchestra.

The dance music was started and the whole hall was soon buzzing with countless dancing people. It was a pleasure to study the many happy faces. However, I didn't have much time for that. I had a lot of dancers. In between, I played the violin or the flute.

A new love affair

Two days after the ball, I went falcon hunting with Magdalena and Friedrich. I was also allowed to try my luck myself with Sahib, the falcon tercel. He slayed a hare and I was happy about our hunting success. Magdalena and Friedrich congratulated me with genuine joy.

That afternoon, Friedrich accompanied me to Frederik. We wanted to fence together.

Magdalena decided to stay at home. "Oh, I'd just get bored there. I'd rather stay here and let Morgana fly."

When we sat exhausted in Frederik's parlour after two hours of practice in various constellations, Frederik had a snack prepared for us, which we enjoyed to our heart's content.

Frederik then left us briefly to get something from his saddlebags. Then Frederik turned to me.

"I think you're starting to need a lover again, dear Vic. Jacob hasn't been with us for almost two years now, but nothing is happening with you. Apparently not even with

Konrad. Although I don't think you're really compatible either."

I sighed. "Yes, unfortunately that's true. Well, I don't need to think too much about Konrad. We really like each other, but I miss something about him. I don't know. There's also nowhere we could meet."

"There's someone else who's been madly in love with you for some years now and will carry you on his hands. I know just the right place where you could meet undisturbed."

I looked at him curiously. "Who do you mean?"

"Don't you really notice that Friedrich always looks at you like a moon calf in love?"

Friedrich?

"But he's only twenty-one years old!"

"Two years younger than you. So what? Do you think he doesn't have enough experience? I don't think so. With his looks, he's sure to have girls chasing after him in droves. I can't imagine him not getting amorous with them now and again. Besides, he's a really lovely person."

The younger brother of my best friend, who I only recently realised had really grown up? The young man whose skills I was so proud of? The one I was so fond of? Was it really a possibility?

"You like him, don't you?"

"But of course, that's no question!" Yes, I actually really liked Friedrich. He was as much a part of my life as Frederik and Magdalena. Without him, I was definitely missing an important part of my life. However, I never had considered him as a candidate for love.

I suddenly remembered my dance with him at a ball two years ago. When he had assured me that Bella would miss me. Now the penny dropped. Of course he did! He was telling me that he missed! Jacob had seen it back then and had even pointed it out to me. Oh, what a ninny I was not to have realised it myself. But I was still married at the time and didn't give a damn about lovesick talk from young lads. I just didn't take him seriously at the time. After all, he was only Magdalena's brother.

I smiled, even blushed. "I think you're right!"

"Whatever you decide. I just wanted to let you know that you can meet at my house at any time and that I will always make your bedroom available to you. You could even use it now."

I hugged him fiercely and gave him a friendly kiss. What could be better than friends who give you security in difficult situations?

"You are a true friend, Frederik. I love you for that."

"I'm glad to hear that!"

When Friedrich was back, I saw him with different eyes and realised for the first time that he was looking at me with a similar look to the one Jacob had always given me. Yes, I realised, he was definitely in love with me. But he was shy because he had never hinted at anything or he didn't want to jeopardise our friendship. I didn't know.

A little later, Frederik signalled to me that he would leave the room if I wanted him to. Yes, I wanted him to. He left to do something important, according to him. I was sure he wouldn't come back without being asked.

I sat down next to Friedrich on the kanapé. He looked at me expectantly and curiously. I took his hands in mine. His expression changed from suddenly blushing to questioning, but he still let me take the lead.

"Can you forgive me, dearest Friedrich, for not understanding what was bothering you for so long? Frederik had to help me. He pointed out to me that you were in love with me. I'd actually been aware of it for a long time, but I didn't want to let the fact get to me."

I looked at our hands and let go of his with my right hand to stroke his face gently.

"I'm not sure if I'm in love with you. But I promise to find out." With these words, I bent my face towards his and lowered my lips to his. In the next second, Friedrich's strong arms enveloped me. Yes, it felt very good. His sigh sounded relieving.

Our kiss gradually became more intense and I buried one hand in Friedrich's hair while the other travelled along his back. He kissed well and I felt great.

Slowly, a feeling of anticipation rose in me. My erogenous zones all over my body seemed to tingle and a long-felt need arose in my abdomen that hadn't even been felt with Konrad, whom I was now also very fond of. But, he hadn't managed to touch my insides with the few kisses we had shared as Friedrich now did with surprising ease.

I thought about it for a moment: what would be wrong if we withdrew immediately? Because of the fencing exercise, I was still in men's clothes, which I could easily put on and take off without help. My hairstyle that day was just a plait.

So, I gently wriggled out of Friedrich's embrace, stood up and then pulled him with me. He willingly allowed himself to be led. We climbed the stairs to the first floor and entered the bedroom that had always been available to me on my previous visits. The first thing I noticed was a fresh rose on the bed. There was also a lively fire burning in the fireplace. There was a carafe of wine and two glasses on a table

I smiled. Frederik had known more than me. I silently praised my friend who had finally opened my eyes.

Friedrich had also spotted the rose and fire. "Praise be to good friends who know what we need!" he said.

He looked at me with shining eyes. "I've loved you ever since I met you. Victoria, loving you is my destiny and being loved by you is my deepest wish."

I prefer to keep the intimate details to myself. That should remain private. But I can say that the experience with Friedrich touched me to the core. He is a very attentive and tender lover.

He looked at me. "I feel like a complete beginner with you. But I really like what I'm learning. You're so beautiful, Victoria. This is a dream come true right now. Please don't wake me up so quickly."

We rested a little and lay closely together on the bed.

"Friedrich ..."

"Yes, dearest?"

"You're an important part of my life that I wouldn't want to miss. I think we're also a good match in bed. You give me a formidable feeling. Like something that was broken is whole again. This morning I still thought I would be alone and now ..."

"This is the happiest moment of my life right now, my love. It's been worth waiting." He tenderly ran his fingers through my hair and over my back and then lightly stroked my backside.

After what felt like an eternity of caresses, he continued talking.

"I was always afraid that you wouldn't want me because I'm younger than you." Friedrich said. "That's why I never made any effort to get closer to you. I wouldn't have been able to bear it if you had cancelled our friendship, which was so important to me. As existential as breathing itself."

I kissed him in response. "You were very important to me right from the start. I just didn't realise how important until today." Again, we exchanged a few kisses.

"All the women before you, that was nothing compared to the experience today. Physical union, yes, but not with such overwhelming feelings. Only now do I realise what it can feel like when both your hearts are in it. I think I've just seen heaven."

"I only really realised that today. Jacob and I had a very high level of mutual respect and we also enjoyed the physical union, but it was still very different. Thank you for this unique experience, Friedrich."

It was a truly great experience with this man, who just a day ago I would only have described as a good friend.

"Do you think we can steal an hour together tomorrow too, Vic?"

"As the time with you is special to me, I will do everything I can to ensure that we can meet up as often as possible before I leave," I explained.

Friedrich gave me another kiss, telling me what he felt.

Shortly afterwards, we got dressed and then left Frederik's house with Katharina.

"Katharina ..."

"I know, Madame, no one will ever hear a word from my mouth. I'm glad that you two have finally found each other. But, it's about time! I felt really sorry for the lovesick gentleman."

I laughed. "Apparently everyone knew, only I didn't realise."

"And I think everyone saw it." Friedrich was surprised. "And I thought I had my emotions under control."

"You hid it well. But sometimes I could catch a longing look that gave away what was going on inside you."

Katharina was a good observer.

Friedrich and I had agreed that we didn't want to let anyone know for the time being. He knew that I no longer wanted to get married and said he would be happy with a secret love affair. The only thing that mattered to him was that I loved him.

In the days that followed, we always found a way to get together at Frederik's and spend intense hours in my bedroom. Katharina was a willing helper. She benefited from this because she was able to spend a lot of time with her friend.

Friedrich, Magdalena, her mother and I were invited to Frederik's for dinner. We had a very nice evening with good conversation and even music. During the meal, Frederik sat next to me and kept teasing me furtively because Friedrich and I was trying very hard to behave as usual. It spoke in our favour that Magdalena and her mother didn't notice.

Friedrich announced that he would be spending the night at Frederik's because they both wanted to do something together tomorrow.

The next day I spent the morning with my friend and then rode off on my own to make a few visits.

Only, I had already completed them all. I rode a few detours to Frederik. There, I spent another unforgettable afternoon in bed with Friedrich. We were in love and happy.

The three of us had agreed that I would integrate my correspondence with Friedrich into the mail to Frederik and that the letters back would also go through our indispensable friend.

The next day I said goodbye to Magdalena's family. On the way to the post office, I had to pass Frederik's house again.

I wanted to pick up Katharina there, who also wanted to say goodbye to the cook. I still had quite a lot of time and wasn't surprised when it wasn't Frederik who greeted me in the parlour, but Friedrich. As soon as we kissed, my lust was aroused to an extent that I would never have imagined.

We made love one last time to say goodbye. We wouldn't see each other again for some weeks.

Katharina and I had an uneventful journey home. I mostly sat on the horse and daydreamed. I never thought that something like this would happen to me again. I was so happy.

Homecoming Seraphia

As always, a letter from Frederik arrived every few days. Only now there was always another one from Friedrich. I was delighted to receive these romantic love letters, which I always answered with great passion.

"When is Aunt Seraphia coming? What do you think, is she in the carriage or on a horse?" my brother asked.

"You know our aunt! I think she's coming on horseback while Heinrich and Apollonia are in the carriage. According to her last letter, they should be here by the end of the week."

"That's fine. I have to go through the books with mamma first while you take care of the new orders."

I became serious again. "I can't imagine how father can derive so much pleasure from his profession as a businessman."

"I can't understand it either. But I guess we'll have to get through it for another while. I'm glad that I focussed a lot on commercial law during my studies. That at least helps me to understand the legal side of the business."

"I don't particularly mind the job itself. But if I didn't have dancing as well, I wouldn't enjoy it."

A few days later – it was almost late autumn weather – a completely hooded figure, obviously soaked and covered in mud, was let in by Johannes.

I tore open the library door and flew round the neck of the new arrival with a cry of joy as she had just taken off her coat. "Aunt Seraphia! Welcome home!"

We squeezed and hugged each other until we were both gasping for air. Only then did we really look at each other.

"I was so excited at the thought of seeing you that I had to come here first before I freshened up in my own four walls." She gave me another big hug and then stood in front of me, beaming at me. Seraphia was   still a beauty. I love and admire her because, despite her fame and acquaintance with the powerful of the world, she has retained her sober outlook and naturalness.

Sometimes, she talks about other dancers who are engaged here and there with minor princes and so have adopted their behaviour to such an extent that they no longer even speak to her, although Seraphia has danced at the French and Prussian courts and even before the Archduchess of Austria and Queen of Hungary and Bohemia, Maria Theresa, and not least before the Russian Tsar.

"Some of your orders from Krümmelbein arrived last week. Katharina has already put everything in its place – as far as she knew – and our Johann has had your house heated up so that you're cosy while cold rain pours outside. Mamma and Christoph want me to say hello to you. They're already looking forward to seeing you and Heinrich for dinner. At the moment they're working on balance sheets and hopefully they'll find the error soon. Oh yes, please tell Apollonia she's been invited to dine with the cook. She and Johann want her to give them a travel report."

"She'll be delighted. Then we'll leave my sister and her son to pore over the numbers and I'll go to my own little house. I'll see you at dinner. See you later. Oh, how I'm looking forward to a hot bath!" She turned around and gave me a quick wave before slipping back into her wet coat, which John held far away from himself, and leaving the house again.

The whole family met in the dining room for dinner. Father has spoken less at the table since his illness and lets us talk more. He told me just a few days ago that he was amazed to realise that he had learned a lot more about his family and their views in this way.

Seraphia told us a few anecdotes from the past few months and made us laugh several times. It was nice to see everyone back home safe and sound.

Fallen girls

When I came back from a ride a few days later, there was a rather pretty young woman huddled around near the outer gate. I could remember having seen her before. But where?

She looked me in the face with a sad expression in her eyes that I couldn't bring myself to simply pass. I greeted her curtly at first, but then reined in my horse and dismounted.

She bowed deeply to me. "Madame, I have come to you in dire need and hope that you can show me a way out."

I was unpleasantly touched to be addressed in such a submissive manner. And now I remembered. I had seen her in the house of a nobleman in Reichenhall. His wife had once invited us to a soirée. I think she was a chambermaid there.

I pulled her up from her bow. "Come with me first. I'll take the horse to the stable and then we can talk."

She willingly let me pull her along. I handed the reins of my horse to the stable boy Friedrich the Little One and then wanted to direct my steps towards the main house. The girl grabbed my arm.

"No, please, Madame, let's talk outside. I can talk better here." The young woman begged me imploringly.

"Well then, let's just go to the pavilion. We can sit down there and at least there won't be a draught."

She trotted along beside me and then sat down on the bench in our glazed summerhouse without resistance, folded her hands in her lap and gave the impression of a lamb being led to the slaughter.

"So, now tell me what's on your mind. I'll listen to you and then we'll work out what to do together."

"My name is Franziska. I've been employed by the Montag family as a chambermaid for the last five years. I always felt comfortable there and did my job without ever receiving a reprimand.

"In May, a brother of the old man came to visit. A cowardly man with cold eyes, who frightened me from the start."

She began to sob and struggled to keep her composure.

"He was stalking you?"

The answer was a vigorous nod. "I fled from him wherever he appeared. But, one day he came into his room while I was stoking his fireplace. He locked the door and ... and ..." Another heavy sob.

"He took what he wanted without your consent and now you're pregnant," I surmised and spread my arms out. Franziska pressed herself against me and cried on my shoulder for a while. I could well imagine the end of the story. After all, she wasn't the first person to come to our house looking for help.

"Yes, I fought back and screamed. But he wouldn't let me out of his clutches. And afterwards he told everyone that I had stalked him and that he had only done me a favour. Now that my pregnancy has been confirmed, my masters have chased me out of the house. They think I'm a depraved woman and a fallen girl. They don't want something like that in their house.

"What have I done that I now find myself without a job and a reference letter and with a child under my heart from a man I deeply detest?

"I wanted to end my life, but the cook stopped me from doing something stupid. She told me to go to you. Even if you and your family can't help me, it would still be early enough to take that last step."

I could only give Franziska limited hope. "Franziska, I can help you by getting you a job again. At Lake Chiemsee, in Rosenheim, München or Augsburg with people who will take you and your child in and not hold you responsible. Your new environment won't see you as a fallen girl, but as a woman whose husband has died."

"I don't want this child!"

"I can understand that, but the law stands in our way. I'm sorry, but I'm not going to risk either labour or imprisonment to help you. But I can offer you the chance to stay with us for some days and then, once everything is sorted out, you can take up a new position. There will be someone willing to take in a poor pregnant widow."

"You would do that for me? Oh, thank you, Madame." Franziska got down on her knees in front of me.

"Please, get up again. I'll help you like I would help any other woman in your situation. I find it dishonourable the way some men behave. But, if they have influence and money, then unfortunately their victims are at their mercy. How I would love to change that!"

With Jacob's network, we managed to place Franziska in a new position within a few weeks. She had made herself useful during her time with us and we were able to provide her with very good references. My mother also took it upon herself to persuade the lady at the house where Franziska had previously worked and had been treated so badly to give her a good reference.

I don't know how she managed it, but I do know that mamma can sometimes be unpleasantly persuasive.

Casanova

Seraphia and I had made ourselves cosy by the tiled stove. The cold had come surprisingly quickly. The mountain peaks were already white.

"Auntie, you promised me a long time ago that you would tell me about this Italian who is rumoured to have every woman who hasn't fled on the count of three. Now that everyone is out of the house, I'm asking you to tell me more about him."

Seraphia winked at me conspiratorially. "Yes, that's right, I promised. His name is Giacomo Casanova alias Chevalier de Seingalt[169]. I think it was during Carnival 1768 when I met him at a ball near Augsburg. He is an extremely interesting man. Giacomo plays the violin very well and has also worked as an orchestral musician. As far as I know, he's about five years older than your father."

"That may all be true, but what's he like as a man and – have you got to know him better?"

"You're quite curious, my dear. If your father ever found out what I told you about the relationship between a man and a woman when you were only ten years old, he would have shut the door on me..."

I interrupted my aunt. "But, then he would learn from me that this knowledge has already saved me a lot of grief – especially associated with my late husband! Now please go on."

"Giacomo is a charmer, no doubt about it, and a clever man. According to him, hardly any woman can resist him. But I didn't feel erotically attracted to him. Perhaps he wasn't interested because he was enjoying our conversation about God and the world too much, or perhaps another conquest was more important to him at the time. I don't know.

Anyway we had several longer meetings where I learnt to appreciate him. I like him a lot and have already helped him out of an awkward situation. Of course, it had to do with a young woman.

"We keep in loose correspondence with each other and occasionally share the news that comes to us. That is very valuable for both of us. He's in exile at the moment, but he's planning to return to Venice this summer."

"Oh, I would have loved to hear an erotic adventure from you. You know such a charming ladies' man – and you don't have an amorous interlude with him."

---

169 *Giacomo Girolamo Casanova, 1725-1798, Venetian writer, adventurer and woma-niser*

Seraphia laughed. "And you really think I would tell you about my intimate experiences? Dear niece, you really don't need to know everything!" She smiled mischievously.

"All right, keep it to yourself. But what else can you tell me about this Italian charmer we keep hearing rumours about?"

She thought about it for a moment and then began to talk.

"You've seen the Margravine Elisabeth Friederike Sophie of Brandenburg-Bayreuth. She is a beautiful woman. Casanova also met her once. He still thinks she was the most beautiful German princess he had ever seen."

"Why didn't you tell me this when we were there?"

"My dear, in Bayreuth I didn't think for a moment about Casanova and his views on the princess.

"Oh, and I remember how he told me at our last meeting that he had visited the great castrato Farinelli[170] at his retirement home in Bologna. Giacomo had heard him once when he was young and had been enchanted by Farinelli's voice ever since, with a range from tenor to the highest soprano. But he was particularly moved by Farinelli's interpretation of the pieces. He is a very special artist. Allegedly, Farinelli was able to sing 150 notes on one syllable in one breath using a special breathing technique. Or at least it sounded as if he didn't take a breath in between.

"The two talked about music for a long time and, according to Giacomo, also played together. Two such different men ... Casanova with his countless women's stories and Farinelli, who was perhaps never really intimate with a woman. Well, of course I can only make assumptions here. I would have loved to have heard Farinelli sing once. They say his singing made people cry, he was so beautiful. He's an old man now. I wonder what he does with all his free time."

170 *Carlo Broschi, whose stage name was Farinelli (1705-1782), was a celebrated Italian castrato singer who lived and worked at court in Madrid for a long time. Casanova and he actually met.*

I imagined the singing in my mind. At least I tried to. I had heard castrati before. But their voices had not awakened any deeper emotions in me. It was more that it disturbed me to hear these seasoned men singing the female parts in voices that were unnaturally high for my ear.

Triebenbach Castle

Mother, Christoph and I had received new sheet music from Frederik. They were trio sonatas and a violin concerto by Maddalena Laura Lombardini Sirmen[171], the Venetian musician.

We practised these beautiful pieces very diligently. After a while, an opportunity arose to perform them at Triebenbach Castle. That day, the von Schidenhofens were having a hunt followed by a party and decided to hire us as musicians.

As word of our work as dance masters had already spread as far as Triebenbach, Christoph and I were also hired for this and were, therefore, at the castle almost a week before the festival, giving dance lessons to families in the area who showed an interest.

To our delight and surprise, our friends Magdalena and Friedrich were also invited to the party. They were known as falconers and were therefore there. I couldn't believe my luck when I saw them. When we greeted them, I showed my excitement about the surprise reunion.

"Magdalena has been my best friend since my time in München. We know her whole family very well. I've often gone hunting with her siblings."

---

171 *In 1779, she performed in Dresden. There she received twice the fee of an Italian singer at court.*

Our host, Kaspar Joachim von Schidenhofen, looked at me questioningly. "Oh, you know about hunting with falcons? I didn't even know that."

I laughed. "Really know about it? I wouldn't go that far. But it fascinates me and I love these birds."

"Then it's fitting that I've billeted you next to each other."

We went for a long ride with Joachim von Schidenhofen, Kaspar's son, and learnt from him that he was in Salzburg more often to visit balls or some friends than we would have thought.

We had finally sold him a horse that he had wanted last year. Now, he sat happily on this horse and was delighted to have such a well-trained mount under his saddle. We, on the other hand, were delighted to have received a handsome sum for it, which further paved the way for Christoph's engagement. In the meantime, we were almost back on solid ground financially. The last letter from Krümmelbein had made us very happy, as the latest consignment of fabrics and yarns had sold well.

In the evening, an informal dinner awaited us with everyone who was already staying at the castle. The evening was very stimulating. Many anecdotes were told, which contributed to the general amusement.

Christoph and I couldn't go hunting. We had a last dance lesson for a leading family in Laufen.

We were back and changed in time for the banquet. Our music was very well received. It was a success, because the von Schidenhofens were delighted.

The evening of the ball flew by. The fact that the Mozarts had also come meant that there was no shortage of good dancers and musicians. As a result, there was a lively exchange between the two professions. As a result, everyone enjoyed themselves and we were able to make music or dance as the mood took us.

As I didn't want our love affair to be publicised, Friedrich and I remained abstinent. But we chatted a little longer at the ball and on another ride. This went unnoticed so far because everyone knew we were friends.

Ball at the Mozarts

In the meantime, our father has been doing so well that he seems to be getting back to his former vigour by the hour – and to his rapid speech, even if he still slips up sometimes. It will still be a long way to go before he finds his way back to his old self. He, who has always placed his trust in everyone, was betrayed in the worst possible way and has not yet been able to fully come to terms with it. I think it will be a long time before he trusts strangers again.

"Tomorrow is the ball in Salzburg. When should we leave?" Christoph asked.

My brother pulled me out of my thoughts and I had to sort them out first.

"As we're both on horseback and the weather is dry, I think an early breakfast will be enough to get us going."

"Yes, that will probably be enough. Have you arranged something with Nannerl?"

"She says we can spend the night at their house. They're already looking forward to our visit. I am too. If we're early enough, she'll give me a piano lesson. She said she would visit us again during Advent and stay for a few days."

The path was dry, so it didn't take us long to get to Salzburg on horseback. In Staufenbruck[172] near Staufeneck Castle, we crossed the Saalach and rode on from there on the Marzoll side. Our two four-legged friends were delighted with the long gallop we gave them. Despite the full saddlebags, we could feel the horses' joy of movement.

---

172 *First mentioned in 1275. Border bridge between the Duchy of Bavaria and the Salzburg archbishopric.*

Nannerl gave us such a warm welcome in Mozart's flat that I was almost in tears.

The ball was to take place in the Tanzmeistersaal in the evening. This hall on the upper floor was accessible from Mozart's flat or via a staircase to the driveway. It had a beautiful stucco ceiling and numerous windows.

Together with Wolfgang and Nannerl, we had already rehearsed a minuet and a gavotte at previous meetings, which we wanted to perform together. We danced through everything again and realised that we could do it well.

As different as we were in character, all four of us had one thing in common: we loved to dance. Each of us also had a certain demand for perfection and so it was always a pleasure to dance in this particular formation. In a way, the Sun King, Louis XIV of France, was also a shining example to us. He perfected the dance and managed to make the whole world accept him as a ruler through his dance and its expression.

The ball in the evening was a highlight in the early winter. The rather small hall was completely overcrowded, but as everyone present knew each other more or less well, it was fun. During the dances, only a few people stood on the sidelines and some of them left the room in a hurry as it got quite crowded.

Our two dances were cheered by the guests, whereupon Wolfgang threw a few crude expressions of joy into the room. Completely heated and laughing, we made our way to our beds at daybreak. After a few hours' sleep, Christoph and I rode home again.

Christoph reflected on our lives. "I am glad that we are among the people with whom fate has been kind. Although we are always busy, we mostly do things that we enjoy. We also get to experience evenings like yesterday."

"According to the latest figures, we will probably be able to make a profit again next year and we will gradually get back the money we gave to our father's business, sister."

I rode alongside my brother. "We're really lucky, brother."

"Are you going to go to München and continue working there as a dance master?" he asked me.

"I haven't thought about it yet. My palace is still rented out until the middle of next year, so I still have time to make a decision. Will you go to München when you marry Magdalena? After all, you have the most wealthy clients there and our friend has a licence to hunt falcons there."

"Oh, I really can't tell you at this stage. It also depends a bit on whether father still needs our support. Although a lot of the work could also be done from München, I think. Besides, like you, dear sister, I don't have a house in München."

"We have to think about our mother, too. She lives here alone with the servants for the summer without us. Father will certainly be back in Hamburg as soon as he is fully recovered, and Seraphia and Heinrich will certainly be on tour for the next few years. We should also consider whether mamma wants to do this in the long term. Now that my father has given in because of my job as a dance master, I no longer have a compelling reason to go to München. Perhaps I should simply divide my time between here and München. But the question doesn't really arise before June."

"Pappa is incredibly proud of you. He was in Reichenhall with mamma the other day. He was waiting in the carriage while she was getting something. Meanwhile he was approached by our customers with their seven children. The couple were full of praise for us and especially for the way you teach dance."

"I couldn't do it so well without you, Christoph. I think it only works so well in the long run with two people."

"That may be. But, whether the second person is me or a Frederik or sometimes a Friedrich or one of our friends shouldn't matter here. Dear Vic, I know that it's mainly because of you that people are so enthusiastic. It's your informal way of dealing with them that fuels their enthusiasm and your dignified demeanour that commands their respect."

"Don't underestimate your part in it, Christoph. I think it's our bond and the wordless understanding between us that makes a big difference."

The winter weather outside was cloudy and cold and wet. I was sitting in a big armchair in front of the fireplace in the library, reading a book that my friend Elizabeth had sent me from England: *"Emma; or, The Unfortunate Attachment"*. It's still quite new and rumour has it that it was written by a highly placed person[173]. In my opinion, it must have been a woman who wrote this work. Men write differently.

It is primarily about an arranged and unwanted marriage from the perspective of a young woman.

This work gives a very good insight into the upper echelons of English society. It is sometimes incomprehensible what is normal there and what is considered reprehensible.

When I read something like that, I am very glad that I come from a family of the lower nobility here in Baiern and have little to do with the high nobility. I'm no longer drawn back to my family by marriage.

I think that many people from the high nobility imagine too much about absolutely irrelevant things. Some of them seem completely degenerate to me. They laugh too loudly and make fun of everything and everyone they don't understand. They have no idea what work is and what it means for their servants to be entirely dependent on someone like them. Without rights and protection. Always dependent on a momentary whim of the master or mistress.

I have met countless ordinary people who seemed more valuable to me than these "master race" people who

---

173 *The book was later attributed to Georgiana Cavendish, Duchess of Devonshire. She was one of the most influential women of her time.*

thought they were the centre of the world. When such people leave this world, humanity suffers no loss. But when a sincere farmer leaves, it is a serious blow to the lives of everyone around him.

Kathrein stops the dancing

At the Kathreintanz[174] in a private house in Reichenhall, we shook a leg for the last time this year. I chatted to an art-loving lady from the aristocracy. She was a fascinating figure and had probably travelled a lot around the world. She had even been to America. But she also had other interesting information to share.

"A cousin of mine lives in Dresden." The lady said. "Her husband is employed there at the Electoral Saxon Academy of Art. A few years ago, the floral still life painter Caroline Friederike Friedrich[175] joined them on a scholarship. This year, this young woman was made an honorary member of the academy.

"Just imagine: Sachsen accepting a woman as an honorary member! I absolutely have to get to know her. Because this woman is definitely a genius. Otherwise she would not be recognised by the gentlemen there.

"I am also fascinated by Anna Maria Schürmann or van Schurmann, who was widely admired as the 'star of Utrecht', the Dutch polymath and most learned woman in Europe in the last century. She wrote poetry, was allowed to attend university lectures – albeit behind a curtain – socialised with painters, glass engravers and copperplate

---

174 In the Alpine foothills, the dance season comes to an end on 25 November (day of Saint Kathterina from Alexandria) with one last dance together

175 From 1783, she was the only female teacher (working under another teacher) at the academy.

engravers and also learned their art. Magdalena van der Passe was one of the artists she learnt from.

"Something important for us women that she wrote has stayed with me: '*Every human being is endowed by nature with the principles or the potencies of the principles of all the arts and sciences. All this is also given to women. Whoever has an inherent desire for the sciences and arts by nature will also be endowed with them. Women, as individuals of the human species, have this desire.*'"

"Yes, they do exist, the female geniuses. But only a few find the recognition they deserve throughout their lives. My father's business partner wrote to us from Hamburg to say that the famous opera singer Margaretha Susanna Kayser had died in Stockholm at the proud age of eighty-four. Have you ever heard her?

My father's mother knew her family – she was from Hamburg – and is said to have once heard her at the height of her art. Grandmamma raved about this voice all her life. The Kayser is said to have had a range of over two and a half octaves. She was even an opera director for a time and also travelled with a touring opera company."

"Yes, she must have been really very good. Madame Kayser sang a lot of Georg Philipp Telemann, whom I also greatly admire. Unfortunately, I missed the chance to hear her. You play the flute, don't you? What do you think of his double concerto in E minor? I'm looking for a suitable partner for it."

And we already had the next topic. We wanted to practise together and immediately set a date for a meeting. This always leads to opportunities that you would never have thought of at the beginning of an evening.

I danced extensively with some very talented gentlemen and overall had a very satisfying evening of dancing.

News from around the world

Father and I were always obsessed with news from all over the world. So we gradually learnt the following:

On 1 December, the boycott of British goods began in the thirteen colonies in North America, as decided by the First Continental Congress with the Articles of Association of 20 October.

"I am very curious to see where this conflict between the mother country, Great Britain, and the American colonies will lead. I fear that if it goes on like this, it will come to war."

I agreed with my father's assessment, but I didn't know of a way out that would be feasible for both sides.

In our neighbourhood, in Austria, things were also happening. It became known that Archduchess Maria Theresa of Austria had introduced "General School Regulations for German normal, main and trivial Schools" on 6 December.

With the permission of Frederick II of Prussia, the abbot of the Augustinian canon monastery in Sagan, Silesia, advised the monarch and drew up the new school regulations. Austria now has compulsory education[176] for children aged six to twelve. This is very welcome.

Here in Baiern, the state commissioner for elementary education, Heinrich Braun, decreed compulsory education throughout the electorate as early as 1771, but there is still a problem somewhere, because I know of enough children who still have to slave away at home instead of learning something for their lives.

"I've heard that we don't have enough teachers here in Baiern. And there's never enough money in the state coffers for everything we actually need anyway." That's what Christoph had to say on this subject.

---

176 *Austrian compulsory education still exists. Unlike compulsory schooling in Germany, children in Austria may also be taught at home.*

Father agreed. "Our servants are lucky that we make sure their children are sent to school for at least a few years. We pay for it and they can all at least write and do maths to some extent."

Winter pleasures

When it was finally really cold, Christoph and I often met up with our friends from the neighbourhood at the "unnamed lake". We went ice skating there together.

It was a great pleasure to glide along on the ice of the lake. Although the surface is not very large, the number of skaters was limited, so we had plenty of space to run riot. The Tonhausers and the Lasser zu Lasseregg were usually there, too. One of us always had bread and cheese as well as drinks in our bags. The latter with alcohol, of course, so that nothing could freeze.

As a result, at the end of those days, we were usually sitting in the saddle of the horses with heated faces and half-frozen, slightly to heavily tipsy, eagerly making their way to the warm stable. One horse or another was a little too eager for the no longer sober rider and so it was bound to happen that there were falls.

However, we were all lucky during these happy days. Both the falls on the ice and the falls from the horses only resulted in bruises that were hardly worth mentioning.

We received an express letter from Krümmelbein in mid-December. He announced his arrival before Christmas. He had good news, he wrote.

That was perfect, because we had invited both the Sieghardinger family and Frederik over for Christmas. In our house, our parents' rooms were in the western part, while Christoph's and mine were in the eastern part.

So I decided that Krümmelbein, Frederik, Magdalena and Friedrich would sleep near us and Madame Sieghardinger with her youngest son Josef would sleep with my parents in the wing.

On 20 December, first Andreas Krümmelbein and then all our guests from München arrived safely. Krümmelbein's appearance had changed significantly for the better since his forced shave by Frederik.

First of all, mulled wine and hot soup were offered in the well-heated parlour. Our guests warmed up gratefully after the twenty or two-day journey. There was a lot of fun straight away. Seraphia and Heinrich had also come over. Everyone hugged each other and had something to talk about. The warm alcohol soon had a little effect on our youngest guests.

Everyone retired for a while. Later, we met up for a late dinner. It was very cosy, even though there were so many of us. We laughed a lot and talked about this and that.

At some point, Magdalena's mother put her foot down. "We're going to retire. After all, tomorrow is another day." She shooed the tired Josef out.

"Friends, I can't wait any longer!" Andreas Krümmelbein silenced us. "You know, good news has to be announced. We're back in the black this month. Before I left, I visited our bank again. I was assured that almost all outstanding debts had been paid and that the business was back on a sound footing. What's more, another large consignment arrived just one day before my departure. There are already fixed contracts for half of it and I have samples of the other half with me."

Father embraced his young business partner with a happy whoop. "Thank you, dear Mr Krümmelbein. You are the pillar of my business. What do you think about running the Hamburg office all by yourself from now on? I would then only visit you once a year for a short time in the spring, together with my wife. A man as capable as you doesn't need the old idiot from Baiern."

Krümmelbein looked happy. "Thank you, Mr von Sommerauer. Your trust honours me. If that's what you want, I'll gladly comply. And I will look forward to your visit every year. However, I can only continue to work so successfully if your whole family continues to support me so splendidly. I have to admit that I wouldn't be able to do it alone."

He looked round. We assured him that it would be a matter of course for us to continue using our contacts to make good sales.

"I have to say, it gives me incredible pleasure to pass on the exquisite fabrics to the right people." Mamma said what I was thinking.

"Even in Paris, the fabrics you've ordered attract attention. You have a lucky hand, Mr Krümmelbein," praised Aunt Seraphia.

My parents also withdrew after this joyful announcement, as my father seemed a little tired. Seraphia and Heinrich also said goodbye because they wanted to leave us young people alone. "I'm sure they have a few things to discuss among friends that we would only disturb."

Mr Krümmelbein asked for our attention again. "I would love to be part of this select circle of friends. That's why I ask you all to call me Andreas."

We agreed to include him in our circle as a special friend.

Now it was Christoph who, after exchanging glances with Magdalena, took the floor in our group of six.

"Nothing is official yet, but we're as good as engaged and want to get married next year." With that, he took Magdalena in his arms and kissed her. Andreas and Frederik warmly congratulated the happy couple.

Friedrich looked at me pleadingly. So I made an announcement too.

"I guess it's my turn now. This information is also for your ears only. You know that I no longer wish to marry. But I never said I wasn't looking for a lover. After Frederik nudged me with my nose during my last visit to München, a connection was made with my sweetheart Friedrich." I took Friedrich's head between my hands and kissed him, whereupon he wrapped me in his arms.

Christoph, Magdalena and Andreas were surprised, but nevertheless delighted that we had come together.

Frederik cleared his throat. "Speaking of openings ... Andreas and I have been a couple since the spring. Even if we don't see each other that often. Of course, we ask for your discretion. In our case, going public could have fatal consequences." Christoph, Magdalena and Friedrich congratulated them again.

It was my turn to come clean. "Oh, just so you know. We have another person in the house who knows our secrets but will keep them. It's Katharina, my maid. She knows about our connections, but has promised not to let anyone know. She looks after our rooms and has organised them accordingly. You can trust her. She is a treasure of a person."

I knew that Katharina wouldn't betray any of us. And I also knew that my friends would always be respectful towards her. What's more, I was pretty sure that Katharina would receive small gifts for her discretion.

We chatted for a while and then retired. Friedrich and I met immediately afterwards in my dressing room. A noticeably erotic atmosphere was already building up there. We only used my bed on those nights. But nobody had to know that apart from Katharina. She was happy that she hardly ever had to heat the fireplace in Friedrich's room and had much less work to do.

The two of us talked a lot. "What do you want to do when you graduate?"

"There's an experienced doctor who wants to take me into his practice. A really good doctor from whom I can still learn a lot. He also works one day a week at the Holy Ghost Hospital. I would like to do that, too. After a few years, I hope to be able to open my own practice. At least that's what I'd like to do."

"I'm sure you'll make a fantastic doctor. You have a feeling for people. You really want to help people and get to the bottom of things. You listen to other opinions. These are the best criteria for a good start to your professional life. I firmly believe in you, my love."

Friedrich covered me with kisses for these words. I felt completely loved.

On the 21st it snowed about six *Zoll*[177]. We went for a nice ride together and took Josef with us. Our horses were full of energy. They all loved snow. We rode to Aunt Maria and Uncle Josef and let our horses gallop from the village Walserberg all the way to Salzburg.

Our relatives gave us mocha and hot wine to warm us up, plus cake and other pastries. Then we strolled around the town a bit, did some shopping and then rode back home.

In the evening, we celebrated the winter solstice. We made a fire in the garden and everyone in the house gathered there.

My father said a few words about the year that was almost over and we symbolically parted with things and people we no longer needed by throwing pieces of paper with corresponding details or drawings into the fire and burning them.

Christmas Eve finally arrived on Saturday. As the snow that had fallen again made the path to St Pankraz's church too difficult, the whole group rode to St Georg's church in Nonn. We attended the Mitternachtsmette[178] there.

It seemed to me to be a truly magical night. The moon was almost full, shining brightly in the sky and the snow crunched under our feet.

We spent a few days walking, chatting and eating delicious food. It was simply a marvellous holiday with our friends.

303

"I do blame our time to rebuff strong and to good actions gifted spirits, only for being women."

Teresa von Ávila,
Spanish female Mystic (1515–1582)

Epilogue

A few years have passed since I wrote this down. Christoph and Magdalena married in May 1775 and are a happy couple. They live in the spring and summer in our parents' house in Reichenhall and the rest of the year in a wing of the Sieghardinger house in München. Magdalena is pregnant for the second time, having given birth to a set of twins just one year after the wedding.

Unlike me, Christoph was lucky with his mother-in-law. She loves her son-in-law and especially her grandchildren. As a result, she is involved in many activities and is never realy alone, even though her other children no longer live at home.

Josef is now in a military academy.

My parents stay in Hamburg for two to three months every spring, until early summer. Business is booming and profits are growing.

Frederik always stays with his Andreas Krümmelbein in Hamburg for some weeks after visiting my parents during his summer holidays from the university. They are still a happy couple and are content to spend some time together every year, while the rest of the year they work a lot and spend time with other friends.

From this year onwards, Seraphia and Heinrich would like to devote themselves solely to their dance students in the Reichenhall and Salzburg region. My aunt felt that she had finally had enough of travelling. She felt too old and wanted to retire before she became a laughing stock.

After receiving his doctorate, Friedrich worked mainly abroad for two years and became a fantastic and highly esteemed doctor. After returning home, he opened a practice in my townhouse. By then, I had remodelled my home a little. Officially, my palace now consists of two units: my residential wing and Friedrich's living and working wing.

My former maid Katharina supports Friedrich as his assistant. She has found fulfilment in this role. It makes me proud when I hear patients singing the praises of Friedrich and Katharina. These patients are predominantly female. In my opinion, this is partly because Katharina takes away a lot of anxiety and partly because Friedrich is a very empathetic person. And he does treat women with respect compared to some of his collegues.

Since my return in the second half of 1775, I have been giving dancing lessons all over Munich and inviting people to practice evenings in my palace.

These days and evenings are very popular and are always fully booked weeks in advance. I have changing partners who support me with enthusiasm: Christoph, Frederik, Friedrich and my former stable boy Felix, who has turned out to be an incredibly skilful dancer and is now working at the theatre after an intensive period of lessons with me. I am very proud of him, as I am of my majordomo Heinrich Summerer, who still lives in my house. He's quite old now, but he never misses the opportunity to organise the events in my house in concert with me. I say both of them are dear and reliable friends to me.

Every year, all of us friends together organise the servants' ball in the Redoutensaal in honour of Jacob. This has now become an institution that has grown to be an integral part of the annual programme. Time and again, aspiring musicians ask if they can play with us on this evening. For the next year I hope to be able to have the orchestre from the Ospidale della Pietà[179] from Venice with us.

Friedrich and I are still a happy couple and I can no longer imagine life without my beloved. A big dream has come true for me. I pray that I can dream this dream for a long time to come. There is only one downer. Our wish to have children has not been fulfilled. But even this is not just a disadvantage in our lives.

---

179 *An orphanage in Venice where girls were trained as musicians. Antonio Vivaldi was also a teacher there.*

I probably won't make it into the history books as a female dancing master, unlike my male colleagues, but that's of secondary importance. The main thing is that I love and live my profession and can bring joy to other people and myself.

Afterword

Dear reader,

I have been interested in feminism and women's issues in general for many years. When I came across countless brilliant women during my first in-depth research into the 18th century, I decided to mention as many of them as possible in my book. I wanted to show that the world is not and never has been the way society still wants us to believe.

Women can do almost everything. Above all, they can do everything just as well as men (apart from physical differences) and some things even better. But – just like most men – they need support from their environment, which they unfortunately receive far too rarely, even in this day and age, to an adequate extent and from the right places or people.

Even today, we women still grow up believing that women had hardly any rights until the 1970s and were unable to achieve anything professionally, but also that all opportunities were now open to them.

Neither one nor the other is true.

Just as there have always been oppressed women to whom men – or society – refused to grant rights, there have also always been women who "stood their ground". Women who (even in the Middle Ages) successfully continued to run craft businesses as widows; women who ruled countries; women who were musicians, dancers, painters, healers, astronomers, scholars and were highly respected and well paid in their day.

However, historiography is still predominantly written by men. And they tend to ignore the opposite sex, which is why we only find out about many outstanding women when we dig deep into history and take a closer look at the subject. Nevertheless, I didn't want to do the same as the male authors and only mention women in my book. I believe that there have always been women as well as men who have created beautiful or helpful things for humanity.

I myself have often experienced men attacking and discriminating against women. Both parties are often not even aware of what is happening at the time. I have probably seen women attack other women and deny them respect just as often. There are many reasons for this. But often they are simply learnt by the example of our sick society.

As long as this society continues to differentiate between children – and not just through colour-coordinated toys and clothing – the still poor situation for women around the world will not change much. The man is seen as an independent being and the woman as an object.

This means that we all have to be on our guard at all times and distance ourselves from the previous behaviour of judging everything by male standards or accepting sayings such as "boys can do it", "boys are just like that", "you have to give them space", which is countered by "girls should keep their mouths shut", "they can't do it anyway" or "it's not suitable for girls".

The differences in the way families bring up their children are still striking. The son is often the pampered and powerful prince all his life, while the daughter is the sweet princess for a few years before she is suddenly and without warning demoted to the powerless Cinderella, who often has to remain in the prince's shadow for the rest of her life because no one helps her out of her dilemma. This game is passed on to the next generation without any relevant change.

I would like to see a society that values every individual and doesn't treat anyone differently because of their gender or appearance. Because we can all learn so much from each other.

So my book is mainly written the way I would like people to treat each other and not the way they usually do.

Protagonists

Family

Victoria von Falkenstein (Vic)
> first-person narrator, true-born von Sommerauer,
> (* 1751, pianoforte, violin, flute)

Christoph von Sommerauer
> twin brother (* 1751, pianoforte, violin, cello / viola
> da gamba)

Regina von Sommerauer
> Mother, true-born von Neubauer (* 1732, pianoforte,
> violin)

Dionysius von Sommerauer
> Father, of lower nobility, international merchant
> (* 1730, basso continuo)

Seraphia von Neubauer
> Aunt, dancer of international renown (* 1737, violin,
> flute, dance)

Jacob Count von Falkenstein
> Husband of Victoria (* 1743, violin, enthusiastic
> dancer)

Josef von Neubauer
> Victoria's uncle in Salzburg

Maria von Neubauer
> Victoria's aunt in Salzburg

Good friends and spouses

Andreas Krümmelbein
> Administrator of the trading house of the von Sommerauers

Angelika von Sieghardinger
  Sister of Magdalena (*1755)

Cecilia von Falkenstein
  Aunt of Jacob

Frederik von Barby
  Companion of Jacob (*1748, bass viol)

Friedrich von Sieghardinger
  Brother of Magdalena (*1753, violin)

Heinrich Winkelmayr
  Dancer and partner of Seraphia (harpsichord, violin)

Johann Baptist Josef Joachim Ferdinand von Schidenhofen
  zu Stumb und Triebenbach (* 1747)

Josef von Sieghardinger
  Brother of Magdalena (*1758)

Kaspar Joachim von Schidenhofen
  Lord of Triebenbach

Leonhard von Falkenstein
  Jacob's brother (* 1745)

Leopold Mozart
  Father of Nannerl and Wolfgang

Magdalena von Sieghardinger
  Friend of Victoria in München (*1752, pianoforte, violin)

Maria Anna Mozart (Nannerl)
  Friend of Victoria (* 1751, pianoforte)

Wolfgang Mozart (Wolferl)
  Friend of Victoria (* 1756, pianoforte, violin)

Servants and further circle

Apollonia
Servant of Seraphia

Erich Hintermeier
Jacob's valet, Palace in München

Felix Hartinger
Groom, Palace in München

Franz von Cottenau
Devotee of Magdalena

Friedrich the Younger
Stable boy in Sommerauer's house

Heinrich Summerer
Majordomus, Palace in München

Johanna
Cook in the house of Sommerauer

Johann
Majordomus in the house of Sommerauer

Katharina Kleiner
Maid of Victoria

Konrad von Ehrenfels
Devotee of Victoria, human and veterinary surgeon
of Anif Castle

Kreszentia von Sommerauer
Cousin of Victoria in Ingolstadt (*1760)

The Lasser zu Lasseregg family
Live in the Marzoll Castle

Luise von Sommerauer
Cousin of Victoria in Ingolstadt (*1757)

Michael and Katharina Tonhauser
Battalion Lieutenant, with his wife

Nina, Kathi and Liesl
    Serving girls

Susanne Schiffelholz
    Neighbour of the von Sommerauers

Severin Schadwell
    Neighbour and brother of S. Schiffelholz

Peter von Sommerauer
    Cousin of Victoria in Ingolstadt (*1748)

Philomena
    Hostess in Erlangen

Sibylla of Murach
    Acquaintances in Bayreuth

Wappler
    Compagnion by Dionysius von Sommerauer

Wendelin
    Fellow student of Victoria and Christoph

Willibald von Dachsbeck
    fellow student and friend of Frederik

Bibliography

Books and writings

Große Frauen der Weltgeschichte – Tausend Biographien in Wort und Bild; Neuer Kaiser Verlag, Klagenfurt, 1987

Beck, Barbara: Die berühmtesten Frauen der Weltgeschichte – Vom 18. Jahrhundert bis heute; Maxiverlag Wiesbaden, 2008

Schad, Martha: Die berühmtesten Frauen der Weltgeschichte – Von der Antike bis zum 17. Jahrhundert; Maxiverlag Wiesbaden, 2018

Lang J., Schneider M.: Auf der Gmain – Chronik der Gemeinden Bayerisch Gmain und Großgmain; Gemeinden Bayerisch Gmain und Großgmain, 1995

Pfisterer, Herbert: Reichenhall in seiner bayerischen Geschichte; Motor + Touristik Verlag München, 1988

Sipos, Mag. Cecilia: Frauen als Instrumentalistinnen im 18. Jahrhundert; Masterarbeit an der Anton Bruckner Privatuniversität OÖ; Wien, 2016

La Beata Olanda – Ensemble für Alte Musik: Musik von Frauen – ein vergessenes Erbe; Auf den Spuren von Komponistinnen und musikalischen Traditionen

Handelsbeziehungen zwischen Venedig und Salzburg am Beispiel der Familien Spängler von Brigitte Heuberger (www.zobodat.at)

Taubert, Gottfried: Rechtschaffener Tanzmeister oder gründliche Erklärung der Französischen Tanz-Kunst von 1717; Nachdruck der Originalbücher I–III, Hrsg. Kurt Petermann, Heimeran Verlag München, 1976

Salmen, Walter: Der Tanzmeister – Geschichte und Profile eines Berufes vom 14. bis zum 19. Jahrhundert; Georg Olm Verlag Hildesheim, Zürich, New York, 1997

Haslinger, Adolf und Mittermayer, Peter (Hrsg.): Salzburger Kulturlexikon; Residenz Verlag Salzburg und Wien, 1987

Maps

Map of Baiern: Von Johann Baptist Homann – https:// www.davidrumsey.com/luna/servlet/detail/RUMSEY ~8~1~290967~90067342:Bavariae-, Gemeinfrei, https:// commons.wikimedia.org/w/index.php?curid=91285674

Salzburg map: Von Johann Baptist Homann – Foto mit freundlicher Genehmigung von Alfred Huemer, Museum Tittmoning.

München map 1740: author unknown – Alt-Münchner Bilderbuch (München 1918),
Gemeinfrei, https://commons.wikimedia.org/w/index. php?curid=5854592

Literature tips

Criado-Perez, Caroline: Invisible Women – Data bias in a world designed for men; Abrams Press, 2019

Opelt, Rüdiger: Die Unterdrückung der Frauen; S.A.W. Edition (www.opelt.com), 2019
Das Ende des Patriarchats – Die globale Gesellschaft der Frauen; S.A.W. Edition (www.opelt.com), 2019

Brunner, Verena; books with CD: Tanzen mit Mozart; Fidula-Verlag Boppard/Rhein, 2001
Contredanses – Tanzvergnügen der Mozart-Zeit; Fidula-Verlag Boppard/Rhein, 2014 (www.fidula.de)

Music directory

Maria Teresa Agnesi Pinottini:
Overture from Sofonisba

Johann Sebastian Bach:
Brandenburg Concertos No. 4
Easter Oratorio, BWV 249
Thus God loved the world

Arcangelo Corelli:
Variations on La Folia

Anna Bon di Venezia:
Flute Sonata I.

Friedrich der Große/Frederick the Great:
Allegro assai from the Flute Concerto in D major

Christoph Willibald Gluck:
Iphigénie en Aulide

Georg Friedrich Händel/George Frideric Handel:
Oratorio Solomon: Entry of the Queen of Sheba
Fireworks Music
Passacaglia, Suite No. 7, G minor, HWV 432
Lascia ch'io pianga from the opera Rinaldo

Joseph Haydn:
L'infedeltà delusa

Jean-Baptiste Lully:
Marche Royal

Marianna Martinez:
Piano sonatas in E major and A major

Claudio Monteverdi:
Vespro della beata vergine or Vespers of the Virgin Mary

Wolfgang Amadeus Mozart:
Il sogno di Scipione, Serenata, KV 126
Pianoforte Concerto in D major No. 5
Ascanio in Alba

Mrs Philarmonica:
Trio Sonatas

Antonio Salieri:
Armida

Maddalena Sirmen:
Violin concertos

Alessandro Striggio:
Missa sopra Ecco sì beato giorno

Thomas Tallis:
Spem in alium, motet

Georg Philipp Telemann:
Alster Overture
Hamburg Admiralty Music
Double Concerto in E minor

Marco Uccellini:
Aria Sopra La Bergamasca in D major by

Antonio Vivaldi:
Nisi Dominus

BAVARIÆ
CIRCULUS et ELECTORAT,
IN SUAS QUASQUE DITIONES
tam cum
ADIACENTIBUS QUAM INSERTIS
REGIONIBUS
accuratissime divisus
per
IO. BAPTISTAM HOMANNUM
Norimbergæ

Sic NOTANTUR

Urbes
Oppida

SEPTENTRIO

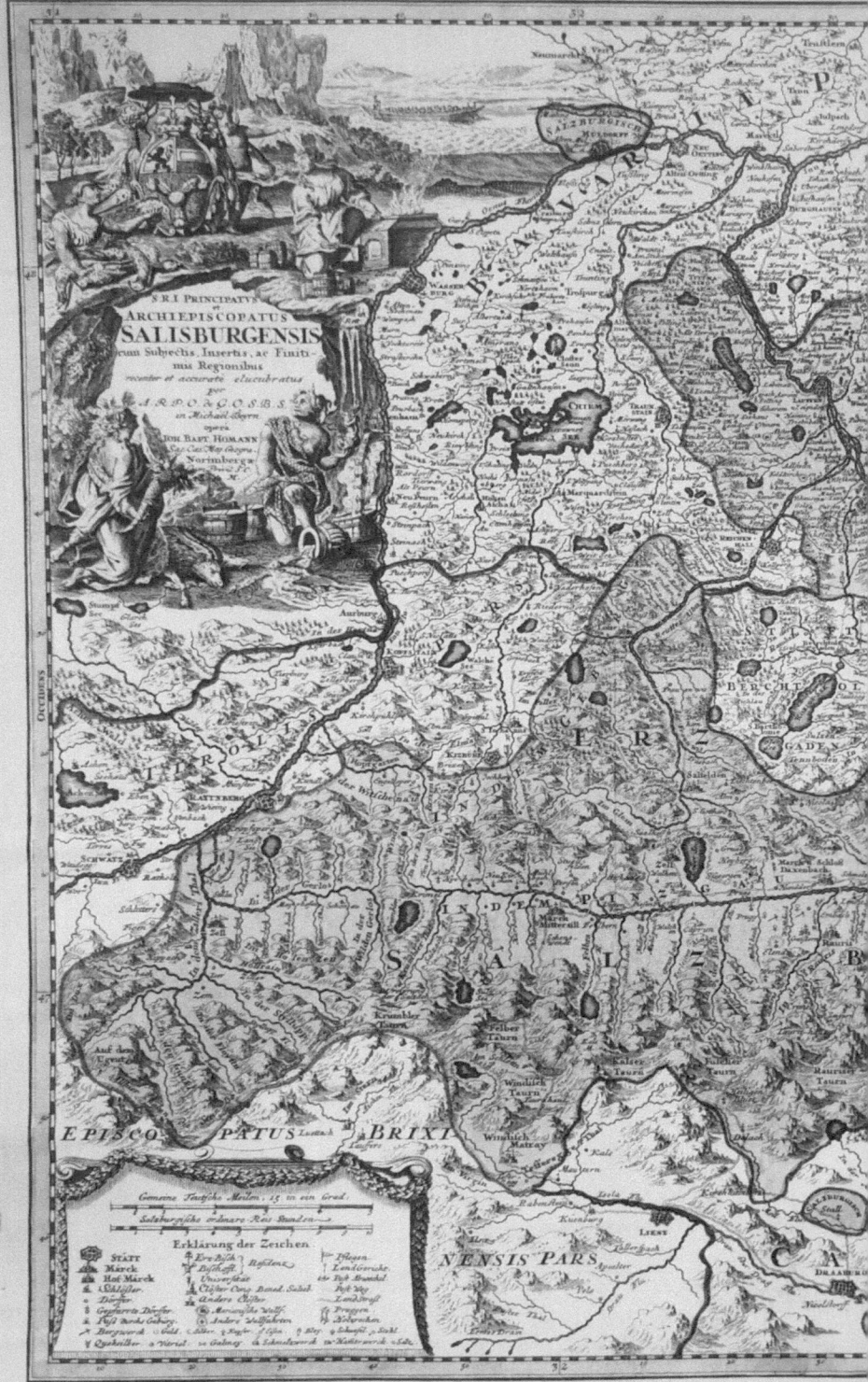

S.R.I. PRINCIPATVS
et
ARCHIEPISCOPATVS
SALISBURGENSIS
cum Subiectis, Insertis, ac Finiti-
mis Regionibus
recenter et accurate elucubratus
per
A.R.D.O. de GOSBS.
in Michael Beyern
opera
IOH. BAPT. HOMANN
Sac. Cæs. May. Geogr.
Norimbergæ

OCCIDENS

BAVARIAP

TIROLIS

EPISCO- PATVS Lottich BRIXI NENSIS PARS CA

Gemeine Teutsche Meilen, 15 in ein Grad.
Salzburgische ordinare Reis Stunden

Erklärung der Zeichen

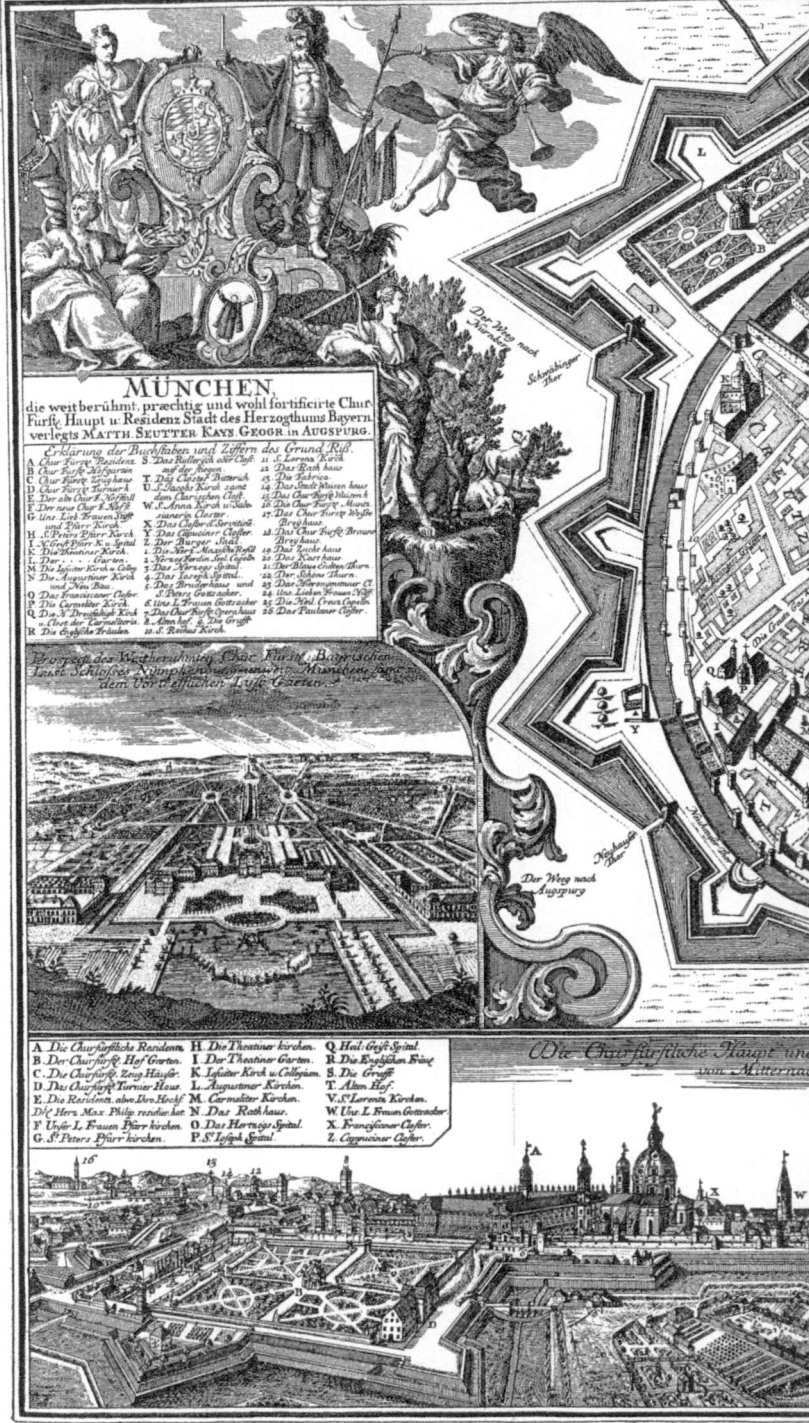

MÜNCHEN,

die weitberühmt, præchtig und wohl fortificirte Chur Fürstl. Haupt u. Residenz Stadt des Herzogthums Bayern. verlegts MATTH. SEUTTER KAYS. GEOGR. in AUGSPURG.

Erclärung der Buchstaben und Ziffern des Grund Riß.

A Chur Fürstl. Residenz.
B Chur Fürstl. Abtzgarten
C Chur Fürstl. Zeughaus
D Chur Fürstl. Turnier H.
E Der alte Chur F. Hofstall
F Der neue Chur F. Hofst.
G Uns. Lieb Frauen Stüft und Pfarr Kirch.
H S.Peters Pfarr Kirch.
I S.t Groß Pfarr K. u Spital
L Die Theatiner Kirch.
L Der 1 – Garten.
M Die Jesuiter Kirch u Colleg.
N Die Augustiner Kirch und Neu Bau.
O Das Franciscaner Closter.
P Die Carmeliter Kirch.
Q S.t Dreyschigk Kirch u Closter der Carmeliten.
R Die Englische Fräulen

S Das Rathaus oder Cleist auf der Bogen
T Das Closter Bieberich
U Das Jacobi Kirch zum dem Carespihen Clost.
W S. Anna Kirch u Salanarsyten Closter.
X Das Capuciner Closter.
Y Das Burger Mast.
1 Die Nor. F. Minxelhe Res.
2 Vor ein Ferdin. Josl. Leipsh.
3 Das Herzogs Spital.
4 Das Joseph Spital.
5 Das Brückerhaus und S.t Petri Ostwacker.
6 Uns. L. Frauen Gottwacker
7 Das Chur Fürstl Thornhaus
8 Alten haf. g. Die Gruft
9.
10 S. Rochus Kirch.

11 S.t Lorenz Kirch
12 Das Rath haus
13 Die Fabrica
14 Das Stadt Waisen haus
15 Das Chur Fürstl. Waisen h.
16 Das Chur Fürstl. Münz
17 Das Chur Fürstl Weyße Breyhaus.
18 Das Chur Fürstl Braune Breyhaus.
19 Das Zucht haus
20 Das Kaer haus
21 Der Blaue Collegi Thurn
22 Der Schöne Thurn
23 Das Nürnpimmauer Cl.
24 Uns. Lieben Frauen Närt
25 Die Heil. Creuz Capelln
26 Das Paulaner Closter.

Prospect des Weitberühmten Chur Fürstl. Bayr'schen Lust Schlosses Nymphenburg ohnweit München samt dem Vortreflichten Lust Garten.

Der Weg nach Nord

Schwäbinger Thor

Nenhauser Thor

Der Weg nach Augspurg

Wie Chur Fürstliche Haupt und von Mitternacht

A Die Churfürstliche Residenz.
B Der Churfürstl. Hof Garten.
C Das Churfürstl. Zeug Häuser.
D Das Churfürstl Turnier Haus.
E Die Residenti. alwo Dvo. Hochf. Der Herr Max. Philip. residiren hat.
F Unser L. Frauen Pfarr kirchen.
G S.t Peters Pfarr kirchen.
H Die Theatiner kirchen.
I Der Theatiner Garten.
K Jesuiter Kirch u. Collegium.
L Augustiner Kirchen.
M Carmeliter Kirchen.
N Das Rothhaus.
O Das Herzogs Spital.
P S.t Joseph Spital.
Q Heil. Geist Spital.
R Das Englischen Fräul.
S Die Gruft.
T Alten Hof.
V S.t Lorentz Kirchen.
W Uns. L. Frauen Gottwacker.
X Franciscaner Closter.
Z Capuciner Closter.

16   15   12

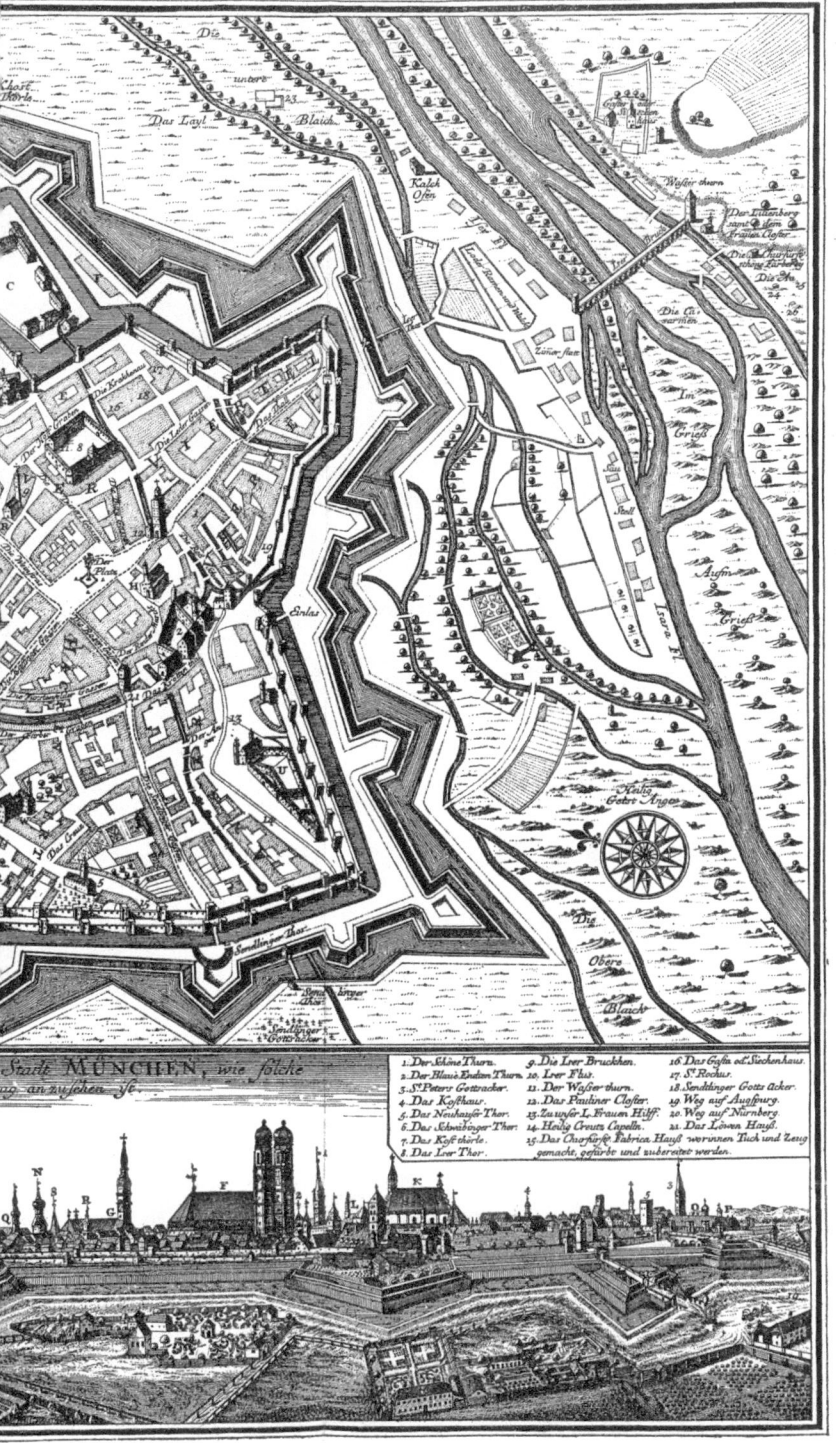

Stadt MÜNCHEN, wie solche
...ng anzusehen ist.

1. Der Schöne Thurn.	9. Die Iser Bruckhen.	16. Das Gisti: od: Siechenhaus.
2. Der Blaus Endzn Thurn.	10. Iser Flus.	17. St Rochus.
3. St Peters Gottsacher.	11. Der Wasser thurn.	18. Sendtlinger Gotts Acker.
4. Das Kosthaus.	12. Das Pauliner Closter.	19. Weg auf Augspurg.
5. Das Neuhauser Thor.	13. Zu unser L. Frauen Hülff.	20. Weg auf Nürnberg.
6. Das Schwäbinger Thor.	14. Heilig Creutz Capell:.	21. Das Löwen Hauß.
7. Das Kost thörle.	15. Das Churfürst Fabrica Hauß worinnen Tuch und Zeug gemacht, gefärbt und zubereitet werden.	
8. Das Iser Thor.		

Acknowledgement

I would like to take this opportunity to say THANK YOU to everyone who was involved in making this book possible.

Firstly, I would like to thank my biggest fan of my Laura books, Michaela Grüner. She was my neighbour and unfortunately passed away far too young. I am glad that I was able to make her happy with the first draft of this novel.

A big thank you goes to our dance master and Mozart dance expert Verena Brunner and the entire dance group for historical dances at the Musikum Salzburg, all of whom I have taken to my heart over the years. Verena has published two wonderful dance books (see page 315) with CDs in the Fidula publishing house and also made her "Rechtschaffener Tanzmeister" by Gottfried Taubert available to me for the work on my book. She also gave me numerous valuable tips for my work.

I would also like to thank the master falconer Josef Hiebeler for the basic falconry knowledge he gave me and, above all, my friend and falconer Rebekka Bloßfeld, who provided me with her expertise for the scenes in this book and answered numerous questions.

A particularly big THANK YOU also to my good friend Alfred Leiblfinger, who patiently listened to the results of my research in countless telephone calls and realised the drawings for the cover fan excellently according to my wishes.

And a special thank you to my master typesetter colleague Sabine Schmidt, who turned my print files into a real fan using screen printing. I love our collaborative cover!

Thanks also to my dear proofreader and author's regular table colleague Lisa Graf (she wrote the bestselling trilogy about Dallmayr in Munich as well as about Lindt & Sprüngli) and my test readers Delly Hierl, Gabi Lutter and Isabell Buttron.

For the English version thanks to my proofreader Peter Longley (Author of the Magdalena Trilogy and further great books) and Nicholas Kester from The British Falconers' Club for his help with the part with the falconry.

Finally, I would like to thank life in general, which has blessed me with all the opportunities that have made it easy for me to tackle some topics equipped with at least a sound basic knowledge. Whether I do something as a hobby myself (dancing, horse riding, playing Trompe de chasse) or know the right people who have been answering numerous questions with enthusiasm for years, both have helped me a lot here.

Daniela Brotsack, 2021–2024

Table of Content

YOUR historical dancing event in Salzburg!

Mozart in Style KG

Allow your dreams to become reality!

Dance events and dance-picnics in
Rococo/Regency style – become part of
Mozart's and Jane Austen's world.
Ask for your personal offer!

www.mozartinstyle.com
myevent@mozartinstyle.com

Historical events as a setting for special occasions:

Do you sometimes have the feeling to belong into a different era? Experience an epic birthday party or wedding in exactly the setting you have always dreamed of. In our dream factory we create tailor made events ranging from Mozart-style celebrations to a Sissi dress for the bride. The location will be original and fine-tuned for the purpose, be it in the palace of Hellbrunn (former summer residence of the archbishops) or Salzburg's old town, where heritage dates back to 900 A.D. Salzburg is a unique gem with an incredible historical and cultural depth.

To be really transposed into a different time we suggest at least events from Friday to Sunday afternoon, but naturally if you really want to immerse into a different age Wednesday to Sunday is best. Even if the normally warm and balmy Salzburg weather restricts outdoor activities, we have suitable options even for last minute alternations in place. The following short programme is intended to provide a general idea – normally we create the agenda to the specific needs of our customers:

Friday: First city tour & preparation evening (optional additional Mozart evening with singing)

Saturday: Salzburg & historical ball with live music

Sunday: Dance & food alfresco (picnic)

What is needed? Clothes in your preferred style, dancing shoes (ball) and relatively flat shoes (picnic).

Further information about the event:

www.mozartinstyle.com
myevent@mozartinstyle.com

*"Dream your life beautiful and
turn these dreams into reality."*

Marie Curie, physicist and Nobel Prize winner
(1867—1934)

*"Be the heroine of your life,
not the victim."*

Nora Ephron, writer
(1941–2012)

*"Don't let them get you down,
be bold and wild and wonderful!"*

Astrid Lindgren, writer
(1907–2002)

.